The Passion according to Renée Vivien

The Passion according to to Renée Vivien

Maria-Mercè Marçal

Translated from Catalan
by Kathleen McNerney and Helena Buffery

Francis
Boutle
Publishers

La passió segons Renée Vivien first published
Columna Edicions, Barcelona, 1994

First English translation published by
Francis Boutle Publishers
272 Alexandra Park Road
London N22 7BG
Tel/Fax: 020 8889 8087
Email: info@francisboutle.co.uk
www.francisboutle.co.uk

Cover image. Smithsonian American Art Museum
"Ophelia" by Alice Pike Barney ca. 1909

ISBN 978 1 9164906 5 9

To Fina who has shared it with me word for word.

INTROIT

"Five years ago I stumbled upon verses of a dark beauty," says Sara T., punctually commencing her disquisition before a completely empty room. But just as the Pied Piper drew streams of kids and rats behind him, her words begin to bring to life a strange, motley retinue of characters, as if emerging from under the flagstones, who proceed to take a seat before her without rhyme or reason. The teller of this tale – or rather, strange miscellany of narrations woven together diversely, which are about to unfold in the following pages – contemplates her creation, Sara T., for a moment as she confronts her nightmare. For surely every reader – whether female or, indeed, male – will have realized that this is one of those penumbrous dreams, charged with dense, burdensome meaning, susceptible to decipherment by experts in the field. Just as if we were to have Sara T. lay back on the proverbial couch, let us follow her in the vision that appears before her.

Propped up on crutches and prostheses are all manner of mutilated and deformed beings: squat dwarves, sinister bigheads, giant creatures with one eye in their foreheads glowing in rum-induced bile. Blind beggars bearing the eyes of Saint Lucy on a plate; goitrous seers, spewing grotesque and hysterical stutterings. Saint Agatha with her breasts on a tray and Apollonia with her torn-out teeth held in outstretched hand. An ambiguous headless page. Eunuchs and hermaphrodites ostentatiously displaying either their excess or their original or supervening lack. He-devils with cloven feet and she-devils with serpents for hair. Lustful apish clowns, all misshapen.

An avalanche of monsters, ogres, trolls; demented females, chimeric and teratological beings displaying sculptured silicone extracted from the worst special effects filmography.

The teller of this tale finds Sara T. at daybreak, relieved because she, too, knows it's just a nightmare. She gets up and looks at herself in the mirror, but suddenly the mirror goes blank. She says nothing, as if a single word might reawaken the unruly, polymorphous procession that has just vanished, conjuring them up once more to ogle her from the other side of the glass. She returns on tiptoe to her bed, convinced she is still dreaming. That is when the Angel appears and wakens her, at last, with a dazzling revelation. Sara T. makes an effort to retain every sound, every syllable, every word of the message she does not yet understand, as if it were encoded in a language unknown to her. When she is definitely awake – or is she? – all has disappeared from her memory. A gigantic eye stares at her, and the pupil holds nothing but a vast emptiness. "Five years ago I stumbled upon verses of a dark beauty," says Sara T. And the teller of this tale leaves her at this moment in order to cast her somewhat squinting and at times sardonic gaze on other characters that beckon her attention. Let no one reproach her for the unequal distribution of caustic elements or biting words over the chapters that follow. Diverse intensities and qualities of light require different filters. The decision to dispense with our sunglasses when faced with paler gleams was taken spontaneously, perhaps due to an irrepressible urge towards compassion. In the same way, every instance of benevolence might suggest secret scorn and every apparent censure hypothetically conceal an undertone of genteel badinage.

The teller of this tale is unable to draw this introduction to a close without confessing her frankly unexpected feeling of failure: like a neophyte photographer who has tried to find all the angles and focal points in a landscape, but is then surprised to have ended up with nothing more in hand than dozens of frames devoid of the most essential element which he thinks he knows. Perhaps if Sara T. had been able to retain and decipher the Angel's message, she could have offered to the teller of this tale a clarity of inestimable value.

first part

TRIALS AND TRIBULATIONS OF AN HONOURABLE BOURGEOIS MAN OF LETTERS

Paris, 21 November 1909

Four years had passed since the death of Madame M. Since that time, Amédée had struggled with a bewildering, sceptical orphanhood, stubbornly determined to deny itself. Fastened to a string no longer tugged by the imperious hand of a woman, he went about his daily rituals mechanically, repeating gestures formed over the years, as if, in spite of everything, some axis had managed to survive in the empty space that now centred his steps. He was like a ship suddenly liberated from a ballast that for all its apparent excess was nonetheless necessary; unaware of being adrift because never venturing beyond the benevolent, tranquil waters placed around him like a picturesque backdrop.

But now, the frail vessel had imperceptibly succumbed to a silent dread, a premonition of troubled waters or a cliff over which it might crash into splinters. It had done so with an insouciance *de salon*, like the weary acquiescence of a lady entering a waltz by the hand of a mysterious and insistent dancer, after hours of making him beg, acceding only when he was about to desist … And now he was gliding above things as if both he and the things had wings, wax wings perhaps, forever destined to melt in the fire and hopelessly attracted to the incandescence of a still far-off pain. This frightful lightness made him both yearn for and loathe – why have you abandoned me? – the weight that previously lent him substance, that of the authoritarian hand at once capable of tying him down to earth and appearing to reign over the waters.

To counterbalance that growing sense of irreality, the child he once was hastened to take refuge in his eyes, eyes that saw everything, touched everything, except for the old man's face in which they shone, a glassy, aquarian blue. A soft face, of polished lines, and white, becoming whiter at the hairline touching his temples and the kindly beard that refined his chin. Eyes that often belied this image of a benign patriarch, momentarily flashing in pursuit of his nieces when they visited and kissed his cheek: "Oh, uncle, your cheek is so sweet! What a pleasure it is to kiss it!" At this he would take their hands to return the kisses: "But *mademoiselles*, the cheek of an old gentleman is unworthy of such rosy lips", he would laugh. And the girls would think to themselves: "Ever since auntie died, uncle is more playful, he laughs more". But they also witnessed him melting away, in waves, due to the intermittency of their visits – all too often announced and then postponed due to some last-minute *je m'excuse* – as if he were burning more brightly, but also more rapidly spent. So one day they would take him arm in arm to the Luxembourg gardens, and another to the cinema on the Boulevard des Capucines. "Uncle, we must go to see *Le Voyage dans la lune*". And he, who had been the first to take them to the pictures, would coyly make them beg: "I'm no longer made for such things, but I'd be happy to serve as escort to two charming young damsels!" Then one or the other would flatter him shamelessly: "Why uncle, you are a poet!"

These elderly coquetries sometimes brought Pauline suddenly to mind. Not that his laughing, lively nieces, out of a Renoir painting, were anything like that strange adolescent who played a Chopin waltz for him fifteen years before, having refused his initial request: "You've forgotten! See? I told you I preferred waltzes, and you forgot. Waltzes are so much sadder than nocturnes. Nocturnes have an unveiled sadness, without restraint…" She would then conclude emphatically: "Waltzes are a great sorrow that bursts into laughter for fear of going mad". In response, he had drawn on Musset: "Nothing makes us greater than a great sorrow". To which she had retorted: "Your beloved Musset… He, like Chopin, is a connoisseur of the heart. Whereas Beethoven, like Dante, is a connoisseur of the soul: at least that's what my friend Violette says… and I couldn't agree more!"

No, his nieces would never have known how to speak like that. They were like their mother when she was their age, barely able to coax out the few easy piano pieces expected of every well educated young lady. He could not deny that Rose, the younger of the two, had recently displayed a certain inclination towards culture, which he had tried to stimulate as much as their brief and infrequent visits permitted. But neither Rose nor, indeed, her sister Berthe, were capable of reading Dante, let alone in the original Italian, as Pauline had done at their age. Nor of translating the poetry, for his eyes only, as a gift ministered little by little in successive letters or read aloud, seated by his side as the twilight hour tinged the windows with violet.

Even so, in spite of the sheer and vertiginous distance between the two different situations, those childlike eyes flashed him an image of himself too similar in weave to the one that shimmered from so many years ago… a looser fabric, perhaps, with threads of a different thickness and texture… One of his nieces had said to him "You, uncle, are a poet", responding with a hint of irony to his amiable phrases, which themselves mitigated, again with irony, the outmodishness of his gentility. Yet once upon a time he had witnessed their amazement to learn that as a young man he had published poems in journals in his native Flanders. "And will you not let us read them?" they had chorused rapturously. He could hardly have made them beg, and so an old-fashioned Parnassian sonnet rang out in well-scanned alexandrines – which he knew to be of negligible value – pinning them like candid moths to the fixed point of a dazzling devotion: "You, uncle, are a Poet".

That day was a Sunday. After an entire week of rain and stormy skies, the sun mustered up the courage to try to peek out between the cracks in the still dense cloud cover. The foliage in Monceau Park, which Amédée could make out from the balcony of his apartment on Courcelles boulevard, oscillated between sparkling greens, the glow of burnished copper and a diffuse shadow that negated all colour, forming an indeterminate sadness. The Wednesday before, a strange event had occurred, one that could probably be explained by meteorologists, but that for Amédée maintained the prestigious aura of mystery. All of a sudden, at eleven in the morning, from right where he was standing, he had seen night swooping down on Paris like a bird of prey, leaving only darkness. Lights began to flicker on in the luxurious *quartier* where he lived, like the little votive candles lit by god-botherers before sacred images and which some also offer to their dead. Omnibuses, streetcars, carriages, and arrogant automobiles added their headlights to the sterile pride of this poor man's light show. Even so, darkness prevailed everywhere, with a cruel and inscrutable cunning until, as if moved by royal caprice, it deigned to retreat just as unexpectedly as when it had made its entrance.

On that Sunday, however, things were in their proper place: a classic autumn day like all the others, with the added gift of an unexpectedly benign angle of sunlight. His nieces had announced a visit. They wanted him to accompany them to the Louvre. Rose had recently taken quite a fancy to art, to the extreme that she had asked him to lend her Salomon Reinach's *Histoire générale des arts plastiques*, and she had actually read the entire work. Her older sister, who was somewhat more indolent in nature, was generally happy to follow on a couple of steps behind. "One day, uncle, you'll have to take us to the museum at Saint Germain-en-Laye. Reinach is director, and he says…" "Very well, I will," he conceded. "But tell me, how did you find out? I can see that your old uncle is no longer your only guide through the realms of the Muses…" She only mentioned a certain teacher, a Mademoiselle Bonheur, but judging by the flush that suddenly tinged lips and cheeks, Amédée suspected some vague, lovelorn young man.

It was just a matter of time now, he reflected with regret, before the girls entered the office of adulthood. However much they resisted, there could be no return. There were those who resisted tooth and nail. Not him, though. Blessed with an innate capacity for compromise, the young Amédée, that child who returned to his memories from so far away, had understood perfectly what was expected of him and what was offered in return, and he had agreed to pay the price. On the other side of the scale, for the longest time he had maintained the intimate conviction that somewhere deep inside his ultimate truth remained intact, always preserved in outline form, inaccessible to the demands of the world. To this inconcrete, inviolable place, he assigned poetry.

When his family sent him to Leeds to study the latest innovations in the textile industry, he had applied himself to the task dutifully. He knew that in a not too distant future it would fall to him to run the business and he wanted to do so in a manner that befitted modern times. This was what the ties of blood and lineage demanded of him, yet the truth is he threw himself into the endeavour with the dedication of a novitiate. The world was changing. The ancient tree with its deep roots reaching down over the centuries would now have to display all of its verdant exuberance in order to take on the challenges of the future! True, this was the time of the parvenu, and American cotton was overtaking the old textiles, but nothing could stem the vigour of this ancient dynasty of wool producers. Amédée accepted the arrival of the new class. But deep inside, he knew he was something else, something much truer to himself, and unnegotiable. Something substantial and undefinable that slipped through the cracks of all his day-to-day structures. Something like … a Poet, for example. Every time he dared to lend his desire a profile as nebulous as that mythical word, it began to unravel. At Leeds, many a daybreak would find him awake, reading old man Wordsworth, who aroused his fervour, or the young Swinburne, who made him shudder from pleasure or repulsion, he wasn't sure which, perhaps both at the same time. He often battled with the blank page himself: the greenest of landscapes imbued with a nebulous melancholy, ethereal nymphs, faraway unattainable loves … It had been years now since he had written poetry. Once in a while the odd verse came looking for him like an old habit refusing to disappear altogether, but it was a weak, ephemeral contact. He knew that at this point he would never be a poet. Not even a poet with a small *p*, having explicitly renounced the emphatic grandiosity of the capital letter. Perhaps he had always known it, but old age finally destroyed all subterfuge and wishful thinking regarding the matter. He told himself he had carried out all that had been asked of him, and that gave him a certain peace: he had paid his debt to the world. All that was left was a vague debt to his own even less definable sense of self. Knowing that it was no longer payable lent a bitter taste to his occasional restlessness.

"Preserve with you always poetry's fragility", Pauline had written to him in a lovely French alexandrine. Pauline, who believed he was a poet. "Dearest Poet and Friend" often headed her letters. And she sympathised "that a Poet like yourself should have to be involved in such prosaic affairs…" It was strange how everything took on such definitive clarity through her adolescent eyes. All that for him was confused and murky, incipient or uncertain, she was able to configure precisely, lending everything the finished and perfect form of the purest crystal. At the same time she confined everything that for Amédée represented the most concrete reality to the absolutely nebulous word "affairs". Once in a while he fantasized that the idealized image she returned to him of himself – in her letters, her verses, her eyes – was a reflection of what he would have been if circumstances hadn't pushed him so relentlessly towards the life he had, after all, chosen. Deep down he knew that what she made dance before his eyes was only a simulacrum of a different kind of life, a fiction that fascinated him with the same sort of unreality offered by those fluttering shadows with which the Lumière brothers had attempted to capture a slice of life. In the dark, they filled the entire space, shutting out the variegated existence of the boulevard, confining it for a while to an even greater unreality. Meaning, or at least a semblance of meaning, appeared to emerge from a field defined by a beam of light, that of the chosen and offered fragment, while the formless mass of acts and thoughts, impressions and sensations, languished, destined to die, like the golden hue of the leaves that an anonymous broom would sweep from the streets, without fail, early the next morning. In a similar way, he had been bewitched by the illusion Pauline offered him of living another life, if only for the briefest of moments. An alternative life that only beyond this world appeared to have the right to exist.

Pauline must have heard the sound of breaking glass inside her brain when he wrote that last letter. He imagined her laughing uncontrollably, leaning over the piano, eking out the saddest Chopin waltz, much sadder than any of the nocturnes. Afterwards, with pen in hand, she would distil farewell phrases full of dark irony, a goodbye he had tacitly agreed to accept as final without a hint of protest. It was the only way. Even so, he had ignored her request to return the letters, photographs, poems and souvenirs. He had saved everything religiously, as the only proof both of his guilt and of his innocence. He only occasionally succumbed to the temptation to re-read them. On one such occasion he had destroyed a letter, one that burned in his hands, seeming to upset the balance of guilt towards a blame that only he would have dared attribute to himself. In it, Pauline undid in just a few words that happy ambiguity where his spirit and sentiment rested. The words remained still, for you cannot destroy fire with fire. The same inner eye that demanded their extinction had unleashed a photographic mechanism, and her explicit request had become an expired ticket to a paradise which only the fallacy of time – as he knew all too well – dared tinge with the absolute.

It had all begun in the spring of 1894. Amédée remembered this exactly, though not by the dates on the letters, which never carried the year but only the day of the week: those hateful English Sundays Pauline would sum up as: "Prayers and roast beef", before adding: "both things equally indigestible to my delicate Parisian stomach". She compared those Sundays to an All Souls Day crossed with Ash Wednesday and a funeral, whose stifling atmosphere made her feel like committing every imaginable excess: "I'd insult someone … just for fun, do a somersault in the middle of the street, to see how people reacted … sing an immoral song during a sermon. I'd go and deliver an anarchist speech in the middle of Hyde Park. Start a revolution, yelling: Down with the Queen and the Prince of Wales and the whole royal family. An insurrection would follow. I'd burn London down and return to Paris! Everyone here is so by the book, so hypocritically devout…" Mondays and Wednesdays were like holidays in comparison. She would go downstairs at eight in the morning to intercept the mail, thus avoiding the scandal so many letters from Paris might cause among servants and family alike.

It had all begun in the year 1894, in a salon on Rue de Vézelay, on the Right Bank of the Seine; an "all" that was insignificant enough, even to the most exacting eyes of any officer given to policing good behaviour. He could only possibly have been accused of the slightest of indiscretions, closer to imprudence than temerity; the momentary product of a blindness that had proven favourable – perhaps suspiciously so – to his desires. As far as she was concerned, her youth was enough to render her blameless, let alone her lamentable family circumstances. Pauline's father was dead. Amédée had met her mother, Madame T., at the very same dinner organized by friends of the family where he had discovered the daughter. Madame T. was American, a splendid woman, widowed for some years; the kind of female Amédée instinctively fled, for they immediately made him feel either too infantile or too old. Next to her, Pauline seemed a touch insipid, with the somewhat banal appearance of a girl in need of a good match, inoffensive and still rather awkward in the arts of the salon. Pauline's sister Toinette, on the other hand, was just at the moment when youth bloomed fullest, when it seems ready to burst toward adolescence without relinquishing the old charm: she was captivating. The contrast formed by mother and little sister against older sister established an implicit alliance between the former that even the most distracted observer would have noticed within a few moments. Amédée, moved perhaps by an innate sense of balance, offered Pauline the arm of a middle-aged gent, given to courteous gestures. As soon as they had exchanged a few words, he realized, to his surprise, that his choice had been the right one. As the adolescent became comfortable with his attentions, her unique voice began to emerge from within the trappings of timidity and dullness; a voice that barely suggested the Pauline he would later get to know so well, but that already captured his interest greatly. At least, he told himself, for the duration of the dinner. As they spoke of literature, she opened her sparkling, eager eyes wide; and his own eyes reflected both the desire to be dazzled by hers and the sparkle of her eagerness, all without ever abandoning the restrained but cordial tone appropriate to a family gathering. At one point, Pauline took his hand to look for his destiny lines.

Months later, she joked about it in a letter, confessing that she always said the same thing to men: they were inconstant and fickle, they always kept some sort of secret well hidden behind the excuse of their business affairs, they couldn't be trusted, etc. Saying such things, she had a ninety percent chance of getting it right, thus establishing her reputation as a seer. That evening, Amédée had protested vigorously, posing as the absolute innocent to the general hilarity and delight of the table, and Madame M.'s rigid smile. On such awkward occasions, Amédée always tended to avoid what he knew to be her severe, commanding gaze. His wife did not at all understand his enraptured curiosity for youth, nor the attraction, understandable in a man without children of his own, that pulled him toward incipient blood and newly emerging spirits. It wasn't so much instinct, more like the will to pass on a legacy, some sort of essential, immaterial inheritance. In his youth he had read Condorcet, Stuart Mill, and even Poulaine de la Barre: it was not surprising, then, that he greatly favoured members of the female sex, who offered him the added possibility of contemplating the beauty of a gesture, a face, a body, alongside their grateful surprise at his acknowledgement of their potential intelligence.

Pauline wrote to him within a week. He took longer to answer. He could not quite fathom what shadow of a scruple held him back. Only this fearful doubt muddied the transparency of the relation. Much later, Amédée attributed that initial hesitation to a kind of premonition, but it is too easy, and surely deceptive, to read the past in the light of what we know to have happened afterwards. In one of her final letters, Pauline evoked a day they took a walk in the Luxembourg gardens. A year had passed since the beginning of their epistolary friendship. An old priest looked at them as they walked, offering them a tender smile. Doubtless he took them for a model, affectionate father and daughter who got along famously. If Amédée had an image in his mind as he answered Pauline's first letter, it closely resembled that one. It was only his absolute certainty that this correspondence would be misinterpreted that made him hide the letters from his wife.

Two or three missives were exchanged before Pauline returned to London. Her mother and sister had already gone, but she managed to prolong her stay, at the house of some American friends: Violette, whose name was so often on her lips, and her younger sister Mary, with whom she at least shared a taste for music... They did not see each other again, but when he found out the day and time she would take the train, he sent white roses to her at the station.

Pauline, Paule, Paulette. Depending on the day and the nuance. The last letter was signed Paulette, as if she wanted to make herself even smaller, and Frencher, in the desperation of her double exile. Fifteen years later, Amédée's memory would forever link her face and words together in a single, vivid image. Even when he evoked her in silence, her words, whether remembered or projected, transformed his vision of her, until that first, all too banal and false picture she had originally offered him was erased completely.

24

Her visage was, in the last analysis, that of a wise or troubled female child, and grave. Yet, there was no indication of that seriousness at first glance. So, the two portraits he still had of Pauline from that epoch were no more than engravings of a girl in the flower of her youth, a pretty, oval, rounded face with velveteen cheeks, and lips that the sepia colour of the photograph could not temper. Her little head rose from an open neckline covered with fine lace and silk flowers. Even though his imagination superimposed what he knew of her, helping him discover the beauty that at first glance went by unnoticed, the image itself remained quite conventional: that of any marriageable girl who might have attracted his attention momentarily in a salon, only to vanish from his memory without a trace at the next moment, in favour of another, similar image.

Of the two pictures, essentially alike, he preferred the larger one, on stiff paper, framed by a narrow, greenish trim... In it, Pauline appeared at once ethereal and sensual – ethereal in the whiteness of her neck and the brightness of her eyes, and with her hair, softly curled and gathered up at the back by invisible clasps. Sensual in the expression of her barely open lips, in the full vigour of her cheeks. The other photograph was smaller and darker, with jagged edges: vulgar. On her head, an enormous hat like a flowery pagoda paid respect to the questionable fashion of the day, with a dress overloaded with guipure lace and garlands of roses to match. The little round face fought in vain to attract attention, like a relic inside a baroque monstrance. Only someone who knew her could perceive a happiness imbued with uncertainty in those almost invisible dots of eyes and the imprecise lines of a smile. It was the last photograph she had sent him from Eastbourne, once she had prevailed in the lawsuit against her mother. The luxurious attire attested to her new fortune. The happiness, to her new liberty. Was it also a new uncertainty that led her to write him that letter, the only one he had to destroy?

It was on an autumn day just like this one that he had received the letter. But the whole tangled skein, which left him with no prudent choice but to cut the thread, had its origin half a year earlier when Pauline returned to Paris in the wintertime and was practically alone. Up to then, their relationship was limited to letters, to the exchange of poems and literary impressions, and to the shipments of books Amédée considered most appropriate for the formation of a spirit he felt to be touched by genius. Pauline's letters were full of confidences and declarations of principles. Amédée remembered her exasperation when he predicted – in the best of faith – that the end of all her troubles, which he put down to a lack of affection, would come about with an ideal marriage. "So you still think the women of today have nothing better to do than be led to marriage like a flock of sheep? I thought you were a true friend…"

The interchange of poems was lopsided. An avalanche of verses flowed from London to Paris, which he commented on and corrected, some of them addressed to him specifically. Amédée attributed the increasing passion they manifested to literary artifice and her exalted adolescent imagination. He participated in the game with a few gallant rhymes and four sonnets regretting his lost youth. Pauline's responses traced elaborate filigree around the theme of springtime and autumn joined by love. If the world were to make such an alliance impossible, then she offered a definitive assignation in death.

The poems always accompanied the letters, like two voices

in a musical score, different yet complementary. Every so often she would express her deepest gratitude for *Atala, René, La faute de l'Abbé Mouret, Une page d'amour*, all courtesy of the well-edited and accessible Collection Guillaume, or some recent book by Barrès or Bourget. From that year there remained a few random details which for him had no logical explanation. For example, the string of letters Pauline had written on mourning paper, with a black border. The explanation she offered, later on, when he uneasily asked the pertinent question, did little to dispel his heedless, imprecise anxiety: Pauline's mother had rented a summer house from an acquaintance in Shepperton, and it was he who was the owner of that funereal stationery which, according to Pauline, filled the drawers of a writing desk; mired in debt, this same personage had lost his mother two months before. The gentleman was also the proud owner of a collection of magazines and books that never should have fallen into the hands of a young lady of manners… Pauline had invoked her universal desire for knowledge in response to her correspondent's scandalized reprimand.

It was while she was at Shepperton that Pauline's letters became more frequent. She intensified the rhythm, and he responded promptly, without losing a beat. She felt almost happy there, she said, in that village on the banks of the Thames. Her mother was in London preparing a cruise with one of her admirers… Alone with Toinette and two or three servants, Pauline felt free. She played the piano, took long walks, went by coach to a nearby town for ice cream, looked at the sky at night, as well as all the sunrises and the sunsets. She cursed the rain that kept her indoors, the showers that rent petals from the rose bushes. And she wrote to him, page after page. Then, the cruise project fell through, Madame T. showed up suddenly at Shepperton, and Pauline fell ill. It was then that everything became more complicated.

Amédée was well aware, even from the distance that now separated him from those goings-on, of the extent to which she held the reins and he allowed himself to be led, flattered and moved; how that child had so unexpectedly taken possession of an intimate redoubt that up to then had belonged entirely to him. And so, when Pauline asked him to write two letters – a false one for Madame T.'s eyes, and another, real one for her – he did so, amused. He also agreed, albeit with less enthusiasm, to write to Toinette. He followed each of Pauline's directions to the letter. He wrote so that his letters would arrive on the day she indicated, whether for objective reasons of security, or for subjective ones: a simple whim of hers. Later, when the mother and two daughters took a trip to Spa via Ostend and Brussels, Pauline asked him to suspend the correspondence, and he did so. For a month, nothing more than a few hasty postcards from her, with a brief text, nourished the longing which was laid bare to him for the first time. At a given moment, a live yearning with sharp edges would take hold of him, and then he would realize that it was one of the days on which he used to receive a letter from Pauline.

When the correspondence resumed, Pauline announced with overflowing enthusiasm that she would spend the winter in Paris. Meanwhile, few letters now arrived at the post box in London with the false name she had asked him to use for the time being. Pauline was alone in Paris, while her mother and Toinette travelled with friends. She could come and go as she pleased. Just as she had announced in her letters, she showed him all her favourite places. And Amédée let himself be led, like a schoolboy on his first outing, above the towers of Notre Dame, where he discovered another Paris at his feet, a Paris completely different from that of his adolescence: his first trip to the capital, when the works of Haussmann were turning everything into a giant pile of rubble. Together they covered the length and breadth of the Louvre, and any passersby, had they failed to notice the age difference, might easily have mistaken them for one of the many timid and proper engaged couples who arranged to meet there. They crossed the Luxembourg gardens in every direction and paused, enraptured before the children applauding wildly for puppets on the Champs Elysées. He visited her at her apartment on Boissière, which he inundated with flowers, and she read Dante in Italian and played waltzes by Chopin. Amédée's situation became stranger by the day: he hid those visits from Madame M. as he had hidden his correspondence, and that made him feel like a guilty man, even though no one could possibly censure any concrete aspect of the relationship.

They went to the theatre only once. Until then they had never gone out at night. They took that risk in spite of Amédée's hesitation, and the fear of a likely indiscretion. But Pauline's insistence and their absolute innocence before any possible accusation seemed to protect them with invisible armour. Amédée allowed himself to be persuaded, won over by a desire for candour he hardly recognized. When the cab stopped in front of her doorstep afterwards, a rebellious, childlike complicity sealed the diffuse but unmistakable pact. The moment was dense and tight, a world unto itself. There was a frame, some limits, that they had implicitly accepted, and their blood pulsed against them. Colliding with them only whetted and turned the heightened impulse into effervescent, winged froth. Amédée had brought her a bunch of violets, which she wore all evening tucked into her neckline. When she got out of the coach, as he offered her his right hand, his left brushed nervously against the spot where her white, slim neck began. The violets passed from Pauline's left hand to Amédée's while their right hands remained clasped for an eternal moment.

Amédée's worst fears were confirmed. It was difficult to identify where the rumours came from. But Madame M. was apprised and so was Pauline's mother, who reacted with an unexpected authoritarianism. The announcement of an immediate return to London produced that tragic episode he did not wish to remember, which was inflicted upon him like a final reprimand, grave and decisive. Pauline took a frightening dose of chloral. She used five times the normal amount for insomnia. The last Amédée heard about it was that irreparable consequences had been avoided, because one of the servants had arrived in time.

A long parenthesis followed. At first, Amédée felt a certain, unexpected relief. Recent events had left him immobilised by the weight of gloom, heavy as lead. Knowing that Pauline was safe and far away allowed him the space he needed to make decisions. Later, her silence simply indicated the strict, invincible control of Madame T., and he began to miss her with a strange violence. At that point he made that stupid, imprudent gesture, which he regretted immediately. When the Goethe book, with a message in German, was returned to him, he cursed his own momentary ingenuity. Obviously Madame T. was not to be fooled by such a simple ruse. Pauline eventually wrote to him a couple of months later.

The first letter after such a long silence was a very long one, in which she explained her escape, Madame T.'s failed efforts to have her locked up in a mental institution, her own lawsuit to get out from under maternal jurisdiction, and her current situation as a ward of Court. Shortly afterwards, the second letter arrived, also from Eastbourne, containing that little photograph with the jagged edges, showing Pauline's whole body, dressed in that flowery frock with too many ribbons and braids and that enormous hat. A certain detail had attracted Amédée's attention from the beginning: she appeared to him for the first time as having an extremely thin waistline, unrealistically small thanks to a corset. But a contradiction was all too evident between that apparent signal of adulthood and the childlike expression on the tiny face that smiled at him from the portrait. In that letter she had let slip the unrighteous proposal that had precipitated an already, perhaps, inevitable ending. "Since I was never your lover, we can bid farewell as friends", Pauline wrote in the following letter, the final one, in response to Amédée's sermon, worthy – as he himself knew deep down – of the most run-of-the-mill moralist… Pauline alternated between a serious tone with an unsuspected hint of cynicism and the most absolute declarations that emerged so frequently from her pen.

Three or four years were to pass with no news of Pauline until he came across her one night at the Opera. Paris was a whirl at the time. The Universal Exposition and the excitement at the turn of the century came together to form an overwhelmingly epochal moment. Pauline appeared, unannounced, in the stage-box Amédée and his wife shared with his cousins. It lasted only a moment: the dense, icy atmosphere wounded the open, warm glance of the newcomer. Embarrassed and dumbfounded by their attempt at hidden and impossible pacts, Amédée did not even dare extend his hand to her. Pauline no longer looked like a child, and that fact made the snub all the more serious. Amédée retained this image of her for several days: she was wearing an evening gown the colour of wisteria, tight around the waist, her shoulders bare, her neck a dazzling white, in the blossom of her twenty years. Later he erased a vision that only accentuated and refined the regret that had assaulted him once before, and burdened him still, even after the sentence had been meted out incontestably, with new elements of punishment: Pauline was no longer a child, and she was living in Paris. Although the coldness of their encounter had, for the moment, prevented him from finding out her address, a chance occurrence like this might happen again at any time. He hardly knew which was weightier, the fear or the desire. For several months he remained alert. Later, things took on their previous contours and Pauline returned, like so much sediment, to the very bottom of his memory.

It must have been a year or two later when Amédée found himself leafing through a book of poems: *Études et préludes*, signed by a previously unpublished author, R. Vivien. His walks often took him by Choiseul Passageway, where he would ferret about among the new tomes of verse, looking for the spark of some young voice that might nourish his hope for the future of poetry. The book was in regular verse and metre, for which he was most grateful in those days when free verse was wreaking havoc among youthful writers. That fact, along with a favourable first impression, made up his mind to purchase the volume.

Several days went by before he found the time for a careful reading. Something inside him seemed to put the moment off. But one morning, he felt a sudden rush to read it as soon as he awoke. The poems echoed a faraway but familiar tone that drew him in, and Amédée resisted the pull, for he did not know where it would take him. He clung desperately to logic, to calculations of improbability in order not to give in to that siren song. But suddenly, there it was, the clearest evidence in the first line of that sonnet: "Elles passent au loin, frêles musiciennes".

Amédée remembered that line perfectly, because he had corrected it; in the original version, Pauline had written "au lointain", leading him to point out that something didn't quite work: it required one to elide a syllable in order for the line to read as a classical alexandrine. She agreed to change it; she was obsessed with perfection of form. Even so, the solution he had proposed was "très loin", he was sure of it, in order to produce the correct syllable count. Her choice, however, was much more evocative, of that there was no doubt.

So, R. Vivien was Pauline. In this light he re-read all the other poems. By then, it seemed absurd that he hadn't realized it from the very beginning: so unmistakable were the verses, so nakedly did that youthful soul throb from within them. The ingenuously Baudelairian tone they often took, the deft use of rhetoric, which upon a first reading resembled so many other poems, published by the dozen, only made her originality stand out: that intimate substance that lends truth to a text, above and beyond literary craft. Amédée had heard an echo of that voice years ago, and now it came back to him like a penitent's reward and punishment, simultaneously. From now on, Pauline's aura would always be nearby, within reach. That in itself inflamed in him, at times to the point of torment, the heretofore muted desire to see the other Pauline, the one of flesh and blood, the girl with the slender, white neck, and an easy laugh countered by sudden seriousness.

Because of all this, when he read in *Le Figaro* that a relatively well-known critic was to give a lecture on new trends in French poetry, and he saw that R. Vivien was one of the authors to be discussed, the impulse to attend unleashed itself inside him, and his good sense seemed to lack the dexterity to pull in the reins. He was not accustomed to such passion. Hours later, the battle was still at an impasse. Amédée searched for the terms and concessions for a truce, but there were only two options, mutually exclusive. He finally decided on the sensible course, and to confirm it he made an appointment with a client at the same hour. The strategem melted in his hands. Half an hour before the meeting, his client sent him an apologetic note saying he would not be able to come. Now his impulse had nothing to restrain it; suddenly there remained just an empty space of time with nothing to do. Chance or luck had tipped the balance with no ambiguity. He was at once choked with panic thinking what would have happened otherwise. The terrifying idea that he might die without seeing Pauline again attacked him unexpectedly and viciously. He rushed out, worried by the feeling that he was already too late.

The lecture was under way when he arrived. The room was crowded, but the first thing Amédée saw was Pauline's curved back in the second-to-last row; her neck, her fair hair pulled up beneath a wide-brimmed, white hat. He recognized her at once. It took him longer to hear the words of the critic, and when he did, he realized that the scholar was enthusiastically praising *Études et préludes* and at the same time assuming masculine authorship of the work. It was no surprise. Amédée himself had made the same mistake until he identified the true author. Pauline seemed to carry her anonymity to the point of putting her words in the mouth of a man. Otherwise, how could one explain the fact that all the love poems were clearly addressed to a woman? It was a time-honoured literary device, of course. Years later, in a famous article on "feminine romanticism", Charles Maurras would raise the possibility that Pauline's poetry was written with her seated before a mirror. Was she, herself, then, the beloved to whom those poems were addressed by a lover to whom she lent her own poetic voice? The speaker of the evening did not address that problem, which would not merit attention until the publication of her third book, when the R. of the pseudonym expanded to Renée. Instead, he continued to elaborate on the sentiments of that young male poet, in love.

At one point, Pauline leaned towards the person seated to her right, as if to comment on something the speaker had said. Her companion was a young woman of about the same age, to judge from the back, with blonder hair, almost silvery; she was shorter, sporting a black hat with feathers that climbed straight upwards, shiny and lush. Suddenly the two seemed possessed by a convulsion. The moiré and lace of their dresses shook violently. Amédée realized at once that the spasms responded to a silent but violent attack of laughter. They appeared to take control of themselves for a moment, but then they exploded again with even more virulence. Seconds later, the two left the room quickly, passing next to Amédée who was seated in the back row. Pauline's cheeks were bright red and her eyes sparkled. She looked straight ahead to avoid stares, her mouth held rigidly under control. He was sure she hadn't seen him. Her companion, however, dedicated a distracted glance his way, or rather a fraction of a glance, since he was merely part of the collective to whom it was directed. Surely, however, on detecting his tense attention, her eyes had fallen, for an instant at least, on his face: grey, incisive, steely eyes, still holding a flash of laughter but now in charge of the situation. The strange hardness of that look contrasted with her slender body and fine features, and matched a smile that carmine lipstick tried to define without accomplishing anything more than to sharpen the enigma.

After that vision, disappointing in its brevity and lack of consistency, Amédée was to acknowledge his error. That schoolboy intemperance, which could have led him to the abyss of ridicule, came from an uncontrolled being that inhabited him without his knowledge, a madman who ignored all limits, and was capable of undoing on the impulse of a moment the wise moderation of his pact with life. He learned his lesson. And so, when he saw that another lecture was to be held at the Hôtel des Societés Savantes, dedicated exclusively to Renée, he declined the offer, thus avoiding the trap of circumstance. Despite the fact that the announced speaker, Charles Brun, was an intellectual of a certain prestige; a capable poet and respected scholar of troubadour verse, who was afflicted with an ardent regionalism which found the faintest of echoes in Amédée himself.

For a long time, the only news he had of Pauline was what

he found and read sporadically, and avidly, in the press about Renée Vivien. So much so that he sometimes ended up calling her Renée himself, as if a single being had doubled into two and Renée was the part life had conceded to him with equanimity. Book after book, her poems kept coming to find him, and he experienced this as an assignation, to which she always showed up with loving punctuality. Afterwards, he would read the criticism and reviews that mentioned her, as proud as a mentor who has been surpassed by a beloved disciple, or an exultant father on hearing people speak of a child who has attained the lofty heights to which he himself had aspired. And every once in a while, there was that regret. The regret that made all the other feelings he dared admit to himself about Pauline ring with the empty sound of a false jewel. The anxiety that appeared suddenly in the form of a radical insecurity about the truth of his link with her, the legitimacy of his rights of possession to that which was his only as long as he felt Renée was his.

Chance arranged for him to see Pauline once more, a couple of years ago, at the Longchamp races. Installed in a luxurious, open convertible, under a grey silk umbrella, she seemed absorbed, with her lowered gaze fixed on her fan of feathers. At her side was an exuberant lady, solid as a Roman matron, visibly engrossed from behind her binoculars by the horses' performances. To judge by her splendid attire, she was a person of high standing. Perhaps someone from Pauline's family, thought Amédée. Her binoculars came down after a while allowing Amédée to identify the profile of the Baroness van Z. de N., the wife of the founder and former president of the Automobile Club of France. Amédée had been introduced to the Baron, and it would have been appropriate for him to approach the car, which bore the family escutcheon, in order to courteously offer his respects to the occupants. Instead, he hurried away from the place while ruminating over the elevated relations literature seemed to have bestowed upon Pauline. When he felt far enough away to be safe, rescued by his caution from the risk of being seen and recognized, he focused his field glasses on Pauline and contemplated her at leisure. The image he took with him from that absurd temerity was terrible: Pauline was troubled, sad, with dark circles under her eyes. What had seemed mere self-absorption or distraction was in fact a strange disorder of the gaze, which fluttered about in nervous flight, not knowing where to land. Her bowed head looked as if it bore a heavy weight, as if her harshly inclined neck was barely able to hold it aloft, keeping it from imminent collapse. Her entire body folded inward, formless, as if no bones remained, and in the absence of a corset, there was nothing to outwardly give it a consistent structure.

Amédée recalled some of the dark, distressing verses from one of her last books, *La Vénus des aveugles*. The image he gleaned at the Longchamp races reunited Renée and Pauline into a single, mysteriously wounded being. It made Amédée think of one of those strange illnesses of the soul that destroy from within, which sometimes have their origin much earlier, in an old sorrow, fermented by secrecy. The idea then crossed his mind: perhaps Pauline still loved him. She had said so very clearly in her last letter: I will always love you. At the time, Amédée hadn't paid much attention, and over the years, he had never seriously considered that possibility. Now it took hold of his mind, against all logic. Perhaps Pauline still loved him. Perhaps during all those years Renée had written the poems she would have liked to receive from him: no doubt she had converted him, in her imagination, into the absolute lover she would have wished him to be, curiously giving herself the role of the vanishing, unattainable woman. For Amédée had never, not for a moment, given credence to the calumnious rumours, full of bile and dictated by the most repulsive envy, that every so often oozed from the press:

The damsel Renée Vivien
sings the pleasures of the rub
as no one else has done
since Sappho first divulged them.

Amédée had tossed that newspaper into the fire, indignant. There had been other such insinuations, attempting to splash mud on a literary reputation whose prestige was constantly growing, as had happened with the very same poet Sappho, mentioned in those vile couplets, whose work Renée had so beautifully translated into French verse. At that moment in Longchamp, while he gazed at Pauline through his field glasses, he felt positively assured that his interpretation was correct. "I will always love you", she had written. Why should she be less faithful to that promise than to all the other unequivocal decisions she had made as an adolescent? She wanted to be a poet, and she was a poet. She didn't want to marry, and indeed there was no ring on her finger. But the clarity of that evidence collapsed after a few minutes, as he struggled not to sink under the weight of a darkly culpable dread.

He never saw her again. But on that November day as he awaited the visit of his nieces, the memory of Pauline had slipped into his apartment on Courcelles Street with its double-edged sweetness.

Carmen, the maid, brought him the morning papers. She left them on the side table and turned to leave, but Amédée noticed that she was hesitating and suspected an unformulated request. He responded with sensitivity before she could say anything. His innate, genteel courtesy extended to all members of the feminine gender, even servants. "Don't worry, Carmen," he said, pointing to the papers, "if there is any news, I'll let you know."

Ever since those dramatic July events in Barcelona, the maid anxiously poured over any news from the other side of the Pyrenees. Amédée perceived her distress, a concrete suffering for someone faraway, who was perhaps in some sort of danger. At the same time he was aware of Carmen's discomfort at not being able to hide her emotion from his eyes, perhaps apprehending that he might judge certain complicities too severely. Her gaze darkened, becoming sorrowful at times, and avoided his as she tried vainly to pretend a merely generic interest in a city where her family didn't even live.

Carmen was very pretty; there was a sadness in her that indicated passion. That is why he had decided to call her Carmen when he hired her. It was the first time he had assigned a name to a maid: while Madame M. was alive, she had invariably called them all Françoise. He had permitted himself that minor whim of a man of letters, convinced that it would flatter the servant. But she remained inexpressive, apparently indifferent: she had probably never heard of Merimée or Bizet, or even of Emma Calvé. For her it was simply the second or third name she had had to get used to since coming to work as a servant in Paris... She did not even know how to read, at least not in French. But she bore a natural dignity, fine as chiselled ivory; a strange equilibrium between intensity and delicacy of spirit emanated from her face and slender body. Amédée had employed her shortly after Madame M.'s death. It would have been unthinkable before: his wife distrusted feminine beauty and she would never have allowed it to cross the threshold into the house. She understood Amédée's interest in sculpture, ceramics and porcelain, and she had even accompanied him to a well-known antique dealer's shop on La Boétie Street, offering her opinion in the choice of a Sèvres vase or fifteenth-century Faience amphora. But his admiration for living forms was not acceptable… Now, however, his eyes greedily followed the beauty coming and going in his presence; he breathed it, sucking it in voluptuously. But surely his greatest pleasure resulted from demonstrating to his wife, under their conjugal roof, how innocuous his aspirations really were and how absurd her gnawing suspicions, which had wounded his deepest sense of aesthetics. This kind of posthumous pact, which Madame M. had no option to refuse, absolved Amédée of the one disturbance he had felt in that carefully watched space over which she alone continued to reign.

Amédée began to leaf through *Le Figaro*. It was his favourite paper. Not because he shared its opinions. He could not bring himself to agree with the editorial line of any of the papers; they were all too partial. But having to choose, he preferred to attribute any disagreement to his own excessive liberality. It was as though he could mentally advance as much as he wished, but with his back covered. Yes, there was a report indirectly related to events in Barcelona: the Council of the Seine had protested the execution of that Ferrer i

Guàrdia fellow, who had provoked so much commentary and raised so many voices throughout Europe. Nothing else. The new budget was approved, the conflict in Morocco, Blériot's latest aerial feats, flying at so many metres of altitude between such and such places … and suddenly, in a corner, just a few lines:

"We announce the death of Miss Renée Vivien, author of *Études et préludes, Cendres et poussières, Brumes de Fjords, Évocations, La Vénus des aveugles, Une femme m'apparut, Sappho, Les Kitharèdes*. She passed away of consumption in her mysterious and funereal ground floor apartment on Bois de Boulogne, amid her multitude of Buddhas, in a deep darkness barely penetrated by the light of a few candles. Several months ago she appeared to have taken leave of her pagan ideal. She was obsessed by mystical ideas."

Amédée was unable to finish reading. Night swooped down on him suddenly, like a bird of prey. Ever so vaguely, in the distance, Pauline still seemed to offer him one last appointment, from which there could be no return.

Private Papers of Sara T. (1)

Where the – seemingly absent – narrator catches Sara T. in the process of composing an extensive epistolary account of her doubts, motivations, considerations and reconsiderations regarding Renée Vivien. And where that which is silenced is more important than that which is said.

Paris, 6 July 1984

Dearest Chantal,

Here I am in Paris again. Tomorrow I'll have been here a whole week, back on my obsessive pursuit of any trace of my Renée. Where did this monumental obsession come from, you must be asking yourself. And I admit I sometimes ask the same myself. I swear that if I believed in demonic possession – or angelic, for that matter – that's what I would be thinking is happening here. Five years now I've been chasing this story, without even really knowing what it is I am seeking any more. I feel more and more lost by the minute. I mean, is it really still of interest to me now, in the present, that is? Or am I simply continuing down a side-track, due to an absurd fidelity to a past interest that didn't come to anything? The very same thing that occurs from time to time when you fall in love: you don't know if it will go anywhere, but you cling to the one thing you do know: where it came from, its origin. As well as to the time, the effort, the desire that you have already invested – and which you cannot resign yourself to recognizing as being definitively lost – on the same number of the Roulette wheel. All the time, failing to remember, unforgivably, that line from Marcelline Desborde-Valmore: *Ce qu'on donne a l'amour est à jamais perdu* – "What one gives in love is

43

forever lost" – and that Natalie Barney Americanized as follows: "The gift of oneself to another is an investment without return". All in all it's a case of a fish trying to bite its tail, because each new day that you persist in going in the same direction, the stakes become even higher, and it's precisely this that spurs you on. As I still can't quite see the wood for the trees, I'm going to stick to the facts and to some pretty simplistic deductions: in a nutshell, I'm in Paris, and for the third time in a row I've decided to invest in this project – without hope of return – my holidays and double holiday pay: it's important not to forget the prosaic details of the matter. So there must be a pretty powerful reason driving me to do so. At least that's what I've chosen to think in spite of all the unease I've been feeling lately. It turns out that my initial project was just too damn simple. As simple as that.

All of this is a roundabout way of saying that the screenplay is still in its infancy. It wouldn't progress even with wheels on. Perhaps because it's me who's putting obstacles in the way. I can't stop myself rethinking the project, over and over again. Only the beginning remains clear to me, and rather more tentatively the ending. As I explained to you before, it will open with the death of Renée. Amidst an atmosphere of Gothic gloom: the apartment all draped in dark blue with violet stained-glass windows, and the stormy night all setting the tone – I don't even need to invent anything. Every time I think about it, I am reminded of the opening sequence of *Citizen Kane*, even though they are characters and deaths that have absolutely nothing in common... Renée died surrounded by people and has had numerous last words attributed to her. All burdened with meaning. There is no "Rosebud" here, and that in itself is perhaps suspicious. As if everyone heard what they wanted to hear. From a resolute profession of her belief in the Catholic faith in her final hour, to a confession of her eternal love for Natalie-Lorély, to a tooth-and-nail defence of her literary vocation and even a suggestive "I curse my mother" that to me, personally, is far more attractive than the others, but highly improbable. How to choose? Trial and error. The very plurality of posthumous messages attributed to a dying woman with laryngeal paralysis is highly significant and not in the least banal.

Renée is one of those mythical figures who has functioned as a screen on to which everyone projects their own imaginary. Me included, it would seem. But, is there any other way of bringing the dead back to life? "Whoever writes of me will be lying without doubt" – *Si l'on parle de moi, l'on mentira sans doute* – Renée once wrote. This phrase, this line that has always been there in my mind, has perhaps also been the reason for such continuous distortion. I have tried so hard, and so in vain, not to justify her fears, that I have become lost in the phantasmagorical wood of words. It is something of a paradox that beings who are so extremely singular in their hard-fought subjectivity should awaken in their disciples a mechanism both of simplification and of radical extrapolation that converts them almost into a generic concept, a kind of degraded metaphor. I have striven to counteract this tendency by accessing the greatest possible complexity of biographical and contextual data. It is a bottomless well.

Returning to the screenplay, I have written and rewritten this first sequence of her death, but can get no further. Even so I am not satisfied with it. And now, to crown it all, things have been made more complicated by the appearance of new events and characters. I know what you are thinking: that I deserve it. I haven't taken your advice and now I am facing the consequences, but I don't know how to work without having all of the threads in my hand and being able to tie all the ends together. Of course I know it's an illusion, that life always escapes you like water through a sieve, but sometimes illusions appear real and that is what really matters. I need a convincing enough simulacrum in order to be able to begin.

At long last, after all the obstacles, I've been given access to the manuscript section in the Bibliothèque Nationale. I had no idea of what I would find there. In the card catalogue there was only one dossier, made up of a collection of letters, photographs, manuscript poems and translations of parts of the *Divine Comedy*. But I met a friendly librarian who told me about another really important legacy, which cannot be opened until the year 2000 due to the express instructions of the man who deposited it. His name is Salomon Reinach, but I have no idea who he is or what research needs to be done in order to work out what kind of relationship he had with Renée. I seem to remember Natalie Barney mentioning the name in one of her books, but it must have not struck me as significant at the time and I didn't record anything. For the moment, however, I have enough work copying the letters from the archive that is accessible. Because I've decided that instead of reading and taking notes from them, it will be more useful to copy them. It's more mechanical, and in my current state of doubt, I worry that my intuition for selection won't be up to the mark. I'm even copying all the crossings out and the ink stains: you can't imagine how suggestive they can be...!

As a result of all this, two new characters have appeared on the scene. One of them isn't that important, I think: just a girl Renée was friends with as a child. She's the one who presents the entire collection of letters, and a section of them are addressed to her, with dates from her teen years. In her introduction, this friend, called Marie, explains how they came to be in her hands and the identity of the addressee of the rest of the letters: a cousin of hers, who was over 50 at the time – and married, to boot – by the name of Amédée. Marie talks of a liaison between Renée and him. From what I've copied so far, I can't really tell the actual dimensions of the affair. I'll give you my three ha'pence worth another time. What do you think of that, though? The discovery that Renée Vivien, the "Sappho 1900", had a male lover, at this stage of proceedings! If my original ideas were already in disarray, then this has contributed to their absolute collapse into a sea of doubt. Even though, in one of the letters there is a minor detail that Freud would have seized on…: in the opening address, instead of writing *ami* she writes *amie*, and then crosses out the *e*… However we read it this new information confirms the need to do as much research as possible.

At the beginning it was all crystal clear: the passion between Renée and Natalie, black and white. Plus a third more shadowy figure – "fate"? – impeding the mythical and definitive reconciliation of opposites. In synthesis, and in rather less romantic and high-flown terms, this is the version given to us by Natalie, the *Amazone*, in her own *Souvenirs indiscrets*. It hardly mattered that the tragic ending, so common in this type of set-up, only affected one of the parties. It almost seemed logical in her story, that the lover of Death, Renée, should be the one to die at the age of 32, whereas the lover of Life, Natalie, carried on living to the age of nearly 100. To each her own: a game of chess ending in stalemate. The three or four poems by Renée I knew and which made me come out in goosebumps – do you remember? – hardly helped me to find my way out of such a frame. I thought that all I needed to do was to uncover the workings behind this unbreakable bond between your typical *poète maudite* and that other figure with her triumphal air, who had somehow succeeded in turning a marginalization into a privilege. Heads and tails of the same coin? Or better, the negative and positive of the same photographic image?

Later, as you know, I stumbled upon Hélène, who Natalie turned into the grotesque and fallacious agent of their contrarian "fate". Most of the writings about Renée I have read are critical of her – not just Natalie, which would be understandable – and insist without scruple on dismissing her on the basis of her physical appearance. You already know what I think, so I won't go into any more detail here. As well as Hélène, there is a whole litany of names that do not appear in Natalie's version. Other stories to nuance the image of sculpted stone, enclosed and without cracks that, I'm not afraid to admit, captured my attention at the very beginning. It makes me laugh now, to think where those initial romantic clichés of mine have brought me. It hardly needs to be said how I felt that first day on emerging from the manuscript section in the Nationale.

Well, I imagine that after this excessively long letter, you'll no longer be complaining about not knowing what I'm up to or where I roam. I know I have only talked about one thing, the thing that all my attention is focused on at the moment. There are subjects I don't want to think too much about so I've, for want of a better word, parked them. All I will say to you, so you don't worry too much, is that Arès and I have taken a break from each other again. I know that we don't seem to be able to get out of this circular pattern: conflict-break-reconciliation-conflict… etc. "Only goodbyes with a smile are definitive", is what the Amazon would say. That's precisely why I don't want to think about it: I've turned it over in my mind enough times. Perhaps in a week or two I won't be able to help myself and then the downpour will come. By letter, or perhaps…

Listen, is there a chance of you coming down to Paris for a few days? Letter writing never quite makes up for a good long natter, even if only by phone. You know me by now! Lately, though – as I think I've already told you – I've had to put a break on that particular vice because the bills were about to ruin me – although they say you can't ruin a poor man – or woman! The truth is that one of the things that make it hardest for me to put myself in Renée's shoes, or for that matter those of the other characters in my project, is precisely to do with economics… I know someone once said, rather pointedly, that at the end of the day Renée had the fortune to be able to torment herself only with metaphysical problems.

Going back to what I was saying before: if it doesn't suit you to come down to me, perhaps I could grab a weekend and come up to Brussels. I could make the most of the journey, too, and see a bit of Flanders. One of my characters lived there for a few years, in Saint Omer. The one I'm referring to was a teacher – and confidant, and friend… – of Renée: Charles Brun, I don't know if I have mentioned him before. I also vaguely recall that there is a village, just on the border – can't quite remember the name now – where Marguerite Yourcenar was born. Have you been there? Do you know anything about it? Oh, and there's another thing I haven't told you and which will make you smile: Yourcenar once met

Natalie Barney and, what's more, she also won the Renée Vivien prize – I just don't know the year – founded and endowed by Hélène, no less... Don't go thinking it's only a coincidence: if I wanted to pursue all the traces of important women who were milling around Paris at that time, I'd end up writing not just one but one hundred screenplays... Only yesterday I went to the Rodin museum, with the aim of viewing the bust of Renée, which I hadn't spotted on previous visits. And I began to think about Camille Claudel: surely they must have met at some point, if only crossing paths on the staircase to his studio...? And that's without going through the whole list of people who used to frequent the Amazon's salon. Apart from Marguerite Yourcenar, we find Djuna Barnes, Gertrude Stein, Colette, Marina Tsvetaeva... as well as Sibilla Aleramo, Marie Laurencin... And those are just a few of the better known names!

But back to the matter of a trip: to tell the truth I don't know what I should do, what should be my priority. Because if I had to follow up all the itineraries that in one way or another had something to do with Renée and co., I just wouldn't have the time, I'd be travelling non-stop across the planet. Although coming to see you would be a good reason to make some sort of a decision, and with the excuse that it might also be useful to me... I'll call you. A short one, though, okay? What's Anna up to? I imagine that when I see her I won't even recognize her. Listen, if we really do manage to meet up, here in Paris, or in Brussels, or half-way, I'd like to speak with you about this whole business of mothers and daughters. In Renée's work there is a strange kind of horror towards maternity. For example, from a physical point of view in one poem she writes of maternity having devastated women's breasts: *Les seins qu'ont ravagé les maternités lourdes / Ont la difformité des outres et des gourdes.* In another she identifies with Belial, "Archangel enemy of births" who on "fertile bellies traces the number 13". Or she exclaims: "Let us throw into anathema the most hateful cry / hence is born the pain of beings to come". And there are more along the same lines. At another moment, however, she says to one of her girlfriends: "I love you because you are feeble and sweet. My arm will be a tepid cradle for you and you will rest there", or else "You are at one and the same time a child, a friend, a sister to me", and other such.

There you go, it's all so very complex and contradictory. If you come, I'd like to be able to talk about all of these things with you – you who are at the same time "daughter of a mother" and "mother of a daughter". That way we won't fall into going over and over the labours of love, as is my usual wont. Anyway, I'll sign off now without asking you anything about your own loves, so as not to give you a reason to fall into the same temptation.

Hope to see you soon,
Sara

THE NARRATOR IMPOSES A WEIGHTY TRUCE ON THE LABILE AND VAPOROUS WALTZ OF A SUPPOSEDLY MERRY WIDOW

London, November 1909

She laughed and laughed, talking continuously. As if she were at a party, someone next to her said. Or was it her own voice, from within? She gibbered and jabbered, and from time to time, she'd laugh. As if she needed to cover the mouth of silence.

Someone criticized her brown dress. "Ladies and gentlemen, my daughter was young and she didn't inform me she would be dying. I've always done what I was supposed to and I've been up to any task as long as I was given the opportunity. Of course, had it been up to her, she wouldn't even have invited me to her funeral!" But she knew very well what her duties as a mother were, even though Pauline had always insisted on seeing her as an evil stepmother: Pauline, poor little Cinderella... She had always loved playing the victim. And she had succeeded in convincing others so that whether they wanted to or not, they became either her tormentors or devout spectators of her torture. The former role had been assigned to her. From the beginning. Ever since that wrinkled, ugly little thing had left her body, executioner of her body, and surrounded her in a network of mirrors.

"She cried and cried, constantly. Like an unending reprimand." Afterwards, she never in her life saw her cry again. Afterwards, she laughed and laughed, but her mirth sounded like broken glass. "And it sliced into you, secretly, underhandedly." Shaken and brutalised as she was still by that violent, barbarous spasm that traversed her from top to bottom, robbing her of flesh and blood, no love could oblige her to enter into that cruel game, in which victim and executioner have secretly agreed to alternate for symmetry's sake. Even so, she had never been able to extirpate the dark root that, since Pauline, was buried deep in her, stuck fast in the mire of a past without name.

She had always fought fiercely against the maelstrom of pain that threatened to swallow her up. Life hadn't been at all easy. It never was, especially for women, but her lot had been excessive. "Life is like following a good or bad dancer; you have to know how to follow with elegance, even if you don't like where he's leading you, or how. And letting yourself be led gracefully is more meritorious than it may seem!" Pauline, in death, was still, maybe more than ever, the extreme force of a heavy, staggering rhythm that clung to her feet like a shadow. She defended herself, holding on with all her strength to that other force, sometimes winged and brilliant, often irregular and awkward, always versatile, changing, fascinating in its light reeling towards other salons, other seas. London, Paris, London, Honolulu, Ontario, Jackson (Detroit)…

Detroit Post, 1876: "A true amorous romance. Rich English gent visiting the Sandwich Islands falls in love with girl from Jackson."

The newspaper clipping parades it, yellowed and pompous; the headlines inscribe it – her "unheard-of" marriage – into the local chronicle with banal rose-coloured ink, spurious and false. They don't mention that the girl from Jackson, Mary G. B., was a girl with no dowry, no mother since the age of two months, abandoned by a remarried father, then picked up on the fly in Honolulu by a maternal aunt, after having passed through the worn-out hands of a tired grandmother and the cold tentacles of a Canadian boarding school. Nor do they explain the enchantments of the evenings on the island she would have to leave: the Oahu of pineapples and sugar cane, surrounded by volcanoes; the feverish, runaway joy of the dances; the variegated uniforms; and at the port, and everywhere, the hodgepodge of races and languages. Nothing was said about her love, abandoned like a nuisance, since the heart isn't even worth its weight, if subsistence leads it to a dark auction.

The "rich English gent" arrived, elegant and good-looking, with no skills but a considerable income, ready to allow himself the luxury of love at first sight, and to legitimize it with a fairy-tale wedding. She entered into the tale, seduced but at the same time sceptical, like a fish confronted with a too-shiny bait. John T. was a Londoner, and his fortune derived from the sale of some department stores created, epically, from nothing by his father and then turned over to third parties the day after his death by his descendants, who had more of a penchant for culture and dandyism, and were obsessed with Greece and the horse races. Nothing in that impeccable gentleman betrayed his obscure family origin in the mining valley of the Tees, nor was there a trace of the *élan* responsible for elevating that lean lineage of ne'er-do-wells to the heights of the most solid bourgeoisie. It was the lyrical intensity of the moment, perhaps, that overcame any regret for an epic far-removed from salon and chamber, and no doubt the full moon shining over the waters of the Pacific was an efficient catalyst to accomplish the transformation.

Mary felt as if she were being transported to the altar on an infinite cruise, and Europe in the distance attracted her like a moth, drunk on its own flight, to the dance of the flame at night. London, the first stop, was disappointing. The grey-black city, submerged in fog, smoke and soot, received her amidst the most hostile autumn in its repertory. Before long, the gravity of her body joined the dead weight of darkness that fell upon her shoulders.

It wasn't easy to distinguish, among the various unfamiliar and contrary sensations, which had to do with her situation as a well-to-do newly married lady with no financial worries, which could be associated with the radical change in landscape, climate, and social surroundings and which had their nebulous origin in her premature destiny of motherhood. The anchor fell to the bottom of the port and the wings of water were deprived of flight, tinged with lead. Her veins took on the weight of a blood at once new and as old as time. Her slim legs inflated and her body became more alien and hostile day by day. Her youth was suddenly swallowed up by a fearful swirl, from the depths of which old age and death shot her malicious winks. The world closed its doors to her and transformed her into a prisoner, a provisional inmate awaiting a definitive sentence.

Pauline Mary was born that summer. It was a difficult birth. And in that moment when all is forgotten, they say, because the baby pulsates some previously unknown chord in the sentimental lyre, releasing a sharp diaphanous note that permits the attentive and ready ear to recognize an archetypally maternal sound, Mary's eardrum remained resolutely deaf. As if, confronted with a crushing avalanche of inarticulate, discordant sounds, fissured by delirium, she had built herself an impenetrable and opaque dam. On the other side, from a supposedly sure dock, Mary struggled to put names to things: "She had enormous hands, out of proportion. Predatory hands that snatch and strangle you, that demand that you fill them and yet at the same time are riddled with holes, a bottomless well. Hands that only give you what they don't have, the void of their offering carrying the weight of regret inside your blood. I have seen those hands before my eyes ever since her birth. I haven't seen her dead woman's hands, but I know they would open up towards me like two carnivorous flowers, seeking bloody sacrifices for their nourishment, yet incapable of resisting the agony of the victim without inflicting on themselves the same destiny as necessary expiation." No love could oblige her to become a prisoner of those hands, to enter into the circle that would close in around her, to yield to the pressure that pulled her down, devoured, swallowed up as if by quicksand.

"Difficult, so difficult, to take flight again, to recompose one's image in the mirror, as if after a turbid night of mud and storms. Difficult to recover the lightness of the body, the vaporous profile of the dance, the agility and sharpness of spirit. Difficult to hold on to oneself, when everyone sees you as other, when you've been alien for months – an albatross suddenly hobbling on land, a bird changed into a tree – difficult to uproot oneself and forget that which had once before been forgotten, and whose emergence endangers the fragile itinerary of crystal and foam. Even more difficult when a difficult child returns the precise and terrifying reflection of a face you don't recognize as yours." Five years went by before Toinette's birth. During that time, Mary had learned to balance steps and cadences as she moved about gracefully and masterfully. When her body again became dense and her throbbing heavier, she managed to maintain equilibrium by stretching her thighs upwards and leaning her head back slightly. Both that gesture and the one which followed, of taking up the infant from between her legs, she made with a singular grace, as if it all formed an inescapable part of the same choreography. The infant smiled in her arms and the pact was sealed.

Meanwhile, they had moved to Paris, and the city's seduction had infiltrated her bones, down to the marrow. All superfluous lyricism had dissipated from her marriage, which had been reduced to a decorative pretext, a household structure of stewardship in which she moved with comfort and ease. Longchamp and the Derby regained their magnetism, capturing the capacity for enthusiasm that John T. had directed toward Mary for a year or so, and the horses seemed more capable than she of faithfully fulfilling his marital expectations of intense, constant emotion, thus evoking a permanent delirium in the man. Only once in a while, usually under the influence of the effluvious spirits of some opulent liquor, did the husband become aware of the essential unattainability of she who, by law, belonged to him. At that point he saw her, exquisite and dazzling, before a host of fascinated eyes, as unreachable for him as for the others and therefore equally attainable to the extent that she capriciously condescended to allow it for a few seconds. Those moments drove him mad with desire and jealousy, and Mary had had to learn to avoid those intermittent pitfalls in her path; she had excelled in this, with an exemplary dominance of the instinctive horror that bursts of emotional violence provoked in her, especially when compounded by incorporeal Bacchic emanations.

Nevertheless, those situations became ever more frequent with John T.'s progressively deteriorating health. And so, willingly or no, Mary joined the abominable, disaggregated ranks of widowhood before she reached her thirtieth year, determined not to allow herself to become imprisoned or trapped again and to utilize to her benefit the lustre of those intense, fair eyes and splendid golden hair, now beneath the dark transparency of mourning veils.

As to the lamentable specific circumstances leading to the death of the father of her daughters just as he was about to enter his fourth decade, Mary let a thick and ostensibly honorific oblivion fall like black crepe damasque. The same oblivion extended, up to a point, to those ten years of her life, like some sort of strange parenthesis, endowing her nevertheless with a train of questionable gold and two saplings that had emerged so differently from the same trunk as principal legacies. From then on, she had to put up with the watchful eyes of her deceased husband's family scrutinizing her expenses and conduct, though the English Channel placed a convenient distance between observer and observed. Her life recovered the festive disorder of her youth, propped up by the faithful inertia of more or less flattering servants. The grief, if there was any, sank to the depths without a trace. "Grief is an expensive luxury that not everyone can afford. It's the only area in which I've opted for complete austerity and modesty."

Pauline, on the other hand, had chosen to belong to that proud elite that looks upon the rest of humanity with disdain from the peak of its shadowy opulence, treasuring like an impassioned collector each ounce of suffering, from the most vulgar drops to the rarest and most valuable pieces. Her father's death when she was nine shone in the midst of it all like a black pearl of imponderable quality and exorbitant price. Without even being conscious of it, like the potentate of a starving country, she created an intemperate and inconsiderate ostentation. No one could accuse her of stinginess, for she gladly shared her bitter treasure at the slightest insinuation. Mary tacitly but definitively refused the perpetual offering, not always at her gracious best. And so it was that the daughter sank into the depths, in pursuit of the grief buried by her mother.

THE BARONESS

Paris, December 1909

Baroness van Z. de N. accommodated her immense body behind the wheel of the brand new Dion-Bouton her expert eye had carefully chosen at the latest Automobile Show. More like a barrel than an amphora, as had been spread about irretrievably by a famous *boulevardier* of the time, Hélène-Betty-Louise-Caroline, a name to suit her corpulence, offered an easy target for sharp tongues, spurred on all the more by certain details about her life she would have preferred to keep private. But the dust raised by her heavy, energetic step failed to dim her gaze one bit, and so much galloping verbiage barely aroused a shrug of her shoulders. So, she was aware from an excellent source – and quality here is beyond price – that an acquaintance of hers, a fashionable writer, had spoken ill of her, calling her an elephantine monster, among other epithets of that ilk… Yet Colette Willy, that dear little *petite-bourgeoise* from the provinces who was lately given to alternating literature with music-hall numbers, was such a delightful creature, just as seductive in one field as in the other!

Soon enough, then, her malicious comment became little more, in Hélène's memory, than the slight buzz of a somewhat bothersome insect, until it melted without a trace, and all without the author ever suspecting any other sentiment in the Baroness than immaculate cordiality and faithful admiration. It was odd, though, that that *sans-culotte*, literally so in certain scenarios – and here the excellent source blushed – should be so scandalized at a few inconsequential happenings. Due to an anecdote she herself would have forgotten had it not been for other very sad circumstances of the moment: while she and Sacha, sporting moustaches and men's clothing, were screaming, in Nice at Carnival, at a group of low-life insolents who had recognized and shouted at them loudly, Pauline, alone in Paris, was engulfed in a crisis that, seen from the present, took on the tone of a terrible premonition. Her faithful maid had had to scrape her up off the floor, and with great difficulty, bundle her into bed. Then she had called Miss G. – "Auntie Marie", as Pauline called her – who, in turn, called Nice, but was naturally unable to reach her... But this was another matter, unfortunately all too recent, and sensitive in the extreme. Furthermore, it had nothing to do with the crushing reply that had been tossed to that bunch of shameless ruffians, with words more worthy of the vulgar ears they were intended for than the lips that sent them forth. Patrician condescension, after all!

Of Rothschild ascendency on both sides, her blood had centuries of practice, in fact was perhaps even genetically programmed to display that Olympian scorn, dedicated by her race to all who might convert the privilege of belonging to the Chosen People into a stigma. She had also grown accustomed to another hundred-year-old legacy that reinforced the first, condemning her also from the pecuniary point of view: a permanent obesity. No need to dwell on this point: her family name and her legendary pocketbook are still capable of awakening a sigh of admiration in the smallest, most remote villages of the continent. But very few know of her dark crucible: like the majority of children in her family, Hélène's mother had taken her when she was very small to the sordid redoubt where her ancestors had incubated the lineage: the *Judengasse* of Frankfurt. It was like a baptism of blood. Even though it no longer existed, swallowed up by time without a trace, Hélène could never forget, by the bright colours with which it had been described, the ignominious frieze the proud Christian city had used to defend itself from the cursed effluvium of the ghetto: in it, a painted rabbi rode upon a sow while a colleague consumed the excrement that the animal shamelessly let flow; below, like a muddied replica of the capitoline twins, Jewish children took nourishment from her udders...

The Baroness still held before the wide-open eyes of a little rich girl from long ago, the image of that long and winding narrow street, shaped like an intestine, which over four centuries had seen its inhabitants multiply by thirty and its dead by five thousand without being able to expand the originally-assigned space by a single inch. The minuscule houses piled up, divided and shrunken... Only then was Hélène able to appreciate the exact dimensions of her great-grandfather's heroism – great-great grandfather on her mother's side – an ex-rabbi of the future infected with ideas from the Enlightenment, which he then plunged into numismatics, discounts on bills of exchange, and the lending business, amid the tumult of German states and cities at war with revolutionary France. Five males survived of the nineteen offspring he engendered, and they were spread throughout the principal European cities, investing in monies and stock, always multiplying the base until they created the first international banking corporation with an unprecedented network of informants, often playing on both sides of the bellicose conflicts that impoverished – and enriched – the century.

Even though she had been repudiated by her mother for

marrying a Gentile, the Baron Étienne van Z. de N., and she never missed Sunday High Mass at the Jesuit house on Madrid Street, where she also had her two sons educated, nothing could extract the vigorous, robust root that, though exiled beneath a field of silver lined with heraldic red, secretly nourished her proud external ostentation.

It must be acknowledged that Hélène managed the dual lineage with the skill of an accomplished charioteer steering two pairs of headstrong, ill-trained horses together. It was not in vain that she had been dubbed "The Valkyrie" ever since the Paris-Berlin rally, which had taken place at the peak of the Bayreuth festivals. And she managed this even though the playing field was not always level nor the mission straightforward. We might recall, for example, the notorious Dreyfus affair, which shook Parisian salons with such ferocity. Fortunately that evil wind, capable of evacuating half the gathering of a reception in an instant if some imprudent member of the other half had dared to make the slightest hint of an allusion, had already abated. The Baroness did justice on that occasion to the motto at the top of her marital escutcheon, fearlessly flaunted since at least the thirteenth century, by the mustiest Belgian aristocracy: *non titubans*. She had not wavered for a second between the two sides that seemed to demand of her such a painful and delicate choice: on the one hand, her race wounded in the person of that insignificant army captain; on the other the mundane froufrou of Paris's finest. Her common sense and energetic character had enabled her then to follow the biblical maxim: the right hand was ignorant of what the left was doing. Her generous donations to the Dreyfus cause were miraculously eclipsed from her memory as soon as she set foot in some gathering in the Faubourg Saint Germain, where opinions about her high Hebrew lineage were hardly flattering.

At the moment we find her, before her luxurious mansion on the Bois de Boulogne, ready to sportingly take on the various stages of the long road that separates her from Nice, Hélène van Z. de N. is brushing fifty, but nothing about her would indicate decline. No matter how much her flesh seems to yield, justifying one of her nicknames, the popular "la Brioche", her long hair, plaited in great amplitude atop her head, crowns with a majesty far from posthumous the density of an entire life. Paradoxically, the progressive softening of skin and pulp had made that nickname less abominable to her; the only one with the rare ability to wound her, without, however, making her lose her compass. The more her flesh started to resemble bakery dough, the harder it was for anyone to see an allusion to a trait of her character that she knew all too well and strove to keep secret: the sweetish softness, like marrow inside the bone that holds it, hidden beneath her apparent toughness, which some impenitent reader of poetry might have been able to perceive in a book published under a pseudonym a few years earlier, obviously at the expense of the author, by a printer on Choiseul Passage:

How I admire poor dogs
deprived of all kinds of petting,
as if in perpetual shadow,
with no peace or resting…
Often so ugly and coated in slush,
Their souls can be utterly lovely!

Memorable verses, especially the liquid alliteration of the ending, no doubt destined to be recovered from oblivion by one of the first societies for the protection of animals…

The fact is that Pauline had encouraged her along this difficult path, lovingly offering her prosody classes; she had helped her polish nodes and edges with unlimited patience… her little Pauline, who wanted to make a great poet of her, back when she still felt like doing something and her memory had not started to unravel… When she thought: Pauline!, emphatically, like that, for a brief moment that infantile face would appear before her, so full of dimples, along with her ingenuously perverse laughter, her little teeth with even eye teeth as if wishing to blot out any indication of ferocity… that fleshy upper lip curved slightly upward, her pug nose and her eyelashes so long that they reached her eyebrows when she opened her eyes wide. Overcome by an unconscious obstinacy, Hélène pushed other, more recent images away from her memory and clung tightly to those snapshots that conjured up a feeling of faraway comfort and well-being. Above all, it was the early scenes that returned to her like a sweet refrain, from when her love seemed to close all doors to a murky past and to erase definitively any possible shadow on the landscape that opened before them.

She had seen Pauline for the first time eight years earlier, in the cosmopolitan and colourful salon of Lady Anglesey. Of course, she already knew who she was. In the spring of that year – she remembered well that by that time winter was approaching – *Études et préludes* had appeared, signed by R. Vivien. No one in that limited circle, addicted to literature and to all things that surpassed the limits of the everyday, ignored the gender of the author whose use of the initial made ambiguous; nor indeed her identity and that of her beloved: the famous Natalie B., that modern naiad with "vague hair" that "floated upon her breast, fluid and subtle like seaweed". The intense echo, awakened in certain sensitive souls by an absolute, and perhaps for that very reason unfortunate, passion directed towards a third person, tends to resonate all the more when haloed by the effective lyricism of a few lines of poetry. In such cases, the real vision is in danger of disappointing expectations that the imagination has generated on too weak a base. Nothing of the sort had happened here.

That day, Pauline was seated alone in a corner of the room, visibly at the margins of the animated effervescence of comings and goings, introductions and leave-takings. She occupied one of the spaces on a so-called "love seat", upholstered in a sea-green silk. Hélène could see her still, all white, like the foam atop a wave. She was sitting on the edge, like a child on an obligatory house visit. Her hair, which must have been placed neatly atop her head at the beginning of the evening, had loosened lock by lock, and this rebellious rain framed an abstract face, eyes invisible behind eyelids and long thick lashes. Her hands rested on her lap; long hands barely forming an ivory shadow on her white organdie dress. Was it her hands she stared at so obsessively with her downcast eyes? Hélène suddenly perceived, as if by revelation, all the fragility of one in whom before she'd only seen strength, of sentiment and words. That fragility – like the empty space on the love seat – seemed to offer her a place, to request her aid in a work of protection and rescue. Without hesitation she accepted her under the rule of a solid tenderness, a compact solicitude. It was easy for her. Pauline had recently installed herself on the same avenue of the Bois, having abandoned the icy, empty nest of her unfortunate passion. Hélène's house was on the even-numbered side of the street, near Porte Dauphine, and Pauline's apartment was on the odd side, halfway to Étoile. Within a few metres of crossing the street, they were at the other's place – Hélène, in fact, always at Pauline's. One evening, just a few days later, Hélène, sincerely and emphatically, praised some new verses that Pauline read to her: "How I do like your verses, Pauline: more than that, I love them." Pauline fixed her eyes on her in an unequivocal stare as she replied: "It isn't the verses you should love, but the poet". Her cheeks and lips turned red, but she didn't blink. Hélène required no repetition of the insinuation. Her generous body enveloped the delicate creature just as the warm, velvet density of her affection had wrapped Pauline's ethereally melancholy spirit in a protective cushion.

Those early days had been "the hour of sisterly sweet hand-in-hand", according to the poetic expression Pauline had borrowed from Rossetti. For her, though, those verses of pallid beauty explained only by half the life of her love, just as the silvery side of poplar leaves lends an argent hue to the whole tree. But there was the other side, too, the burning sap that scorched their veins. "Overcome by the ardours of a lioness / the forest vibrates and abandons itself / to the scarlet kiss of autumn…": lines by Paule Riverdale, that hybrid being born of the two of them, of their two sistered plumes merely a year later…

When harmony installs itself between two very different beings it's because an unconscious, mysterious wisdom has regulated the play of forces, making opposites work as complementary, stressing and heightening each and every similarity. That had been the case with them. Pauline stumbled through the real world because she couldn't avoid it; with the same inconsistency, Hélène inhabited the world of poetry, the only coveted field that had resisted her efforts until now. It was a tacit pact: each one took her respective helm, toiling to get the other to participate in their realm; the relative failure of the task could only be attributed to a tendency, perhaps innate, in nature, towards economizing means and dividing functions. This result further welded the symbiosis. The common family circumstances of orphanhood – Hélène had lost her father before her first birthday; Pauline at nine years – and the conflictual interaction with their mothers were elevated to the category of the symbolic. Hélène's belonging to a race at once privileged and abominated, cosmopolitan and without homeland, had aroused in Pauline a vision of parallelism with the common lot of poets: exile.

Pauline saw the Baroness as a "sister of the queens of yore / exiled amid ancient splendour…" The vision was an accurate one. That vague sensation of affliction that had once assaulted Hélène, the feeling of being a stranger surrounded by luxury and profusion since the cradle, became more concrete, more permanent and intense since her love for Pauline. It was only when she was with her that she felt herself to be in possession of both a land and of true wealth. Like the return from an age-old exile or the redemption from an indigence only now identified as such. The sentiment spurred on her natural generosity: she gushed forth like an endless fountain, with no recognition of what she was giving, which in her eyes had no value and was fair compensation for all that she was receiving. She also knew what she couldn't give. But that external, limiting element formed by the conglomerate of her domestic and mundane obligations acted as a sluice in the river, raising the level of the water to deviate part of its volume to a more sensible use. Or like one of those devices in navigation canals that facilitate passage at a change in level. For there was definitely a difference in level. But in those early days, the disposition of the elements at play made it almost imperceptible, as always happens when the more avid being is also the one with more obstacles to overcome.

Hélène sometimes thought that for three years it had all been too regulated and complete: perfect. Nothing left to desire. Perhaps that which constituted the force of their love was also the source of its weakness. Pauline had received from her the certainty of a presence. Water for the feverish thirst of a convalescent. The soft weakness of arms around her neck that returned the image of her own power in the mirror. "I've made my heart childlike in the innocence of our love…" she wrote. Further along: "I love you because you are feeble and sweet. My arm / will be a tepid cradle for you and you will rest there". There were also those shining moments of physical excitement aroused by an unexpected or lengthy separation. In the beginning, that had been a strangely violent and necessary aspect, almost obsessive, compulsive. Hélène had been astonished by the discovery, and by the revelation of sensations inert until then, of newly awakened flesh. Her old passion for Natalie had given Pauline all the paroxysm of sentiment, had hurled her from abundance of the heart into the void. The body, on the other hand, had offered itself for the first time without self-knowing, like an inessential extra in this heightened self-oblivion. Everything was new in this realm: Pauline's eyes, wide open or closed in the confines of pleasure, her panting, her grateful smile like a satisfied baby, her hands, grasping enough at first to leave scratches, and then relaxed on the hills of Hélène's breasts. And Hélène's own pleasure, a sounding-board, a cascading and trembling spasm suddenly unleashed from an older, darker nucleus, as primitive and absolute as a pact of blood. Then the gratefulness for the pleasure and the gratefulness for the gratefulness for the pleasure, and the pleasure of gratefulness.

Aside from those tingling nights, tender and rough at the same time, everything beyond the limits of a stable well-being was engulfed by literature like absorbent paper. Pauline worked during those years more than she ever had. Every so often Natalie's shadow was perceptible in some of the poems. Memory, regret, desire, all in the past tense. Hélène wasn't jealous of any sort of dream. When Pauline sometimes fell asleep by her side, she liked looking at her at leisure, watching over her, as if the inaccessible abyss where sleep carried her became inoffensive due to her attentive vigilance. As for the other kind of dreams, she sensed intuitively that they were necessary nourishment for Pauline's poetry. And she believed, perhaps too ingenuously, that poetry itself could be an effective spell to keep the worst phantasms at bay. Since she didn't let her guard down in that arena either, she was the first to find out about Natalie's return and to inform Pauline of it.

In the beginning, that occurrence appeared to have no repercussions in her life. Pauline stubbornly refused to see Natalie in spite of the theatrical scenes she staged to try to change her mind, as well as Hélène's own entreaties, for she was in favour of looking straight into the face of the enemy. Even so, and in spite of the fact that nothing had changed between the two of them for the moment – except perhaps for Pauline's increasing insistence on reaffirming her link with the Baroness: like a shipwrecked person might grab hold of a solid, stable rock – Hélène blamed all their subsequent troubles on that return.

Hélène's memory, now that Pauline was dead, dwelt stubbornly on that point. She wasn't capable of any more grief, even less for a sorrow that bore no fruit. After all, she was a woman of action, with a preference for turning nostalgia into lasting works, so before heading for Nice, she left a letter for the next mail:

Mrs Antoinette A.
24 Hyde Park Street
London

Dear Toinette,

I do not wish to burden you by making you aware of a suffering that would perhaps have the sole virtue of supporting your own. I will only say that during the last month or so since the death of our beloved Paule not a single night of sleep has come easily to me. It is as if sometimes the dead were petitioning us not to let them fall for a single second into that apparent void that is oblivion; and demanding that we continue taking care of them, as if in their eternal sojourn they might still require our meagre assistance. Perhaps it's just that we imagine them subjected to this human limitation that is found in all loss, leaving us with the proud illusion that they still need us. Be that as it may, I've given a great deal of thought to what we might do to honour your sister. During my long visits to Passy cemetery, where I go whenever my numerous obligations permit, and where flowers have never been absent since that woeful day, an idea has taken hold of me. While the family tomb that holds her is perfectly adequate for a young woman of her position, that is, for a normal young woman, it is much too modest to perpetuate the memory of a great poet, the memory of that exquisite and inspired being that was Pauline. It is true that she loved the modesty of violets and professed her disdain for showy displays, but she also loved beautiful surroundings, and I feel we should dignify her love of beauty, allowing it to be reflected it in the dwelling place for her remains.

I've dreamed for a moment of a little chapel, nothing luxurious – I think Pauline would hate Marie Bashkirtseff's byzantine tomb, so insultingly opulent and so close to hers. A small gothic chapel that would arise, svelte, with violet stained glass and a few of her divine verses engraved on the walls, like a little sanctuary to poetry, where her devotees could gather in the shadow of the chestnut trees.

It would have been excellent to have a marble bust on the frontispiece displaying her adorable features. But, unfortunately, Paule refused, in spite of my insistent entreaties, to pose for another sculptor after the unhappy experience with Mr Rodin. As you must know, after having put up with the deplorable conditions of his study, the result was terribly disappointing. He was asked once and again to re-touch it, but to no avail… The work was returned to him, despite the exorbitant price we paid: it was truly a horror. You're familiar with the reputation of the artist, that's why we chose him. But those hieratic, lifeless features had not the slightest resemblance to a face so charming and intensely intelligent. It would do little more than lie to anyone who, in the future, might search for a reflection of the one who was our Pauline.

Without having a suitable bust at our disposal, then, I believe that we could make up for it, at least in part, by placing on the interior a copy of the marvellous portrait of her done by Lévy-Dürmer that combines exact evocation with the vagueness of a dream.

As for the selection of verses, Mr Charles B. would be notified at the proper moment.

I am convinced, dearest Toinette, that both you and your husband will understand my desire and will be touched by my ardour to see the memory of your sister thus honoured. I also ask that you speak of it to your mother as soon as possible. The Labatie firm, whom I have taken the liberty of contacting, will begin the work as soon as your consent arrives.

We leave for Nice tomorrow, my husband on the express and me by automobile. You know how crazy I am about this new invention our times have favoured us with. Within three or four days, we'll be completely installed for the winter, until the end of February or beginning of March. Write to me as soon as possible so I can make all the arrangements, and let me have news of your health, along with that of your family.

Most cordially yours,
Hélène, Baroness van Z. de N.

PRIVATE PAPERS OF SARA T. (2)

Where the narrator slips stealthily into the pages of a melancholy, lyrical and passably emphatic diary.

Paris, 9 July 1984

I have been to the cemetery at Passy. This small plot of thickly covered and uneven ground, filled with decaying tombs, as apparently disordered and chaotic as the work of death, accumulates years and sorrow between its grey walls sparsely covered in new vines and ivy.

Not even the sudden flame of a red geranium, nor the burst of pink and green of the hydrangeas manage to do anything more than emphasize, by contrast, the desolation of this strange settlement where each corpse is like the absentee landlord of an uninhabited cottage, diminutive and ostentatious, with dried flowers on the gate and cobwebs on the roof. Here is the door...

Voici la porte d'où je sors...
O mes roses et mes épines!
Qu'importe l'autrefois? Je dors
En songeant aux choses divines.

I have gone to your cemetery at Passy, Renée. And I even almost brought you flowers. Lilies, as Berthe used to do, until just a few years ago. Or violets, to feed an appearance of pious legend. How to choose? Trial and error, again. To plump for voluptuousness, ephemeral turgidity and touch, or for the gravity of a dream, hidden carnality that is painfully made scent? *Femme damnée ou femme sauvée?*

I feel that I am trapped in a snare to which I was drawn by the brilliant lure of a false dilemma... you yourself scattered the clues that lead to this dead end. But you left me others, too, that unravel the edges of every canvas, until they undo it, taking us to the heart of what was at the same time your hell and your paradise.

I was on the verge of bringing you flowers, something I haven't done for any other dead woman, or man, for that matter, once the tomb has swallowed them: once the visible, tangible border that separates us has been sealed – more uncertain perhaps, the more our physical proximity makes us feel its stone solidity.

Many years ago, when I was just a girl of ten who possibly carried too much wisdom for her years on my shoulders – this weight that now seems so much lighter, but no doubt erroneously so... Electric blue nylon overall, a boarder surviving on inedible meals, hair cropped like a pageboy and arranged like a precariously hung heron's nest. Braids lopped off only recently, and left far behind, between tobacco cloth... Years ago I was trying to come up with a present for Mother's Day. My mother, absent, far away, much further even than those twenty kilometres or so that distanced me from the village. As remote as that little girl was now, seated before a rural hairdresser's mirror, watching the strands fall one by one, of that ambiguous symbol – crown or servitude? – that until then had been her most distinguishing feature. They fell lock by lock, mingling hair and days. The latter, melting like ice in a flame, all of a sudden binding together again somewhere else, to become the object of vicious bargaining between birds of prey – memory, forgetting, and even a third bird without name. The former, gathered with care and destined to become a fossil trace, denied life yet a sharply intense symbol, erected hopelessly in the path of death.

Mother's day. Day of stone. Day of ghosts. Day of subterfuge.

Two sisters appeared with a large bunch of flowers. A nun was helping them to put them in water. They were for their mother, they said. Flowers ... that would never have occurred to me. And like a spark that ignites the tinder, the idea took in my tiny brain and put an end to my fruitless search. "Does she really like flowers, then?" I asked. The nun's significant look and gesture stopped me dead in my tracks, just before the elder of the sisters could remind me of the meaning of the length of black ribbon she had sewn on to the collar of her blouse...

Is this in fact the origin of my unceasing association of flowers with love, and of love with the dark and insidious shadow of blame and shame?

I have never been at the tomb of my father, not even on the day of his burial. There are those who, when they saw him laid out, dead and cold, turned their head away: no, it's not him any more. I simply looked at him. Death, strange midwife, had torn from him painfully, with a force without any hint of weakness, the fruit: all of the fruit that remained possible. The fruit of that hyper-inflated belly that reminded one of the larval state of life, and that he surrendered with a rhythmic panting, regular, progressively more intense, like that shown to future mothers in preparation for their hour of labour. Lethal germination, atypically unstoppable germination, that left, on one side, an inert shell and on the other just an obscure and intangible regret in our empty hands. Even so, it was here that real life could be found, in that now rigid crust, in that petrified past, in that wax doll. His life, my life. I had no idea then of how true this was. Nevertheless I couldn't stop looking at him.

Was it not I who had strangled in me the obedient daughter of the father? Who, then, was this bricked-up prisoner who was hitting me from the inside, mortally wounded, perhaps, with gnarled fists, perhaps, but nevertheless still living? Was it his death which was returning life to her, as if the last breath that had escaped from his mouth had clasped itself to her lungs, demanding of her both life and death, leaving her torn between the impulse to substitute him and that of allowing herself to fall silent by his side, shadow against shadow, dust against dust? Is it she that has been keeping watch over him since then like a faithful dog trying to drag me back to the tomb of my father, which I have never visited? Together, these lovers without remedy have left me alone, like a strange jellyfish, without a carcass, without bones, viscous flesh, formless, without contours… As if I were (re)turning against myself to the state of a sketch.

Le charme douloureux des ébauches m'attire.
The sorrowful charm of sketches attracts me.

You said this, Renée. You regretted having ever left this simultaneously truncated and limitless state, characteristic of the unfinished works of artists, which time has left us incomplete and fragmentary. A space for the unsaid, for the unreal, for dreams, for vertigo. For the invisible wings of an ancient mutilated Victory.

I have gone to your tomb, which is also the tomb of your father. He died when you were nine years old. Not far from there, at the back, going down the narrow stairs and along one of the strait avenues flanked by trees I do not recognize, with black velvet trunks – how strange to find a cemetery without cypresses – I would have stumbled on the tomb of Natalie. *Ma taupinette* was what Berthe called her, the faithful maidservant who accompanied her for more than fifty years – I realize that, automatically, without thinking, I have written "faithful" alongside "maidservant": that adjective that normally accompanies servants, dogs, women, like an epithet… *Ma taupinette*, Berthe must have been thinking, as she approached the simple tombstone, with her heart in one hand and flowers in the other. I, however, have refused to do this.

What a contradiction in terms, to seek the tomb of Natalie! What put me off once and for all are the words that, from what I know, she had engraved on her tombstone: *Je suis cet être legendaire / où je revis* – "I am the legendary being in whom I live again". Even so, somewhere inside me there is a sense of regret, a shadow of a doubt. Perhaps only her tomb would have the virtue of offering me a certain sense of her humanity, the exact measure of her humanity, even. Little Mole, little moley of mine – I could then say to her – you incorrigible creature who excavates tunnels from your lair to us, infiltrating our blood, to seduce us still… Just look at me defending myself with tenderness, the strategy to which we have recourse in order to bring down to size the beings we secretly fear. *Tout-petit*, she – Renée, Pauline – called you. *Tout-petit*, and she then would sign Paule or even at times Paul. What led you, at the end of your almost secular life – and there is no adjective that suits you less than this one –

what led you to trouble with your proximity, here, in the cemetery of Passy, the repose of she who you had abandoned, to follow your own path, seventy years before? Was it the gesture of a sovereign finally conceding an alm of light to a beggar whose eyes are now completely blind? Or were you obeying one of those unwritten commandments, like that which sooner or later leads the criminal back to the scene of the crime? Did you come to take final possession, publicly and solemnly, of the ashes, the dust – of a soul and a nothingness – of the lot that had been explicitly left to you as a legacy? Or was it that after having avoided it skilfully during so many years, you finally accepted your debt in the game? "You will wither one day, O, lily of mine!", Renée wrote. After all, whoever bets on death, will in the short or the long run always have the winning hand.

IN MEMORIAM PAULINE M. TARN, I have read under the ogive over the entrance to this narrow pseudo-gothic chapel, so like all the other ones, were it not for the impossibly white smoothness of the stone, as if polished but a few years ago, and for the privileged place where it stands: on the wide balcony formed at the highest part of the cemetery, which showcases it as in a window display, on stage or on a podium. The final destiny of a valuable object, of an actress, a queen – beheaded martyr, even? Theatre of shadows that draws me in and spits me out. Masked ball that fascinates me and leaves me outwith its secret, always locked and inaccessible, of the tomb. Where to seek you, then, if not in words, yours, those of others, my own, sent out like a badly tamed pack of dogs to hunt and capture a ghost? How to give you a body, to incarnate you, to root you, to make my blood run through your shadow and, without substituting it, convert it into life, into sap, into movement?

From a reflection that twists deep in the water, where the only thing I can make out clearly are the traces that return to me my own image, deformed, stretched out of shape, misshapen or magnified as in a fairground hall of mirrors, how can I return you to yourself, beyond this strange jigsaw puzzle of movable pieces, which I am trying to put together in the libraries, the museums, the streets of Paris, its bookshops, and the Bois, in tourist guides, in maps of the Greek islands, in the scenographic reconstructions of the cinema... Mutable, ungraspable pieces that dance as if in a game of musical statues, fleeing from me and coming closer, disappearing and recreating themselves, in continuous metamorphosis. Mobile pieces made of fragments of fixed and of torn paper restored, documents in which the rats have made their nest and whose most intact pages are blank, photographs where often the most significant face appears blurred; written testimonies that are often acts of defence, of accusation and always of self-justification; houses that have been demolished, streets that have changed names. And your own writings, masks upon masks upon masks. Even so, between the cracks, from deep inside, like a great red cobweb, there is the wound, seeping and invading everything with its colour of sunset and of wine. The wound that appears, like a dark accusation, at the end of your epitaph:

Voici donc mon âme ravie,
Car elle s'apaise et s'endort
Ayant pour l'amour de la Mort,
Pardonné ce crime: la Vie!

WHERE MONSIEUR B., A TEACHER, SOON AFTER
CAREFULLY CHOOSING VERSES FOR RENÉE VIVIEN'S
TOMB, STRAINS ALL HIS MEMORIES THROUGH THE
SIEVE OF GOOD CONSCIENCE.

Montpellier, December 1910

"Renée Vivien would not have approved of the lines that follow. Yet we would be lowering her to our level if we implied
this to be because she hated 'modern publicity' or that the
procedures of 'industrial literature' especially repulsed her.
That disdain and that hate remain very common today, con-
stituting little more than a species of elementary ethical
integrity. Furthermore, they tend to combine well with a certain gentle and ironic indulgence. No, it was the very fact of
confusing admiration for the literary work with curiosity,
however deferent, about the life of the author that was for
Renée Vivien a barbaric profanation."

Charles B. lifted both his pen and his eyes from the text he
had just written. Through the window he could see the dark
silhouette of the church of the Blue Penitents outlined
against the pale grey winter sky. Downstairs, Eugénie was
puttering about. He enjoyed hearing her measured movements: it was a familiar rustle that gave rhythm to his vaca-
tion time – or rather, work without a fixed schedule –
wrapping his restful moments with a light hum. In his youth,
when he had courted her, he had been imbued with a kind of
troubadouresque fervour. Sometimes, in situations like this,
close to the archetypal scenery from which they were born,
the pale images of that remote past came to life. He remem-

bered how, rooted beneath the statue of the Three Graces, he had watched for her for hours in the horse-drawn carriages that circled the Place de l'Ou; how he had stubbornly tried to follow her vanishing trail among the throngs congregating at Les Barques in August to watch the jousts on the Lez; how he had tirelessly watched her stroll down the Esplanade on Sundays beneath the sycamores, and gazed upon the sensual maturity of her rest as she reclined in the seat of the open landau that carried her to Peyrou. She was older than Charles, and married. His verses preceded any timid incursion beyond the platonic canon: but she was the one who took him in, open, and with the dark simplicity of the land. She was the one who closed her former life without calculation or mistrust, placing all of it in Charles's hands with the same confident, sure and dignified gestures with which she would have taken an abandoned child under her protection. Her fortitude dispelled all fear in him, at the same time as he felt the weight of an unknown burden on his shoulders. Charles realized then the extent to which he had wanted to avoid what was happening, as if it were beyond his will, but this did not provoke in him the slightest movement of protest.

Suddenly, everything had changed completely. Up until then, his desire had led to the ways of his ancestors, almost instinctively. The pleasures of trobar e domnejar, the art of poetry and love sung from afar, like the ancient poets of his land, dazzled in their discovery of la Domna, the gilós who made her barely accessible, and their sublimation in verses composed by beardless ephebes... verses in the language that was being revived at the hands of Aubanel, Romanilha, Mistral... The language that, in Paris, he could speak only with Eugénie.

For she had followed him to Paris. She had taken the decision to diminish and distil herself enough to carve out a tiny but concrete place in his life. Light enough that her rustle would not get in the way of his steps, but dense enough to cover up the fissures of anxiety. The impossibility of legal matrimony seemed to maintain an openness to this protected space between four walls and a roof of tenderness. Like the missing tile the ancient Cathars left out of the roof so their souls could take flight freely at the hour of death. Only once – and he still struggled to forget it – had Charles been strongly tempted to flee through that opening, afflicted by the feeling of death that accompanies every passion. But years had passed now since everything had returned to the same precise contours and clear customs, affirmed by time. The laws had changed, and the possibility of socially sealing their bond had appeared at the most opportune moment. Oddly, Eugénie had presented a soft but stubborn resistance, perhaps because she belonged to that order of beings that extract all their strength from the exercise of moderation and are afraid of any excess…

At first, Charles thought he was confronting a mistrust that had its origin in recent jealousy, the irrational fear that paralyses and inhibits even the action that would leave all danger behind. Perhaps that unfortunate episode had aroused in her a recognition of the limits of their union, and of the richness their relationship strangely derived from remaining indefinite and therefore plastic and adaptable to changing reality. Who knows whether she felt she was depriving him of something of value – children, perhaps, unfeasible earlier because of the situation and now due to age, but not only children… – and it was her generosity that made her resist signing the act of definitive expropriation. Or perhaps the necessity of legal recognition after so many years seemed to invalidate the very thing she held sacred and had taken root within her like an innate sign of nobility: her original offering of herself, absolute, with no pledge or token. Charles had stopped trying to understand that dark agglomeration of extreme humility and extreme pride. Perhaps he wasn't capable. But he was able to convince her with what was perhaps an even darker manipulation, responding point by point to her latent opposition. For this, paradoxically, he had needed the intercession of Pauline – which is the name he often called her privately, whereas out loud she was always "mademoiselle".

Pauline had known how to emphasize the need he felt to offer her some sort of recompense: in her arguments, it wasn't Eugénie who was in jeopardy, but Charles. If she didn't agree to marriage, she was arbitrarily depriving him of a way to self-dignity. Perhaps between the lines Eugénie read reparation, redemption for a fault too illusive to be formulated. That way, if she finally agreed, she wouldn't have to feel like a beggar accepting alms that her pride kept her from seeking, nor the usurper of an illicit legacy. On the contrary, the act would be inscribed with complete consistency in her long trajectory of dispenser of all kinds of gifts: her best image of herself would thus be reinforced forever more. At the same time, Pauline had minimized the importance of legal and social recognition. She had strangely, perhaps even somewhat cruelly, insisted on the "maternal" aspect of Eugénie's tenderness toward Charles, which he had invoked in favour of his proposition. But in this case, the supposed cruelty had acted as a balm to the most livid point of the wound. Once again, it was his weakness and vulnerability that appeared in the forefront, requiring the firmness of her support, the security of her commitment. The children she thought she had deprived him of melted away before the rights of that real infant, the man child she had adopted *de facto* so long ago, whom she could not now deprive of papers that were in order, with all i's dotted and t's crossed. The fact that things appeared so clearly, outlined so precisely by such a singular witness as Pauline, convinced her, but not without a last touch of regret.

That had been five years ago. At the ceremony, Eugénie shed a few tears and her face, framed by hair that had been greying for some time, was sweet, like a dying ember amid the ashes of a peasant fireplace. Pauline had recommended her own dressmaker: a pearl grey silk outfit placed Eugénie somewhere in between Sunday best and severe; but she had insisted on wearing a Saint-Léon hat from her old milliner on Montpellier's Grande Rue. She would never be a Parisian, and Charles couldn't avoid projecting in that conviction all the nostalgia that tied him to the land of the Erau River, and to the sea and mountains that Montpellier hints at and sees without ever touching. He would never be a Parisian either, especially not in Paris. On the other hand, when he was in Montpellier, he seemed to partake of an essentially Parisian substance that made of him, by definition, a hybrid spirit: he continued to grasp on to his roots but at the same time felt his sense of identity melting away, however clear and unequivocal it was when he was far away. That tended to happen especially when he spent some time there, as he was doing now. When he came for just a flying visit, as was often required for some conference or other – invariably about regionalism – the theme itself established an immediate connection, clear and inescapable. He was a "regionalist", and that word embodied his past "Felibrism" as well as his present Proudhon-influenced federalism, since he belonged to that vague community that not only northern Frenchmen know as the Midi: *Lo mieu-jorn*. His long stay in Paris had soldered his sense of belonging and at the same time had displaced him imperceptibly toward a prioritized political translation, to the detriment of the linguistic and literary dimension. He felt different in Paris, in spite of speaking French every day – except for the intimate, private redoubt embodied in Eugénie – in spite of his writing all of his poetry in French, and of the favourable reception offered to him by the cultural and political elite of the capital.

There was something else, beyond the language that defined that land of Oc, a sort of essence emanating from the countryside, living in the blood of the vineyards, in the breath of the Mediterranean, in the classical inheritance that brought together with no apparent contradiction the dark symbolism of the *faidits* of Montsegur or the martyrs of Béziers, in the troubadour lyrics in Occitan and the epic song, in French, of the Aliscans and the knight Vivien. It was important to work towards creating a political form out of that reality, which was not in itself unique to the 'hexagon': Flanders, Brittany, Corsica, the Roussillon, all of which had seen their own languages reduced to the category of patois by Jacobin centralism. Normandy too, Burgundy, High Savoy... all victims of that macrocephaly that inflated Paris at the expense of all the rest. As if in a field one planted and fertilized only a certain spot with the excuse that, time after time, it always yielded the most.

Charles placed a possible linguistic recovery – desired

more with fervour than ingenuous credulity – immediately behind this political objective. It was obvious that the language of Oc was in danger of death. In moments of sharp pessimism, or perhaps lucidity, he felt the agony in his bones. People were moved to tears listening to *Mirèio*: he had seen that well the year before when Arle celebrated Mistral's jubilee with Emma Calvé singing "*O Magali ma tan amado…*" For a moment it seemed that the poem, which expressed the absolute constancy of the lover and at the same time his capacity to adapt to the most capricious metamorphoses of the beloved, took on a symbolic meaning: that of the fidelity of the people to their language, latent and irrevocable beneath a changing appearance. That's why he couldn't avoid a lump in his throat at the moment when Magali, wishing to test her lover to the extreme, announces to him that the next metamorphosis will be death. Charles felt himself to be completely one with the bold voice of the lover in his blunt reply: if you become the poor dead one, I'll become the land. That is how I'll have you. The poor dead one…

Sometimes Charles caught himself strolling along the Montpellier streets with pricked ears, hoping against all hope for some contradiction to that intuition, trying to capture in the air even the tiniest indication of health in familiar words. Yet this timid sounding never did anything more than sink the root of his despair a little more. There had been the "Félibrige" movement, for sure. But in spite of its prestige – which Mistral's Nobel Prize had raised to its height – it had not been able to stop the downward slide. Someone had even insinuated that with his fiercely apolitical stance, he had precipitated it. It was necessary, then, to start a new way that would return pride to the offspring that France had treated more as a stepmother than a mother: the children defeated so long ago. That is how he became an apostle of federalism. And that is how, so far from the land of his birth – first in Paris, then for several years at Saint-Omer, and sporadically all around French territory – he could continue to work for his homeland.

But this time, the stay in Montpellier bound him to Paris in a special way. Not the real Paris, but that germination of ideas and written papers that constituted culture and that found its magnetic nucleus in the capital. He had to write about Renée Vivien. He had committed himself to doing so. Just a little booklet. The publisher Samsot had argued insistently: they could not allow her to be swallowed up into oblivion. "And you are, without a doubt, the best man for the job". It was true that that child, that complex and extraordinary being, had passed away practically unnoticed. Among the small circle of friends and followers, there remained a confused and painful feeling of not having fulfilled a funeral rite, however ephemeral and formless, as required by some unwritten law. Still, Charles resisted carrying out Samsot's request: for a biography and literary commentary. Regarding the first, Renée Vivien herself had condemned, through one of her characters in *A Woman Appeared to Me*, that kind of "public espionage organized around the life and work of a writer". Furthermore, during the final years of her life, she had enclosed herself within a silence almost without fissures, she had prohibited publishers from selling her previous works, and she had reserved her new poems for her circle of closest friends. Charles had heard her complain bitterly and sarcastically about the painful office of a "woman of letters" which, she claimed, offended her most sacred privacy.

So, the possibility of taking on a biographical narrative represented something of a sacrilege to him. He invoked Renée: sometimes he liked to call her that, the ambiguous-sounding name without sex or gender which he himself had helped her find; in doing so, he left behind that Pauline of the earth which the earth had taken back – far from being her real personality it was her involuntary, material personality – to bring forth the angel: an angel like Baudelaire's albatross, so awkward when it abandoned the immensity of space. An angel that, paradoxically, had been able to give form to the most beautiful cries of sensuality but at the same time could sing of the white chastity of the violets honouring the name of a dead friend.

In order to do so, he had to fight against other memories, precious memories that he had been treasuring for the ten long years during which he had been spectator and privileged confidant of Pauline's life. He had to keep himself from re-reading her letters – page after page after page written in her hand, at first with the writing of a diligent schoolgirl, later liberated and made personal, and recently, those bewildered and bewildering hieroglyphics. To invoke Renée and not Pauline meant to see her, in spite of everything, during those last terrible times, to converse softly amid the sultry atmosphere of incense, in the candlelight, beneath the eyes of the great Buddhas, already disconnected from the earth to which she was barely held down by an almost immaterial body.

Truly, it made no sense to write a biography of one who had lived for literature alone. Her verses were the autobiography of her soul. But Samsot had been unshakeable: most of her work was unavailable. He had the rights to a few collections, but these were far from her best. Expectations had to be created, a demand, in order to promote new editions of her best work. Obviously a study of her books could have accomplished this task, but to bring it to fruition with at least some dignity would require much more time. The only solution seemed to be to walk the tightrope. To set aside multiple, superfluous anecdotes: just enough information to link Renée to a flesh and blood being born in a concrete time and place. To propose a few lines of meditation via works he knew like the back of his hand, and to probe the essential: the study of the soul.

He picked up the thread of his writing and finished the paragraph:

"I would not wish for anything in this study, necessarily brief and analytical, to stray from a tone of sacred gravity."

THE PRIVATE PAPERS OF SARA T. (3)

Paris, 11 July 1984

At this stage of the game, I find myself asking for the umpteenth time what it is that has led me to become so obsessed with this story. An unhealthy attraction for the defeated? But is it even fair to think of Renée in terms of the defeated, however much she refers to herself as such in various poems; however much everything seems to lead one to see her as an antithesis of the triumphant Amazon...? Surely this can't be the best way of defining her. What strikes me most about Renée and I am trying to express in this word is her absolute incapacity to take the measure of reality – in the sense that is given to the latter by those who in one way or another call themselves "realists" – or to conform to a single one of its demands. The logical consequence of this? Reality expels her, exiles her, destroys her. It is true that there is in her a militant attitude, of explicit rebellion, but her revolt is to be found above and beyond ideology or conscious will... It is as if Revolt had become flesh and blood and bones in her, and she had only had to accept, to give her *fiat*, after the fact, to this new incarnation. To choose to be a "martyr" – trial and error, again – because, as in all witnessing, she cannot unknow this knowledge.

Never would Renée have accepted the miserable and unadorned definition of reality I have placed in opposition to her as her victorious adversary... Most probably for her the real was of a completely different nature. In spite of this not at all insignificant discrepancy between words, there is at least agreement in identifying the antagonist: everything that lies above and beyond the purview of Desire.

Revolt incarnate, I have ventured above. Is it the excess of this concept taking over the body that turns it into a life of suffering, into passion? Is it simply the enormity of this failed effort by the body to coincide in every way with the word, to cover with life, matter, seconds, minutes and hours the entirety of its immaterial extension, beyond time? Is the body, then, trapped in the prison of the soul, torn out of joint on its torture rack?

Or is the reverse true? Is it that her woman's body speaks an obscure language without an established code, without possibility of access to a symbolic dimension? Pain, then, of the soul interrogated from the body without any possible response. Pain of a lack without terms... Were poetry and literature, then, little more than highly imperfect translations into the dominant language, into the language of the (masculine) other?

I realize that this very question – why my attraction for the "defeated", for all the speech marks it requires – might have been one Renée herself would have pondered. When I speak of the defeated, I am above all thinking in the feminine: hers is an obstinately feminine memory. A quest for the stages in an invisible genealogy that inseparably joins the feminine, revolt and pain. Together with power – an ephemeral power, conquered and lost: only the gesture remains of it, and at times, the word. Processing through her texts we find Lilith, the first rebel; dethroned queens – Vashti, Cleopatra, Elizabeth Woodville, Jane Grey and Anne Boleyn; women poets: above all Sappho and her doubly sapphic world – feminine love and poetry – driven, in the end, to suicide. It is symptomatic that Renée should have accepted this part of the legend, despite it being no more accurate historically than the other (which, in contrast, she rejects in indignation): her supposed motive, that is, the love of Phaon. It makes sense that the rebel – for her, Sappho is a rebel – should choose death, but to have been restored, to adapt herself before this to "normality", what nonsense!

Is this exorbitant price, the punishment and the defeat, ultimately accepted by Renée because it is the slurry that inevitably accompanies every precious mineral?

I recall her story "The Lady of the She-Wolf": a male passenger on a ship sets out without success to seduce the only woman on board. She has with her, on a lead as if it were a dog, a she-wolf, who keeps men at bay and is obviously an alter ego for the protagonist. The vessel is shipwrecked, and the strange woman is faced with a dilemma: if she wants to get into a lifeboat she must leave the animal behind. She rejects this possibility with disdain. The narrator can still see her trying to save herself, with her arms around the she-wolf and clinging desperately to a piece of flotsam… All in vain.

Also of great significance is her particular version of the myth of Andromeda and Perseus: the damsel does not wish to be saved from the dragon. Does this mean she instead desires death? At the very least she prefers it to the fortune that links her inevitably to the deeds of the hero. Once this choice has been made, it is not difficult to imagine the next step, to transform everything that is the inescapable alternative into a desirable and desired option.

Is the attitude of Renée simply lucidity that burnishes with heroic pomp that which is no more than the choice of the lesser evil?

Or is there in her pessimism a more obscure feeling of blame, of self-condemnation, which makes it impossible for her to imagine any possible escape, a revolt without expiation? Is it simply the self-hatred common to marginalized groups?

All of the "victors" have to submit themselves, in fact, to the laws of reality, in order to turn them to their advantage. We can perceive the shadow of submission in the cross-light of their victories just as we can see a gesture of nobility shining in the routing of Renée. There are those who have the virtue of exemplifying both positions. The figure of Napoleon comes to mind... Why so? Perhaps because just a few days ago I saw a photo of Missy – one of the more peculiar characters in Renée's entourage – who takes from him his gesture, his attitude, his wardrobe... Or perhaps because in one of the many papers I have read, it occurred to someone to compare Natalie with him in his imperial brilliance... But Natalie is, of course, a Napoleon without Saint Helena, that is, she knows how to preserve for herself industriously, with innate virtuosity, the grandeur of tragic heroes. A hypothetical, doubtful grandeur, but one that is irresistible in its attraction... at least, that is how it seems to me. To contemplate her, as is the case with the ancient Athenians or the pious followers of the *via crucis*, involves a double affect, like that often hidden beneath the word catharsis: to share vicariously in an endeavour, a trial, of a purity and of an extermination that are alien, and at the same time to experience the relief of feeling one's own invulnerability as a spectator.

Renée herself at times evokes in me the grotesque history of the Cathar women: with the inquisitorial persecution in full flow they flee in disguise and manage to get away. A potential informer, who is on the lookout, becomes suspicious and decides to test them. She leaves them a couple of live fowl and tells them to kill them, while she does some job or other. Nobody would have dared recriminate them in a situation like that one, if they had decided to break the prohibition in order to save their own lives. But they were unable to do so: it was beyond their capability.

Absurd and ephemeral, their gesture gains in death an absolute dignity. Their radical purity rests precisely in the fact that they were incapable of doing anything else. In Renée, too, it is every cell in her body that rebels against what she calls "the stupid and necessary law". To do anything else would be to not be herself, this extreme incarnation of the trial that summons annihilation and as a consequence becomes a form of denunciation. And this alone is enough to make one forget her lifelong lot of tribulations, lies, hesitations and impossible accords between diverse fidelities.

Is this why I have turned towards Renée and not towards Natalie? On the one hand, the temerity of an impulse that pays heed to nothing but itself, that throws itself blindly into a stormy sea of troubles. And on the other, the gesture of the athlete who glides above the diaphanous surface: shipwreck or surfer?

It is also possible to see in Renée the figure of her own executioner. Ultimately, she obeys the implicit order of the world: adapt or disappear. There are many ways of disappearing.

Victory itself is without doubt one of the most defensible ones, perhaps the only one. The only one that seems to permit some form of accord or equilibrium, between servitude and power.

There must be a more "rationalist" way of looking at things – with that nineteenth-century rationalism that so captivated Monsieur Émile Zola: Renée defies the natural law of adaptation to the environment. Perhaps she is a "mutant" who does not yet know how to live and dies due to her extreme vulnerability.

Natalie, on the other hand, appears to have the capacity to anticipate herself. As if she had intuited the conditions of the future and had adapted her own conduct and thinking in anticipation. Postmodern *avant la lettre*. That is why she seduces like a "girl from the future", as Pierre Louÿs called her, like a prefiguration of what will later be. But how far is she a cause or just a "premonitional" effect? To that worldly dilemma, adapt or disappear, she seems to respond: neither one thing nor the other, in the sense that she does not in fact adapt to reality as it is, but in many ways defies norms and makes her own law. And so she succeeds in postponing indefinitely the dilemma with the fertility of her wit. With brilliance, she dares to deceive the judge with sleights of hand. But is not seduction, in fact, the ability to adapt in anticipation of the most secret fantasies of the other and to represent them, embody them in their eyes, with the greatest fidelity possible?

Nothing resembles Natalie more than the fluidity and mobile consistency of mercury. Renée, on the other hand, is alternately flowing and clotting blood.

Paris, January 1912

The letters were in the mahogany secretaire in her cousin's
room. Marie had had a hard time finding the key. There they
were, amid dried flowers and a yellowed silk handkerchief
with lace edging and embroidered initials. There were two
photographs as well. The surprise left Marie stunned. At first,
she felt the sort of exaltation artless girls experience when
met with a juicy fact about someone they know. "Well, well,
well, cousin Amédée surely had some secrets: his wife was
right to act like a drill sergeant!" Because it jumped right out
at her as an affair of skirts. Not that Marie was surprised. Her
cousin had been a good-looking man until the day he died,
elegant and delicate, with that distinguished air of a business
graduate from the École polytechnique, and no one could
have failed to spot the effect he had on women.

At this point, Marie had no illusions about the fidelity of
husbands, young or over the hill: she was a realist. But a one
night stand or even a rakish affair with some actress of shaky
morals, from the demimonde, as they say, was one thing. It
was daily bread for those of his social milieu. However, that
species of reliquary, kept, it was crystal-clear, for years, pointed to an affair *dal cuore*. Marie was an opera enthusiast, and
even though she preferred the French, romantic matters
strangely always came to her mind in Italian: perhaps because

97

they had so little to do with her, in her daily life as a well-to-do Parisian. Italian helped to situate such matters within a lavish, exotic frame. And, what is more, when a clearly operatic theme such as that one made its way into her own everyday life, it could not help but activate the little distancing mechanism that would permit her, at a second moment, to enter fully into the spectacle. But in this case, as has already been intimated, that second moment had a tremendous effect on her: the pictures, the handwriting, the initials. Her eyes went back and forth, from paper to cardboard, from cardboard to silk. There could be no doubt, no matter how strange it seemed: it was Pauline.

Her instinctive reaction, after the initial shock, was to prudently take a few steps back: no need to make wild speculations without basis. Perhaps that first impression had been false. She was not aware of, nor had Pauline ever mentioned, any correspondence with her cousin, but that didn't mean anything. He was an older man, who could have been Marie's father – or indeed Pauline's, since they were the same age… The secret could be explained in several ways. But what about the handkerchief – where Marie could still detect a faded perfume – and the dry rose petals, the bunch of darkened and flattened violets? Everything had the air of the kind of amorous gestures that, though made in a strong emotional context, have less to do with the present than with an effort to furnish an uncertain future with memories: "The day she gave me the violets from her décolletage, or the red rose from her sash, or the little perfumed hanky!" Poor remains, now dead and disconnected from the memory that gave them meaning. But what meaning? Marie was not capable of making sense of it all, that day.

She had the two packs of letters side by side in order to compare the dates. She had to do it: so different was the Pauline revealed through her letters to Amédée from the Pauline Marie remembered from the letters addressed to her at the same time. This she resented. Pauline had been one of her best friends. She'd loved her so much that she had shaken off her aversion to writing and ended up penning letters as long as a day without bread. Pauline knew that perfectly: she joked more than once about the heroism letter-writing meant for Marie; she compared her with Joan of Arc or Charlotte Corday…! "I know that not everyone was born with pen in hand, like me!" That retrospective sensation of fraud was painful to Marie now. Of course, she would have felt overwhelmed by all that anguish, all that limitless sadness, and she wouldn't have known what to do with it. At the time, she probably wouldn't have understood at all.

It was hard enough for her to get used to some of the things she did know: for example, Pauline's absolute incompatibility with England. Her fervour for France seemed fine to Marie, who shared it and with more reason. After all, Pauline was French only by adoption. But the insistence with which she demanded to be called *Mademoiselle* and not *Miss* on the envelopes of all those letters! And the ring she wore on her little finger with the three colours of the flag…! Perhaps that exalted patriotism was, after all, the only thing in common between the letters to her and those to her cousin. Her French patriotism and rejection of the English. Everything about the latter bothered her: their boredom, affectation, rudeness and stubbornness, their glassy eyes, puppet-like voices, guttural noises… And she often complained that her mother and her sister Toinette had "gone over to the enemy".

What most surprised Marie was that during all the years she'd lived in England, she hadn't made any friends. As if she had refused altogether, for some mysterious reason. She didn't think Pauline was unsociable at all. Her sense of humour was delightful. Maybe a bit timid at first… Between them, obviously, there was intimacy. They'd known each other since childhood: they were only four or five years old when their families became close, both living at Luchon. Afterwards, they'd vacationed together often: at Dieppe, Cauterets, Evian… especially while Monsieur T. was alive. Marie's image of Pauline was with braids and a short skirt, much clearer to her than the other, hair done up, full long skirts… and her waist made slender by the corset stays. Basically, she had rarely seen Pauline dressed up as a *mademoiselle*.

The last year that they kept company together, before the sudden break between the two families that Marie was just now beginning to understand, she'd seen glimpses of the great temperamental differences that no doubt came between them. Pauline, along with those other American friends of hers, Mary Wallace, and especially Violette, whom Marie barely knew, couldn't stand parties and dances and were only interested in culture. "Knowledge is power" she repeated like a litany. What power? Marie wondered. She felt powerful at times, when she led the cotillon, or when her schedule was stuffed full of dates, and she danced to exhaustion for an audience with eyes dazzled by her image multiplied by mirrors. The only thing she would have traded for all that was a dream of magenta and gold that a vague aureole diffused around the edges: to be the great Sarah Bernhardt for a moment, before a real audience, to rend hearts and provoke an overflow of spiritual admiration from a true proscenium.

She'd seen her a thousand times: in *Camille*, in *Phaedra*, and, cross-dressed, in *Lorenzaccio*, *Hamlet*, or *Aiglon*. She preferred the feminine character, Circe the Sorceress – that's what they called her – but there was also something disturbing and irresistible in her ability to embody the other side of the human experience. As if a single being could personify totality unwound into multiple forms… as Pauline would say. To be the great Sarah, or even, more modestly, Emma Calvé, or the very same Cléo de Mérode whom Pauline could not stand ever since they'd seen her together in the ballet *Thaïs*: always with her black hair in two bands that Pauline found so dreadful and in those "so uncomfortable" poses… Cléo de Mérode: Marie had seen her again, performing her famous Cambodian dances, during the Universal Exposition. She'd gone with Pierre, shortly after they married, and both of them were equally enraptured. Marie interiorized every one of those fortuities, which she continued to favour with ardour and which seemed significant to her in the new life she was beginning.

In that epoch, she had left behind her dream in some tightly closed attic, along with her eyeless doll and the cobwebs. And she felt happy about it. The truth was that she never really aspired to the life of those artists. All she envied was the moment of appearing on stage. All of them had unusual, strange origins, as if their very births marked them out for a singular, special destiny, off the beaten path. No one knew, for example, who Cléo's father was, nor for that matter, Sara's, and that led to wild speculation. Marie, on the other hand, belonged to a normal family, and deep inside she hoped to find her place in the world, without complaint, on a path exactly like her mother's, a lady beyond reproach from the

Elysée district. Even so…! "My dearest great *tragedienne*," Pauline's letters began. In the end, all of the correspondence she kept, perhaps due to a latent fidelity to the past and some vague regret for those times of ebullient living, spoke only of their theatrical stagings of invented tragedies on Monday afternoons in the old apartment on rue de Vézelay. Always tragedies and always in exotic settings. "Dear Sultana" headed another letter, which Pauline signed as "The Sultan", after having embellished her with an entire bouquet of Asiatic compliments: moon-like eyes, flowering palm tree, eternal rosebush, fount of living waters, desert dove and… comfortable camel!!

That was in 1894, the year of the anarchist attack on Carnot – Marie's memory was exceptional: for dates as well as for learning by heart the roles in the tragedies. Once, a fortune teller had told her that it had to do with the constellations of her birth. But the assassination of the President took place in June, and Pauline, along with her mother and Toinette, had spent part of the previous winter and the entire spring in Paris. It was the first time they'd seen each other since the family had moved to London. Marie had heard a lot – always in low voices and whispers – about the death of Monsieur T., Pauline's father, whom Marie remembered as tall and elegant. She had also overheard whispered criticisms of the widow's "excesses". Marie always had a weakness for Madame T.: to her, she was a charming and attractive lady who dressed with extraordinary grace: she remembered her especially in mourning, wearing a black velvet dress and jet jewellery, as blonde as antique gold and with skin of porcelain beneath the veil that burst from a hat sporting ostrich feathers. She thought, during those waning years of childhood, that it couldn't have been much of an honour to have one's husband die of *delirium tremens*. That little expression that sounded so terrible had come to her via an indiscretion of the servants, along with so much other information. Indeed it was they who had half-explained its meaning. The charges against Madame T. were more equivocal and it wasn't until later that Marie caught a glimpse of their significance. In any case, her worldly-wise family never openly showed any kind of reticence toward that lady, even though they privately blamed her for some hidden reason. Afterwards, due to legal requirements in the paternal last will and testament, they'd had to go to England, and so they hadn't seen each other again until the winter of their seventeenth year.

Once the time of playing hoop-rolling and hide-and-seek was over, what she had in common with Pauline was reduced to those private dramatic sessions, in which they sometimes included Toinette, or their habitual attendance at the opera or the *Théâtre Français*. These were family outings, most often Marie's family, since Pauline usually came alone or with her old piano teacher. Just once or twice she had brought her American friends, whom Marie wanted to meet after hearing so much about them. What was really fun – Marie remembered – was when her cousin Gaston, who up until then had a crush on Pauline, was suddenly crazy about Mary Wallace, whom, if truth be told, she thought was a little simple… But he didn't have time to take too much of a fancy, for the appearance of the two sisters was short-lived…

Pauline's letters preserved well the trace of those evenings, the other activity they had in common, which, after all, was one and the same as their private play-acting. On the other hand, there hadn't been the slightest indication of that other type of conversation, the kind decent girls weren't supposed to engage in, until one night when Pauline stayed over... Marie was perplexed at Pauline's ignorance of such things, and at her incredulous panic and horror at their revelation. Even though she'd stayed in boarding-houses, just like Marie, surrounded by gossipy and malicious servants, where it came to matters to do with men, flirting, love, and that which was pompously called "the secrets of birds and the bees", Pauline seemed much younger than she did. And yet the letters to Amédée were from the same year... How could she make sense of both images together?

The letters were, of course, quite innocent: secrets of a lonely girl told to a sympathetic ear but infused with a sort of subterranean coquetry. The poems, however, had a distinctly amorous tone, especially those that weren't explicitly addressed to Amédée... If Marie had initially been incredulous, astonished, at the evidence of the bond shown by that correspondence, the information the letters furnished were hardly on a level with the rash flight of her imagination. Pauline stated literally in the last of the letters that she had never been Amédée's lover. But was it true? Or had it been a subterfuge destined for other possible eyes – his wife's, for example... After all, it seemed they had used similar tricks on some occasions: real letters beside false, "official" ones. And even though the rest of the text did not seem to lend itself to that possibility, her doubts remained. In any case, leaving aside Pauline's naiveté about the physical aspects of love and the possible scruples that might be provoked in a man of elevated spirit like Amédée, one also had to keep in mind that Pauline was a minor, and the prudence and caution seemingly inherent to her cousin's personality was anathema to such slippery territory. In the end, everything about it was pure speculation…

What really upset Marie were the passages that made her rethink altogether her previous image of Pauline's personality. Especially those that referred to Pauline's stormy relationship with her mother. Marie had known nothing about that until now. Pauline never made the slightest mention of the matter. On the contrary, their letters were often carriers and receivers of affectionate greetings between Marie and Madame T. There was even a clearly written and funny comment about how Pauline would turn herself into a dragon to defend against all drones her "beloved and beautiful mammy…" True enough, she often spoke ill of her family, but Marie had taken all that in reference to the English, to the relatives on her father's side. In no case did she assume, when Pauline said she'd have loved to "divorce" her entire clan, that such a love-ly and affable woman as Madame T. would be included.

Marie read that whole trail of explicit and implicit complaints with suspicion and disbelief. That her mother's arrival at Shepperton literally made Pauline sick was inconceivable to Marie. And those exalted paeans to her liberty and solitude when Madame T. was absent! Marie imagined life in that little summer village with horror. The image of Pauline obsessed with the piano, poetry and the *Divine Comedy*, with no more company than that collection of busts of composers – Chopin, Haydn, Beethoven, Schumann, Grieg… – and the reproductions of portraits of Dante and the Gioconda and the little statue of Joan of Arc… All those strange literary loves, splashed with imagined jealousies, between her and Petrarch, Ronsard, Dante, and even Monsieur Zola! Marie could imagine Madame T., in her gaiety and vitality, interrupting the unhealthy dream Pauline was having of the agony of Albine in *The Sin of Father Mouret*, the paroxysm of aesthetic pleasure: death by floral asphyxiation… What an avalanche of madness and eccentricity! Any mother would have felt compelled to stop its course, by whatever means… Marie thought of her adolescent daughters and raised her ire against any invisible danger that might threaten them; so Pauline seemed to suddenly embody some vague danger that she had to exorcise. Instinctively she took sides with Madame T., whom Pauline presented as odious in her letters, especially one of the last ones, without either date or heading, posted in Eastbourne:

"It has been so long since I've shown signs of life that you probably thought I was dead, locked up in a madhouse, on my way to America, disappeared, poisoned or God knows what else! In fact, there has been a bit of all that during the months of storms and tempests I've been through.

I'll explain it all, beginning with the unfortunate book with its baneful German inscription which fell into the grasp of Mrs T. We'd just arrived back from Swindon, and all the mail that came during our absence was waiting on the little table in the vestibule. Mrs T. entered first and put the book in her pocket without even saying it was for me."

Marie didn't understand what the fuss about the book was. But she understood perfectly all the hostility expressed by that distant "Mrs T." referring to her mother. The letter went on:

"None of my friends speak German, she knows that very well, so it wasn't hard for her to figure out where that book came from, since our friendship had been cruelly given away, betrayed, in Paris. I omitted to say that Mrs T. didn't figure out any more than I did what those German phrases meant.

Even though I do know a little German, I don't write it or even read it fluently. On the contrary, I'm like most polyglots who only know a bit of one language and some thirty or so phrases of the others they claim to know. So, I was able to get my hands on the book and examine it in hiding, but in spite of all my efforts I could only figure out a few words: *Ihr Wunsch ist jetzt unmöglich*. I thought I recognized the word 'Paris' below, but I wouldn't swear to it. The mutilated message is as mysterious to me as the enigma of the Sphinx."

Ihr: his. *Wunsch*: desire. *Jetzt*: now. *Unmöglich*: impossible. Curiosity submerged Marie in one of her cousin's thick dictionaries. She had managed to figure out the meaning of the words – but not of the message – for she was even more ignorant of Wagner's language than Pauline; truly ignorant, in her case. Because she had no doubt it was modesty talking through Pauline's pen. As usual. Her friend always tended to undervalue her abilities. Marie remembered all the feverish praise Pauline lavished on her for her grace in choosing clothing and in dressing up and applying make-up. She spoke of herself as some sort of awkward duckling. "You are so feminine, Marie," she would say, "you seem American: the Americans know how to spruce themselves up, adorn themselves, the art of the threads! I'm American on my mother's side but I missed out on that inheritance. And just look at her! You're more like her than I am!" Marie protested and said it wasn't true, that Pauline looked nice and if she didn't look even nicer it was because she didn't want to, it wasn't a question of inability but lack of interest… at the end of the day she thought other things were more important! Even so, Pauline insisted; and it was due to that sort of humility that in those Monday afternoon tragedies she always resigned herself to masculine roles. On the other hand, when Marie reminded her of her obvious superiority in matters of books or music, she would shrug it off as if ashamed of showing off her knowledge. Just as she did now, in the letter to Amédée.

The tale continued: "I was desperate when the book was returned. For a while, I said nothing, but everyday life, full of obstacles, meanness, vigilance and even spying, put an end to my patience and my strength. In one of my day-to-day scenes, I told Mrs T. that I had decided not to live with her any more, that I'd had enough, that I was ready to run away at the first opportunity. She locked me up as if in prison. Every door in the house was securely fastened. A useless precaution for a young person of my spirit. Put locks on the doors and they'll slip out through the windows. That's what I did. One day just back from a walk, they came to tell Mrs Tarn that someone was waiting for her in the sitting room. She indicated to me that I should go practice piano in the big room next door. She couldn't see me but she would know I was there by the sound of the instrument, which I beat on with indignant, rebellious bangs. Suddenly, I got up. The large room had a sort of terrace on the second floor. It's difficult to explain to someone who isn't familiar with the orientation of English houses. Our terrace communicated with a series of others, separated only by a low grate that was easy for me to climb over. Two houses down there was an open window. I went through, into an empty room! I went out and found the stairway without running into anyone. Apparently, the people were out. I got to the street. Up to now I hadn't really thought about it, I simply obeyed my instinct and escaped like a bird flying from an open cage, with no plan or premeditation. Once on the street, I thought only of getting far away from the house, the sooner the better."

"Then I started to think on my feet. I sold a brooch and a ring I was wearing and started to look for a place to stay. I wandered from one street to another, knocking on every door that bore the sign 'apartments', always getting the same answer 'impossible, all the rooms are occupied' until I finally got lucky and found an old Scottish lady, very nice and above all, respectable. She started out by saying she could tell I was French" – at this point Marie smiled, in spite of herself, with a touch of tenderness for the pride that showed through the words of that fanatical Parisian by adoption – "And that it was sad to be a foreigner, alone, in a big city like London. And that even though she didn't usually take in unaccompanied ladies, she would make an exception for me. For my part, I told her a lovely tale, that I had friends in the countryside who would come to pick me up, a nice little fairy story of the clearest azure. I had just enough to pay for five days, with nothing more than breakfast in the morning. I had a minuscule room, where I stayed all day long with nothing to do but watch the rays of the sun move along the parquet from one hour to the next, and cry over the beautiful hours spent in the Louvre, the Luxembourg gardens… which I would never see again. Then I'd remember a wonderful night at the theatre and my poor little room would fill up with all the perfumes of the bouquets I received in Paris… And every time I heard the postman arrive with his special way of lifting the latch, I thought of the friendly letters I hadn't received for a long time. At that point I would start sobbing, and the goodly Scot would hear me from the next room and come in to comfort me. 'Oh, my pretty one, don't cry like that… it doesn't do any good and it'll make you sick.'

On the fifth day, I paid the bill and exchanged my new

dress and hat for a nasty old black dress like Cinderella's, worn, torn, dirty, and ten years out of date. It was the gift of the cleaning lady who had graciously traded this elegant outfit for mine. I looked like a beggar; no one could possibly recognize me. I was a bit unnerved to find myself on the cobbled streets of London, this time without a cent. I expected some copper to throw me in the slammer... that would have been fine, at least I'd have a place to sleep. I was too desperate and feeling too wretched to worry about what might happen to me. I was walking straight ahead when I had an idea. When it got dark, I could throw myself into the Thames. Now I knew where I'd sleep that night. I kept on walking while I waited. After a few hours of wandering along the banks of the river, watching how it flowed and waiting for evening, I found myself face to face with Miss Francourt, the lady Mrs T. had hired to accompany me after my emancipation in Paris. That poor woman had been searching for five days through all of London's most sordid areas. There were policemen everywhere following me. When I saw Miss Francourt, I suddenly fell ill. They took me home unconscious. I was terribly weak, since I'd barely eaten anything for five days – a cup of tea in the morning, an egg and a bit of toast, that had been my daily meal!

You have no idea of the terrible feeling I experienced when I awoke in a room on Hyde Park Street. It was jail, prison, a cage! Death, in short. Miss F., who took care of me with abnegation, kept me company and we chatted. Suddenly, she revealed something that made my hair stand on end. Mrs T. had spread the rumour that I was crazy – that very morning, the doctor had visited me to check on my health. In an instant I saw all the horror and dread of the trap she wanted me to fall into. That woman, as you know, doesn't have her own money, my father was unable to leave her anything because my grandfather, an energetic businessman who made a fortune, forgot to include in his will some kind of guarantee for the wife of my father. If she had me locked up in a madhouse, my money would end up in her hands. Apart from that, she could see clearly that when I gained majority I would escape, since I never felt any tenderness or respect for her, nor any trust or real love. Indeed, for more than a year all my actions had led down that path. She knew I was gifted, if it can be called a gift, with an ardent imagination, very heightened, very impressionable – so she never stopped telling me about striking cases of madness in her family. That got inside my head and affected my nerves, as she well knew. She encouraged all my little eccentricities of behaviour to take advantage of them later. I'm quite sure that if she deprived me of money at this point it was to drive me to expedients that make one say about a girl: Look at her outlandish ways! She's touched in the head, that young lady! She did it on purpose, annoying me, making me feel miserable, taking advantage of my exaggerated, violent outbursts to make a case for my madness. I'm convinced she'd been doing it for months, to goad me into the supreme revolt, which is what happened. The day I left, she went to all my relatives and friends, spreading the good news that I'd run away from the maternal home, having taken leave of my senses. Imagine the consternation of those good people! One of the most overwhelming proofs was the known and confessed suicide attempt in Paris, when I had taken chloral. What could possibly justify such an action?"

All those accusatory paragraphs, in which Pauline made

herself out to be the victim of the most lachrymose melodrama, provoked sharp irritation and a firm gesture of protest in Marie in support of that mother blinded by worry. A seventeen-year-old daughter involved in that sort of adventures… it wasn't at all strange that Madame T. tried everything to protect Pauline from her mental disequilibrium. All the more so if there were other cases in the family.

"I had no doubt, no hesitation" – the letter went on – "My trustees had come to find out my reasons for leaving the house, and I declared to them that the situation was no longer sustainable. I told them that relations between me and my mother had been very tense for a long time. I described my childhood, totally deprived of any maternal tenderness, my unhappy early years, always blamed and punished, and I spoke of my misunderstood adolescence. I accused Mrs T. of neglecting me, of leaving me alone in Paris and other places while she travelled around with friends, and a youngster thus exposed to hazards and circumstances of all kinds, I ask you all, does any of that give credence to the image of a self-sacrificing mother? In short, I requested that my trustees make me a Ward of the Court of Chancery. And after a trial of several months, that's what happened.

So instead of being locked up in a sanatorium in Jersey, which was my mother's plan, I now live with Miss F., the companion I mentioned before. We've been in Eastbourne for three weeks. It's a town with very pretty streets…

I'll spend the winter here perhaps; whatever I do, I have no intention of going back to London. I can't leave England for at least six months – afterwards, I'm not at all sure of being able to live in Paris for even a month per year. Do you know why? Because when you're a Ward of Court, you're not allowed to take up residence outside of the British Isles. Imagine my tears, seeing my exile here prolonged indefinitely… I have a delightful guardian assigned by the court, an unselfish friend of the family for whom I feel great friendship. Things have changed so much, so very much! This ideal guardian gives me all the money I need, gets me beautiful dresses and hats – I've never been so well-dressed in my life! – All my whims are satisfied; in a word, I have everything I want except for the most essential thing, which is the air of Paris, the joyful vision of France. I'm homesick for it and I can never get over that old illness… But with such a nice guardian, life can go stumbling along! I'm tranquil, if not happy, I write poems, some elegiac and others even more so, I live with my beloved memories, along with the dream and the nostalgia of the two worst and best months of my whole life…"

A final paragraph went on to describe in detail some of those specific memories. Then, the text ended abruptly, with no goodbye or signature. Surely the ending of the letter was missing, thought Marie.

Six months later, her daughter Berthe came home panting: "Mama, do you know what Mr Dalbert told me?" She jabbered away, one word bouncing out over the other. Her nose was frozen and cheeks red with cold.

That's how Marie found out. Suddenly everything made sense. The perplexity that had invaded her since Amédée's death, when she discovered his secret bond with Pauline, solidified now to the point where she was immobilized. Monsieur Dalbert was the neighbourhood bookseller, and it was through him that Marie intended to figure out who that mysterious writer was that occupied so much space in her cousin's library: Renée Vivien. That name sounded vaguely faraway, in the ears of a respectable woman, but with intense wisps of sulphur, mixed with a jumble of other names that were esteemed and stigmatized at the same time, like a certain Liane de Pougy – the courtesan novelist – or that mannish Marquise of Morny. Marie associated them with unspeakable scandals, with ambiences cloaked, for her, in the dark and unavowed prestige that vice holds for some virtuous women, leading them to root them completely out of their deepest thoughts. Now she found it looming before her, redoubled in size. She also knew – how? she couldn't remember – that Renée Vivien was a pseudonym. Perhaps finding her identity, she guessed, would bring some light to the subject. Of course Amédée was passionate about poetry: his zeal as a collector perhaps explained everything. But in this case the zeal seemed suspiciously exhaustive. More than twenty volumes of prose and verse, an entire shelf of his library, sometimes including second editions.

Marie intuited something dark, she wasn't sure what. And after reading Pauline's letters the murky areas surrounding her cousin took on, in her eyes, the attraction of an unsuspected mystery close at hand. That liberal-minded man, though always well-intentioned and honourable, had left her, along with his private papers, in a state of complete stupefaction. Now it was all clear. Both reasons for her amazement had become one. Renée Vivien was the same Pauline of the letters written to Amédée, just as the Pauline who wrote to Amédée was the same Pauline who wrote to her, Marie, as if she'd been another person. One image superimposed over the other, the two in conflict, aroused a troubling incredulity in Marie. Her daughter Berthe had supplied the last piece of the puzzle. Perhaps with calm, she would be able to glean something from those waters, stirred up afresh. Perhaps certain happenings would begin to make sense, in the light of a previously unsuspected explanation.

In a flash, Marie remembered one day, ten or twelve years ago, when she had run into Pauline one morning returning from the Bois de Boulogne. It was the last time she'd seen her. She was sure it was Pauline, settled into a luxurious carriage with a shield of nobility engraved on the door. When Marie ventured a warm greeting, waving her hand and asking the driver to hold the horses, Pauline turned away as if she hadn't recognized her. The carriage went by indifferently, haughtily. Marie had resented it. Even though she tried at times to believe that Pauline really hadn't seen her, the reaction of wounded sensitivity remained and left her undeceived. Marie hadn't understood that brutal breaking between the two families at all until she read Amédée's letters. The coldness her cousins and her mother had shown to her friend the day they ran into each other at the opera, for the premiere of *Salammbô*, left her disconcerted. She hadn't known how to react to that and could only muster a stiff smile… But that was no reason for Pauline to ignore her later on with such pride. Nothing from their youth could make Marie believe that the airs Pauline put on due to the elevated position Marie assumed she had reached could have gone to her friend's head like that.

Now Marie understood the real dimensions of what she had considered an absolute defeat. It wasn't pride, but shame when confronted with her own innocent childhood, embodied in Marie; that's what made Pauline turn away from her. The humiliation of a sullied person in contrast to the harmonious life Marie represented. And she saw that she had been right in giving Madame T. the benefit of the doubt. Faced with that troublesome trajectory, how could one deny her the clairvoyance of having perceived the imbalance affecting her adolescent daughter?

Then there was the poetry, of course. But could there be any work that justified the absurdity, the waywardness of sense and spirit, the collapse of an entire life?

She picked up one of the volumes, as if to fulfill a last pious duty toward a deceased person loved from afar, petrified in the distance, impenetrable. It had a soft title, like a prayer, and it was dedicated to some mysterious initials: H. B. C. L. She opened it at random. The brutal answer, the unexpectedly alive words, lashed her right in the face:

I WEEP OVER YOU

Evening has closed like a shadowy portal
Over my delights, my desires of yesterday.
I evoke you, O splendid daughter of the sea,
And now I come to weep for you, as for a dead woman.
The storm and infinity that once bewitched you,
Were they not perfect enough? Had they any less value
Than the conjugal peace of meals by the fire
And the nearby safety of a vulgar spouse?
Your eyes have learned the art of the warm, soft gaze,
And the lowering of eyelids in submission.
And I see you, languid, in the depths of the gynecium,

Eyelashes made up, and eyes shadowed by khol.
Your gestures, meek or wounded,
Have charmed the thick, lazy, satisfied sleep
Of the man who was showing you a stupid pleasure,
O you, once the sister of valkyries.
Today your husband can show off your eyes, once so haughty,
Your hands and your neck, svelte like a swan,
As one would show wheat, gardens and vineyards
For the admiration of obliging friends…
Abdicate your reign, then, and become the wife
Without will before the wishes of your spouse.
Free your fluid body to diverse whirls,
Be ever more docile to his jealous ardour.
Cling to this poor love that knows not how to deceive
Your spirit, once possessed by dreams.
But never again take up the rugged road of sand
Where algae sway to the rhythm of the censer.
Listen no more to the voice of the sea from afar,
Through the shimmering dusk shrouded in gold…
For the dusk and the sea will speak to you still
Of a glorious and lost virginity.

Paris, 13 July

Today I visited the Bois de Boulogne. Chantal has been in Paris since yesterday and she came with me. We went to the Grand Cascade and hired bicycles. Afterwards, we strayed off along the side paths where one loses sight of the asphalt and no car can shatter the idyllic simulacrum. Acacia flowers rained down from above us, and just looking up towards the cloud-embroidered sky through the yellowing lace of the tree-tops, our eyes lit upon a timeless scene. Up until then it had been impossible, even when the odd horse-rider or amazon rode past and the dense smell of the animals hit us like a whiplash, to try to imagine the cortege of horses that used to meet here a century ago, the groups of people on horseback and the ladies in bustles, corsets, and crinoline, promenading with their sunshades open, amidst the foliage. In vain we sought a new gleam, capable of illuminating all that remained in the shadows of paintings exhibited a few years ago in the *Jeu de Paume*, or in the pages of Zola that Renée once read, when she was still just Pauline, at Shepperton in July 1894. *La curée*, for example – *The Kill*? How to translate such a precise word, which alludes at the same time to the part of the hunt that is thrown to the dogs and to the bellicose struggle of the whole pack over its victims, whatever they might be?

Coupés, victorias, landeaus, phaetons, tilburies, carriages, people on foot before the emerging *ennui* of that other Renée who, around 1860, was returning from the Bois vaguely disposed to render herself a new Phaedra. An anachronistic figure, devalued by her context. A woman hell-bent in pursuit of the intense flame of a semblance of Passion, which only the tragic ending granted by her author allowed her to dignify posthumously. A proud gesture, indifferent to the fatuous pomp of the Second Empire, whilst Haussmann was busy disembowelling old Paris and the packs of speculators were fighting tooth and nail over the prey. Did a fragment of the memory of that unworthy young lady, of closed and consumptive life, remain in the revolt without escape of an adolescent who six years after reading the novel would choose this name for her beautiful pink and green pseudonym?

Where the interested party succumbs to a temptation which she had been able to resist up to now with a strength of mind worthy of all praise.

Paris, 16 July 1984

Dearest Chantal,

I have done everything I can to avoid talking about this matter. During the two days you were in Paris I controlled myself with an efficiency that was at the same time perhaps absurd. Deep down it is true what you always say: what you put out the door always comes back in via the window. But it was like a challenge I was setting myself. I have to repeat to myself over and over, I have to convince myself, that love is not the only truly important thing. But when the obsession for love leaves me, I am hit by anxiety about death and the idea, surely closer to the truth, that the latter really is the only subject, and that everything we do is nothing more than a way of exorcising its presence. Maybe all that has happened is that I've caught Renée's obsessions...

When I knew you were coming I said to myself: I'll spend time with her, we'll wander along the *quais*, we'll speak of projects, go to the cinema, have a sandwich in the Quartier Latin, look at clothes, etc. All of it has a value, you must not allow anything to cloud the harmony that always, I know, makes us feel so good together. And it had been a long time, anyway, since we had been able to spend so much time alone together; ever since you left Barcelona. Six years now. The same that have passed since I met Arès. I remember that when you left you said to me that you were happy to leave me in such good hands... And to a certain extent you had a point: if there is anyone in the world further from the *garce* genre it is her. There is a nucleus of truth in her, hard and precise, that reaches me in spite of all of the conflicts. There is a solid understanding between some part of her – the part that I, of course, see as most authentic – and a part of me, the part that also seems the best to me... But what on earth is authenticity all about? The existentialists were very clear on this point, and I think I was too at one time... Now I don't know what I'm up to when I use these words, but I have to be able to say it in some way: "Words are only to understand each other, not to understand them..." Maybe that's the case.

If I look back in time – and if these kinds of breaks in a relationship serve any purpose at all, it must be this, to mull things over, to recapitulate – I realize that this has been the most important love affair I have experienced up to now. That's something everyone always says about present loves, and you know my tendency to dive in head first ... without even knowing how to swim! Then things turn out as they turn out. But I had never made as much of an effort as in this case to learn. And I think the same is true for her. But if that is the case (why should I doubt it?) then it's as if we had wanted to learn at the same time one of us breaststroke and the other butterfly... all the time clinging one to the other: obviously it's been total chaos. Or perhaps a better way of expressing it is that together and at the same time one has tried to swim on top of the water and the other underneath. Curiously, I, who have always panicked at the thought of real water, am the one who has tried to swim underwater metaphorically! This simile, which might to you seem trivial, helps me to understand her terror every time I have tried to come up for air... But what is the use of trying to comprehend these things rationally? Altogether it makes me remember some heart-rending lines by Renée Vivien...

Viens, je t'entraînerai jusqu'au lit du flot clair
Et je t'adorerai, comme un Noyé la mer.

It seems that she at least knew that she would die of drowning...

Taking up again the thread of my recapitulation... To summarize I'll say I have lived at the mercy of passion for four years. Of a spiralling passion, like one of those whirlpools that sucks you in... (all passion is like that, you must be thinking). And at the same time, as if in a circle of mirrors: the passion of one woman for another woman. The mirror effect, mirror, miracle, mirage: If you possess me it is I who possesses myself. If I possess you, you possess yourself. What I give you, pain, pleasure, comes back to me like a boomerang. I leave you, I leave myself. You leave me, you leave yourself. You choose me, you choose yourself. You betray me, you betray yourself. And vice-versa. If I leave off thinking about you, or gravitating around you, I inflict on you non-existence and death. The blame falls on me, and I stop feeling myself. I stop existing. Or in reverse. How to escape this illusion? How to break the mirror without destroying ourselves?

These past two years I have tried to escape, but without wanting to give up Arès, or our relationship. For my good, for her good, I thought – still the mirror effect? – I tried it and managed quite well to protect myself with one of those rigid suits of armour that preserve you from your own desire, from yourself... And her from me. A shell that moulds your actions

122

and feelings. As with Chinese girls' feet, time, I thought, would take care of the rest… I remember that at first everything was very strange. I went around like a ghost, as if only that hollow shell existed, empty and untethered. Disciplined, I tried to give myself some sort of content again: I took meticulous notice of every single one of my most basic movements, of every tiniest sensation: "Now you are touching water. Now you take the clothes out of the washing machine. The clothes are wet. You open the door. Your hands feel cold. You have goose flesh…" With all of this I tried to fill the space previously occupied by my omnipresent desire. It was the proof I still existed in the world. And all in order to undo that equivalence: "I desire, therefore I exist (because only perhaps desire tells me that I am not you)".

It is strange: my contention did not have the positive effect I had hoped. Perhaps because I was riven with resentment, with wounded pride. Depending on your perspective, in some ways it might even look a bit like a form of revenge. For me it's true it was more about rebalancing forces: pulling her without respite towards the passion from which she was defending herself tooth and nail consigned me to remain constantly with my head under the water. I was drowning. "You win, we'll swim on the surface…!" Her suspicion, instead of waning, began to multiply. As if it were all no more than a trap. Or as if I had betrayed her: I was not in the place that I had sworn and double sworn I would be – and she had believed me…

Well, the submarine metaphor can be stretched no further. Perhaps it's something far simpler, a case of "when I pull you, you ask me why I am pulling you, and when I don't, you ask why not". The truth is that time has had its effect and now we are in a different place entirely. I don't know whether it's for better or for worse – from the point of view of our relationship, that is. To kill the passion has been to kill many other things. I would love to know how to feel in another way: to eliminate the dark side of emotion and leave only the intensity, the wonder, the flight… But it is impossible. Along with the one I lose the other, and, worst of all, the first thing that returns, in the moments when I lose control, is compulsive suffering. Every time that it happens to me, over and over again, I push the dragon back into the water once more with my foot. And I continue floating, with the emptiness on my back.

Contrary to what I had thought, we haven't reached a better understanding of each other. Rather a link has disappeared, a conflictual but clear nexus, an axis around which we struggled but which at least provided clear paths to follow. And, "thank goodness summer is on its way", as Christiane Rochefort would say.

The truth is that these last weeks, because I have another obsession, I spend very little time thinking about all the rest of it. Directly at least, because deep down this entire project about Renée and company leads me to the very heart of the matter. When I started on it I believed in passion. I mean to say that only this way of feeling love seemed to be worth living. And perhaps I had deluded myself into believing that by coming to understand the mechanisms that had led the passion Renée had for Natalie to a dramatic end, I would myself be able to experience my own *happy ending*. Right now I really have no idea what a happy ending would consist of, nor do I know very much more about the mechanisms. When for an instant I imagine that I do, everything seems as automatic as a computer programme. At times like that I say to myself that I'm behaving like the man who in order to discover the secret of beauty takes a beautiful body to the dissection table. A happy ending – would that consist of achieving what I thought I desired? "One can at times have what one desires, and it is not what they desire", quoth the ever so wise Natalie. (I barricade myself behind her maxims: as someone once said, plaster over the cracks made by life. Renée, on the other hand, lives through these holes and the blood that they pour forth.)

Oftentimes I am besieged by the suspicion that my desire is a pierced hand or a bottomless well, but I would at least have liked the chance to prove it. At no time, faced with the lack of viable options on offer, have I ever thought that what I was asking was excessive. In the absence of "universal" measures, I take as a model that which I see around me: the distribution of time and space, sharing things... Living together, for example. A common space as an affirmation and ambit of radical complicity, for every woman. For a long time this was the concrete milestone that for me encapsulated something far more vast, more global. Perhaps the very affirmation of a "normality" against the "marginality" to which context seems to condemn you. For, in the margins there is pride, but at the same time greater hardship, greater pain. (As if in the absence of moulds, of a predetermined, structuring skeleton, it were necessary to secrete a shell externally, like a mollusc, or to go out into the world as an invertebrate...)

Perhaps it's true that wanting to live together owes itself entirely to pressure from the most widespread model on the market, but at least it would have been an ending and a beginning: two well-defined stages. A milestone, as I was suggesting before. Or a symbol. Without milestones and symbols everything is just desert. Now I don't know what the next stage is. Sometimes I feel like a very young girl wearing her mother's heels. I get lost in them, I stumble, my feet twist beneath me. It's funny, isn't it? Before I was talking about Chinese women's feet and now I'm running into the opposite image. My problem must, then, be this: how to find the right measure, the shoe that fits perfectly.

I know what you will say: they don't make shoes like that, and perhaps I should just try walking barefoot: that is, free from all moulds... A relationship is always with a concrete being and, at the end of the day, one must always invent it from scratch... It's possible that these praiseworthy alternative slogans are right. I've said them over to myself a thousand times. But I have spoken of passion, a type of emotion that laughs in the face of respect for the other's liberty, which is the refrain that always follows. And what about when it seems to you that the other's freedom – and now I am talking specifics – at times stands for and expresses a capitulation to the demands of society much more serious than that of adapting to available models (models that, when it comes down to it, you are withheld the right and legitimacy to assume).

"Fervour does not measure, it creates. To forget that I look at her. To make her, more than mine, hers. To precede her towards herself, not to be shipwrecked in those ecstasies that have so little to do with us". Apart from the reference to ecstasies – because it's true I have a certain attraction to mysticism, I acknowledge this, and perhaps that is why I fail where the Olympian Natalie triumphs in all earnestness – I recognize myself in these Barneyan good intentions to liberate all alienated and oppressed women. But it's been some time now since I stopped being foolish enough to believe myself when I feel like that. The word alienation, whether for good or ill, is long out of fashion and, what is more, in my case, it just isn't possible to "liberate" someone against their will. All this reminds me of those right-on guys who used to be so prepared to do you the favour of de-repressing you on demand… And who will liberate us from our liberators, I wonder? Whatever the case, it must be necessary to apply a good strong dose of seduction – now there's a subject that has also seduced you – and to seduce with efficacy you must have the cold blood of the Amazon and not be at all vulnerable to "ecstasies". This is where I take the wrong path, no doubt. And I swear I'd run a mile if a generous Natalie appeared on the horizon, determined to help me find myself.

As you can see, I'm doing little more than flailing around in a puddle, and I have no idea how to get out. Perhaps I should do with this subject what I have done at times with a plant: leave it in a corner to see what happens. Impatience has often led me towards more radical practices, of the "kill or cure" type, to no avail… The little plant just carried on in her own merry way regardless… Until when?

Well, when you receive this letter I will have set off, on my way to Lesbos. To see whether the ghost of Sappho entraps me, too. I'll keep you posted, of course. Perhaps I'll find a delightful "lesbian" there and we'll weave *le parfait amour*… as you and yours always say. At the end of the day, people do always associate miracles with places of pilgrimage. And what have you to say about your trip to Prague, pray tell?

All love,

Sara

THE LADIES OF THE LAKE

Paris, 1912

The train had arrived at the Gare de Lyon a little before noon. In the precipitousness of her escape, Mary Wallace was carrying precious little luggage. No matter. If her stay in Paris were to become a lengthy one, she'd do the necessary shopping. After all, her entire wardrobe was out of style; everything she'd left in the closet and the few pieces she'd hurriedly stuffed into a suitcase, not to mention the mauve travel outfit she was wearing, with a good label but worn out by age and disuse. Mary thought about all this distractedly, from a secondary level of consciousness, as she looked out from the carriage at the elegant women who populated the Paris that was greeting her now with the bluest of springtime skies. Suddenly she was astonished and ashamed that her thoughts had taken such a frivolous turn. But nothing in the boisterous air invited gravity. Mary experienced this sudden lack of adaptation like a sharp blow to her legs, as she got out of the coach at the Hotel Albe. That was where she'd stayed every time she set foot in the capital in recent years. Always as in the blink of an eye, and always with Marcelle.

"There are days like islands," she thought while the maid helped her settle into a spacious room with a view of the Seine. "Like islands". The phrase came to her from some old forgotten reading, wrapped up in confused references. Perhaps it conjured up a sudden familiar vision of l'Île-de-Saint-Louis. For she didn't really know whether the island referred to that day, so unexpectedly solitary and enclosed in a soundless convulsion, or rather the seven years spent outside the hustle and bustle of the city, on the French bank of the

Léman. Those seven years now formed a unit of enchanted and impenetrable harmony enfolded onto itself, and bathed in light. They were an island like a lake, suspended in time, half water and half sky. Both water and sky forming a liquid envelope around the solidity of a name to which she clung, as if to the nucleus of all existence.

She'd left the three of them back there at the castle: Marcelle, Mabel, and John.

From her new solitude, everything she had left behind seemed a formless conglomeration of murky sensations, difficult to make out, that suffocated her, run through by painful and shining spindles like tongues of fire. She instinctively cried out: Violette! – Violette, a hard, brief, fleeting point of certainty. Violette always knew what to do. Violette projected an incisive prism of light over all things. Mary Wallace saw Violette intensively in the depths of her voyage. But where could she find Violette?

That same afternoon she went to Saint Germain-en-Laye. But she didn't find Violette there. All she found was the palid memory of an April day in 1901. The cheerful little cemetery, enamelled with geraniums and giant begonias, received a mourning party as an unprepared host receives inconvenient guests. A new tomb had been opened in the American section. The gravestone bore two dates: 1 April 1877 – 8 April 1901. Mary evoked her own desperation and her unsteady gait between Marcelle and Pauline as if they were someone else's. Pauline, loved by Violette. Marcelle who loved Violette. Pauline was dead now, too.

A little bit yonder, by the chestnut trees decked out in new leaves, she caught sight of her parents: a pig and a cow, as

Violette always said, laughing and fortifying the wall between generations with Olympic scorn. A pig and a cow, erect and dignified, dressed impeccably in black, inflicting ceremonies on their deceased daughter that she would have explicitly forsworn. Pure-blooded Americans, scandalized that the two of them only wanted to speak French. They thought it was fine to acquire a thick veneer of European culture – Europe was culture, especially Paris. But those two incomprehensible damsels they had engendered had crossed the line: they only used English when it was absolutely necessary, and then with a French accent! And so the afflicted parents made every effort to supply them with English governesses, one after the other. Pauline, who spent a few days with them in Paris one spring in the mid-nineties, and couldn't stand English or the British either – "It's only the great poets that save that language from horror," she went as far as to say – made fun of Miss Perkinson and compared her to a telegraph pole or a ship's mast… Since the poor Miss didn't know a word of French, because the ignorant head of the family and his wife thought that would force their daughters to use the language of the other side of the Channel, they heartily laughed at her right in her face. All of that led to an unfortunate return to the United States, where she and Violette were truly separated for the first time, for a long time. Interned in different boarding schools, they stoically suffered pitiless immersion in an atmosphere where everyone spoke the language that by origin and birth should have been theirs. It was during that double exile that Mary Wallace met Mabel.

Perhaps without the forced parting from her big sister, the intimacy between the two would not have germinated. Indeed, perhaps their bond had grown because of Mary's dominant double longing reflected in a single word: Violette, pronounced *à la française*. All Mary's conversations revolved around her. "When you meet Violette!" The future of their friendship always vaunted that particular landmark, like a lighthouse on a thick night, like a point of certainty, solid within their vague adolescent fluctuations.

Mabel asked her: "Is Violette pretty?" Mary didn't know how to answer such an inappropriate question. "Pretty? … No, I wouldn't say that, it's a word that doesn't suit her at all. She's… brilliant, the most intelligent person I know, and you can see it imprinted in her face. There's no other face like hers. Her great interior life, and exterior life, she dominates with supreme self-confidence. Just imagine: she learned Greek on her own so she could read Plato, and German so she could understand Wagner, and I don't even know how many philosophers she is familiar with. Mathematics fascinates her: she says it's pure Beauty. Not to mention music, even though it's the only field where I have the advantage: at least that's what our piano teacher said. Pauline and I were more on the same level. Pauline is a friend of Violette – Mary clarified. – Miss G. always said that Pauline put more heart into it, but that my technique was better… Violette preferred listening to us to playing herself… but in the end she wound up understanding music better than either of us. And literature, and art… and history and… she really does know everything!"

Mabel looked at her with a hint of disbelief in her wide-open eyes, filled with expectation in spite of herself. She was a little suspicious of the charm that such sage people might have: for her, living was more important than knowledge, acting more than wisdom. "But Violette makes life exciting all the time. She can be more fun than anyone, and she has no respect for behaviour imposed on her by outside norms! One time – she continued – when our parents had gone out, we ran off and went to dinner in a private room at Maxim's. And you know what she said to father, who was so angry he looked like he was about to have an attack of apoplexy? That the things we'd seen that night couldn't be learned in books or museums! And she really believed that: she loved adventure, and to figure out the how and the why of everything.

Years earlier, when she was a boarder at Fontainebleau with Pauline – that's where they'd become such good friends – they would sneak out of the house to see the sunrise in the forest, or to go naked bathing in the river under the stars. Just as everyone else was getting up, they went to bed as if nothing had happened". At that, Mabel took the risk of mentioning her favourite subject. Maybe Violette... Mary was scandalized: "Men? Men don't interest her at all: pigs, piglets or boars, that's what she says. A mix of bestiality and hypocrisy with the mere appearance of civilization! In a woman, you can find both beauty and intelligence, whereas in a man... if he's good-looking, it's because he looks like a woman. Have you seen Leonardo's San Giovanni? It's gorgeous. But even so, as soon as you imagine him in real life, a little physiological mechanism would in a matter of moments transform beauty into the grotesque. Because, you see, Violette knows physiology... theoretically, of course... she never forms opinions out of ignorance".

Mary not only repeated Violette's arguments, but endorsed them with the fervour of a disciple. "About that physiological mechanism: have you heard about the *castrati*? They're also called *tenore alto*: it seems one of the Catholic popes prohibited women from singing in the churches of Rome, but at the same time he didn't want to diminish the beauty of religious ceremonies. And how do you think he could get a masculine voice to sound as lovely as a feminine one? By making a man not a man anymore! As I was saying before, can you imagine a woman poet getting inspiration from a man, like Dante got from Beatrice? Never. It would be impossible for her to find in him the ideal of Beauty. Violette is convinced that's why there are so few women artists. But even for men to do it – I mean what Dante and Petrarch do – they have to eliminate their own animal dimension. Why do you think the Catholics made the Virgin the feminine ideal? And not just the Catholics… Because they know that men, with their gross animal zeal, never elevate women, they only degrade and sully them…"

Mabel listened, amazed and dazed, drawn in in spite of herself by that torrent of words. Mabel, who, when she met Violette, had also felt her overwhelming power of subjugation, while Mary had stepped back a little, modestly, with a subtle shiver of voluptuousness.

Mabel, who had married a few years earlier (what had become of their old, secret pacts?), was now at the castle by the lake with Marcelle. Mary struggled uselessly to erase the image that kept coming back to her, painfully, like the repeated attack of a sharp-edged dream. From deep down in the waters confusing faces appeared before her wandering gaze. She fled from them to slip away from the death which blurred the contours of all things, possessed in the manner of drunken birds in October, confounded by the elements, and vainly seeking the boundaries between water and air, diving into the lake and coming out again, like scared, swift arrows. Bewildered, she had fled death. And there she was, facing a stone slab, seeking the imprecise aid of a dead woman.

It was at Cannes, while Violette was dying, that Mary met Marcelle. Violette incessantly begged for Pauline's presence. But it was Marcelle who watched over her at the bedside. That young woman with a tenacious gaze, often quiet and distracted, hadn't left her alone since they met at the Sorbonne, both of them passionate about Mathematics; she was familiar with every step of Violette's intellectual inquiries, which lately – or maybe always, in different forms – obsessed her. She had followed her along a zigzagging path through Nietzsche, Lucretius, Schopenhauer, Buddhism, Taoism… she was there during the unexpected, feverish pirouette towards a Catholic faith verging on ecstasy when at death's door. As if that religion, which hadn't helped her live, could now help her die. Rather than the arid reading of Pascal, it was mysticism and the cult of the Virgin that attracted her decisively, perhaps from way back when. Reasons of the heart, no doubt. Just as reasons of the heart, strong as religion, led Marcelle to stay with Violette to the point of her passing, without fear of a dreadful contagion and with an abnegation bordering on sainthood. Pauline, on the other hand, waited until the last minute, tortured by guilt. In response to Violette's persistence, who repeated her name constantly in her delirium, a telegram was sent to notify her that the end was near. Violette died without recognizing her. And Pauline had never been able to console herself.

They still spoke of her the last time Mary saw Pauline. They always talked about Violette, whenever they saw each other. Even though they'd known each other since childhood, and for three years Mary and Marcelle lived in the apartment above Pauline's on Bois Avenue – mourning Violette – what united them most was the memory of the one who had died. That memory was like a net that seemed to suspend the passage of time. Mary remembered each detail of that last encounter, four or five years ago, as if it had awakened a hidden sense in her that heightened her awareness of an exceptional occurrence. It was at the end of the summer, at grape harvest time. Pauline was just returning from a trip to Constantinople and Mytilene. She was travelling with Hélène, by way of Italy. They had to go through Geneva, and Mary and they had made a date to see each other. Marcelle had stayed in the castle. There was a kind of incompatibility between her and Pauline, and neither one of them did anything to hide it. It was a fallacious resentment rooted in mute irrefutable accusations buried in impossible recesses of memory. And so, they avoided each other.

Mary made the boat trip from Evian alone. It was windy and sunny. When she disembarked in Geneva, Mary caught sight right away of the bejewelled bulk of the baroness next to Pauline, dressed all in grey with a bouquet of violets at her belt. Mary thought of Marcelle, and how that detail would have infuriated her. Hélène seemed upset, and for the first time, at least for Mary, lacked the aplomb that usually distinguished her. Later, when the baroness left them alone for a moment with some excuse, Pauline confessed that she hadn't gone to Mytilene alone, as she had told Hélène. She had made the trip with Natalie – stubborn Natalie, who has never known defeat, Mary thought. She remembered her, humiliated and furious, the day she saw proof of what she feared from her window on Bois Avenue: Pauline and Hélène embracing in the garden. Now it seemed her time had come to respond... – Pauline went on: "Natalie came to meet me in Bayreuth a year ago... and proposed this trip: I resisted at first but finally... It was like a dream. But it's over now... one doesn't put one's life on the line twice. You know how much Hélène loves me. Her love is exclusive and jealous, the way I used to love Natalie. I haven't told her about all this, but she knows. It is as if she can read into the depths of my eyes. And she suffers, you know? This time I've made my choice, definitively," she concluded.

It wasn't the first time Mary had heard her say that. Perhaps only death made it the last time. But that day, she continued in a dark voice: "Because of Natalie I was late to Violette's deathbed. I still can't forgive myself. But I couldn't leave her alone in Paris. It wasn't just for fear or jealousy: without her I was nothing more than a disembodied shadow." Mary remembered how her sister's death had brutally and violently thrust Pauline into a senseless, opaque agony.

It was Violette who introduced Natalie to Pauline. Both wanted to be writers, they both wrote poetry: they had to meet, she decided. One winter day she invited them together to a matinee at the Théâtre Français. Afterward, they'd taken the obligatory walk through the frozen Bois de Boulogne. Mary remembered that, at Violette's request, Pauline read a very sad poem that started like this:

I'll sleep a sleep long and sweet tonight.
Close the curtains tight, keep the doors shut.

Mary once again felt the strangeness that the texts of her friend always provoked in her: why did Pauline, such as she was, write that sort of poetry? Until Violette's death, she had never seen her overcome by any kind of anguish. She had a happy character. But Violette, who knew her better, said that Pauline did indeed have a darker side, an acute sensibility and the yearning for the absolute found in all great poets. That's why she was so dismayed when she suspected Pauline's passion for Natalie, when she guessed what had happened, which for some odd shame or scruple that was hard to understand, her friend had kept a secret. Their friendship, their "soul sisterly" affection, was based on an implicit pact of sincerity. In those straits, Pauline thought the only solution was distance, trying to hold to the pact by delaying its implications. At least that's what could be deduced from the pages of *A Woman Appeared to Me*, the novel Pauline was to publish some years later in which Mary recognized Violette beneath the transparent Greek name Ione. In that text, Pauline justified herself, now that Violette wasn't around to absolve her, for all the pain that she had unwillingly inflicted. For there was no doubt that, excluded from the circle she had contributed to creating, Violette had suffered greatly and in silence. Pauline was only semi-conscious of it at the time, or perhaps she thought it was a suffering that was inevitable but temporary. Typhoid fever had drastically robbed her of any possibility of making amends.

Mary herself had also introduced Mabel to Marcelle. Mabel and Marcelle, now together at the lake's edge. Something about Mabel related her to Natalie. Some recondite thing, not visible on a superficial level: maybe that capacity to turn all events in their favour, as if they both held a secret dominion over destiny. And a sort of hard edge that made them invulnerable to the pain caused in others by the fulfilment of their desires.

Mabel, Natalie... Was it all, then, simply repetitions of repetitions? Did everything roll down the same slope again and again toward the same unchangeable paradigms, the inevitable, ordinary lot of the everyday? During the ten years she shared with Marcelle, Mary thought she had escaped the rites and oscillations of normal unions. Normality implied gregariousness. Like the famous Llangollen ladies a century earlier, they had taken refuge far from the world in a perhaps illusory attempt to recreate paradise on a human scale, though without the previous exaltation of a novelesque flight. The mirror, the miracle – the mirage? – of the lake had reflected their invariable idyll and enclosed it in an azure case. Between the two of them and all others there was always a transparent, almost imperceptible limit, like the glass of a showcase protecting an object too valuable, offered only for dazzling contemplation. Violette was the only benevolent and permissible goddess of this world returned to its first innocence, as if the atavistic sacrifice of a virgin had redeemed it from all culpability. Her name always rose above them and liberated them perhaps from the madness of seeing each other's naked soul, one in the other, as if in unending, repeating mirrors. Instead of that, like the Léman's still waters, Violette's name reflected back to them the calming image of two faces, side by side, gazing at the same fixed point of a multiform and changing universe. Love was simply to double their gaze on all things.

Like the impact of a hurled stone or a bullet, Mabel's arrival burst upon a space that now appeared unexpectedly vulnerable, fragile. The memory of the bond she too had held with Violette apparently gave her a credible, confident right of entry. The presence of her accompanying husband was probably irrelevant. "How can you live here, all cloistered up?" she exclaimed as soon as she arrived. For a moment, paradise seemed reduced to the lowly category of a prison or a convent. Marcelle's voice unexpectedly caught it in flight and raised it up once more: "It's in Paris that we felt cloistered, not here. It's hard to explain but that's how it is. All this has a charm that you discover day by day..." The stones, the panelling, the heavy furniture, all overwhelmed the newcomer. But Marcelle insisted – and Mary approved, relieved at not having to carry the defence herself – "You haven't seen the lake from the tower yet... And the garden: we've become first-class gardeners. We have more than fifty varieties of roses! We'll show you!" And she alternated her gaze between Mabel and John.

"Let's go down to the garden," Mabel said. Mary raised her eyes from the score as a sign of assent. Her fingers continued oscillating on the keys. Mary had instinctively delegated the role of host to Marcelle. The morning concert of four hands had given way to one of those solitary sessions that she insisted on preserving in spite of everything. She kept on religiously for an hour, running through pieces by Grieg, Mozart, Brahms. She hadn't the heart to take on Chopin. Later, she decided to join the others. She found John reading the morning edition of the *Journal de Genève*. He was unexpectedly alone, by the little pond adorned with waterlilies about to open. His expression was somewhere between worried and furious. What a change from the previous night, when with a crafty look and an ample smile, he had broken out into Leporello's aria from *Don Giovanni*!… "*Madamina, il catalogo…*"

The evening had been most agreeable, at first surprisingly festive and merry. Later it evolved toward the elegy: Marcelle's lovely voice had seduced the small audience with a series of arias for *tenore alto*, ending marvellously with the most famous passage from Gluck's *Orfeo*: "*J'ai perdu mon Eurydice, rien n'égale ma douleur…*" Mary had alternated, accompanying both John and Marcelle on the piano. Mabel alone had limited her role to that of spectator. Mary saw, though, that she enjoyed following along with the metronome at hand, enumerating Don Giovanni's conquests, and then listening, completely entranced with shining eyes, to Marcelle's little recital…

They had gone to bed after midnight, and all except her had slept late. She took great care instinctively lest that surprising parenthesis in her social life alter the daily rhythm of things. She got up at the usual hour and had given orders to the servants before she sat down at the piano… Now she noticed the remnants of breakfast on the marble table. Three places. But Mabel's and Marcelle's chairs were empty. Mary addressed some empty phrase to John; lost in thought, she mechanically picked up a bit of cold toast and rang the service bell. When the maid left, Mary's strong suspicion of the day before was confirmed: John's gaze softened in Chiara's presence and his eyes followed her with an eloquent expression; then he made some comment about Italy, entirely out of place. That evoked a secret scorn in Mary as she recalled the looks her father used to bestow upon the young servants. How could Mabel accept such matrimonial usage? They'd only been at the castle for a week, and a banal adultery was looming on the horizon. She made some excuse and left him alone. Then she headed off down the path that disappeared beneath the high arch of the magnolia trees.

Near the parterre of violets, just now blooming, she thought she saw Mabel and Marcelle very close together, seated on a stone bench. They formed a reddish grey spot against the soft purplish of the flowers. Suddenly the grey silhouette separated brusquely as if disposed to jump out at Mary. Or as if to flee something. Because Mary realized right away that she hadn't been seen. Marcelle came toward where she was, her eyes moist and her face red. Mary shrank back as if she wished to disappear behind a tree trunk until Marcelle had gone by. She was suddenly afraid, although she wasn't sure of what. What kind of power did Mabel's words have over Marcelle? At that moment, she didn't even dare suspect that there might have been more to it than words.

"Madame, if you please…" Mary Wallace was startled. A man with a solicitous attitude was at her side. The guard said simply that the cemetery was to close at six, but if she wanted to stay a bit longer they'd find a way… Mary felt gratitude toward that man who had obliged her return to the present.

When she left the cemetery, she went along Rue de Pologne towards the new market. She knew Saint Germain well. It was a usual summer resting spot for people sojourning in Paris, and they'd stayed there from time to time since her childhood. The same year Violette died, toward the end of August or beginning of September, she'd come here with Pauline, who had a true obsession with being physically close to the dead woman. She'd have spent the whole day at the cemetery if Mary hadn't dragged her on the kind of itineraries that were more of a relief for her. She herself had never felt the presence of her sister when she stood before her tomb. But for Pauline, the dust and ashes of Violette were like saints' relics to Catholics, tangible links to what was impalpable and immaterial. They lodged, those days, at the Aigle d'Or Hotel, on the corner where the picturesque street of the same name crosses Rue Vieil Abreuvoir. It was the hub of the town. The spacious, light rooms of the second floor opened onto a patio with a few trees that Mary recalled as dark silhouettes against the sky on her sleepless nights – Pauline, drenched in chloral, slept, but moaned in her dreams. Nearby, just down Rue Saint Louis towards the square was the castle, converted into a museum, and beyond, the gardens of Le Nôtre and the terrace over the valley of the Seine.

Rather than the trips of that terribly sad year, Mary evoked other scenes, when Violette was still alive and they travelled in an open landau all the way to the Mare aux Canes, to the pond surrounded by yellow narcissus in the midst of the forest. Or their strolls along old avenues where ancient aristocratic palaces from the long regal epoch of the Louis succeeded each other like a string of stone jewels, with carriage gates of carved wood, sculptured corbels, musty shields, and names that were magical to the ears of young North American girls, dying to be European. Violette always wanted to pass by the Maintenon Palace, which shone with the legendary prestige of the Grande Dame of letters, and had a lovely wrought-iron balcony which did not correspond, however, to the period of construction. "That's new," Violette would say, "it's only fifty years old, at most". They'd gone through the museum innumerable times, and they'd bicycled to the end of the Terrasse or beyond Avenue Loges. Walking lightly through those scenes with the indefinable odour of old Saint Germain, and such a clear sky above her head, Mary could now – at last – feel Violette's breath near her; along with footsteps that were in step with hers, on tiptoe so as not to make a sound. It was just an instant. The feeling dissipated the next moment, like those white plumes of dandelion they blew when they were children, which dissolved in the air, and they called "angels".

At the station she thought she saw the curator of the museum, Monsieur Salomon R. He was a very highly regarded man who had probably held that position for twenty-five years. Once, when they were very young, Mary and her sister had gone to the museum and had run into him in the vestibule. Violette had been harbouring unresolved doubts for days about the Dame de Brassempuy – a lovely ancient ivory figure she couldn't get out of her head – and she accosted him with polite audacity. Monsieur R. seemed to puff up and strut, all inflated... It was very unusual, he said, to find such bright and daring young girls alone at the museum. He asked them lots of questions and accompanied them all around, answering every one of their enquiries untiringly. More than twenty years had gone by since then. There was no chance he would recognize her. Mary lost sight of him as she boarded the train.

During the trip, the images she was trying with all her might to suppress came back to her: the light of the oil lamp from the tower window, herself, suddenly awake, Marcelle absent. The beating of a monstrous, deafening heart which suddenly stopped pouring out and pumping blood. Had she fainted? She didn't know. The scent of cologne on her wrists still made her nauseous. And the two of them, Mabel and Marcelle, tangled together in a corner of the grounds, protected from the stone slabs only by their intermingled delirium. And a stain, red as a pomegranate, on Marcelle's lily-white chest. "Mabel suggested we see the lake at night", she'd said at the moment of unnecessary explanations. Mary cut her off abruptly with a glance. At that, Marcelle lowered her eyes, as if Mary could have read some terrible secret crime in them, buried through the years. Then she raised them again with a begging gesture and said in a thread of a voice: "I don't know what it is, Mary... Never before..." She didn't finish the sentence. To Mary's look, dressed with an almost priestly dignity, Marcelle's nude sincerity could only come across as squalor or obscenity. Both were intolerable. Mary searched for something to say, and just like couples in an unwanted divorce invoking the children, or like the pious who always have a saint's name ready for any disgrace, she asked: "What about Violette?" Marcelle didn't understand. To no avail she sought some clue in Mary's expression that might help her decipher that unexpected message. Mary jealously hid the link that only she knew was broken. And she felt as though Violette was dying for a second time.

It was dark through the compartment windows as the train entered Paris. Suddenly, inexplicably, Mary felt light, as if she'd left behind in Saint Germain all the ballast of the past, turned to shards of glass.

When Mary got to the hotel, she found a telegram. John and Mabel were gone. Marcelle was waiting for her at the castle. It was odd: that laconic message made her feel anxious and unhappy. She had to decide what to do. She well knew that she'd go back, but not yet. Not until… until what? She'd think about it tomorrow. She had time. The others had already decided. Who had decided? Marcelle? Mabel? Or maybe John, in the last instance; the pre-established limit against which the ardour of the two women could crash without danger, like a rock that absorbs, immutable, the constant lashing of the waves? All three of them seemed far away from her now, very far from her life. She would not return. Paradise had melted away. Violette was dead. Definitively dead, like Eurydice in Greek mythology… She wouldn't come back to life, as was the case in Gluck's pious fantasy… At the lake's edge, Marcelle was all alone, waiting for her. Mary turned over, becoming tangled up inside the sheets, like a mollusc in its opaque shell. In the distance, she could see a very small girl, lost in the night. Outside, the Seine flowed, slow and dark. She shivered. She couldn't leave Marcelle alone at the lake's edge.

Private Papers of Sara T. (6)

Where the narrator surprises Sara T. in the bar of the Gare d'Austerlitz, cooking up the most earnest of abracadabras and galimatias on ephemeral paper serviettes.

Paris, 26 July 1984

Whenever I try to put my finger on the essence of my chronic dissatisfaction in all of this our story, there always appears to me a triangular schema – is it not a triangle, also, that frames the eye of God in pious representations? The triangle, which limits our grammatical perception to the three persons of the verb. The triangle, which irrupts into the harmonic or tense immobility of the two thus bringing movement and, hence, conflict between itself and the agent of change. The triangle, which at times opens out into other triangles, like Catherine wheels in fixed firework displays, forming and dispersing constantly, superimposing themselves, interpenetrating, intersecting. The triangle, image of perpetual choice – trial – and of perpetual betrayal.

I'm not talking now of that triangle that has become such an unerring and clichéd staple of vaudeville and melodrama. Though it's fair to say that my experience of events has taken on a melodramatic tinge seen up close, or vaudevillian, when distance allows a dose of humour into the picture. And indeed that the classic but hackneyed image of adultery might serve me as a starting point, like any other triangle that takes on a concrete and defined shape. I have felt, in this our story, as if I were permanently the "other" without there being any one – female or male – at the other vertex. In fact, I'm sure that if there had been a "one", it would have been easier

146

for me to resign myself to the fact and to attempt to adapt to the situation; to fight; or to simply let things go and break up.

The precision of that which interposes itself in the way of desire and the will makes things appear so much simpler. Even if at times such a simple fact can be a sign of a greater subterranean struggle. But what does that matter. It serves its purpose, and that is good enough, I suppose. Yet that which I have felt permanently between you and me has always been imprecise, multiple and changeable. On the other vertex of the triangle I could only place a word that has such a wide meaning it is almost meaningless: "the world". Often I have had the no doubt fallacious sensation that outside of this complex, all-encompassing and powerful "world" – which, lest we forget, imposes a hostile law on the kind of love you and I have tried to live – the majority of conflicts that have stood in our way would have been inexistent.

It is true that a good part of the problems, distrust and misunderstandings stem from the different way in which each one of us relates to the "third party" in our presence, even when this takes the form of an "absent" presence. From the different pacts that each one of us has established with it. And from the different trials and betrayals to which we have subjected any pre-existing complicity. But, what would remain of us if we eliminated this referent that is so necessary for all real existence? It is perhaps this tug of war with the world which defines us in the most singular manner. There is no escape, there is no "outside the world": for an instant, passion, freeing you from the prison of yourself, dissolves the limits, refuses all law and denies all blame. For passion's sake, forget oneself, forget the world. Or make a truce with it: with the private and the social as articulated by institutions such as

147

marriage or other such... To extend to the ambit of the emotions that which under the rule of law is a constitution.

I have oscillated over the last years between these two solutions (?). I have had the sensation of living the worst of each of them without any of their respective advantages. At the end of the day, this hybridity brings with it the monotony of perpetual shock, of a lack of projects – of a common project – and the installation in a continuous present just as routine as in the worst of marriages. All that uncertainty and anxiety about one's own place, the discomfort at having to make a continual effort, as absorbent as passion, as mechanical as any sort of habit... Is this hybridity innate – not exclusively so, though – to those attachments which "the world" has declared as being against nature? Is it the absence of a legally and socially recognised "constitution" that establishes the power struggle in its pure state, as the savage articulation of each and every one of the extremes? Or at the other end of the spectrum, is there only the possibility of imitating – and imitation always becomes grotesque – that which, with our own particular evolution, we have sought to avoid at all costs?

WHERE THE NARRATOR PLACES CHARLES B.
BEFORE AN UNDOUBTEDLY SPURIOUS MIRROR, FROM
THE DEPTHS OF WHICH, NEVERTHELESS, A SMIDGEON
OF SENSE SEEMS TO EMERGE.

Saint Omer, July 1912

The *Mercure de France* always got to Saint Omer a couple of days late. Almost immediately after the article about the correspondence between Reboul and Aubanel, the eleventh "letter to the Amazon" occupied pages 110–112. Rémy de Gourmont: all of learned Paris commented on the hypnotic power that a woman of very odd habits had acquired over that man confined within himself and his dusty books, with the permanent company of a cat and the intermittent company of barely a handful of friends. That inexpugnable fortress on Saints-Pères Street hid a face disfigured twenty years before by lupus, a bothersome stutter that tripped up his words, a scornful pessimism about everything that moved, and a well-known misanthropy. Even so, the sharpness of his pen, ground in that secret "granary" on the Left bank, made his indomitable Voltairian spirit visible and assiduous to devotees of Lady Literature, among whom he reigned supreme as the most recognized Pontiff.

It goes without saying that Charles B. held an unreserved admiration for that sacred monster, seasoned several months ago by a touch of gratitude and a goodly splash of flattering complicity. A small opuscule had fallen into his hands, *Je sors d'un bal paré*, in which Gourmont made his admiration for Renée Vivien explicit beyond doubt: "A young woman who was also one of our most penetrating poets and who carries

149

the divine melancholy higher and further than anyone..." He then went on to recount the anecdote of the tuft of violets... Charles B. knew it better than all others in the world, except perhaps for Marie, Pauline's maid. If he'd had any doubt before about the identity of the legendary Amazon celebrated by all of Europe, that text would have erased it immediately. No one but Miss Natalie B. was capable, if she'd proposed it, of taking Gourmont to a masked ball, with his head wrapped in one of her green silk stockings like a turban, and of arousing a devotion that scandalized all, from strangers to intimates. Charles also knew from another source that it was through Gourmont that Natalie B. had published some poems in the *Mercure* in memory of Renée Vivien – perhaps the few poems written by her that Poetry had deigned to visit. The episode Gourmont related, documenting the origin of violets on the island of Lesbos, was known by very few people. Miss B. was never tight-lipped about secrets that, at the same time, shed light on her own dominions. And Sappho's island formed part of the legend that indissolubly tied her to the memory of Renée Vivien...: Charles had heard her scatter to the four winds the project, hypothetically shared with Pauline, of founding a doubly-Sapphic colony on the island. Gourmont did little more than assume the role, willingly, of a fervent, humble chronicler.

Charles couldn't help but smile a little bitingly at that strange idyll between a ferocious, awkward intellectual and a woman unreachable for him by definition of her Amazonness. Not even reachable for the other supposed "Amazons": one had only to remember Pauline's complaints – Pauline, defenceless before her own fascination for that fleeting being, who was, perhaps for that very reason, rendered a substitute for the absolute. It was quite odd: Charles had never succumbed to the dazzling adhesion that Miss Natalie B. seemed to demand of all in her presence. His ironic character, at times cryptically ironic, formed a formidable armour, and explained this unheard-of heroism. The admiration he undoubtedly felt for her – who could avoid it? – wasn't enough to disarm him, and the toughness of the adversary spurred him on. It was only compassion that placed a limit on his causticity: the respect aroused by the suffering of others in those who know they themselves are susceptible to suffering, and who do not try to hide their own vulnerability to love and death. It was this sort of compassion he had felt excessively for Pauline, never diminishing his admiration for her, but, in fact, illuminating it from within, as if an image sculpted in stone was suddenly animated by life and blood. Thus, he could be mordant with her, making her laugh, to get her to take some distance for a moment from a world that could never be fair to either Renée Vivien or Pauline T., and that wounded her so often with incomprehension and hostility. But he was incapable of the slightest irony towards her, about her. In the case of Miss Natalie B., things were very different.

Charles had met both of them within a short time of each other, about twelve years ago. The North American ambassador, father of one of his students at the Lycée Saint Louis, had introduced them in the company of Miss B.'s parents: he could be the good teacher of French prosody, prestigious and patient, that their daughter needed to solidify some wobbly literary debuts. From one day to the next, his amazing pedagogy spread to a new student of English origin. Natalie had introduced her as "my friend". Charles was quick to glean the special meaning of that expression.

In a long poem from his early youth, Charles had responded somewhat humorously to an imagined question about his first love. The humour covered up both genuine nostalgia and a half-truth. To call the dazzled fascination of a boy of ten years and four days "love" for the figures on a tapestry was a way of playing with words and concepts. But Charles didn't feel it was a game, or if it was, it took on for him the seriousness games can have for children. He liked nothing better than to get to the bottom of things, and now that he was an adult, to reflect on the importance of a word – love – returning him to a childhood experience, so small yet so exorbitant. The tapestry hung in the salon of his house. It was the only exotic element in that old manor that always smelled of lavender and wildflowers. An interminable line of Chinese girls with too-bright dresses, too-tight shoes and too-big tortoise combs chased each other endlessly along the old wall. They carried blue and white fans that almost looked like wings, and their violent and ethereal tones attracted the marvelled gaze of young Charles like a magnet. He'd have loved to pull them off the wall, teach them to walk, and then run far away with them. He dreamed of who knows what joy, a distant vision beneath immobile lacquered skies, along a river of colours on the edge of unknown stars… Porcelain pagodas, golden steeples, swaying palanquins: an entire Orient, vague and strange. And in the evening, the Chinese girls with the flame of their black eyes and the scent of a rare plant…

Sometimes when he closed his eyes, far from those trifling, ridiculous chimeras, and occupied with more serious affairs – which would perhaps seem ridiculous to the uncompromising eyes of the daydreaming child he once was –, a compassionate memory would come to him of those Chinese girls with the minuscule feet, chasing each other the length of the wall, indifferent to his fascinated gaze. In light of all that had happened to him since then, at the side of Miss Natalie B. and Pauline, that old, childhood dream almost seemed like a premonition.

The eleventh letter to the Amazon began on page 110: "To speak of love with a young woman is one of the pleasures of our delicate civilization. One would have to be the last of the Methodist pastors to not find pleasure in it". Charles would have liked to be capable of imagining one of those private conversations between Gourmont and Natalie B. that culminated in public letters. "But there can't be many women who don't find it too, even with the least seductive of men, even those women least disposed to let themselves be seduced, even she whose physiological nature makes her unseduceable".

He became more specific further down. "It's you I'm talking to and about, Amazon, and to myself as well. We know our spirits have a sex, as we know also that it's the cause of their pleasure… It isn't even necessary for both of us to be equally convinced; my own conviction is enough to colour the relations of our souls. When a man converses with a woman in intimate tones, he takes on a certain femininity in his nervous contexture. A charming agreement is established between those two beings who touch each other only with the tips of their antennae and interpenetrate perfectly, above all when they reject any ulterior motive and neither one imagines arriving at the great union. Who knows if the kind of friendship I'm describing isn't such a profound desire that it becomes obscure, like those wells in which one sees nothing but senses the reverberation of the sky. But it is a desire which allows itself to be contemplated serenely. Far from muddying the waters, it clarifies them; far from making them boil, it calms them. It is the ferment of peace, joy, serenity. The tranquil character of friendships of men for women has been doubted because of the suspicion that the desire therein was synonymous with anxiety and interior confusion. But it is forgotten that often the milieu into which it falls is not favourable to its development, and thus maintains its growth within limits. Love that is unaware? – they say – Indecisive passion that trembles at its own shadow? Can words characterize in fairness sentiments so particular that they escape the very expressions that would imprison them?"

It was through those lines that Charles realized how Gourmont struggled, and half succeeded, to capture in words a sentiment and intimate bond of the kind that had linked him to Pauline for so many years. It wasn't often, though, to find a relationship like that between a man and a woman; one that escaped all conventional provisions. That is basically what made them similar. But between the two of them, there was an essential component that could by no means have been present between Gourmont and the Amazon, from what Charles knew of both of them: Pauline had turned him into a confidant from very early on, the only confidant that Pauline allowed herself. In his presence, she unclothed her soul, removed all veils and artifices, and was naked in her vulnerability, armed only by the power of her complex truth. He knew her verses as well as her life in their imperfect state; he witnessed her efforts, always failing in her own eyes, to reach perfection, to capture the ever-fleeting ideal. The ideal incarnate in Poetry or absolute love, the love for Natalie B., to which she clung as to a solemn vow: only death could free her from it.

One of the letters Charles found most moving – in spite of his sceptical reserve when confronting proclamations of extreme sentiments – and which demonstrated the intensity of their friendship, spoke of a failed suicide. It was shortly after the death of her friend Violette. Pauline had refused to follow Miss Natalie B. to the United States, where the latter's family beckoned her. The year before she had accompanied her enthusiastically. Charles knew all about the disappointment through letters: Natalie went to and fro all day long, from one party or engagement to another, dancing till dawn, bouncing around and flirting without pause… while Pauline languished in a corner. Only the splendid American sunsets managed to console her a little, plus the discovery of Sappho's verses, introduced to her by Eva, a childhood friend of Natalie's.

During the entire year after her return, she had battled with Greek under Charles's attentive supervision. Natalie was becoming a source of restlessness and anxiety day by day. The last news Pauline received of her since she left for Washington was of an engagement, signed and sealed, to a broke European aristocrat, surely on the hunt for easy money. Violette's departure, on the other hand, had left Pauline with a mixture of suffering and remorse: Mrs T., Pauline's mother, had gone so far as to tell Pauline that she was responsible, indirectly, for that death. In such a frame of mind, she had left the apartment on Rue Alphonse de Neuville, which Natalie's absence made intolerable, and had moved to Avenue Bois de Boulogne, a large first-floor apartment with a tiny, charming garden – over the years, Pauline had populated it with dwarf

Japanese trees. In the same building, a floor above, was Mary Wallace, along with a friend her deceased sister Violette had bequeathed to her. Pauline herself had lived in one of the many apartments for a time when she was small. It was in the middle of the move that Pauline wrote to him, dated September 16, 1901:

"My dear friend and esteemed Mentor, your letter arrived the day after my suicide… for when I sent you my poems yesterday, I had decided to die…

I had heard about asphyxia by flowers – so I bought lots of bouquets of spikenard, and with doors and windows closed, I wrapped up my head in a big, thick shawl full of blossoms. I had fastened the shawl tightly around my shoulders and taken chloral so I could sleep deeply, passing softly from sleep to death. To die breathing in perfumes, what a sweet dream! – I had nothing in my soul but the far off grief of having lived. Can you believe it? I woke up this morning without the slightest headache! My robust Anglo-Saxon health resists all trials. I'm made of wrought iron! I'll never succeed in killing myself.

Everything you say to me is truly amicable and charming – and I thank you from the bottom of my wounded heart. Thank you for weeping over my sorrow. How can you say that death is banal and without lustre? The hour of my death will be the only ray of absolute joy I've ever had or could ever have. Death bears the sweetness of solitude and silence and the charm of sleep.

I'm obsessed with death. You want me to live. Why? You speak of people who love me – no one loves me in the great, sacred sense of the word. I have loved Natalie, I squandered everything on her exclusively, but she didn't love me. Who, then, could love me? There are people who like me a little, who perhaps feel some slight contentment when they see me – and there are those who have exploited, entangled, and deceived me. Two sincere friendships are precious to me – Violette's little sister's, and yours.

But one doesn't die of friendship, one dies of love. Friendship doesn't kill, but neither does it make one live.

I love Natalie, that's my desperation. Each hour brings me an old anguish renewed. Known and confessed sorrows come with silence, solitude – I have to bear the thousand natural shocks, troubles, and futile ills of a weary existence.

I obsess over where to place furniture, which cloth to choose, what to have for dinner or supper. And I deal with all that while I agonize in silence.

I am shattered, my friend, shattered. The voices all around me! – Oh, they give orders, argue, scream about simple, trivial things. Oh, to not hear anything at all, ever again!

My eyes are sick from abuse of chloral, my skin is ruined by excessive alcohol – and my forehead slashed by an ugly scar. I fell down unconscious some two months ago, and in my fainting I hit my forehead violently against the corner of a table. I'm telling you this so you won't have a disagreeable surprise next time you see me, if that ever happens.

Thank you, again, and forever, for your good, loyal, and precious friendship."

Where the lover, with a vague and ethereal intention to set things straight, examines all the harms and blames against the beloved or, perhaps, against that which has come to be called love.

Barcelona, 2 August 1984

"Those who say their love is infinite, actually love infinitely little".

"Avoid that romantic trap: saying more than you feel, forcing yourself to feel more than you've said". (Natalie Barney)

I have to intone a confessional and committed *mea culpa*. The punishment is perhaps now this love without words.

Barcelona, 3 August 1984

I have been to your house. Of course, I knew you weren't there. But I suppose I vaguely hoped to find you there. As I didn't see a single note or message addressed to me, I began to sort through drawers, without really knowing what I was looking for. Suddenly I found myself in some letters I wrote to you five or six years ago. I am, in fact, an other. Where is she now?

"In the end, a great passion often becomes too much of a burden to carry. It weighs down on us, and we weigh down on it. Who will be obliterated first?" Natalie hits the bullseye again: it's been some time now since I have installed myself, immobile and tense, on the very needle of the balance. On a dead point.

"To live or to wish for another to live on the dead point of a feeling: to fulfil without desire the gestures of love.

Conclusion: to allow oneself to do so is horrible; to deny oneself is horrible".

It isn't true that I no longer know how to say the great words to you. Perhaps it is just that they are no longer necessary. More than that: one should relegate them to the attic and burn them like old furniture on the night of the summer solstice.

"The Romantics appropriated for themselves all of the great words, only the small ones are left to us."

"And yet it is more difficult to find the small beastie than the great one."

I have read a note I left you after returning from the dentist in which I basically said, in words more alive, that to remember you had been the best anaesthetic. Another where I celebrated a normal day as a feast day because you painted it red with your very presence. Cheap ingenuities, which from a distance would seem ridiculous if they didn't inspire in me the most violent of jealousies.

I do not know whether what I lack now is the great words. But I am sure I miss that intensity, the strange vibration that electrified all things, that dilated tremor that extends, even now, through the longest letters I wrote to you, and flashes for a moment in the shorter messages. The joy and the fire, salt and pepper of love, as someone once said.

There are those who when they cannot find the words simply borrow them. To read you, then, all that the lover I once was wrote to you. It is what today, were I capable, I would like to be able to say to you.

PRIVATE PAPERS OF SARA T. (8)

Dearest Chantal,

As you can see I am writing to you from Mytilene. I arrived this morning on the ferry – which, incidentally, bears the name of Sappho – and am still getting my bearings. One time, a friend you do not know told me it wasn't to Lesbos that I should go to find Sappho: in fact she penned this to me on a postcard from Lesbos! I have no doubt she was right. But at first glance this island has a real charm, if only the indefinable attraction of those places that haven't yet been affected by mass tourism. And wouldn't you believe it, unconsciously, and still weighed down with my travel bags, I ran into the statue of our poet: she carries a lyre in one hand and looks out to sea. Perhaps my friend, who, according to her, had given up trying to find her in vain because nobody was able to give her a hand with her search, had not been able to forgive the deception she felt. As for me, I think I am capable of making my peace with such modest and naive kitsch. A few metres further on past the statue, in the port, I came across the Hotel Grande Bretagne and, oh what a miracle, I was able to stay there. My exclamation stems from the fact that it was precisely here that Natalie and Renée spent a few days, before renting their famous villa…

The hotel looks like it hasn't changed one bit. The only difference is that then it must have been the only one in town that was modern and more or less luxurious, whereas now it is a run-down relic, somewhere between the rustic and the decadent, quite charming. And, luckily for me, one of the cheapest hotels on the island. Upon arriving they told me there were water restrictions. But I have an incredible view from my room: the port and the medieval fortress – I think it is fifteenth-century Genoese – which rises over the ancient town. Tomorrow I'll climb up to the Aklidiou which, as far as I can tell from the town plan, is a district on the outskirts, to see whether I can find the house…

I would like to be able to lend the episode on Mytilene special importance in the screenplay. It ought to be a turning point, the fulcrum, of the story or stories. I suppose that it is in many ways that very "outside the world" which mythically rubs out an angle – systematically the victorious rival – of a triangle. I've talked to you about this theory of triangles of mine, haven't I? I don't know: before coming it seemed to me that things were finally falling into place. When you left Paris I was in a much better mood. The only thing in my head were your contacts with the feminist producer and the possibility of passing the screenplay on to her… Then I had some more difficult days: the whole thing about the crisis in my relationship with Arès poured down on me again, as if I had opened a dam… And these kinds of emotional deluge have never permitted me to do anything much. When I was beginning to recover and returned to work… well, something else happened: a little episode I have decided to leave as a cherry, for the end of the letter.

The point is that when I set foot in Greece, it seemed to me that I was crystal clear about the structure of the screenplay. And about the ending, which in this case is the determining factor. I had pretty much decided to make Nice the place where, at the very end, after the death of Renée, all the characters would converge: Mediterranean clarity, sun, a diaphanous sky, the bluest and most transparent of seas, set against the Gothic beginnings, the scene of her death. Nice as a kind of symbolic double for Lesbos... And, in between, everything else.

To a certain extent, this was to be a happy ending. It is curious, isn't it, that I should be so determined to extract a happy ending from a story of which at least two of its three parts are tragic and the other, if it can be considered comedy, is as black as can be... You see, I needed to find meaning – yes, that's it, more than a happy ending, a meaning – behind all of Renée's suffering, all of her excess, to think that it hadn't all been in vain... And, of course, it won't have all been in vain, in so far as my own immersion in it serves some purpose for me... For me and for whoever else. "To serve some purpose", I have just written, and I don't like it at all. Perhaps in fact the beauty and singularity of an endeavour lies in its very gratuity... like "the fallen star that is shipwrecked in the night" Renée speaks of. In other words, my "serve a purpose" has to include that, too.

Back to the point, though: as I was saying, I liked the idea of this luminous ending: as if what Renée had captured in a few brief moments in Lesbos irradiated in some way, after her death, the lives of the other characters... Obviously, I couldn't transport everyone to Mytilene. Nice, in contrast, would have been perfectly credible: Parisians of a certain class would often spend the winter there... But the island has another essential characteristic lacking in the Côte d'Azur, which is precisely that it is an island. From here it is impossible to forget this, as I became fully aware overnight on the boat: perhaps it would have been less obvious if I had come by plane, as I had originally planned. Do I need to say how glad I am that I couldn't get flights? In spite of the discomforts – which, in their own way, have a certain charm: sleeping on the floor without a sleeping bag, the ferry full to overflowing, ladies in mourning clinging to the legs of a pair of scandalous chickens, whole families with children milling here and there... But an island is an island and, at least the first time, it is important to arrive with the slowness and circumspection of a boat if you want to capture this essential aspect. It surprises me now that I should have undervalued aspects such as these, even from the outside... Now I'll have to go back to the drawing board.

Self-discipline has its virtues, but it is important not to abuse of it. And I have managed to get to this point without having let slip anything but the slightest insinuation, just to get your saliva flowing. I am sure you can already imagine what the fuss is all about...!

Well, you are right. Just a few days before leaving Paris I met someone. It was all very strange. I went back to that café-bookshop on the Rue de la Roquette – the one with the fairy-story name: Carabosse. Do you remember how I was unsure whether to buy some books and in the end I left them...? Well, as an aside, I'll tell you that I returned to Barcelona with a monumental rucksack on my back, all full of books. The same thing gets me every time: I'll hesitate over a book, leave it, and then the next time I'll be back again to take that one and a couple more. Anyway, the day I went back to the Carabosse, I saw a shelf with some copies of a journal I didn't know and which we hadn't seen on the day you and I were there: *Masques: revue des homosexualités*. On top of that, it was one of the numbers from a few years ago, dedicated in its entirety to the Amazon... for the tenth anniversary of her

163

death. I bought it, of course. But, before doing so, as I was browsing, a girl came and stood next to me and started to talk to me about the journal and to show me books related to the same topic – such as Djuna Barnes. She recommended, with a complicitous giggle, the *Almanac de les Dames*. As an aside, I ended up buying *Nightwood*, which I carry in my bag and read as if it were a breviary…

But back to what I was telling you: my immediate thought was that she worked in the book store. I was a bit shy and embarrassed. It's always the same. When someone catches me looking into certain subjects, I still have the tendency to blush inside and out… Whoever I'm with. In this case, I think I was shaken by the frankness of her gesture, by its directness. The girl, wait for it, is called Renée – weird, isn't it? – and however much I repeat to myself that Renée is a very common name in Paris, I can't help looking for meaning in this coincidence… What it means exactly even I wouldn't venture to say, but, as you can imagine, metaphysics is beginning to take me on a merry dance. Well, contrary to what I had been thinking, it turned out Renée was not one of the store assistants, and she told me she was going to take tea at one of the tables – you remember the ones, at the back of the shop? – and if I wanted to, when I finished, we could talk for a while. I went over and found her writing in some sort of notebook. I thought she was writing something about me, I don't know…

When she raised her head that's when I really saw her face for the first time, because before, crouching by the bookshelf, and with all my inhibitions, I had only really caught a brief glimpse. She's very French-looking, a bit like Mireille Mathieu, and she has a look about her that I can't quite describe, as if she had green eyes but not quite... strange, intriguing! Anyway, up to here, everything was going fine. She talking about "ses marginalités", as she called them – on reflection, this way of alluding to it isn't the most prepossessing – and I was even worse – very prudent, guarded and not really saying anything of interest to the discussion. That is to say I really didn't reveal anything about myself: at the end of the day the fact you are interested in a particular topic doesn't necessarily mean anything. Or does it? No matter. You know I'm not particularly "secretive", but an identification that was so clear, so brazen, alarmed me, perhaps because I'm not used to it. The sensation was similar to the times I've gone into Island's on my own or into some other bar on the scene. Suddenly it is as if all your possible expectations, your vague desires, your fantasies, were being placed on display for all to see. As if you were transparent. It's curious, because objectively that could give you an advantage; assuming there is anything resembling objectivity in such matters. But in my case if I get the sensation that my brass is on display, that my desire is too unequivocal, there is nothing to be done, I curl up like a snail inside its shell.

Anyway, let's go back to my supposed conquest. After these preliminaries we began to talk about literature: about Proust, about Wilde, about Colette, and then Djuna Barnes again... The conversation began to hobble a bit: nothing special, just the usual pauses, that get filled with conventional phrases as you begin to run out of things to say... Faced with this scenario, no doubt, she proposed that we meet another day and that I should ring her. I did so almost immediately and we arranged to meet at her house a couple of days before I was due to leave Paris. I confess I thought: if something

165

happens – it really looked like something had to happen… there were those, I don't know, vibrations… – if something happens, I said to myself, there won't be time for me to lose my way… everything is nicely delimited. And, depending on how it goes, I would still have a full day, and best case scenario, I could always change my ticket.

The truth is I always get lost in these kind of pre-considerations. I don't know how to simply go along and see what happens. No need for me to tell you the knots I tied myself in over the three days that passed between the day of the book store and our date. I cursed my bones for not having known how to do what I never know how to do: to simply go with the flow when the opportunity arises. Because I'm sure that if on the day of the book store I had known how to make things go more smoothly… As you can see, I liked the girl, and after such a long time of "marital" fidelities – of a "marriage" so very troubled and unrecognised, at that… – the perspectives that were opening up to me certainly had their attraction. What is more, I don't know if I ever told you, but one of my all-time fantasies goes along these lines: suddenly a stranger comes over and… The problem is that behind all of that I always place, candidly, incorrigibly, the idea of eternal love. Otherwise, the fantasy would be much easier to enact and wouldn't generate so many headaches.

Anyway, the day came… and nothing of what you imagine actually happened. And all because of the bed: an enormous bed, covered with a kind of furry white bedspread, that occupied most of the space in what was the tiniest of apartments. The truth is my legs had turned to jelly and, even before I had the time to say a word, I saw that bed, as monumental as a bull ring, and it turned me to ice. Absurd, isn't it? And, then I was stuttering when I said hello! She told me to sit down… on the bed. I did so, on the edge, as tense as can be, and I drank a couple of sips of an orange juice she placed in my hand. And then I don't know why (?), I started to talk and talk: about the School of Cinema, the production company, my marriage, my ex-husband, men… At some precise moment I realised that I was scattering false clues everywhere and then I spoke… about my abortion of seven years ago, about wanted and unwanted pregnancies, even about the home-birth movement. This was an "authentic" clue, because it was at the planning stages that I met Delia. But not her, she could not know that… And I didn't even have the time to explain to her that "ma première femme avait été une sage-femme". Suddenly, as if an alarm clock had gone off, she said that she had work to do, that if I wanted I could phone her some other time, and then maybe…

Before leaving I had the time to do a little bit of tourist propaganda for Barcelona: about Gaudí, about Miró… And the next day I phoned her, as punctual as a clock, and, obviously, she couldn't make it. It was just as I expected. I had gone over and over the matter and the truth is her attitude was much more comprehensible than my own. But the fact I expected it did not prevent me from being very disappointed… disproportionately so. It's always the same, of course, after all that anticipation! I'll only say that I had spent the entire morning spring cleaning, because my studio was in such a state you couldn't even get inside… And then there's all the time I had spent deciding what to wear…! Using only the toilet mirror. Where it comes to clothes, I'm bad enough to warrant you hiring out chairs: I get absorbed by the process, three hours pass, and then suddenly I get the obsession that it will be too obvious I've spent so much time over it, so back I go to the drawing board. Over and over. And all for that result.

In the end, I decided to take advantage of my last day in Paris to go to the cinema. And didn't I only elect to go and see *Identificazzione d'una donna*, by Antonioni: as if I couldn't quite bring myself to leave the subject behind at home... Even so, I calmed down and, when I left the cinema and was seated at a bar, I wrote to her: one of those letters in which, I suppose, one sets out to "seduce", and does so by drawing on every semblance of sincerity. I hit the bullseye. That very night I sent it, and, within the week, back in Barcelona, I received the reply. Right now, just about everything is possible... I may return to Paris, she may come to Barcelona, we may meet in Honolulu or – can you imagine I've even considered inviting her to this island with its cursed name? – as long I don't end up ruining it all with my strange contortions... As you always say, I will never learn!

How are you, though? I am really impressed by this fantastic job of yours, which seems to take you everywhere... From what you say about it and from the postcard, Prague must be really beautiful. You are right, I must add it to my list, but it will have to be after Istanbul: another Vivienian "altar" which I still need to visit. As for you, have you no plans to film a report on this island from which the "femme damnées" take their *apellation d'origine*? The interrelation between the current reality, the history of the island and the myth. It would be really interesting. Now don't go saying that I haven't served you a good idea on a plate... Don't worry, take no notice, or I'd have you mixed up in one of those never-ending projects like mine that never actually take shape... and which, if there are all the possibilities you say there are, you will probably end up having to give me a hand with yourself anyway. Once the screenplay is finished, that is. I don't think I'll manage to translate it all into French by myself.

Well, then, I'll be going now. Whilst writing the letter it has got dark and I can hardly see a thing. I've switched the light on, but the bulb must be a 25! Tomorrow I'll have to fix that, because if not, I don't know how I'm going to be able to work. Now I'll go downstairs for a bite to eat and, later, a walk around Mytilène-la nuit! Right now I'm very happy to be here. I'll write again soon.

All love,
Sara

The teller of this tale would now be obliged to don the humblest livery of an antique lackey to publicly announce with triple stroke of ceremonial staff, each and every one of the titles and distinctions that adorn the personage who, having enticed us from the beginning from the shadows, is about to enter directly on to the scene. She will limit herself, however, to naming those which, earned fair and square, efficiently lifted a wild girl from Cincinnati and her name of limited reach and low condition, Natalie C. B., to the heady pedestal of legend.

Shining above all of them, rescued in its purest sense from the millenary archive of names and with a vague ring of cruelty at the tip of its arrow, the title of "Amazon" was conferred by a high dignitary of the hermetic Palace of Wisdom and proclaimed by himself to the four winds with the equivocal modesty of a herald fascinated by the hero he precedes and announces.

A trail of names follows, in no precise order, inscribed in their moment, using a vast range of inks and all due pomp, in the annals of memory: "Miss Florence Temple", alias "Flossie", alias "Moonbeam", all conferred by her royal highness of the Folies Bergères, Liane de P., in the wake of her conditional, but no less total, surrender before an imperial barrage of kisses and tender grasps in a tenacious siege. The second name, "Flossie", was accorded, and offered for all posterity by a captivated Madame Colette Willy, who freely wrote with her pen: "My husband kisses your hand, and myself, all the rest".

Listed in the celebrated *Ladies Almanack*, the designation

"Evangeline Musset" defies the inexorable, devouring passage of time and highlights her spirit as forced pioneer of a new religion without further sacrificial offering than pleasure, no other eucharist than feminine bodies and the subtle emanations of these bodies, known as souls, as the only sacerdotal officiants. A religion that, unlike the others, prohibits martyrdom, without denying its own martyrs; for surely those unable to follow the exemplary steps of the foundress in this extreme deserve only indulgence. It is here that we arrive at the meritorious title "Triumphant Tribade", so strikingly exceptional amid a tribe of tired and troubled tribades, culminating finally with the categorical, definitive, adamantly curial "Pope of Lesbos".

Like all the mystics of every epoch, past, present and future, Pauline-Renée, reborn by the waters of an ad hoc baptism, and having sworn, like Christ's soldier, Vivien, not to recede a single step before the enemy Infidel, found herself in a difficult and complex relationship with this Church and its Hierarchy. It seemed to her too acquiescent to the powers that be and a virtual traitor to the original message, but at the same time she depended on it as an infallible point of reference to ward off the mutable spectre of Madness.

Like every heterodox, she invoked before the Holy Office, impalpable in this case, justifying antecedents, and a long list of validating ancestors – crutches for moments of faltering firmness and pebbles for her frequent insecure stuttering. No one better in this case than Sappho, the lesbian, responsible for the subtle blush that colours, every time it is pronounced even today, the name of the island and its patronymic. It is thus that the modern poet spoke, like a medium, through the mouth of Sappho, and that the personage who occupies the narrator from the first lines came to adopt in her verse the more modest persona of "Atthis", the loving female disciple. This was not simply an imagined, compensatory artifice to stand in for a seemingly opposed reality, but in this too, she followed to the letter the steps of the mystic: walking, intoxicated, in the sublime, incorporeal footsteps left by the Divine Victim, while the supreme pontiff is resigned to putting on the solid and earthly sandals of the fisherman disciple. Stranger yet is the process that led her to identify that representative on earth of Goodness-Armed-with-Power with the ultimate Temptation of the Serpent, the seductive and destructive voice of Lorelei the siren, and the terrible image of Our Lady of Fevers. Perhaps in this case an inversion mechanism was at work, similar to that which transforms a real image into a photographic negative, thus exposing the minuscule click that separates the asexual angel from the hermaphroditic devil.

Here, the teller of this tale must overcome her born terror before innate victors, and her obsession in her distress with seeking out the secret defect that makes them vulnerable at some unsuspected point; the invisible heel that might finally explain their external power to be little more than a supremely efficient defensive façade. No, the narrator will risk looking straight at the dazzling star tracing its stellar path in a grey sky, with the sole protection of a modest filter before her eyes. No need to go to the extreme of being blinded by the one who – for Renée Vivien – was the "Venus of the Blind". Let us, then, return to origins, back in far-off Ohio, whence came into the world, under the fearsome sign of the Scorpion, she who would one day be christened "girl of the future society" by the creator of *Bilitis*. It must be said that, even though this future was completely indeterminable and the title intended only in a figurative and symbolic sense, Natalie made every effort to reduce those dimensions and make them concrete. If she took leave of this life only a few years before reaching the age of 100, it was no doubt due to her old habit of leaving a meeting before it was over because she had an engagement elsewhere.

But that was to be nearly a century after that thirty-first of October, Day of the Witches, 1876, when, the first-born of a well-heeled bourgeois bon vivant and an artist of brushes and of life, Natalie took her first steps toward the light, with effi-cacy.

There are many questionable signs and gestures we might consider from her childhood, but we'll limit ourselves to those that seem to have most significance in the light of her later trajectory. The narrator confesses her many unresolved doubts, however.

In the first place, there is Natalie's immoderate love for a mother who lived and let live; together with her worries about the dangers her progenitor might encounter when boldly entering the nightwood, without escort or protection from the faithful page she herself was prepared to embody. Let it not be said, however, that her desire went unheeded altogether, for the complaisant mother had the figure of Natalis the Page immortalised by one of her favourite mas-ters, and thus, perhaps unconsciously, sanctioned and validat-ed the girl's most secret investiture.

As for the father, according to our heroine he demonstrat-ed the consuetudinary paternal love by alternating gifts and bruises that left their bond rather less harmonious. We need only recall the episode fuelled by perfumes of wine and jealousy toward a wife suspected of excessive admiration for the beauty – she said artistic – of young men. Incapable of reenacting the role of a poor operettic Othello, he instead decided to mimic, also excessively, the tragic destiny of a modern Medea. Grabbing his two daughters he boarded a train of uncertain destination, and half-way along the journey attempted to jump, dragging his descendants along with him on his trip to Nowhere. Since this was a plan on which she had not been consulted and therefore could not offer the decisive contribution of her Will, Natalie showed no hesitation, by the side of a little sister reduced to useless tears, in making the train stop in its tracks by very calmly activating the alarm.

There are other creditable actions which also deserve a mention here, destined to place a limit on immoderate masculine presumption, and witness to the forging, from her tenderest years, of a character resistant to any form of yoke. Among them is one that arrested the arrogant pride of a little cousin who smirked at her due to some flaps of flesh hanging from his groin, conferred on him by nature for some incomprehensible reason. Natalie was amenable to a pact – she would stop ignoring his insistent lure as she had done heretofore – but she laid down the conditions. She tied a string around the incipient tender appendage and, like an expert tamer who gets the bear to dance in circles, she led him to make rings around her before an invisible audience of women humiliated since time immemorial, all of whom applauded at full throttle and full sails.

Three governesses, three, like the three graces, had the privilege of teaching her, one after the other – and, occasionally, of being taught by her. The first, a French woman, passed

174

French on to her such that it instilled an intense affection that was later to become chronic. If it has been said that when they die all good Americans go straight to Paris, Natalie, unprepared for a wait she assumed would be lengthy, and sceptical about what the inscrutable laws of the great beyond might hold, saw the Seine before she was a decade old. On that first trip, she discovered an odd bathtub for dolls the French called bidet, with a little fount in the middle which soon revealed to her other more exciting water games.

She also became acquainted with the common lot of young ladies of good family in a deservedly famous boarding school at Fontainebleau, where, after mentally feminizing a biblical precept which has no gender in French, she learned to intensively love her fellow women, some more than others, of course, and above them all, one who while rolling her eyes up to heaven, lovingly called her "my little husband". It should be said that nothing specific justified such a, perhaps excessive, appellative. It was at Fontainebleau that Natalie's family recruited a second governess, a German, who after a while began to sleepwalk, and was particularly skillful with scissors on her nighttime excursions, after which one might find feminine hair chopped off or men's hats slashed to pieces. Natalie learned a very valuable negative lesson from that Fräulein, who was quickly sent back home: the ill effects of not realising one's desires in a state of consciousness while privy to reason, abandoning them instead to the uncontrollable and random realm of dreams.

With the third governess, a Viennese who yearned for a vague fiancé who was probably not really waiting for her on the continent, she developed the subtle art of consoling those afflicted by love-sickness, and she marvelled at her discovery of the ecstasy that can come from a good deed. One should say that, after Fontainebleau, she had made inestimable progress in her dominion of touch, that essential sense too often neglected due to incapacity or negligence. Natalie perfected her wonder-working skills in surprising form in her mother's studio while the latter was painting the portraits of Washington's most distinguished ladies. These would hardly have been able to hold such excellent poses without the aid of able little hands that applied inspiring massages to arms, ankles, or other strategic places. The close alliance between body, heart, and mind was in this way favourable to art, as always. In a more precise way, she began to read Sappho, by the hand of a summer friend at Bar Harbor named Eva, who was, according to her own expression, the mother of her desires, mortal by definition.

Three trips, three, like the Cardinal Virtues, each with its respective emblem, she had made to Paris by the time she was twenty. The first, as described above, was a declared tribute to the Faith, of the sort that requires no proof of its fervour, nor works to perpetuate it, for it is its own nourishment. When she returned from Fontainebleau, Natalie had found a credo, and this was the first stage in her fulgurant process of initiation: to believe in that world still floundering in pre-genesis chaos, and to see it – in her mind's eye – offered in the future to her creative, organizing, orchestrating instinct. The second, and especially the third trip deserve special consideration for their close ties to the facts the narrator wishes to focus on with her left eye, notably crossed.

Under the tender green pennant of Hope, Natalie set foot for the second time in Paris, which was already hoisting its Tower of Iron in the Field of Mars, along with the much less contested figure of Liane de P., a living tower of ivory in the sacred, plumed field of Venus. If we have said "much less contested" and not "beyond contestation", it is because, contrary to the ferrous fantasy of Eiffel, Liane was faced with double competition, not all of it disloyal, at times with intimate complicities and truces signed between silk sheets. For Natalie, the superiority of Liane, an "angel ripped out of a Fra Angelico painting", over her rivals was unquestionable. And, in keeping with her ancient exploits as page and defender of damsels in distress, she set out to restore to her, in peculiar form, and settling once and for all the age-old Byzantine question of their sex, her angelic quality. For that to happen, she had to rescue her from the life she was leading, unworthy of the purity of her soul and bodily form, but fertilized economically by the manure of venal love. Other nourishment had to be found so that the flower could live without languishing, having been transplanted and irrigated by Natalie's love. The latter, at the time, did not dispose of the necessary resources herself.

The solution seemed to be personified in a young suitor the American had brought along from Washington, dazzled and disconcerted, who in principle was well disposed to accept all conditions in exchange for a privileged place at Natalie's side – even as observer, in the first row, of course. He retreated, like a coward and with manifest perjury, from the final proposal: an immaculately pure marriage and fully legal adoption of Liane as the unilaterally incestuous daughter. There was nothing to be done. The epic deed that might have gone down in history as a brilliant new contribution to the immemorial Ransom of Captives was reduced to a bare "Sapphic Idyll" that Liane offered to the public two years later, somewhat watered-down in depth and a little overwrought in form, but with a certain indefinable and irresistible charm. "It's not because I don't think about it, it's because I do, that I don't like men," Natalie concluded, in the face of the inexplicable desertion of the young man. And like the soldier who succeeds in crossing enemy lines carrying his own flag, she returned to America waving an intact Hope above her head. "Spes ancora vitae" was her motto from then on.

Natalie had heard it said many times by sensible folks of goodly ways that true Charity begins with one's own chassis. Incapable of adopting such a coarse point of view, but perhaps even less disposed to offer herself in sacrifice to other people's needs, she was left to divining that imaginary point on the horizon where two lines, usually seen as parallel and irreconcilable, converge. And so, when she met Pauline during her third voyage to Paris, she immediately recognised the common interest that united them and would tie them together with an indestructible knot. Wagging tongues would characterize it as a slippery noose, due to the fragile neck of the English young lady... Natalie knew instinctively what Pauline needed, and that was, curiously enough, what she herself needed to give. For, as happens with shuddering frequency, the word Love becomes an opaquely unique screen for the most diverse shadow games. If there was error, it was only on the level of consciousness: in the perception of what kind of substance might fill the avid void that is necessity in each case; which was the water and which the thirst. The impulse that developed in Natalie, according to her own admission later on, as with Liane de P., was essentially an impulse to save the other. Like one who snatches an intended suicide from the loving arms of death, Natalie fought ferociously to rescue her prey from the powerful Unknown One that clung to Pauline and hovered over Renée's poems. Imperceptibly, in saving her from death, she herself was to occupy the place of the Meaning of Life. Pauline abandoned herself to that meaning with all the passion she had formerly dedicated to the meaninglessness supreme – All is Nothingness – that Death personified... And when the meaning embodied in Natalie proved unattainable, the saviour from Death took the place of Death herself, now clothed in the prestige of Love and Beauty: Lorelei, the siren.

Who could reproach the generous impulse of one who saves an attempted suicide? Who would dare blame them for not having judged accurately their disposition to take responsibility, like a provident god, for that being on whom they have conferred or inflicted life? To play the role of god when the attributes assigned by metaphysics to the divinity are whisked away ends inevitably in failure or ennui. Imprisoned in Pauline's arms, Natalie often envied the divine gift of ubiquity: to remain in that loving prison, yes, but at the same time live all other possible lives, not lose a single drop of dew, nor miss caressing a single hair, or spirit, with the tip of her most sensitive antennae. This was shortly their first meeting, after having told her, one winter day as she returned from the frozen Bois, in response to Pauline's admiration for her poems: "It's not the poems you should love, but the poet". Pauline had caught the insinuation in flight and responded with the fervour of a neophyte and an acolyte. After nights of white, red, blue, and all manner of colours and shades, Natalie tried to get her to understand that the harvest for reaping was vast and she only had two arms. She couldn't abandon the rest of the field to la Grande Faucheuse.

Sorrow, given to eternity exclusively, according to the poet, occupied the intermittent void of the tireless reaper in Pauline's bones, medulla, lymph, heart, and guts. Sorrow, the juice squeezed from a bitter grape, fermented, stored, and offered in libation to the absent divinity, imbibed on the rebound until intoxication. Thus Pauline became a Bacchante of sorrow. Pauline's suffering, perennial as the laurel that crowns the immortal mortals, became a fixed point for Natalie, an axis she escaped from but still gyrated around, as if tossed by a centrifugal force against external, rigid, invisible limits.

The furthest point of that amorous circle which enclosed her was a year spent in Washington, where Pauline refused to accompany her for some reason, totally incomprehensible to her. Natalie invested the time very profitably in elucidating and establishing the terms of her future. Her father, moved by clairvoyance rather than myopia about the singular nature of his daughter, dreamed of straightening her out by means of a marriage of convenience. Various rumours circulated and suitors emerged from under the stones. Natalie went along with it, charmingly. Mistress of the art of all that is ephemeral, she offered smiles that seemed promises, lighting up gazes and hearts, only to later coldly dictate the rules of the game. One by one, the suitors displayed an almost insulting insufficiency for her love. The only one prepared to accept Natalie's conditions was a young British aristocrat escaped from England after a tragic trial which led his lover, an extremely well known and fashionable writer, to Reading Gaol.

In order to quiet all that gossip, Lord D. had spurred the other side of his erotic possibilities, and it was in the company of a delightful feminine compatriot that he had carried out his escape to Paris. The young lady, amphibian and ambidextrous, soon found in Natalie the ideal complement for her versatile nature. Again, matrimony, far from representing for Natalie that insufferable corset employed by patriarchs of every epoch to subdue the blood, presented a good solution for a bad problem of which after all she was not the cause: for several reasons not relevant to the case, the marriage between Lord D. and his companion of delightful battles was not viable. Natalie offered to take the place of the bride only in a legal sense. The rest of the pact was easily deducible. In this case, the lack of accord did not come from either of the interested parties in the affair, ideally suited in their respective demands and mutual concessions. It was Natalie's father, instigator of that matrimonial brouhaha, who totally opposed it, convinced that the cure would be worse than the disease with a bridegroom like Lord D. In Washington, people refused to greet him and the mere mention of his name made ladies blush in embarrassment.

In the meantime, Pauline had stopped writing her those long epistles, so very monotonous and full of reproach, memories, desires, suffering, and promises of eternal love. Their dark, dull rhythms had lulled her from afar, like the sound of a sea rendered innocuous by distance. Then, after a very different letter, full of insults and incomprehension with respect to Natalie's hypothetical matrimonial plans, which had come to Pauline's ear second- and third-hand, suddenly there was silence. Not long after that, *Cendres et poussières*, a newly published book by Renée Vivien, gave her to understand that Pauline's love for her – in poetry, at least – was conjugated in the past tense. Disturbed, and with her mother's always so convenient help, Natalie once again placed her feet on the stool humbly offered to her by the ground of Paris. The snake of the Seine slithered along, dominated by her presence. But an unexpected Obstacle, eminent and monstrous, stood in the way of her path to Pauline. It was then that Natalie felt the sting of pain. It was as though, in making inaccessible she who, in her mind, embodied her, the part that corresponded to her from this universal lot – up to this time deflected from her head by the lightning-rod of a symbol – suddenly struck her with all its power. But just as a sharp lash spurs on a good steed and a strong blow of the tongs lights up the fire, Natalie was pushed by her suffering to the very pinnacle of her powers, whence she watched over the enemy camp and readied herself for battle.

We must not imagine that, in being confronted with her own pain, Natalie would forget her generous, redemptive disposition. What ultimately moved her, even now, was the conviction that anything that was good for her and emanated from her will was good for Pauline too, even if Pauline, at that moment, refused to recognize it. The persistence of the Obstacle that separated them, to whom Pauline clung like a timorous newborn to the voluminous bosom of a corpulent Breton nursemaid, or like a martyr to the torture rack, dishonoured both of them. On the one hand, Natalie had been expelled from a space unforgivably before she herself had deigned to leave it, and on the other, the specific substitution to which she'd been subjected redoubled her humiliation on account of its unworthiness. And the indignity of the choice fell squarely on Pauline in ignominious shame. Linked together again inextricably, then, by the Desire and Will of Natalie, it was merely a matter of imposing once more, upon the world and upon Pauline, evidence of the tenacious strength of the bond that existed between them.

The teller of this tale will forego a detailed account of epic gestures, of deeds small and large, of messages, pledges and tokens, of charges and all manner of assaults. We will only say that four full years tested her tenacity, four full years of maintaining her siege without pause. At the end of those years, the wall, already weakened by numerous cracks, burst open.

The teller of this tale is aware that happy endings depend only on the concrete moment at which the word "end" appears. Let us leave, then, the "Triumphant Tribade" at the high point of her victory and make note of a date and place – 1905, August, the island of Lesbos – in indelible ink. Then we'll make haste to place a final full-stop on this chapter of only moderately epic proportions.

Where the narrator once more falls into her obsession of spying on and scrutinising the aforenamed character through her thoughts as transcribed in a diary with naive trust.

24 August 1984

I have come to Mytilene. Lesbos – the island with a difficult name to pronounce naturally – continues to offer, for the initiated eye, its lyre-like form girdled by intense blue. On its beaches, perhaps, the invariable beds of dry seaweed still receive the embraces of a pair of anonymous and forgotten lovers' bodies, similar to those rich and beautiful foreigners who at the beginning of the century sowed curiosity and stupor on the island. I have come here alone.

Mytilène, parure et splendeur de la mer – "Mytilene, jewel and splendour of the sea".

I have been up to the Aklidiou district. It wasn't difficult to find the house. Clambering down the rocks to the Varia road, which goes along the sea-line, separated from it by the thinnest of strips of beach, I made my way along the ancient track. At the invisible inner door, off its hinges, which time has swallowed without leaving a trace, the air and the salt has not been able to erase for my eyes the name etched deep into the wood in Greek characters: Paradise. I have stepped over the threshold with a thrill. In front of me, the orchard, abandoned and wild.

"Orchard of Mytilene where no man may enter".

With my back to the sea and forgetting for a moment the damp of the breeze on my skin, the house, solid and clear, with its great door closed without remedy, and the patina of the years, has reminded me of my father's house, which I have not entered for centuries: the years that separate a girl with a still unforeseeable future from the woman I now am, absorbed by her own path. If I entered, though, I am sure I would not rediscover the paradise I feel to be lost without ever having possessed it.

And even if I had been able to enter into the heart of this shelter which had fleetingly provided safe haven to a feminine couple, the secret would not for all that have been given to me.

"Orchard of Mytilene where no man may enter".

And where even the watchful gardener had to make himself invisible and clear the way stealthily, silently, as a counterweight to his inevitable existence. His spirit must still keep watch, who knows whether vengefully, between the exotic trees and hundred-year-old pines, today without cages or golden birds of multi-coloured plumage.

I have no memory either, from the inside, of the garden of my father's house. I was expelled too soon. Ever since then, I have seen it from the other side of the gate, inaccessible to my steps and tempting to my eyes of an exile without memory. I have not dared to transgress the implicit prohibition in order to enter it as a thief. My feet have turned to lead. I have been halted by the shadow of wings over my head, the imprecise threat of the calm, a sudden blast of wind, like a peremptory warning.

Today, here, in Mytilene, I have entered the garden. The gardener must have been dead for years. But what sign of his remote presence scratches its way across the immobile, glass-like air, rustles in the delicate whisper of the foliage rocked by the sea breeze, and settles in the endless screech of the cicadas

185

that perforate the silence? What strange regret pervades the grass that advances to bury my feet? I can sense his single eye, like that of a minor god, invisible bird of prey. I have not dared venture any closer to the house.

Without a sound, creeping up behind my back, fear has silently clasped itself to my body. I have fallen still for a moment, like a bird secured by the mistletoe in a trap. Afterwards, walking quickly, but without breaking into a run, so as not to raise suspicion in this intimidating nobody, I have made my way towards the distant beach. The shadow snapping at my heels, in this luminous zenith without shadows. I have returned to the centre of the town, every so often checking behind me: my gaze furtively sifting the opaque air. I said to myself that I would return there, all the time convinced that I would never find what I came here to seek. There is no imprint, there is no trace. There is only that which has come here with me. Only the landscape has received me, with its hospitality of light, but its memory is immaterial and no image has formed itself into the clarity of a memory or a dream. For a moment I thought I saw a carriage and the golden halo of two heads of different shades of blonde, on the round flank of an ochre and green hill, against the diaphanous summer sky. Fleeting vision, which only the words have captured, imprecisely. By the sea, once again I almost caught one of those snapshots that mimic fallaciously a moment of eternal happiness. Pauline laughs, naked, close to the waves, and splashes Natalie who speaks to her with eyes of a too tender grey.

"I dream of the splendour of your free and naked body," Pauline would say with regret when the piles of clothes swathed the body of the siren once more. Now the siren is just a girl of 23 years of age in love who makes the discovery that the proportions of her own body – yes, the body of Pauline – have the harmony of a Greek Venus. "Because you love my body and it pleases you, from now on I too will love it, and it will be pleasing to me…" No hostile world surrounding and besieging her, here, under the vivid blue, in the golden clarity of the day. The two of them and nobody else.

I, alone, think of you now.

There are many types of yearning. A yearning without thorns, made of certainty, that demands touch, an unequivocal shoulder on which to bury the shock of loss, the concaves of a body to which one can couple the concaves of another body, in the night, in sleep. The grotto of a hand for a hand, a palpable gaze and the tessitura of a voice. The soft relief of a face beneath entranced fingers. Yearning demands all this, all that which has been subtracted due to some accident of fate, but which it knows belongs to it, that it rightly possesses, somewhere far away. It is a longing formed of confidence, the confidence that comes from certainty. There is another type of yearning, disturbed and traversed by phantoms, whose presence conjures and stirs up absence. This is the longing that makes us face an ancestral shame to which love had conceded us a pardon. Without the ritual signs of this pardon to actualise it, once and again, doubt begins to take root and a strange torture brings together victim and executioner in the same blood. Sorrow is the price of an illusory ransom. There is also the yearning that does not call itself yearning. The denied longing that refuses to recognize separation. Turning the other into an interior image that accompanies and nourishes, and is itself nourished, deep inside. You live because you live in me. Far away, you, the being of flesh, have only a fic-

187

tional, untranscendental existence. Then there is the yearning for that which was and is no longer, for that which memory has selected and shaped into what was and is no longer. Finally, there is also this other longing, the most sterile of them all: for that which could have been and never was. For the paradise lost that has never been possessed. This garden without prohibition and without blame that, perhaps, I have come rather fancifully to find in Mytilene. All of these yearnings blend into one alone, now, facing the sea.

Now I am thinking of her. Why do I address myself to you and speak to you, in my imagination, of her in the third person? Perhaps because you are already in me; embodied in a piece of the past that has made me, the only country that is really mine, towards which, like Renée, I cannot help but continue to look: *Reviens dans la maison du passé, mon amie –* "Come to the house of dreams and of the past…" My dreams, however, have been robbed of me along the way, and the blame has fallen on my head, because the thief was No one. I think of her – who is she, though, in reality? Just a ghost who permits me, for a few moments, to believe that there is a road, somewhere, apart from you. I think of her and suddenly everything seems possible again: "Vertiginously, I attain the stars". A strange innocence struggles to take hold of me. And at the same time a capacity to pervert all things, radical and powerful. The eunuch without desire, self-punished for his ancient daring, suddenly possesses all the sexes of the earth, of the skies and the deeps, and bathes in the burst of blood and of the spring. And you are not here to tell me that I have no right to anything because you yourself think you have no right to anything.

She has not yet spoken.

For I, it seems, unconsciously, have wanted to delay the moment of the word. Of the abolished word that speaks from the body and also from the blood. This language that I fear and which is at the same time necessary to me.

From afar, the moon appears like a powerful ally, mythic, full. Like a goddess at once virginal and pregnant. I am afraid of the moment when the waters break and of the birth, of the bearing of fruit and the inevitable mutilation. I am afraid of repeating, cyclically, like the pious devotees of the Saintes Nafres and the Seven Words of the Divine Agony, all the steps in the passion according to Renée Vivien.

Second part

Paris, September 1919

"The guy's fallen for her, you know. Hook, line and sinker. Lianon already gave me the lowdown. But then I found the letter when I got back from Montecarlo. Imagine, he wants an interview. Truth is it's caught me right off guard, but I suppose we'll have to put a brave face on it… Lianon says he's prepared to grease the wheels, if necessary. Oh, and then it will probably be your turn: that's why I wanted to talk to you about it. I'm never entirely sure, in such cases, whether to dish all the dirt, or… You have more experience in dealing with savants and folks of that ilk. It even surprises me he didn't ask you first. But I suppose he must be going in order of appearance… in poor Pauline's bed!"

Janot laughs and licks her absinthe-coated lips. At this hour, the "Brasserie du Hanneton" is still quite empty. The mirrors on which time has left its imprint in the form of spider webs multiply the scarlet, velvety walls. No spiritous haze, no opium smoke of cigarettes yet fills the air. A tango sung in a nasal voice sounds out from a half-ruined phonograph, but not very loud. At this hour, you don't have to yell to make yourself heard, as you do when the place, just off the Place de Pigalle, fills up around midnight.

Janot's table companion, Mimi, is around fifty, same as Janot. The distance that separates them at first glance is still

193

abysmal, even though the years have reduced them by degrees that are barely perceptible. Nothing would relate that red-faced, good-natured little gnome, affected now and then with a touch of braggadocio, to the elegant, sensual lady by her side. Mimi, who in another time was the super-famous Émilienne d'A., looks at her with a somewhat distant smile, half complicitous, half mocking. Her round face, carefully made up to maintain a creditable freshness, her full lips pursed in an impertinent and fun expression, her little pug nose. They haven't lost one bit of that inimitable air imprinted on them by the ambience of Montmartre passed through a very personal sophistication, purified and refined. Janot can still see her now with the casual, loose tie, the rascally look, the monocle at her left eye and the provocative and facetious pose that made her splendid body undulate. She could imagine perfectly the delicious hullabaloo on that first day when she found a basket full of orchids in her dressing-room at the Folies: "The very idea, sending these ugly flowers instead of roses. It looks like they're sticking their tongues out at you!" Thus had begun, for that daughter of a concierge from the Rue des Martyrs, the brilliant career of a kept woman suddenly elevated to the highest level. The card that accompanied the unappreciated gift was that of the Duke of Uzès... to be followed by the king of the Belgians, the invariable Prince of Wales, and a grand duke of that Russia of the tzar, which, a few years after the wreck of the *Titanic*, had itself suffered the worst of shipwrecks...

If the democratizing effects of time in the field of beauty – which ascetics and critics of all kinds of vanities usually take pleasure in blaming – have not abolished the most obvious, external differences, the language of the two reveals a subtle

194

family air that betrays a common origin, and which the scene where the conversation is taking place invites us to draw out.

"When did you say you last saw Lianon? I haven't heard a thing since last year, when I went to meet her at the Majestic. Ever since she bagged that insipid little excuse for a prince… dethroned and broke, it's as if we're all beneath her. She received me well enough, of course, but she herself never goes out of her way…"

"The 'ivory princess' turned into a real princess! Not someone to mess around with, I'll say…But let me tell you, I'm not sure if you know, I was the one who helped her reel that particular bloke in."

"Come on, Lulú" – sometimes people called her that too – "There's no point showing your accolades to me. As if Liane couldn't do it on her own…"

"She's capable and more, don't be getting ahead of yourself, I know that well enough. But it doesn't change what I'm going to tell you now about how things went down: he always showed up late. I mean, they were involved, but it didn't look like they'd end up tying the knot. The deal is he would make a date for two and then show up at six, at the earliest. Day after day. Lianon was beside herself, but she put up with it. One day I was at her place, Lianon's, that is, at the hour of the supposed date, and she told me all about it, and I said, that can't go on, who ever heard of such a thing? And then she gets all excited: 'Janot, you have a car, don't you?' 'Yes, of course,' I answer. At the time I had that Renault Cab that looked just like Pauline's, remember? I say yes and off we go on a ride through Saint Germain-en-Laye, to the woods…"

"What does all that have to do…"

"Let me finish, here's the best part: well, after that, I took her to Versailles to have a snack at the Deposits, and we came back around eight. She wasn't really in the mood and wanted to go home, but I said to her: come have dinner with me. Not that she was enthusiastic, but she finally said okay. I'll spare you the details… But when she got back to her place just after midnight, there was the guy weeping his eyes out, hungry and out of his mind; and that was it, or so Lianon told me, that day he finally got it into his head…"

"Yes, I know, that he couldn't live without her, end of story, curtain and applause. It's a good one, but too simple… Listen, Lianon has always had the upper hand with men, and not only with men… She hardly needed lessons from you! I know her better than you think…"

Janot knew it, all right. Like everyone in that milieu, she knew all about the sweet rivalries that had once made them inseparable. Even now, when she spoke of Liane de P., Mimi's horny little eyes made her look like she was ready to pounce:

"Do you know if the life she leads really is… respectable? I mean that's what she would have me believe, but it seems to me like she just wanted to maintain her distance. Besides, you and I both know all about so-called respectable people. My poor Jacques, who was just a whistle away from his… holy mother, and the libations he came up with for me. And your viscountess, the Portuguese one I mean… she'd have married you too, if she could have! You had her in the pot, and well-done, for sure. I mean, I just don't buy it that Lianon has turned over a new leaf and settled to walk the straight and narrow with a little oaf of a husband, like a provincial bourgeoise on her first flight."

"Yes and no, depends on how you look at it… But I don't know, those are things…"

Mimi lost her patience:

"Don't tell me you're going to get all prudish, now, I know you better than that, sweetie-pie!"

"Okay then, it seems… but hold on a moment, did you notice that blonde over there at the bar, the eyes she's making. She's there every time I come here, gobbling me up with her eyes… You'll see, later on she'll ask me to dance…"

"Come on, don't get distracted, spill the beans…"

"I'll tell you all about it, okay? But did you see? There she goes again… she's not bad at all, right? A pity! I say pity because it's been a while. My Charlie keeps me on a short leash. Not that I'm complaining, but when things fall into your lap, I hate to let them slip through. Okay, okay, I'll get back to Lianon. I said yes and no, and what that means is that no one, but no one, is allowed to touch her below the belt – she says that's sacred and belongs to her husband alone, but I'll bet anything he's a dud… Have you seen him? For sure his thing is dead… And yes, she has her little girlfriends – which is what I am sure you want to know – but only from the waist up! I know quite a few of them… and some of them she shares with Flossie and everything."

"Don't tell me we're back in the realms of *Sapphic Idyll*. After all, I too like the delicacies and delights of look-but-don't-touch, who doesn't, but the thought of nothing going beyond that, and to top it all, celestial chastisement! I just hope things don't end up as badly as the novel. That's something I always criticized Lianon for… Ever since that uptight Mr Zola made Nana die in such a bloodcurdling way – and in such bad taste, no matter what they say – a trend began that if you aren't careful… Lucky that we know exactly how Nana died, the real one, I mean. Liane told me he had to end the book that horrible way or no one would have published it. Vice always has to be punished, you know, ugh!"

"I don't know, myself, how Valtesse died, isn't that what she was called?"

"Like a queen…! Didn't you get an invitation to the funeral?"

"No… I really only knew her by sight. At best, we exchanged a few words."

"Well, the funeral cards were divine: with a golden border and gothic lettering. And the finest quality paper! Oh, she'd had them made up some time ago. She only left the date blank… And then she wrote it in herself, with her own hand, just hours before she died… Hey, watch out for your glass… It's all go tonight…! What I don't know is whether Valtesse had time to address the envelopes or not…"

"Let's change the subject, okay? I don't feel like talking about dead people or death right now. I've been thinking about it for plenty of hours, now, and all thanks to Mr Salomon R. He's some voyeur, all right, sniffing around under the skirts of a dead woman! I've heard that some people, some men, like dead women. Did you read *La tour d'amour*? Yeah, you know, a novel about that stuff, a lighthouse-keeper who did it with drowned girls and kept their hair… Doesn't matter, I don't remember what they call people like that, but he must be one of them…"

"Well, he'd have had no chance if Pauline were alive!"

"Too right, he wouldn't! Did she ever tell you the one about men just being dogs in heat? Or that she couldn't stand the way they stank of leather? Or that men's voices always gave her a headache? She went a bit too far, for sure, but she was delightful, there was no one to match her… She's been pushing up daisies for so many years, poor thing…"

198

"Those well-to-do girls can allow themselves every kind of luxury… I couldn't afford to be so fussy… men made me rise to the top like foam… and I'm not one to be ungrateful. But, it's true you have to know how to choose… And if I told you everything!"

"You're telling me. I like having a guy in the bed once in a while: not for the thing itself, but they will ask, and I just say: yes to this, no to that. Nothing makes me feel more, what can I say, more woman! It's all so very simple! Because where it comes to my heart's pearls, besides not being able to say no to anything, sometimes they make me forget what I am…"

"I'm not surprised, with your plumage… but are you really sure you don't just take the fairest birds of our feather?"

"As if! You wouldn't believe the success a specimen like me can have with men… though I know I've never been quite your type… have I?"

"Let's not go into that one. Besides, I'm not a man, so I wouldn't really count… You could always give it a shot with this lover of Pauline's. I doubt she'd mind a bit from the great beyond…You were saying he's got cash, and he must be a piece of cake."

"Charlie would kill me. I'd rather risk it with the blonde. At least she wouldn't smell all inky and musty."

"You're just like Pauline, you and your obsession with smells. But listen, what the hell is it with Charlie? Because you used to be just like me: forget the chains and a free field for all!"

"I'll explain it some other time, but it's not the first time it's happened. And when I get it bad, I stick like a tick. You wouldn't want me, just because she's got it worse than I do, to toss it all out for one crazy night."

"Look, to each her own, everyone has to be her own doctor. But what about Pauline? Isn't that what you wanted to talk about? At least that's what you said. Uh-oh, looks like you've lost your blondie… she just got company."

"Who? A dried-up thing that she just swallowed up, with her sad eyes like a boiled fish? She comes in every day. Here's the scene: that one turns up, the blonde gives her a couple of caresses, and after a minute or two, she comes over and asks me to dance. I don't know what game they're playing. Nor what would happen if I went along with it… But the way it goes is that the other one waits without taking eyes off her, and in the end she always leaves with her…"

"You come here a lot, don't you? I haven't set foot in the place for ages. Not since before the war. Imagine. That's why I got all excited… Besides, I was born just around the corner. And it's quite a coincidence; last time I was here it was with Pauline herself… It's all very different, the ambiance, I mean. Pauline was dying to know this corner of the world… Of all worlds, I guess, because I reckon 'la Brioche' must have shown her another one altogether…"

"Gosh, it really has been a long time, because since Pauline died we've witnessed pretty much everything, things you'd have never dreamed…! Now that you mention 'la Brioche'… what do you know of her? Me, I've been out of the loop for years, the last I heard was about the Russian woman…"

"Wow, you really are out of it, my girl: she's had at least three or four since then. And, those lassies are always the same: they cash in and then they kiss her goodbye. Yachts, hotels, cars, jewellery, whatever. They even say she bought one of them a chit of a husband. The Russian, when she left, made the excuse she'd seen Pauline's ghost!"

"What a devil. But then, 'la Brioche' is pretty brainless. And with that physique! You'd have thought the other would crumble in her arms…"

"I always thought they went the English way, not that that means anything anymore. Listen, what about that pair of turtle doves? Remember? Yes, one of them was a good friend of Pauline, and one year at Nice…"

"Oh yeah, I remember, what a riot, those two that Margot called 'the nuns of Léman'… I lost track of them years ago. They must be just the same, because sisterly vows are forever, I think…" She lets out a good laugh, then lowers her voice: "Oh, look here she is. Didn't I tell you?"

The blonde was headed straight for the table. She had very short hair and was wearing a black velvet dress, sashed and low-cut, with an amber pipe in her mouth. The nails on the hand holding it were polished with a wine colour to match her lips. She encircled Janot from behind with the sinuous whiteness of her arms. Janot got up and let herself be led to a corner where some couples were now moving, entwined, to some sort of jazz rhythm. The blonde was a whole head taller than Janot, whose own head rested on the bare shoulder of her companion. Her lips, now without the pipe, seemed to suck something invisible from Janot's hair…

Mimi turned her gaze toward the other woman, supposedly the blonde's friend. Her eyes were lowered and she looked obsessively at her long, thin hands, sort of olive coloured, twitching in a repetitive movement on her blue silk skirt. She sat hunched over, with depressed shoulders and her neck tense. She was small, like a Japanese woman, fragile, very young. She suddenly raised her dark, tiny eyes that shone from the depths of two purplish, shadowy circles and looked straight at Mimi. She visibly avoided the sight of the two women dancing. Mimi made her a friendly enough gesture with her hand and eyes. She smiled back, timid and grateful. Mimi's presence that evening with Janot must have been calming for her. Mimi amused herself as she confirmed how appearances sometimes lead to conclusions quite contrary to reality… For her very presence might be enough to force Janot into a fully-fledged demonstration of her capabilities. She knew that well enough. For a moment she felt an impulse to interfere in the play. Not so much out of compassion for the little victim as for her own malevolent satisfaction in shoving the events along so she could take hold of the reins.

Suddenly it occurred to her that Janot had only invited her to witness the spectacle of her conquest. Pauline was just the excuse, or maybe the instigation… In spite of Janot's veneer of crafty affability, she surely couldn't have forgotten that long-ago night in Montecarlo, when the vision of Mimi and Pauline embracing in the garden of the casino put an end to her lucky winner's euphoria. When they returned to Nice, Janot had drunk until she couldn't stand up. Pauline, with the help of her chamber maid Marie, had got her into bed. She then returned to the hall and locked the door. Mimi remembered the feverish, rosy, moving smudge of their nude bodies in the great mirror framed in bronzed wood.

It hadn't lasted long, but it was intense and tender, with fun and fire and sweet cheating… "Poetic," Mimi told herself, who had a soft spot, secret at the time, for poetry. Her little volume *Sous le masque*, published the first year of the war, had spread this relentlessly, with a wealth of details.

Janot came back. The blonde didn't want to let her go, but Janot whispered something in her ear and finally she desist-ed. With unlit pipe in her mouth she returned to her table. She lit it parsimoniously.

"I had to promise I'd dance with her again later, or she wouldn't have let me go on any account. Today it's all the way, that pearl of mine... And I'm liking it!"

"Okay, then, tell me what you wanted to tell me about Pauline and I'm out of here... I don't want to stick around watching your comings and goings..."

"Don't get cross, you can see I'm not to blame..."

"Blame is always a dark matter. And we'll have a drama yet. Didn't you see what a face the other one was making? It wouldn't surprise me if she had a knife in her purse."

"Are you kidding me? I'm not buying that. She looks pretty lily-livered to me..."

"Go ahead and stick your fingers in her mouth to see. She's just a bit subdued and curled up in her own cocoon... and the other one doesn't give a damn. But I'd like to see..."

"Come on, forget about it... Back to what I was telling you about Pauline. I just want to know what you are going to tell this Salomon R. about it all... It's very odd, isn't it, that the guy is such a good friend of Lianon, and that he has such a fixation on Pauline? When the two of them couldn't stand each other! Of course, Flossie did everything she could to get them at each other's throats. In any case, I'd just like to know what details... I don't know, but look: there are things about Pauline that are better left unsaid... even if it were the year two thousand. That year at Nice... the twenty-six year..."

"Yes, yes, I remember perfectly. Your streak of twenty-six. You bet twenty-six I don't know how many days in a row, and you always won..."

"That's what I'm getting at... do you know why I always

bet twenty-six? It was just a little secret, an erotic one...
between me and Pauline."

"Twenty-six? I don't know what that is, kid, I simply can't
imagine. And if I don't get it, I don't know who... Good thing
it wasn't sixty-nine, or the casino would have collapsed in the
scandal..."

"Hold on now! If we'd got to sixty-nine, maybe we would-
n't be here to tell the tale. The record was twenty-six. Twenty-
six in one night."

"Oh, that's what it is... wow! Don't tell me about it, I hate
the finger-counting thing... it's so vulgar! I could believe anything of you, but I'm surprised Pauline would go down that
path."

"Well, you didn't know her very well if you can say that!
Where it comes to all that kind of stuff we got along perfectly. She was like a naughty kid. A bonfire. She wanted to try
everything, and she never had enough. She always pushed me
to tell her rude words and to show her what they meant. We
laughed so much! How plastered we used to get: she concoct-
ed some cocktails that would knock you on your arse..."

"Yes, I tried a few of those cocktails, but our relations were
more delicate, more poetic."

"Well, I still haven't told you everything, because those days
in Nice were something else. Pauline had a very funny book by
that guy who made Flossie famous, the one who wrote the letters to the Amazon. A book Pauline found greatly amusing,
because it said something about males not being necessary in
nature, that it was the females that mattered, and stuff like
that. You can imagine Pauline reading that... well, that book
explained how all kinds of animals do it... fish, birds, frogs,
spiders, butterflies... I can't tell you how much we laughed,

trying out all the possibilities, in our own way… The dragonfly suited us best…" She guffawed. "Haven't you ever seen them? I have. When I was little and lived in the village I never tired of watching them… Everything's useful, in life! But for me, the very best are the snails. They're a marvel, really, they have all they need, and sometimes ten or twelve of them do it in a row… the male to one is the female to the other, and so on…"

"If you tell all that to Pauline's boyfriend, he'll die of fright. Believe me: it's best to be very careful about certain things. People probably won't believe you anyway, and you'll be the one who comes out losing…"

"That's why I wanted to talk about it… You must believe me, though… If not, one of these days I can always give you a demonstration… privately, of course."

"Hey, here comes a better candidate… I see the blonde with the pipe is coming back… Give me a cigarette, and let's just hope nothing happens to you."

"Shhh! If I get lost, don't come looking for me."

Mimi watched as they disappeared together in the reddish shadows. In the mirror, the little brunette was wilting – what name should she have? She was like a little blue forget-me-not blossom under a cloudburst that was too strong… Forget-me-not, Myosotis. Yes, she liked that. Or if not, maybe an oriental name, as brief as she was: Li, for example. Li would be capable of carrying a knife in her purse… As for Myosotis, there'd be nothing to be done there: she'd wait, faithfully, in spite of all the evidence. She made a bet with herself. If it was Li, any possible outcome was sweet: the startled blonde, the sprint for recovery, Lulu's game upset… or maybe even better, to end the night at the opium den on Rue Chaptal, with the little brunette asleep, trembling against her breast.

"Everything is nothing. Only death exists, and the fumes of glory," the wise Salomon R. used to say, of whom mean-spirited voices assured that he only knew the nudity of statues, whether Greek, Roman, or Babylonian. With an illustrious surname, ennobled by the King of Prussia just before his kinfolk decided to establish themselves in the capital of the Seine, his lineage was closely related to the two great scandals of the Third Republic: the crash of the Panama Canal Company, which made of his paternal uncle a banker's elegant cadaver by way of a bullet of doubtful origin; and above all the notorious "affair" in which his older brother waved the baton of the most stringent Dreyfusism.

Salomon R. took his universal curiosity much further than the limits considered appropriate to a new pontiff of the ancient goddess Reason, in order to act in accordance with *de omni re scibili*. This unexpected aspect of his personality must be emphasized as both counterweight and complement to his enormous work of research and dissemination – from Greek, Etruscan or Hittite vases to the sarcophagus of some unknown Nefertari – and to his commitment to the patient teaching of "Latin without suffering", "Greek without tears", "French without pain" and a well-digested philosophy to the little "Paulines" who wished to go beyond a few piano pieces for under-occupied young ladies. Without fail and with a true spirit of service, Salomon the Wise gathered and prepared a legacy for the archaeologists of the future, destined for those who, once distanced from the passion of morbidity to which the present entrusts its fruits, would know how to confront serenely the mysteries of Lesbos and the secret sanctuaries of

Aphrodite Urania. Closed and sealed until the year two thousand, all tokens, remains and relics that fell into his hands, so avaricious and at the same time so splendiferous at moments of pouring out easy money, await their time to see the light – a secret magnified by mystery – as if they were a bed of precious minerals that someone had hidden, but with filtrations beyond the control of an obstinate will. And so, the secret so assiduously defended might have melted away imperceptibly, pillaged by adventurers, explorers, or necrophiles, or, in being revealed, it could have lost all its power of seduction or left us just the feeling of an even bigger secret, this one truly inaccessible forever to our capacity for knowing. In the meantime, though, let us permit the privileges inherent to the role of narrator cast an indiscreet eye through the veil of the temple and the seven inviolable seals of the Bibliothèque Nationale – an invincible obstacle for the patient inquiries of Sara T. – to read, in invisible ink, some pages from wise Salomon's *Violet Notebooks*. Transforming ourselves into amateur archaeologists, we can endeavour to reconstruct the rest from just these few fragments.

Boulogne-sur-Seine, 5 January 1920

And so I begin this the seventh of the violet notebooks, corresponding to the first part of 1920. Up to the present, each year has brought me materials *grosso modo* to fill two of these files of papers, specially bound in Moroccan leather of the colour of Pauline's beloved flower. Thus, it has now been more than three years since I began, and I have maintained, without interruption, this precise chronicle of everything that had anything to do with Pauline, whether directly or indirectly. These papers have the vocation of becoming at once the catalogue, the repository of materials, explanatory breviary, research diary, memoir and commentary of my successive discoveries. Located at the uncomfortable crossroads between this whole series of textual specimens, my notebooks, which have for several reasons a morphology much less systematic and more apparently anarchic than might be expected, must accompany with modesty but also utility, my future legacy. My age and my state of health lead me to suspect that, unfortunately, that future is not far off. And if I have let this strictly personal plaintive note slip out, contrary to my usual habit, in the midst of writings that have no intimate character at all, because it is a consideration that affects absolutely the possibility of carrying my task to term in all its definitive dimensions.

A little more than three years ago, I began to register in these notebooks every step I took – too clumsy no doubt – in the wake of Pauline's winged footprints. But in truth I first encountered her much longer ago. In the beginning, howev er, obsessed and dazzled by the discovery, bewitched suddenly, like an idiotic, devoted, love-struck fifteen-year-old, the strict, marvelled contemplation of my object of admiration was enough. When I realized with absolute clairvoyance what sort of task I needed to undertake and what sort of service my fervour would have to entail, I even, in my haste, failed to register that it was an ancient and beautiful Greek amphora that had led me to where she seemed to be waiting for me. Forever and a day, the enamoured dolt would say. For at least fourteen years, the stuffy academic infected with precision would correct. Strange chance that brought her to me, strange chance that had kept her books from me until then. That the loving heart gave in completely to the meticulous library rat is demonstrated by this very oversight: no lover writing with the blood of his heart would skip over the relation of antecedents, the exact time and place of the revelation. So now I will allow myself to mend this *lapsus memoriae.*

It was the far-off year of 1888 when the desire to see a Greek amphora took me to the house of an acquaintance, Madame Beulé. It was there that I found, by chance, Carole Lassier, who had been a widow for a few months and who would remarry five years later to become Madame R. Some time during 1910, even though I systematically refused all invitations, I accepted to go to dinner at her house. Pauline had died just the year before, but I was unforgivably completely unaware that she had ever existed. At that dinner at Madame R.'s house, I met Madame Brimont, and we got on famously right away. Four years later, on an autumn day that would have been pleasing to Pauline, I accompanied Madame Brimont, by now a good friend, to the Salon. At one point she recited some verses to me: "They are by Renée Vivien," she said to me when she noticed the impact they had on my expression. I bought all her works – difficult to find, and now I completely understand why – and I daresay I devoured them. Madame B. took me to Flossie's house, and Flossie revealed to me *Sapphic Idyll*... Thus it is that I distantly owe the imponderable fact of having discovered Pauline and got to know Flossie, Liane... to a Greek amphora: the noblest of heralds of which they were more than worthy and a perfect match for my interests, to boot.

Pauline's books, each and every one of them, had been waiting for me for more than thirteen years. Of course that hardly constitutes excessive antiquity for me, accustomed, as I am, to count by millennia... Nevertheless, when one attempts to recover the vestiges, the remains, the ruins of a human life, the years seem to multiply their effect, in relation to those of the stones, in a vertiginous way, so much so that they start to seem like centuries. All the more so with the havoc wrought by the war in between, tangling up all the threads, erasing many trails and sowing mistaken indications and fallacious clues.

Thirteen protracted years, then, to which we must add the twenty or so that she lived before publishing *Études et préludes*. It is possible that once, during those antediluvian years before the turn of the century, we may have crossed paths at some point, on Bois Avenue; she returning to the family *pension* on Crevaux Street and me to my apartment on Trakpir Street, three blocks beyond. She, on her way to meet a fragrant Flossie, a gold and white lily among the other lilies in the room. And I, on the way to my desk where the task before me never seems to give me the slightest break, then or now, and which has helped me to understand deep inside the real suffering of Sisyphus. Who knows whether, one autumn or spring morning, our carriages crossed within a hair's breadth, by some ironic caprice of fate, beneath the Arc de Triomphe or at the Porte Dauphine?

It hardly matters: if one of those fleeting encounters did occur, it left no mark. It was through her books that she revealed herself to me. All that remains of us is to be found in books.

16 January 1920

I have been given access to the "Blue Notebook" number five and have written to Liane, my Eva of indescribable beauty, thanking her in the name of all those who will read her one day. They too, if in the remote future the taste for *belles lettres* and lived history still exist, will say, captivated: "I belong to Liane." And perhaps they will hold a grateful memory for the one who first spoke to her of the twenty-first century, of the duty and pleasure experienced in making the effort to please and remind them of what we were and how we suffered during these unfortunate, anguish-filled years we are now living. At this point, I think I can begin to work on the indices of name and theme that I aimed to complete. Without a good index, even the best works remain unusable for the most part.

I have made only two observations to Liane: in the first place, if my eyes are destined to pass systematically over the notebooks, it is inevitable that she will stop exercising the liberty of giving her sincere opinion about me, out of tact. Hence, I have proposed that she write a few pages, which I will keep scrupulously with the others, but will not read, where she can expand on her critical sensibilities, which I must surely arouse more than I would like.

My second observation concerns Pauline directly. I realize that Liane does not wish to write anything about her that might cause me excessive grief. I have told her from the beginning that my cult for Pauline is in no way an idolatry; I judge her quite severely when I think of her ruined health, of her squandered life. Abandoned by Flossie, she should have remained a widow or remarried; her years of picking up passers-by are quite lamentable. But nothing that concerns such a great genius is indifferent, not even her accepted humiliations: "By humiliations to inspiration", Pascal would say, and in this case I am tempted to agree with him. Even so, suspecting that in spite of these arguments, she might still resist emptying her cornucopia of memories into my hands, I have again made the same offer: I will not read the pages that she dedicates to this theme.

24 February 1920

I have just copied new letters by Pauline which the kindness of Natalie B. has allowed me to have in my hands and which occupy the annexed folios 125-154. I think they are admirable, as always, if also rather crazy. They betray in Pauline, as far back as 1901, a kind of persecutory mania and extreme credulity when it comes to suspecting ill of her friend. Consider, for example, the supposed engagement of Flossie in America, and the torrent of insults it provokes. It seems she did not understand – she, of all people! – the true nature of the Amazon. Flossie must have responded, affectionately, with an offer of her friendship; that can be deduced from Pauline's irritated protest reminding her of the miserable exchange of receiving friendship when she has offered love. As if Natalie could give something she did not possess, that perhaps she never possessed! It is in these incomparable letters, too, that the first mention appears of Liane, my Eva, from which it is easy to infer the profound motive for the abyss between her and Pauline. Pauline really believed, to judge by what she says – and mistakenly, in my opinion – that Liane had been loved by Flossie with the sort of love that had been denied to her: "Just think, you did love once, you loved Liane."

Even Liane agrees with me, though she is convinced that she meant more to Flossie than Pauline did. "The complete opposite to what has happened with you, my dearest Nathaniel," she recently said to me with cunning. Without daring to disagree, I reminded her that it is thanks to Pauline that I stumbled so fortunately upon her. Returning to the previous theme: when last Christmas, Liane offered me the gift of a letter Pauline wrote to her (folio number 118), oozing bile, she told me that Flossie spread her passion to the four winds, but that one could always count on her tenderness… And then she let me read the haiku she had fabricated for that "inconstant faithful one":

Dazzling moon,
how, in the distance,
you seem more beautiful!

I can imagine the Amazon, when she received it, raising one eyebrow in that peculiar gesture of hers…

Getting back to Pauline's letters, all of them, whether in French or English, are written with fire, far beyond that of the letters of the Portuguese nun or even those of Julie de

Lespinasse. What verbal genius even amid the worst madness! I cannot hide the satisfaction it gives me to find the time, in spite of all the obligations that weigh me down, to copy these works of art of passion. True enough, literature has its place here; Pauline, without saying so explicitly, considered herself an abandoned Sappho, and she expresses herself thus, at times using vocabulary taken from the poetess she so admired, of whom she no doubt thought she was an incarnation. But where is there not literature?

21 February 1921

Thanks to my excellent contacts, I have been able to find out the identity of the Eminé of Pauline's poems. With the happy occurrence that the lady is living in Paris at the moment. Her husband, an important diplomat, was assassinated here a few years ago. Since she belonged to the Sultan's household it is unlikely she will be tempted to return to Constantinople for now. The lady who gave me the reference is an exiled Russian, the Countess of O., whom my wife greeted on leaving the Opera, at the premiere of *Boris Godunov*.

For some reason, she already knew of my interest in Pauline: sometimes it seems Tout-Paris knows. That has caused more than one ironic comment, I have no doubt, but it has also helped greatly with my research, and the discomfort occasionally provoked is a small price to pay for what I have gained. In any case, the Countess told me that her sister-in-law had known Pauline. The lady referred to – her brother's wife – is a well-known Turkish lady of high lineage who fled the harem a few years before the famous "Disenchanted Ones" of Loti – to be more precise, before the living protagonists of real history, less "syrupy", in Pauline's words, than the fictitious history told in the novel. I had heard talk about this intrepid precursor, but since her flight from Turkey preceded Pauline's trips to Constantinople, I did not think it necessary to investigate in that direction. Instead, I had tried to follow the trail of the hypothetical Turkish princess through the acquaintances I had made in Constantinople as a result of the excavations at Mirina and Imroz, just as I reported in earlier notebooks. All in vain. It seems Pauline was absolutely discreet on this occasion. Charles B. assured me categorically that the Turkish lady existed, that she was no exotic invention, fruit of the fashion of that moment. He also knows that Pauline stayed at the Pera Palace: all the letters he has that she sent to him from Constantinople bear the hotel's letterhead. So, now it has been confirmed. I wrote to the lady in question and today I got a response. She tells me that her relationship with Pauline was quite superficial, though she retains a charming memory and she believes, as do I, that we are dealing with a great poet. But the one who really knew Pauline, she assured me, was her sister Kerimée. And as I said at the beginning, Kerimée now lives in Paris.

THE SULTANA

M. Salomon R.
Director of the Art Museum…
Saint-Germain-en-Laye

Paris, 7 November 1922

Distinguished sir,

Finally I have found it in my heart to send you the narrative you requested in your kind letter of more than a year ago.

The agitated situation in which my country finds itself immersed has struck my spirit with terrible anguish and my memory and pen with extreme hesitation. I realize that you have not asked me to compose literature, and I know, as well, that it is not a gift with which I have been favoured. I know too well the works which the Word has blessed with a long visit over the centuries to mistake that point. Renée was visited by the Word. She was aware of that, and she blazed her life away in honour of that Guest who had chosen her without her feeling worthy of it. She tried to be worthy, desperately and in vain. She did not grasp the humility of simple acceptance, the giving of thanks without question. The triple reverence of mouth, heart and mind before the Inscrutable. This fact brought us together. During that time, a diffuse and wordless revolt had taken root within me. And she possessed the words. I was also dazzled at first by her lack of moderation, but this would later become one of the major obstacles between us, perhaps even the dagger that would sever the fine but resistant gold chain that held us together for four years across the miles.

Yes, I know you did not ask me to create literature. But even so, I cannot evoke the most literary, most beautiful episode of my life, so often monotonous despite appearances, without making the effort to give my words a tessitura and colour that will not betray altogether, in my own eyes, the vividness of a completely unfaded memory. Its strange music still blossoms in my bosom. But my fingers have the greatest difficulty in reproducing it, in bringing it forth from the strings of a sleeping lute. Surely you perceive at least the trembling of blood in my pulse in the shadow of these words.

You have been in Istanbul – permit me to call it that, by the beloved name of my people, and not the more frequent here, Constantinople. I am sure you know the historical richness of our city, of the stones that bespeak a glorious and remote past. This is the Istanbul that has not changed its face, the indestructible jewel amidst the ravages caused by the war and its aftermath. All the rest is unrecognizable at this time. I know this, even though I have been far from the city for so many years, and my heart insists on maintaining an old, permanent and faithful image. But I cannot but believe the voices that speak to me, nor deny the sadness transmitted to me in letters from those I love. Women I love. Women who, like me, yearned for deep-rooted changes in the world. And in spite of so much painful turmoil, in spite of a law proposed which still does not arrive when the weight of deeds has gone beyond its reach, life for women has have barely changed at all. I mean concrete, everyday life. The life that confines and negates any aspiration beyond the closed space of the *haremlik*, but at the same time offers the leisure and the means for the spirit to travel and soar without limits or borders. I speak of women of my status, of course, the ones I know best, those who have felt in recent times the impulse of liberty.

I belong to the generation of the "Disenchanted ones" that Pierre Loti gives voice to in his novel, too dramatically perhaps: the majority of Turkish women find less romantic, less novelistic outlets from an all-too-real dilemma. Such is my case. That does not mean that there are no Zeynebs, Meleks, or Djananés of unfortunate endings, nor that something of their revolt without pact has not found its nest in each one of us. The Occidental model, which I know well from my stays in one embassy after another while my unfortunate husband was alive – from Saint Petersburg to London and Albania, and most recently Paris – and which has become too prominent in my country since the defeat and unhappy armistice, does not seem as desirable to us, seen from close up, as books had made us imagine.

Do you remember Renée's poem "The Walled Women"? When I read it, it seemed she was speaking of me, of us, of all women who languished and still languish behind walls and wooden shutters along the shores of the Bosphorus. Of the shadow that chokes their timid laughter, of their living death, of the lichens that consume and devour their hearts. And yet, she was speaking of herself. And of the invisible walls that imprison the spirit of women of your culture – which I feel is also mine, in part. "A prison that is everywhere but nowhere," she used to say.

At the time I couldn't quite understand her. I saw her as an example of a free woman, subject only to her own decisions and the consequences of her own actions... "I only feel free behind the doors of my house, with the windows closed tight. Outside, it is as though I were nailed to a pillory, hatcheted, condemned to public shame for a dark crime, exposed to the hostility of the world. Sometimes I envy your charshaf that makes you anonymous, faceless, and protects your steps out-side of the norm from accusing gazes." Those are not her exact words, but they express what she meant. And that terri-ble feeling that oozes from one of her most harrowing poems:

> *I was nailed to a pillory for a long time.*
> *I suffered and the women laughed at my suffering.*

The women in the poem laugh, they laugh at her, even ingenuously. The men, more fired up, throw balls of mud that hit her right in the face. But it seems that the passive and happy assent of the women hurts her more than real mascu-line aggression. Renée expected nothing from men. "I have no male friends," she told me in one of her letters, "there is no friendship without esteem and I have never found a man who could inspire that in me." I am sorry to say that to you, for I am sure that you are an exception in that group of humans that she found so loathsome, as is proven by the long devotion you profess to her memory and her verses. On the other hand, I am not telling you anything new: you know perhaps better than I do all that she wrote. The only ones she excluded from her absolute disdain were poets and artists, who, for her, tran-scended their gender. She believed that of herself as well.

Would it surprise you if I say that she signed some of her letters "your guy" or "your lover-boy"? That fact, as you know, did not keep her from an extreme femininity, or from a soli-darity with other women that reached unsuspected limits. Because of that I think she was fascinated with the feminine complicity sealed by the *haremlik*, that "sisterhood" as she called it, favoured by a common and exclusive space, that bursts forth in the form of games, dances, and shared perfumes, baths and grooming. In mutual unending visits. In readings in common, where the verses of the poetesses Zeyneb, Mihri, Leyla, or Fitnet alternate with those of Abdülhak Hamid, Baudelaire, Verlaine or the countess of Noailles. In heated discussions in which the *Qu'ran* is sifted through Kant or *Zarathustra*. And above all in the pact of secrecy, a secrecy artfully impenetrable to the outside eye.

Paradox, which the wise say is the patrimony of the divinity, also seems to form part of the deepest root of those beings who, like Renée, have taken on the divine prerogative of creation. I have mentioned one of these apparent contradictions above. But there is no need to stop at anecdote: a radical ambivalence pervaded her from top to bottom. From that subterranean source she derived her strength and her weakness at the same time. I say that because for all the admiration Renée had for the secret that binds together the women in the enclosure of the *haremlik*, she seemed to contradict herself with the publicity that her verses gave to very intimate aspects of her life. But those same verses seem to suggest her reply to us:

Standing in the public square,
from which came an odour
of dried fish, one morning I sang.
But in the headiness of my song
I did not hear the noise of the market.

At other times, however, she could not help but painfully live what she called:

The shameless spectacle of public souls.

At the moment of deciding to write the narration that I send with this, I could not help but consider the point to which, in doing this, I am betraying the tacit agreement of secret and mutual discretion all intimacy brings with it. Even though one could object that Renée respected this pact only relatively, the fact is that the poems I inspired always maintain my anonymity; in them I am like the shadow of a Turkish woman behind veils. It takes a discerning and persistent eye like yours, and perhaps the help of capricious fate to make out a concrete face and eyes and assign a name and surname. By contrast, in my words she is a face, a body, a name exposed to the crude light of day. On the other hand, the mere beauty of her verses would justify an even clearer indiscretion on your part. My words have only tried to clothe with dignity and modesty the most beautiful memory of my life.

So, I have reluctantly decided to speak. I am not an artist, nor have I had children. All that I am and have been will one day disappear with me. I know that things still exist and have a life as long as a heart or a mind nourishes them with memories. By the year 2000, nothing of what I have lived will be supported by memory of me. Can the written word be simply that other memory that lasts longer than we do, giving our death a bit of respite? It is your commitment to keep my tale secret until that date that finally convinced me. And even though I understand the magnitude of your sacrifice, I accept your sensitive offer not to read yourself the pages that follow, trusting completely in your promise. Without that, I never would have dared to divulge myself with the liberty I have used, limited only by elementary norms of good taste and respect, so necessary always but especially when we penetrate themes so often objects of gross incomprehension. Your prestige is my guarantee and pledge, as is the unanimous consideration in which you are held by people of my highest opinion.

As far as the letters are concerned, which I do have in my possession, and which have served as points of reference that nothing could substitute for my narration, I must respond in the negative to your proposal. For me they are a priceless treasure, the harvest of a bright time that still nourishes my eyes and heart with its charity of golden light. I could not let go of them even for a few days. I could copy some of them for you, not all, since there are more than a hundred and some of them are very long. The loveliest ones, then, could form a part of this legacy that you are so generously preparing for the next century.

Consider these lines a testimony to the admiration and great sympathy that I have professed for you for years, even more so since I learned of your interest in Renée and your obstinate task of research and investigation. I remain, then, at your disposal with a cordial greeting,

Kerimée T. P.

Kerimée's Tale

1

Begun on 8 March 1922

Memory is beautiful like a ruined palace, Renée used to say. But it is not the beauty of that which is only a vestige or ruin that makes me turn my eyes to those days. It is not a hopeless nostalgia for that which is definitively lost.

On the contrary, it is the sensation, perhaps illusory, of returning life for a few moments to that which existed fully, to that which possessed the rare and intense perfection of a rose of Saadi. And which, like her, was also the mistress of a single day.

It must have been at the beginning of the year 1904, 1322 according to the Hejira. It is strange: now that I am faraway, and I know that the bright Eyüb cemetery will not watch over my rest when the hour of my death comes, I feel a dark, yearning pleasure in counting months and days for myself in terms of the Muslim era. At that time, though, one of the signs of revolt and breaking away from the atavistic customs that distinguished our generation was the adoption of the western calendar. In the year 1904, then, one of Renée's books fell into my hands by chance. I seem to remember that it was *Évocations*, but my memory may not serve me faithfully on that point. I do know that it captivated me from the first word. I have always liked poetry and my ear has been sensitive to the music of French verse since childhood. Before my

223

sister and I took the *charshaf*, we knew entire Ronsard poems by heart. But those verses by Renée had a strange quality that made them mine, an incisive yet diffuse sadness that penetrated me deeply, unto the marrow of solitude that at that moment coloured my hours with bitterness. I ordered all the other books that author, unknown to me, had published up until then from a Pera bookseller especially well provided with French novelties. And the miracle was repeated; it was even more intense and vivid. It was not only the latent revolt and sadness that were a magnet for my blood. There was also another aspect that at the time I left in the shadow and confessed only in part, but that from here and now I know acted upon me with an even more powerful magnetism: her clear and diaphanous affirmation of feminine love.

I was young and all forbidden fruit had the brightest and liveliest colours in my eyes. To reach out and leave the imprint of my teeth in them, though, was not as easy as it may have seemed. It is true that among us, fingers, faces and bodies play and touch each other in waves of joy, or consolation in grief, with a liberty rare in the west. The sensuality of the common bath in the *hamman*, the loosened hair, the massages and perfumes sometimes evoke a fallacious image in a European imagination. Transgression of the norm demands an initiative, a daring that are infrequent. Sometimes it is even difficult to outline one's own desire in the mind, to discern an exact, vigorous impulse amid the cloud of unlimited, vague sensations and tremblings. And to name them and give them a right to exist. Many times I had felt that light, brief flame that runs through the body from head to toe due to an almost imperceptible contact on the skin's surface, or a gaze that suddenly bares your soul. From a tender word. Or from the shared tears in a prolonged embrace. But they were sensations that seemed to fulfill themselves without requiring more, no urgency led them anywhere. At times there were also furtive words, caught on the fly, or jokes half-understood among the jumble of laughter and fuss that accompany the gatherings of the baths, sparking for a moment like unanswered questions. Renée's books answered a question even before it had been formulated. And, faced with the answer, the question dared to present itself with force.

I obtained her address and wrote to her. It was easier than I thought, though no difficulty would have stopped my sudden determination. My letter was a demand, an imprecise, open cry out to the unknown. Renée had no face for me. But I felt I knew her soul, perhaps better than my own. While I was struggling within a formless effervescence, she presented herself to me with the force of the word that gives order and shape. Her soul was, in the end, the beauty of her verses. And in the magic of that mirror, I searched for the unknown features of my spirit.

A singular desire, more urgent perhaps than any other, was born in me to put a body and a face – so different from my own – on that soul so like my own. That is why, from the very first letter, after telling her of the impact her books had produced on me, I asked her for a portrait. She refused. Her reply, which arrived sooner than my most optimistic reckonings, said among other things:

"You very kindly ask me for my photograph. I am not vain at all, O most exquisite Unknown One!, and I have no likeness to send you – I would prefer that you fashion an image of me to your own liking. Adorn me with your dreams. Thus will you more fully relish what everyone desires and seeks in friendship and love: her own fancy. That way I will be a reflection for you of your own beauty."

That is how it all began. I remember it was toward the end of spring. It was about a month and a half since my sister Xereff, whom I have mentioned earlier, had run off to Europe. Everyone was still talking about it, in bursts of indignation or murmurings of envy. Her first letter came to me one day before Renée's, also from Paris. The ink was completely smeared from my tears. As the letters blurred, the image of her face appeared with rare precision before my eyes; her face, beloved beyond all measure, and the sharpened audacity of her gaze.

It was more than a year before I got to see Renée's face, that face of a "daughter of the north" which appears before me often now like a vast bolt of lightning, young, smooth, white as a musk-rose that ardour tints suddenly with vivid pink. I can still trace her soft profile with my enraptured fingers and softly stroke her long eyelashes with a silken touch over her eyes. Linger on her smiling dimples with barely open lips, kiss her receding chin.

But I am going too fast. I could thus create a false image of what that year before our meeting in "flesh and blood" was like. I do not say "real meeting" because perhaps the reality in this story was, and is, our letters, hers and mine, and the entire world of suggestions they opened for each of us. And the true connection, the encounter, happened in that space in common generated by two dreams entwined through words. On the other hand, unreality, the atmosphere of dreams, always surrounded the intense fleetingness of her visits and the short, avid, slow fire of our bodies in love. And in fact, from within the heart of the fire, memory of the written word fanned it like a powerful wind, and afterward the written word prolonged the dominions of time, out of time, and at once became the seed of new incendiary memories.

All that I explain is fruit of that all-encompassing gaze permitted by closed episodes of the past when seen from a present that crumbles in our fingers. Day to day, things bring uncertainty, the unforeseeable, a tension that makes them alive and changing. That year that I have wrongly presented as previous had the exaltation of a first loving fulfilment, accompanied by a feeling of possession and plenitude that has nothing to do with the anxiety we associate with waiting. I seemed to know Renée's soul from the beginning. From then on, I came to know and treasure greedily all that her mind and heart offered me, brimming with richness and excess. If her verses had given me the marvellous design of a delicate and complex tapestry, accessible to everyone's eyes, now I alone could have access to the warp and woof that supported it. In one of her first letters, she wrote:

"I am twenty-seven… I have never wanted to marry. Nothing compelled me towards matrimony. I had a certain fortune: I was free at twenty-one. That is when I found Vally. She reigned over my entire destiny. For eighteen months I lived the strange dream of our turbulent love. I loved her ill and I hated her: I did not value her properly. I regretted that, and hated her a second time. Then I found Eva. Here you have my whole life."

And a little later:

"I am sending you *A Woman Appeared to Me*. It is the story of my ardent and painful life, of my life in love and my life disappointed."

I read the novel with passion. Many aspects of that story were completely incomprehensible to me at the time, especially the disturbed, dark love she had for Vally. It is true that pain often binds more forcefully than pleasure – or is it that a strange, shadowy pleasure expresses itself through the intensity of suffering? The fact is that, not too many years ago when I met Natalie B., the legendary Amazon that Renée always called Vally in the letters she addressed to me, everything suddenly became clear. It is impossible to imagine two more opposite natures. Renée felt guilty about not loving her well, of not having been capable of accepting her as she was, without demanding that absolute, total love that Vally, in fact, was incapable of giving. Added to that was a feeling of extreme impotence for failing to inspire that kind of love, an impotence that was also pierced with culpability.

The truth is that a profound accord between two such different beings could only have been possible at an exorbitant price: the renunciation by one of the two of her own uniqueness, her personal way of feeling. But the end of the conflict surely would have brought about the end of love as well, for there are loves that bury their roots precisely in conflict. In this way they imitate the unending, tormented idyll that for centuries had bound ancient Istanbul to the wind of the Black Sea that batters it without respite and spoils its springtimes. Renée understood that, and her lucidity fed an awful fear, a sacred terror of Vally. "One does not risk one's life twice," she said. That is why she fled and clung to Eva like a protective shield held up between herself and death.

I never got to meet the Baroness, always called Eva by Renée when she wrote or in person. I have heard all manner of rumours about her in the salons of Paris, most of them hardly flattering. But the image that came out of those early letters was one of a beneficial, positive presence:

"I live like a savage, almost like a recluse. Aside from my professors, I only see three friends – not to mention the dearly beloved one who is close to my heart. She is the very soul of my solitude."

"You ask how I spend my time. Oh, my God, in everything and nothing. I read, I write, I am with Eva – never without Eva – she accompanies me everywhere. We are inseparable. In the evening, I sit by the fire with my soul a bit idle and I dream infinitely about you."

Later on, jealousy and turbulence muddied that bond, tied "at the hour of sisterly sweet hand-in-hand." And the port in which the skiff was anchored became high seas in the midst of a tempest.

But we are still in the summer of 1904. The preparations for the season and my stay at the *yalı* that my husband had near Beykoz, on the Asian shore of the Bosphorus, coincided with the beginning of our feverish epistolary idyll. I said earlier that my first letter was an open, imprecise demand. Renée saw that right away and channelled that current of undefined margins. So, a bit roguishly, she insinuated:

"I still wish to ask you whether another Captive Princess has ever been able to lighten your chains with her loving smile. If perhaps that way you were able to forget the idiotic tyranny of the owner... Feminine lips attract each other urgently and sweetly, they say, in the shadows of harems..."

To my more or less veiled questions about a subject that silence had marked with its seal, she responded with the clarity of passion made into words:

"You ask me, O my faraway princess!, whether happiness is found in the sacred love of women for women. I know that the most profound and sweetest happiness nests there, for I myself have found it. Ever since I realised I have a heart, I have felt attracted by the sweetness of women."

And her words led up in a dizzying ascension to more ardent places:

"One day I will hold you in my feverish arms – and my lips will search for and find your lips – And your eyelids will close under my kiss. I will show you how vehemently and softly Psappha caressed Atthis and Eranna – for some of us have conserved the rites of Mytilene. Our love is stronger than all loves, because it is eternal. And when we love, we give and take at the same time."

I let myself be pulled along little by little into that free, impetuous flight, seduced and astonished, and also safe, protected by the distance that conjured those too imminent dangers. Faraway, Paris, which had taken away the longed-for presence of Xereff, ever more remote, brief and laconic in her news, offered me in exchange, enclosed in an iridescent case of dreams, the voice at once sisterly and lovingly voluptuous.

Warm words alternated with confidences. Thus it is that in August I learned of her trip to Bayreuth, and of the encounter that took place, enveloped by the music of Parsifal:

"By the strangest of coincidences, I ran into Vally at Bayreuth. I am seeing her again, and of all that ardent past, there remains for both of us a great, sweet sadness. We have exchanged our two sadnesses. She believes she loves me because I avoid her…"

I know now that things were not that simple. Renée had refused to see Vally for a long time, believing that she could defend her peace that way, the peace she had constructed out of Eva's love, like a wall between herself and the tormented shadow of a latent desire. Just as she feared, the encounter meant the melting of the mirage. The gift of peace is not conceded to everyone. There are beings who seem to grasp intensely and without palliatives that seminal struggle that moves the threads of everything in nature and life. Harmony is out of reach, patrimony of extreme simplicity of heart and spirit, or of the wisdom that lays bare and bows its head at the threshold of mystery. But can poetry be born of such a clear fountain? The strange, tempestuous, dark sentiment that Renée had for Vally had found, on the other hand, its only release in the torrent of words.

At the time, all of this was vague and very faraway for me, and I did not perceive the extent to which the growing vehemence testified by her letters could be another way of avoiding that desire without remedy. Like a preventive antidote, that is, the same poisonous substance taken in small doses under one's own control. There was something like that going on in the beginning, perhaps. But what love has a completely pure origin? And that was not all it was. An essential affinity soon manifested itself between us, a coincidence of thought and emotions that I had only previously felt with Xereff and had attributed to carrying the same blood. Desire took root in this good earth and was nourished by time and waiting. It grew and matured like fruit in season.

"I will come to Constantinople," Renée told me that autumn. And further on she specified: "in the spring."

2

She came in August. A series of problems had delayed the trip. Especially Eva. Renée told me that Eva did not trust her,

231

that she could see my image in her eyes… Finally, Renée took advantage of the Baroness's family obligations along with the excuse of a literary project for which she needed documentation.

She had already translated and adapted fragments of Sappho. Now she wanted to write a biography about her and she needed to go to Mytilene. The island, like all the others in the Aegean, had been Turkish until a few years ago – but I do not wish to speak of this present time, which breaks my heart. Renée arrived in Istanbul by the Orient Express and from here she was to embark for Lesbos. Shortly before, she had written to me:

"My sweet princess of the Orient, my mysterious rose, the thought of finally seeing you has given me bouts of luminous vertigo. Something sings and weeps within me, disconcertingly, of terror and desire. Who knows toward what radiant sufferings I am headed so blindly… You alone, in the universe, this is where I have arrived. You alone… I am living an exquisite and mortal fever: the fever you know too…"

It is true, I, too, felt impatient. And also a little intimidated. During that year I had sent her two photographs of myself. In one, I was dressed *à la Turque*, with my face half covered by a muslin veil. Later, feeling more daring, one I had taken with an ivory-coloured silk dress from Doucet, with marvellous Lalique jewellery in which I could be seen with my face uncovered, *à la Européenne*. In fact, most of my wardrobe came from the best houses in Paris, those on Rue de La Paix. But contrary to what I expected, it was the first she liked the best. She enthused about it. So much so that she asked me to dress, above all, in the oriental way for our first encounter, with my face covered. She had continued to refuse to send me a photograph of herself and I had no image of her, not even an approximate one. But I did know her small handwriting in great detail, the way she jumbled inner *u*s, *v*s, and *n*s in a single sketch, and prolonged in a free downward design certain consonants, especially at the end of a word. I tried to imagine a silhouette from that writing, some features or gestures, but I failed. I mixed up the faces of all the young Anglo-Saxons I had seen, the Parisians from postcards or books, and since the resulting image was a distant one and did not produce the familiar, close sensation of the letters, I superimposed that of beloved faces, especially the progressively blurry outlines of the one which was also too far away and that I suspected I would not see again for a long time. Perhaps never.

When I learned the day of her arrival, I rented a private little salon in the Tokatlian Hotel with the utmost possible discretion under an obviously false name. In fact, it would have been easy to invite her directly to my house, since it was a woman, but it seemed more suitable for a first encounter to find a place completely removed from my everyday life and protected from unexpected interruptions. She had told me that she would stay at the Pera Palace, and I sent a servant with a message detailing the rendezvous. I dressed with great care, a loose silk dress of pale reseda and mauve shoes embroidered with golden arabesques. And a veil of indefinable yellow, soft like a ray of winter sun. Then, beneath the *charshaf*, I became a dark, anonymous shadow. A caïque, then a rented coach, took me to the door of the hotel an hour early. I remember that I was trembling all over, but little by little I calmed down. An intense odour of magnolia mixed with jasmine wafted through the window. I had them prepare coffee with cardamom on a low little mother-of-pearl table next to a divan, along with Lukums, rose preserves, pistachios, and some Egyptian cigarettes I was especially fond of. I took off my *charshaf* and waited.

Renée arrived early as well, so loaded down with white roses one could barely see her eyes behind the bouquet. She was dressed completely in white, and the veil over my face lent her a vaguely golden hue. She must have thought she would arrive first; she was surprised to find that I was already there waiting.

After a few banal words of greeting, stammered clumsily and timidly, she offered me her flowery, perfumed arms. I took the roses, not all at once but one or two at a time… placing them in an empty crystal vase that seemed to be waiting for them, with a slow tension like the string of a bow. Little by little her face came into view from among the roses, and her lips, like another smaller rose barely opening, flesh-coloured. The silence at that point was dense and vibrating like the wings of a nocturnal butterfly. When there were only three or four roses left in her hands, Renée made a jerking movement and the roses fell to the ground. Embarrassed, she quickly picked them up, hoping to erase that awkward gesture, murmuring confused words of apology, visibly humiliated. She held them out to me with lowered eyes. I suddenly had my first view of those eyelids that she unknowingly offered me, unaware of the vulnerability and extreme beauty thereof. I felt a crazy impulse to kiss them. I did not dare. My kiss went astray and landed on the whiteness of the flowers, remaining there for only an instant. But when I made the gesture of putting them in the vase with the others, I realized that the thorns had become entangled in my veil. I was too nervous to untangle them without tearing the gauze. Renée, trembling, approached to help me, in vain. We started to laugh nervously, quietly at first but then with more confidence until we burst into unstoppable laughter like boisterous children, when a clumsy movement rocked the vase and almost made it fall to the floor.

Renée, Renée. I still remember how you laughed. With your eyes, your lips. With your face, and your whole body. And how, later, I took off my veil still stuck to its inseparable roses. And I remember that other sudden silence, different now, soft and velvety, warmly open, which first united our naked gazes.

My memory of the hours that followed is not so precise. I do recall that she was much more timid in her gestures than she had been in the written word. Strangely, I felt more secure, as if it were up to me to guide the course of things, and finally, to decide. In fact, all was decided within me from the moment I saw Renée. And I was fervently thankful to her for being pretty, svelte as a young cypress, and that she curled up at my feet defencelessly, letting me play with her hair and the fine fuzz on her neck. I thanked her, too, for her voluptuous trembling, and for finding me pleasing, so that in the dark alchemy of desire, the word was made flesh.

I remember the vertiginous slowness of time. The undone sashes and our hair mixed together on the divan. The Lukums half-devoured and the shared cigarette that made Renée cough and made us laugh again. Her delicate mouth, reddened by the blood formed by her ardour. And her sweet kisses, seed of a delirium that grew like a flower of living foam. And the trace of preserves on her lips, at their corners, which I erased with playful tongue.

The dance of gestures that spread with the oscillating rhythm of a young flame. The caresses that ventured for an instant through the fragile, vaporous frontier of fabric, receding the following instant, wisely fearful, hovering over the silk and lace and muslin. Then the skin crying out its most taut, iridescent note, as if all the pores stirred in pursuit of fleeing fingers, at once urgent and diffuse in their demand.

A last redoubt of modesty held us back. But I had decided in advance to enter into the depths of that forbidden place that I now had at hand. Since the sun was beginning its decline, fortunately slow in the summer, I decided to invite her to my house. At the time, my husband was out of town, as happened once in a while, and my friends often came to see me and stayed overnight, since once the sun has set, no Muslim woman would be on the street. Renée accepted right away, with eyes shining. She sent a message to a friend who, she explained, was accompanying her to Mytilene and was expecting her at the hotel, and she followed me.

We went on foot to the caïque: she was totally white, the folds in her dress slightly wilted, a diffuse reddish shadow on her neckline and a little slit my nail left near her shoulder. I was next to her like a dark, faceless shadow, but with all senses alive and roused by a sustained anxiety. The caïque went down along the Golden Crescent, and seated side by side with a slight, vibrant contact, imperceptible to indiscreet glances, we saw how the old Istanbul, crowned with sumptuous cupolas and sharply pointed minarets was gradually sinking into darkness, while on the other side, Pera and Galata were tinted with an incandescent rose blending into mauve and amethyst. The voices of the muezzins in nearby mosques were slowly making themselves be heard, calling to the day's last prayer. I will never forget that strange sunset and the concise sweetness of the few words we said to each other.

Once at the house, I took her to my favourite spot: a covered balcony overlooking the Bosphorus, protected from the exterior like all rooms in the *haremlik* by a wooden grating where wisteria draped down, having lost their blossoms some time ago. They were just beginning to show a lilac colour in their clustered pomes when Xereff came to tell me goodbye, the year before. Then they bloomed again at the beginning of the following spring. Now they were green turning to black against the blue of the night that was spreading little by little over the water. We looked at each other in that clear penumbra. And the rapturous tension of the wait projected violently, at that point, the desire of the one into that of the other, like two flaming arrows converging in the night.

A month later, Renée evoked the moment in a letter from Florence:

"The Florentine night has made me think of that other night overlooking the Bosphorus ... The foliage on your balcony sheltering our trembling joy... I can hear your feeble and sweet sighs... Love's silence is all around us. Your eyes seem even more vast and profound amid all this shadow. And you murmur, ever so softly: I love you. I am taking you to the stars. The night is ours.

"The memory of your flesh exhausts and enchants me... I cannot forget the taste of your lips...

"Oh the marvellous corolla of your mouth in the secret burst of your lips – other lips!"

A few hours later I wrote in my diary.

ten o'clock

Renée has just left. All has been sweet and sharp at the same time. My fingers still carry a trembling memory: the fine, delicate flower of grass moist with dew.

Noon

That which I previously called forbidden fruit has a strangely familiar taste. By that, I do not mean it resembles anything I have lived before. It is a sensation like the one of arriving at a place we are convinced we have been before, without any confirmation from memory. The feeling of marvel comes as much from the unexpected familiarity as it does from all we perceive as unknown and new.

seven in the evening

Renée, Renée. You passed through like a shooting star and now the darkness is darker. There is a void, hard and precise like a fist beating my temples, my belly, my legs. You intoxicated me with words. I had you, you had me – still intoxicated – for an instant. I have glimpsed the threshold of another intoxication. And now?

darkest night

I curse Sappho, who takes you away from me. And still and all, her words are with me:

The moon has set
and the Pleiades. It is
midnight. In vain
have I waited. I lie alone.

Renée had gone, in a disconcerting hurry. I did not understand it at all, at that moment. She had told me that her trip to Mytilene was her excuse for coming to me. And now the excuse had become the inescapable imperative that brusquely separated us. In vain I asked her to wait for another boat. She undid herself in confused justifications, beneath which fear was seeping out. Fear of Eva? Fear of being disappointed and thus being expelled from her dream? Fear of disappointing me? Fear of falling too much in love? I remember a sentence referring to Vally: "She only possesses when she passes, and she passes the better to possess." Did she perhaps want to stimulate my desire by making herself inaccessible to me and to be for me what Vally had been for her? Quietly, that suspicion made way for itself and generated, as the days passed, a dark distrust mixed with yearning and grief. Like a constant dripping of bitterness into a glass of hydromel. Two weeks later, when Renée let me know she was back in Istanbul again and would catch the Orient Express that same day, I did not go to meet her.

3

Something was going on with Eva. It was difficult for me to decipher reality through the letters, even though they were full of confidences. But they were only half-confidences. After our very short encounter and her stay in Lesbos, Renée went to Holland, where the Baroness has a castle. She wrote to me from there. The whole thing seemed most illogical to me: Renée had not written a single line to me from Mytilene, where the danger of being caught by Eva did not exist. It is true that mail from the islands is most deficient, but Renée told me later that she had gone to Smyrna for a short stay, where there is no problem with mail. By contrast, oddly, a shower of passionate letters came to me from Utrecht, where according to Renée, Eva was on the watch, mistrustful and jealous. My suspicions petrified into an obstinate silence. But the power of her words, which knew how to polish and smooth the most livid memory, slowly left their mark on the stone:

"You belong to me – do not forget that for a single second – for with ardour, fever, and madness, I have made you mine. You must not forget me, because I will never forget…"

"I love you with passion and tenderness. You are my marvellous dream and my divine memory. Take into your hands my heart, ardently submitted to your beauty. – I close under my kisses your divine eyes of oriental shadows." Beneath the effects of such sweet pressure, I broke the silence and wrote to her a first time.

Throughout September Renée travelled with Eva. Cologne, Basel, Florence. As a matter of fact, she was always a great traveller. I still have postcards she wrote me from many countries and cities. Even from Egypt and Jerusalem. On that occasion, though, the tour was shorter and ended up in London in October. During the course of that voyage, Renée's letters bear witness to an especially upsetting time in her relationship with the Baroness. Despite my partial information, I will try to sketch the basic traits of the process. It seems Eva had serious problems with her husband. According to what Renée said, the baron had caught the two of them some time back in an excessively tender conversation by telephone – "that perfidious modern invention". Since by now I know a bit about Paris high society, I do not believe that the conflict was even remotely related to feelings of jealousy. Perhaps the problem was more because the chatter and gossip about his wife were growing unstoppably and now surpassed tolerable limits. There was even a brouhaha about the *mise-en-scène* of a more or less explicit text by the Baroness. And it was Renée, also, who had initiated her into literature. On the other hand, it seemed Eva had no fear of scandal, and I imagine that her passion for Renée, which at that time knew no bounds, did not make her in the least prudent. The fact is she was more than willing to face a separation, and Renée was terrified, for complex reasons that partly escape me, of that possibility.

According to her, my image and her love for me were transporting her further and further from Eva, and the breakup of the latter's marriage would no doubt have made their bond closer – too close: Eva had a domineering temperament and nothing would have kept her from dedicating all hours of the day and night to a Renée I now imagine trapped between a strange mirror effect and a dark feeling of blame: How could she extract herself from the power of a love that shared her own extreme determination to defy the world? What caprice of the heart insisted on denying that sentiment to precisely the one who would have been the most deserving of it? How could she be for Eva the exact same evasive, inaccessible being, that Vally had been for her? To inflict the same pain on Eva without feeling any blame would have been to absolve Vally on the rebound. And if Vally were in fact innocent of all the suffering Renée had experienced because of her, the blame once again went right back to Renée, for not having been able to inspire enough love in her: I believe she veered from one pole to the other without respite, unable to escape from this bitter condemnation of herself.

Early in the autumn, she had written to me from Utrecht:

"I am wounded, torn apart, by a terrible scene between Eva and me. She threatened to kill me and then kill herself. Then, tears and more tears full of desperation.

"I do not know what to do. A reconciliation is under consideration between her and her husband: it would be totally platonic, the spouses living under the same roof for the sake of the children and for fear of what people would say. I try to push Eva in that direction. Not that she listens to me much at the present time."

Bewildered by all of this, it took me a few weeks to respond, and shortly after I did so, I received an answer from London that took my breath away:

"Your letter arrived at a moment in which Eva is between life and death. She tried to kill herself for me... I do not know whether she will be alive when you get this letter... And it is my love for you that has killed her... I forgot her for you, I abandoned her for you... who have only written me two letters in two months... She always had a revolver nearby. One night, the temptation was too strong. And she used it. And I have chosen between the dying woman who has loved me so terribly much, and the living one who has only thought about me twice since I left..."

It is difficult for anyone to understand the exact state of my spirit, confronted with that bizarre mix of complaint and farewell. To believe that I could have been the cause of Eva's failed suicide would have been excessively presumptuous on my part. But to think that Renée would use that sad occurrence just to reproach my silence would be to attribute an excess of bad faith to her. Both the first and the second assumption had two sides: the one that flattered me was common to the two. The love that she affirmed and the silence she criticised bespoke a place in her soul that was precious to me. The other – the slant of blame attributed to me for the delirious action of someone I did not even know, or the possible tergiversation of deeds and motives alien to me – was easy for me to leave in the shadow. As far as her "choice" was concerned and the farewell it implied, soon enough I had the most overwhelming refutation in a shower of postcards and letters from Naples, Capri, Corfu, Athens, Smyrna, Jerusalem, Alexandria… Her letters displayed the same torrid tone as before the tragic incident in London. She wrote this to me from Basel in September:

"Oh, your nostalgic eyes of a captive princess! Your mysterious nocturnal hair and your lips of a temptress, herself tempted! I love you to the point of madness and I am willing to do anything for you. Your lover and friend."

Then, in the middle of January, from Nice, she announced her imminent visit and her trembling, unbridled impatience with these words:

"Finally the wondrous hour approaches. I will see you again. I will newly possess you…You will be mine, fatally, inexorably. A loving and terrible destiny binds us, for suffering and for joy."

4

Renée arrived in winter this time. The wisteria behind the glass meandered up the balustrade with branches still nude

243

and odourless. I remember that it was a benign winter. And even though no gift can placate the avidness of Desire, those short days vanishing like a waning moon were still able to nourish it with sumptuous provisions. In the springtime, when my balcony over the Bosphorus was in full bloom, all blue and fragrant, with that intense perfume the wisteria pomes offer when they open, she returned. And again, later, at summer's end. That was her longest stay. And for the last time, at the beginning of autumn. I was never to see her again.

I often remember that year of my life with nostalgia; each season was graced with Renée's presence, as if she wanted to leave her image on every changing hour, as if she wished to become a loving marker of the passage of time. That memory, in the present, is like one of those palms of fire that open against the night during the festival of Bairam, from the gardens of the Dolma Bachté palace: they suddenly rise from an invisible fount, spread out in a fan for an instant in all their splendour, to change in the following moment into a luminous shower over the Golden Crescent and then fall and melt into the darkness. No other meaning than its own brief beauty and the sacred brilliance left in eyes that know how to make themselves childlike.

But that vision cannot stand up to the much more complex testimonial of my pen. Earlier, I turned to the pages of my diary. This notebook bound in mother-of-pearl and gold that still keeps me company in my hours of solitude is a relic of my adolescent life. It has a little filigree lock, forced open by my own hands one day when I could not find the key anywhere and the diary was locked. I still have not been able to figure out how I lost it. But from that day I have had to take the most extreme precautions to keep it secret. It was written in French as a first protective measure, and only Xereff had enjoyed the privilege of reading it. In fact it was spilling over with the sort of dreams we both shared, that led her to take on that novelesque flight, and me to accept a marriage full of hope: the world of diplomacy seemed to open doors to a future different from that of my friends – cosmopolitan, exciting, new. But after my wedding I no longer opened the notebook: rereading it was painful, I am not sure why. I was incapable of writing anything in it, as if that which I felt and thought did not belong to me, and according to an unwritten pact, hidden from me, had been given over to a stranger along with my virgin body.

When Xereff left Istanbul, I felt the impulse to pour out all my pain in it. But the most intense pain is mute and the page obstinately remained blank. I took up writing again with Renée's first visit. The diary follows faithfully the intermittence of her visits, along with a few other moments when an impulse perhaps capriciously took hold of me to record happenings and feelings into the modest little casing of my word. Specifically, for example, when Renée spoke to me of Zenour and Nouryé, the famous real "Disenchanted" ones who followed Xereff's example and fled the country through Belgrade and Sofia a few years later.

30 January 1906

I must write to feel that all of this is real. As if to say: this existed and I swear to it. I just saw Paule, Pauline, Paulette, Renée. All together and one by one, one after the other. She arrived yesterday on the Orient Express and I went to meet her this morning at the Pera Palace. She leaves on Thursday. She will stay in Constantinople only three days. She received me in a spacious, warmed-up room, dressed only in a Japanese robe of white silk embroidered in purple and gold. It is glacially cold today and on the way, the wind cut like a fine sharp knife. As soon as she saw me come in, numb and shaking with cold, she came running to me, embraced me, and began to kiss my fingers, lips, and earlobes, frozen and without feeling. This time no timidity haunted her. With delicacy she made my blood recover its feeling and return to life. Then she had me sit by the fireplace and took off my shoes. She sat on a cushion on the floor and caressed my feet and ankles, kissing them a thousand times, then she wrapped me up in a soft, warm cashmere shawl.

In the meantime, having recovered a little, I looked at her. Her hair has grown since summer. Her skin is even whiter, almost livid, and her gaze, darker. At a given moment I feared her fragility, in such brusque contrast with her unexpected solicitude, as tender and strong as a young mother. She got up for a moment to stoke the fire, and then, when I saw her right before me, I noticed her little breasts beneath the silk and I had an impulse to feel their freshness of a wild rose, to grasp their little taut button between my teeth. Memory, so vividly intertwined with her presence, caused me to imagine the rest of her body under the folds of her gown. Desire dragged me beyond delirium. I clasped her body close to my own, so as not to lose myself, so as not to lose her. Her body, like a pink and white garden, warm with milk and wine. I found her and she found me in the most hidden folds, in that secret flower of pale, rosy gold, where my lips planted the seed of pleasure.

You are away again. You said you would come back soon. I have your poems with me. I like the one where you evoke "the sisterly kisses that follow the spasm".

Yes, I would like to go to Mytilene with you. I did not say so when you asked, but I would. I did not say so because I saw the excess in your eyes. As if you were dragging me with words into a dead-end street. Yes, I would like to set sail with you to the island, not to die there, but to live. And I know, as well, that it cannot go beyond the phase of a dream. One of those dreams that gild and lighten prisons, but that cannot substitute them without unleashing the cruellest of shipwrecks.

3 March

Renée has written me a letter full of fascination for the flight of Zanour and Nouryé, which fortunately has ended as well as Xereff's. She sends me a clipping from *Le Figaro* where the first part of the tale comes out. She seems overwhelmed with impatience to meet them. She asks whether she may use my name to introduce herself, for she is prepared to offer them economic aid in name of "the great feminine solidarity". She makes an inflamed panegyric to their heroism and says textually that she feels infinitely grateful for the fine courage it took them to liberate themselves. I think I am reading a sort of veiled reproach between the lines, addressed to my supposed cowardice. It is not that she says anything, but I know what she must be thinking and feeling. I have never told her up to what point I tortured myself when my sister left all alone, and how much I envied her determination, so bold to my mind. Now perhaps Renée will meet Xereff as well. And I am not sure why, but that frightens me.

20 March

Renée has met Xereff, Nouryé, and Zenour. She says they are charming. She compares Nouryé to a little Winged Messenger and Zenour to a Fragile Flower. I have the impression that Xereff impressed her even more vividly and intensely, for she says nothing. There is a sentence that worries me. She says she will not court them because she has my image in her heart… It is odd that a sentence intended to reassure me has brought about this unease.

15 April

Renée's arrival has been delayed until May. She has to correct the proofs of her next book, where the poems she dedicated to me will appear. My longing is feverish and turbid. Unhealthy. Suddenly they are together in a kind of Eden not accessible to me. And I, the only one to blame for having been excluded, do not even have the consolation of repentance.

23 May

Renée is here. She wanted to cover herself with a *charshaf* and we took a caïque to the sweet Waters of Asia. Together we saw the low hills blooming in red heather and the violet flower of the calyx sprouting amid the new grass. And we strolled, happy and trembling, under the giant plane trees. It is strange: in the last letters she wrote me, instead of using her characteristic paper with violets printed in a corner or a garland of them all around, she used paper with a Turkish anagram: a crescent moon engraved in gold. And she told me she wanted me to show her the whole city and its surroundings and the lovely, hilly cemeteries beyond the wall and the gateway of Ederne. She wants to know all the baths and to buy Turkish perfumes, traditional silk dresses, Circassian embroidery...

We came here afterward, all wet because we got caught in a springtime downpour. The strong odour of wisteria flowers invaded the room from the open balcony. We took our clothes off laughing and dried ourselves with a great linen cloth. We ended up all wrapped up, nude, and we saw how our bodies fit together softly, delicately: my breasts under hers, my head in the angle her neck forms with her shoulder, her lips on my eyes, her chin on my forehead. And if I pushed up a bit and she lowered herself, we inverted the fit and I was the higher one and could kiss the curls her damp hair formed on her forehead. And we could still make our breasts touch at the same level, and our mouths, our foreheads, our navels and our knees.

We made love, captured by a rare and sudden intoxication, like the rain.

25 May

Renée went to Mytilene today. I could see clearly that she wanted me to go with her. She did not dare to ask, for she knows it cannot be. She will return in four days, just passing through, but we will see each other at her hotel. We have not accomplished even a small part of our projects. She has promised me that she will return in the summer and spend more time here.

You are far away again. I will remember and miss those hours when we cradled, adored and devoured each other.

29 August

Renée has been in Constantinople a week and I have not yet felt the need to write. I suddenly feel that my pen is clumsy, unfaithful, incapable of leaving in these pages a trace worthy of what I have lived. But today, anxiety has made an appearance. Renée told me she wants to come and live in Constantinople. She said it in a moment of exaltation, it is true. I had just given her one of my loveliest oriental dresses: the one I wore for our first meeting, a year ago now. She tried it on and wanted me to take her right away to a photographer's studio in Pera to have her picture taken. She said that wearing that dress was a little like getting inside my skin. Then she started to repeat that she did not want to return to Paris, that she would stay with me, that she could live a few months in Constantinople and a few in her villa in Lesbos. I do not know whether she read the terror in my silence and in my eyes.

3 September

Eva came to reclaim Renée from Mytilene, where her yacht is anchored, and she took the first ship. Her attitude is odd. Just the day before yesterday, when she had not yet received the telegram, she insisted on her intention to come and live close to me. Again I felt the same fear, the terror that smothers you when faced with an undefined threat. And now, on the other hand, she left without hesitation and I miss her with a rare fury and virulence.

8 September

Renée has returned. She brought me grapes, figs, and pome-granates from Lesbos. Her skin is darker and her hair lighter, with a salty taste. She talks obsessively about coming to live in Constantinople, as if she wanted to wrench an assent out of me, which she knows is impossible. I have buried my anguish in her embrace. And from within the confines of pleasure, she sobbed.

18 November

Today has been a terribly sad day. I had not written in this notebook since summer's end, when Renée was here the last time. Now she has come back. The first day we saw each other, it was like a rapture, an abduction of passion. First, her: I had never seen her like that. She seemed crazed. I even felt a little violated, wounded, and that left me frozen. Then I grasped the anxiety that traversed her desire, and it pierced me like a thorn, deep into my body, as if it were my own anguish. The thought came to me that this was the first and last time we made love. At that point, I became crazed as well, and the madness shook my heart and body like a savage wind. Afterward, everything took on tones of a gray melancholy. Today, Renée insisted on visiting Eyüb cemetery; she wanted me to show her the place of my tomb. She said to me: "if I had come to live in Constantinople, I would have wanted to be buried near you." I could see that she was speaking of a remote idea, confined to a past already far away. Suddenly, I do not know why, I had the certainty that this was her farewell. I wanted to look into her eyes, hoping they would refute that impression. But they were inaccessible beneath the black veil of the *charshaf.*

A few days later Renée left. I never saw her again. I have divined the mark of that last day of autumn in one of her poems, which ends like this:

She smooths a fold in her dress, laughing…
And I evoke her naked body, matured by light
close to mine in some uneven cemetery
in the shade without terror of oriental cypresses.

And in the same poem, a few verses above, the imprint of our last nights:

The caresses have such cruel enthusiasm,
and shivers and laughs of desperation…
And later, sweetness falls like twilight.

From then on, our correspondence alone barely maintained a contact that was melting away. We never mentioned that tacit ending which she decided and I accepted. Her letters, however, took on a different tone and became less frequent, more laconic, full of vague confidences like a muffled chronicle of her discouragement and disenchantment. So, in July of 1907 she said to me: "There is no woman, other than the Baroness, in my existence of a tired woman – tired, so tired of everything and all of them." And later, the following February, when her bond with Eva had definitively dissolved, she confessed to me: "I have a lover – officially – but I do not love her." Some months later a brief message arrived in which I read, with sadness: "My strength has betrayed me, it is such a struggle to live!" Finally, in August, nearly three years after our first encounter, she sent me this last letter from London:

"Kerimée, my poor beloved one, forgive me. This letter – or rather, these few lines, all too brief – are my last message to you. By Saturday or Sunday I will have ended my lamentable life – with profound regret for having lived at all. I beg your pardon for having offended you – but forgive me as one forgives the moribund. For my mortal agony has already begun. Once again, I beg for your forgiveness."

I am still not sure whether these words were anything more than a dark fantasy. I confess that during those four years I had got used to all manner of allusions to death from Renée's lips and letters without blinking. But those lines had an irregular, lax slope that betrayed a true disorder and that strange insistence on asking me for pardon startled me. The guilt she seemed to accuse herself of was inexistent for me; furthermore I believed myself to be the one deserving reproach. And I was convinced that the outcome, which she had tacitly already initiated, was the only one possible, in the long run. That conviction helped me endure the pain of the earliest days and liberated my yearning and regret from all shadow of resentment. Memory had clothed itself in a golden, intensely rose-coloured light, like her lips and hair tangled up in love and the fuzz of silky gold on her aroused skin.

How can one understand a begging for forgiveness from someone who has made us an offering of excessive love, a gift that perhaps we were unable to deserve? By now, I believe those exculpatory words were not addressed to me, but rather that she was appearing before the rigorous tribunal of her

253

own self. It was not my measure of love that had disappointed her, but her own. To cease from loving me meant abdicating her Dream. But at the same time, and above all, abdicating me: to abandon at the hands of my fear that part of me that for her was the best of me, the part that made me rebellious and unfortunate because of my destiny as a woman. That was the offence she believed to have inflicted upon me: to have stopped believing in me and in the truth of my revolt.

Nothing of that sort passed through my imagination at that moment. But I lived through some anxious days until I found out that Renée was still alive. It was Xereff who informed me. And it was also through her that I learned, a year later, of Renée's death.

Kerimée's text, written on lovely parchment paper of a light salmon colour and in a literary French as impeccable as that of a former model student of the Sisters of Sion, ends here abruptly, at the end of a reverse of a sheet. The narrator cannot guess whether there was another page that has been lost or if this is the true ending Kerimée wished to give to her tale. If the former is the case, one must acknowledge the opportune gift that fate sometimes affords.

THE NOTEBOOKS OF SALOMON THE WISE – II

21 August 1923

Natalie B., the incomparable Flossie, has unfortunately just published a page in the *Mercure*, which I will cut out and file in any case, in which she gives in to the worst tendency of indulgence and weakness, using the minimal effort, as characterises our epoch. Lines that are neither prose nor verse, a confusion of imperfect sounds and nebulous ideas... The deplorable tyranny of free verse cannot be reproached enough; so in keeping, however, with the signs of the times: the dominion of sloth and incompetence... The author took care not to send me the text: she knows with what a string of elegant insults it would have been received.

I cannot help but miss, faced with this show of poetic (?) negligence, Pauline's Natalie, of the *Acts and Entr'acts*, in spite of the weaknesses that often betray her laziness, a vice seemingly inherent in the Amazon, notwithstanding her one-time taste for sport... In that long-ago work, the beneficial but alas ephemeral literary influence Pauline had over her is evident. By contrast, it seems Natalie made Pauline lose her taste for the only sport she ever practiced. At the beginning of their relationship, in the last year of the century, Pauline used to ice-skate at the Palais de Glace. Flossie went with her a couple of times until it became obvious how well she knew some of the other skaters...

17 January 1924

I reread the last story from *The Tendrils of the Vine* which Colette dedicated to Renée. Some time back I thought I had discovered there the probable origin of the malevolence my Liane professed toward the author, which went so far as to cloud her proven literary judgement. Colette's sharp and subtle evocation of a period spent in Montecarlo brings before our eyes, fascinated by her verbal talent, an entire series of beauties of the era, including my Eva, which the author forces to pass through "Claudine" forks without pity – but using velvet-covered claws, of course. I have searched there and found the evanescent shadow of Pauline. Her house in Nice, as I have reported elsewhere, welcomed with great hospitality the one who was no longer Madame Willy.

25 September 1924

Yesterday, taking advantage of the magnificent weather presented to us by the beginning of autumn, Liane came to get me and we went in her automobile to the "Mare aux canes…" There, we strolled around the pond while my Eva indulged in a magnificent evocation of her times past. It goes without saying that the name of Pauline sparkled on her lips for an instant from time to time. Emotion is a great enemy of the scholar. I was so touched, and still am when I think about it, that the precision of my retention melted like wax in a fire. On such occasions, I start to speak the way that makes Eva tease me, saying "faish" instead of "face" as if I had a hair on my tongue. The ascetic is sometimes like the ingenuous schoolboy: one, because he still goes, the other because he returns, at times not having arrived at the supposed end of the trajectory. Other centres of interest deflected me from certain areas of knowledge well before I could decant off the saturation of excess.

At this point, when certain falls are somewhat more than

improbable – and when Nature seems to want to compensate by making others extremely easy if one forgets one's cane or, in its absence, an umbrella – I conserve, toward those spaces that I have never known except most imperfectly, the virgin, curious gaze of a child, the trained circumspection of an old man. My emotion, however, was more that of the archaeologist that I am before an important, as yet unknown site, at the very point of beginning an excavation. But human mobility demands a quickness of reflexes that the immobile solidity of stones has never required. And in this case, something betrayed me. A friend of exactness, I will not try to reconstruct anything. All my powers of persuasion will be addressed to convincing Liane to tell the tale herself in her notebooks. Her current daily life has such little interest if we compare it to her incomparable past!

Boulogne sur Seine, 5 June 1925

Yesterday Pierre Louÿs died. Three years ago I went to question him about Pauline. I knew from Flossie that during the first year of the century, the two of them had presented their respects to the creator of *Bilitis* and had offered him a Lalique vase of orchids which, alas!, disappeared, devoured by the house cat. Pierre Louÿs was also one of the ambassadors to whom Natalie had recourse when Pauline avoided her so determinedly around 1904... It is strange how the most astute of beings can sometimes deceive themselves about the most elementary things: I had occasion to copy (folio annex 158) the letter in which Pauline reproached Flossie, filled with indignation, for having offered the spectacle of what she called "our sad, mutilated love" to a man.

257

Perhaps I am the one who is mistaken to undervalue the Amazon's perspicacity: to arouse Pauline's indignation was a way like any other – and clearly effective, as it turned out – to coax her out of her persistent muteness. Other efforts, though more appreciated, did not render such good results. At least for the party concerned. The flirting of souls (just of souls?) that resulted from the intercession of Eva P. – Natalie's childhood friend – secured for the unsuccessful reconciler a splendid poem, "To the Sunset Goddess": "Goddess of the sunset, the ruins, the night…!"

No less splendid, if more critical and plaintive, is the poem dedicated to the other complaisant messenger, Lucie Delarue-Mardrus, whom I identified some time ago as the addressee of "I Weep over You". It is quite strange, none the less, that Pauline should weep in those magnificent alexandrines, retrospectively, over the marriage of the lovely Norman when it had taken place years back, long before they even knew each other! I learned from the irreplaceable Charles B. that this writer supplied the inspiration for the brunette Doriane in *A Woman Appeared to Me*, one of the characters who alleviates the wounds of the abandoned protagonist… And that it was during her subsequent idyll with Flossie that the latter asked her to act as ambassador to Pauline. One can never be sufficiently surprised. Liane let me know that she had refused to play that same role, after dissuading Flossie with obvious arguments… all of which seemed to go straight over the head (?) of the one concerned.

To return to Pierre Louÿs: I did not record in writing after our interview an impression that seemed fleeting to me at first, but that has become firm with time: the divine Pauline, the first woman after Sappho to openly sing of feminine love, did not inspire the least sympathy in the author of *Bilitis*. It seems that circumstances – and perhaps an intimate and irreducible viscerality – had made him choose, with no turning back, between her and Flossie. He did not hesitate in his choice. Fortunately, I have not found myself in the same predicament: Pauline is a link, perhaps the principal one, between Flossie and me. This impregnates and colours my entire vision of her. I cannot avoid, whenever I observe her life – a pleasure she dispenses to me all too avariciously – putting myself in Pauline's skin, or rather installing the latter's verses between my eyes and the moving image, brilliant as mercury, that is always slipping away. My Flossie – how do I dare use a possessive, not at all presumptuous in any case, for the most unpossessible being anyone could imagine? – *my* Flossie is, after all, Pauline's Flossie, with the added advantage of my having been able to conserve the sangfroid and parsimony appropriate to the tenacious scholar.

This is not the case with Liane, my Eva, who with her notebooks – in which Pauline unfortunately has played such a small part so far…! – holds a most lively interest, unmediated by any other image or word. Her prose has an abundance of what I would call "style vitamins". Great masters of the pen lack this ingredient, yet the "Blue Notebooks" derive all their charm from it.

30 November 1925

Love is the passion of those who have nothing to do –
Theophrastus

I have often been tempted – with Pauline's pardon – to agree with the old Aristotelian who extracts his conclusions, like a good naturalist, from close, attentive, and perhaps dispassionate observation of living beings and things. I might, however, with less expedience, temper this agreement, eschewing the touch of scorn that betrays a secret envy in him. As a person who is wholly occupied with things very different from love, I can understand the witticism. But even though many consider it a fallacy, I still try to ensure that my personal relationship with the objects of my research does not affect my conclusions. Love is essentially an illusion that leads us to exalt beyond reason its object. This illusion is explained by the often unconscious finality of love, which is not only the perpetuation but also the improvement of the species (from which comes the preference handsome men and beautiful women are objects of). Upon this crude truth, literature and art project their most seductive veils. We owe so many marvels to this happy alliance of gross passion with refinement and the prestige of the imagination that it would be absurd to speak ill of it, and absurd too, to wish the day would arrive when the senses would seek their own satisfactions without cooperating with the spirit.

I admit that this theory has difficulties in justifying what moralists term *amore contra naturam*. I would call them, rather, loves above nature: as long as we are not confronted with a crude case of pure inversion – that which is commonly suggested by the names of those towns in the plains swallowed up by the Dead Sea, and which we also occasionally find in animals – we must rise up to the high spheres of Plato's Academy or its feminine equivalents. And here we ought to evoke the case par excellence of Sappho, who served as model to Pauline. In antiquity, Martial, Juvenal, and Seneca were already speaking horrors of women with a masculine disposition. Concretely they offer the name of a certain

Philaenis, doubtlessly a Judaizing Phoenician who became famous for a strange speciality: she did with young men what Zeus did with Ganymede. There is also an indirect allusion to this peculiar invert in the epistle of Paul of Tarsus to the Romans – a fact that to my understanding testifies conclusively to the authenticity of that text, so problematic from the philological point of view. Paradoxically, the Latin authors mentioned, to whom one should at least add Lucian and Ovid, call this type of abominated women lesbians, all the while defending Sappho of Lesbos against any sort of infamous accusation and putting in her mouth claims of the purity of her love for Atthis, Mnasidika, Timas, etc. This kind of love, the tenderness that rises above nature, as I have already suggested, with disdain and disgust for gross temptations is obviously what we find in Pauline. Even if for some reason she gives in, it is only to lament it right away and free herself from it:

> *From my crude lip I felt the sudden regret…*
> *My soul dreamed of tenderly leaving*
> *on your body where the light lingered at length*
> *the breath of a mystic kiss, vibrant and trembling.*

These divine verses contain Pauline's two main aspects: the Terrestrial Venus and the Celestial Venus. Perhaps it is absurd to claim that the last reigned exclusively – Liane reminded me one day, faced with my rejection of the filth of some aspects of their lives, that one needs manure to feed and cultivate a lily. But it would seem no less absurd to exaggerate, in accordance with the most explicit testimonies, the importance of this ingredient in the marriage of souls.

261

MONSIEUR LE MARQUIS

The automobile of a strident, raving red stopped in front of the Café de la Paix when the opera had just ended. From among the people still mingling together for the banal but imperious magnetism of commentaries and gossip, understood or misunderstood, a shadow of rigorous etiquette slipped inside while the chauffeur ceremoniously held open the little door.

"Monsieur le Marquis…"

And the voice, vaguely virile, with a trembling in the throat, politely specified:

"Go along the Champs Elysées, toward l'Étoile. And then, down Bois avenue."

The car slid down the boulevard of Paix to Vendôme square, ready to follow the strange order without a hint of doubt or hesitation. Inside the vehicle, the mature face of a strong-willed man, seemingly petrified into an expression of wisdom – and irony – balanced between hard and soft, where the aquiline nose and gaze weighed against a round, smooth-shaven outline, looked out stubbornly into the August night fading among faraway stars and tiny intermittent lights. Monsieur le Marquis lit a havana parsimoniously. The odour and smoke enveloped him intensely and thickly, like a layer of padding inside a red lacquered box. He was comfortable in that solitude, which the presence of the chauffeur only underscored. Now he could face that vexation that had caused him to flee and at the same time gave rise to the appointment toward which he was now rushing – with his feet constrained by the triple layer of stockings meant to make them fit into the enormous shoes that constituted his everyday pedestal.

Monsieur le Marquis had seen Salomon R. in the vestibule. The posthumous sweetheart of Renée Vivien pursued with the tenacity of a schoolboy enamoured for the first time any trace the dead poet might have left behind in the most hidden corners, even resigned to finding insides and entrails of his idol without the inevitable odour of their contact with the air discouraging him a jot from his thunderstruck acolyte's genuflection. Monsieur le Marquis had formed the alarming impression that the erudite Israelite wanted to address him, and with an innate quickness of reflexes he had managed to avoid the encounter: the inexpressive, neutral visage with which he responded to the friendly gesture addressed to him from afar by the supposed investigator must have sown doubt in the illustrious person's mind, who would have been suddenly perplexed, as if faced with some statue of dubious authenticity. Monsieur le Marquis disappeared among the crowd, not allowing the pertinent questions to be asked.

A week earlier he had seen Liane, Princess G., an old acquaintance from before the war, when she was one of the three queens who vied for the sceptre of Great Mad Paris – the only one who with time had been able to exchange one royalty for another, even though it was a step down, contrary to all norms and laws of age. Liane, who exchanged letters with the eminent academic and was, at his request, noting down reminiscences of her shiniest epoch destined for the year two thousand, had mentioned his interest in her own memories of Renée. "One of these days, Uncle Max, we could organize a get-together, right here..." the Princess had offered, since she knew that his relations with Salomon R. had not gone beyond the initial stage of having simply been introduced, such an uncomfortable stage for timid souls. She called him that with a familiarity – so much more appropriate for his ripe old age of sixty than the more traditional Missy – and a confidence worthy of old accomplices.

It must be stated, though, that their complicity had never gone beyond an invisible dividing line firmly established by tacit, mutual accord. The marriage of the old "horizontal", of unusual distinction and culture, to a young Romanian prince, delicate, sensitive, a friend of beauty, and of high birth but empty purse – exactly the opposite of Liane, a fact that had provoked comments of every sort –, had added a special touch to that light link, saturated with a not altogether apparent hierarchy which had been restructured most artfully. She had called him "Uncle Max" for some years now, as did so many worldly and demi-monde folks; but also, at times, "father-in-law". This other denomination, which accentuated the kinship even more, incorporating the adoptive filiation of her husband as a mitigating element, had appeared for the first time in the dedication of a memorable portrait, in which Missy sported the clothing and imitated the pose of their illustrious common ancestor, Napoleon the Great. "For my daughter Liane, from her father-in-law," was written on the back.

This flawless cordiality, spiced with the touch of theatricality with which she so liked to flavour her life, to the point of sometimes making it the main ingredient, had unexpectedly been affected by the inopportune discrepancy between his cigars and the migraines Liane suffered obsessively since her marriage. And surely, as well, by the malevolent intervention of some third parties who entertained themselves by provoking a series of well-understood innuendos about them. For a long while they stopped seeing each other, with reason but without reasons or explanations, softly, almost imperceptibly.

Then Liane had suddenly written to him as if nothing had happened. And so, they had reinstated their contact to the obvious pleasure of both sides. Who knows whether Salomon R's interest had had something to do with that sudden initiative...! The two things happened very close together, and if there was no cause-effect relationship, they had at least coincided suspiciously. And so vexation had reared its head. For the moment it had been danced around, but without knowing how to quiet the request that had caused it. Liane had not insisted, and even though she was aware the subject continued to be present in the background, Missy would almost have forgotten the matter had it not been for the chance encounter with the scholar leaving *Boris Godunov*.

It was odd that the man, who said himself that he led an ursine life, had decided to abandon his lair and his territory, covered with printed papers and notable antiquities, and venture across the Seine for a social ephemeris. Surely it had to do with his wife's Russian origin, a renowned doctor, she had heard, but even less visible in society than he was. The bear was there, in any case, and in the role not of hunted, but of virtual hunter. It was not Renée Vivien and the memories she had of her – quite skimpy, most of them faded by time, often second-hand or filtered through the sieve of words that were livelier than the events they portrayed – that produced such a sense of unease in Missy: it was the other memories, her own, from an epoch in her life whose beginnings and ends were practically framed by Pauline's presence in a diffuse but constant background. Like an inessential but significant milestone in the foggy distance from which she viewed those years which only the name of Colette seemed to illuminate.

She hadn't wanted to think about it much. Events had taken place one after the other without pause, and so, her memory was blind: fragments were evoked without a sense of the whole. Salomon R's request pushed her down the paths of history, almost to the point of archaeological reconstruction, and she at first resisted the push. But at that very moment she was crossing Paris in pursuit of an empty stage. Perhaps to show that it no longer existed, to prove its death beyond all reasonable doubt. Perhaps to conclude and give testimony, thus, to the very death of love.

She had always known intuitively that Colette did not and would never belong to her. Paradoxically, that was the guarantee of their bond. Perhaps she also knew that some day the darnel grass that had been pulled out for now would resprout: the desire to be taken by passion like hunted booty, with a voracious, pillaging ferocity. And then the relation would end.

Like a worried mother, she had watched over each symptom, trying to save the presumed patient from her latent wish to die. Over and over she had lovingly accomplished a mission that filled her with a boundless pride: to see her come in from the world entrapped by anxiety, by that exasperated and demanding desire characteristic of a being dispossessed of itself and at the mercy of obscure hostile forces; to possess her for an instant, just enough time to prise her from the claws of an invisible bird of prey; before returning her to herself and to the world, and seeing her go off again, soothed and strengthened, with her eyes brightened by the best image any mirror could have ever shown her, trembling in happy gratefulness. That was her power; and thus, her love. Yet, in spite of it all, her zeal had not been able to save her. The sick patient had succumbed.

It was only an apparent, temporary death. She had survived like a cat against every forecast, and without Missy's help. Colette had recovered without her protection. The surprising outcome even seemed to rescue her, if with an inelegant vengeance, from twelve years of humiliation under the yoke and boot of the tyrant. In this case it was a young whippersnapper, her own stepson, who took Colette in with stingless love. Surely he wouldn't possess her either. But neither would he be possessed, perhaps. Afterwards, Missy realised how necessary it was for her to be able to watch constantly, solicitously, generously, always successfully, over her girl with the eyes of a fox never quite tamed. She perceived it when Colette began the defence of her anguish with tooth and nail, stubbornly clinging to her rights to abdicate from herself, like an unruly child who rejects the blanket intended to protect it from the cold, exposing itself, lightly dressed, to the claws of an intemperate autumn.

At that point, her embraces were powerless to bring the consoling peace of her former liberty, like an inheritance without mourning. It was only then that she wished to possess her, at the precise moment when she saw a fearful Obstacle opposing the free dance of the Vagabond. As if to protect her from herself once again, this time permanently, from the part atavistically consecrated to ensuring the female's servitude to the male: the part that calls for the right to suffer, the freedom to offer one's own liberty in sacrifice to a god without measure. To extract her again from the very same place from which she had saved her with her love all those years ago.

Suddenly she felt thrust into her breast, as if her own, all the pain she would not be able to draw away from Colette. Just as she had so often felt in her blood and in her sex, as if her own, the spasm of pleasure she offered readily, her fingers trembling with solicitude. A dark gasp responded to that pain, as it had formerly responded to the pleasure, imperceptible to others but gnawing on her bones; a pain that proceeded to take root in what seemed to be her most recondite feminine nature, beating frantically against the thick layer of rubber that so tightly girded her too opulent bosom. The latter, like a suit of armour, strangely representative of that which she had established between the world and the hidden "she" within the apparent "he", constituted an effective defence against outside eyes and a useful fiction before her own during most of the hours of the day, like a habit does for a monk or protocol for royalty. But Missy knew how night and the amorous gaze of a woman returned her immediately to her radical nudity.

All those sensations, like fragments of mutilated columns deep in a still lake, seemed to emerge slowly, not only due to the decisive impulse of an archaeologist in waiting, who at that moment would be beatifically experiencing Mussogorski, the madness of the czar and the atavistic suffering of the Russian people, but also in response to recent news of Colette's divorce. The spontaneous end of that sorry story, against whose beginnings she had fought in vain, underlined, retrospectively, her impotence as a visionary without credentials, a poor Cassandra consigned to witnessing the havoc she predicted – even before one hundred years, its end – without anyone lending her any credibility. What appeared before everyone's eyes were her confessed fears and her inconfessable desires, and a series of strictly individual motives that no one interpreted as generosity. The interested party had spread it that way, thus forgetting the nature of her love, which she herself had previously captured in words: "Look, Missy, you've given me the flowers disarmed…!" Colette had exclaimed before a bouquet of eglantines from which Missy had removed the thorns with the soft, trembling fingers of a timid adolescent and the steady provident gaze of a good fairy. That misunderstanding of her motives, suspiciously opportune for Colette's good conscience, had been like a wall of ice between them for two years. All relations between them had broken. Afterward, little by little, had come the thaw.

The voice of the chauffeur made itself heard again with an urgent demand:

"Monsieur le Marquis…"

They had come into view of the Bois de Boulogne.

"Turn down the side carriageway to Rue Villejust. Then stop the car at the corner."

The avenue, one of the widest and most majestic of all Paris, dated from the epoch of Napoleon III, Missy's "uncle", and when she was born it bore the name of the Empress Eugénie. With the Republic, it had lost its imperial denomination to the more modest, soberly elegant, functional one which everyone still used thus disregarding the new onomastic tendencies imposed since the Great War, so recent still, that had filled Paris with names of majors and generals, more or less providential and heroic. The great trees, planted nearly three quarters of a century ago, had seen both the parades of horse-drawn carriages to Porte Dauphine and their progressive substitution by triumphant automobiles. Missy recalled the old pageantry, gilded in the present by a tenuous melancholy with light wings; she remembered also the landau pulled along by two white mares, her very own "Garlic" and "Vanilla", which refused to be swallowed by oblivion.

The car stopped just steps away from the house where Renée had died. The adjacent building in which Colette had lived had been demolished long ago. The two houses were linked by an interior garden at the end of their respective inner yards.

That was once upon a time a few years after the turn of the century. Around 1906... Missy met Renée through Colette, but unlike her, she took a great liking to the girl with the systematic smile, wily and stinging at times, who hid her sadness with the same modesty with which Missy hid her gender. Both performed under the same rigorous disguise of a dissident in her own country or a spy in enemy territory. A manifest sadness proclaimed every day to all the winds, risks the banality of being confused with the external signs it uses to show itself, or of being identified with the non-essential motives that have apparently unleashed it. With all those elements removed, its melancholy purity remains rooted in mystery. For Renée, this was the space of poetry. Missy's case was a similar one: contrary to what could be apprehended from superficial observation, her clothing, habits, the masculine attitude and pose which she so carefully and efficiently adopted and imposed on her surroundings, only accentuated her profound, unfathomable, secret femininity. Hers was a mystery of joy and pain hopelessly searching for signposts not in words, but in the bottomless mirror of love.

Missy had intuited this secret similitude, but without really understanding the terms, and had attributed the spontaneous cordiality to other, more epidermic affinities which were perhaps just the visible derivations. Their common passion for violets, for example, converted into a transparent, diffuse symbol among those in the know that Renée carried to extrapolation. Missy recalled how scandalised the latter had been to learn that Marie Antoinette couldn't stand those flowers, nor their perfume. Distantly related to the illustrious beheaded one – her blood happened to have been mixed with blue globules of incredibly diverse origin, often due to the most fortified and elevated bastardies – Missy had confided to Renée the secret, erotic habits of the queen by way of Lesbos, which Parisians had proclaimed to the four winds in no time at all in order to add insult to injury. "That can't be, it can't be so," Renée exclaimed in tones of stubborn candour, "One of the two things has to be false, surely!"

The flower's symbolism spread to its colour, and the few letters Missy still had in her possession were written in violet ink. For her, Sappho hoisted the epithet "weaver of violets" as obstinately as each and every god waves his standard at all hours in Homer's Olympia, and nothing could dissuade her from a conviction that was for her written in stone. Because reality seemed intent on contradicting her, since, at least around 1900, the plant in question was unknown in Lesbos, she did everything possible to adjust that sorry fact. Defying the vigilance of the strict Turkish customs officials, she herself introduced a violet bush into the island tucked away inside a clump of roots and earth deeply hidden in her bosom. Later on she would be able to offer authentic violets from Mytilene, dried inside the pages of a book of verse, to Missy or some other nearby member of the initiated.

Colette detested the whole floral epic, which, like so many other of Renée's usual attitudes, she could only qualify as puerile. She herself was a little forest faun, voracious and eager for strawberries gathered from the earth, who licked her fingers after sucking the cream off the milk, and did not understand the finicky, fragile kid who goes to the utmost lengths to keep from tasting a single thing… She, who drank in the sun with her eyes and flesh like a little, satisfied salamander, made a great fuss over the strange grimaces of the blind kid who wants to play in the darkness, groping about without recourse to light. So she distanced herself and called her puerile, she who at the same time was whispering in Missy's ear: "Know what? I'm your baby, the one you've never had and never will have!"

Colette had wanted a maternal Missy, with that myopia of a momentary amphibian who only knows how to transfer its own properties to the borrowed milieu. And Missy had felt maternal, thinking that perhaps the word captured something of the mysterious substance that slipped through her fingers every time she thought of the feminine singular in the first person. That very same feminine that was curiously situated so far outside and yet so deeply inside of herself, so much so that she often forgot its very existence: outside, well-defined and concrete, not only because of her civil identity but especially due to a public who censured her, scandalized, or applauded her, entertained; inside, occupying that vague space with no signs or previous clues, without an alphabet or language of its own, that seemed to beg for alms and trembled gratefully before the slightest indication. "I like your cute little feet, so feminine!" Colette would say to her. And suddenly, femininity seemed to rise from the soles of her feet like unexpected sap. It was odd that only women had the capacity to make her feel like a woman. And not only through love.

Not long ago, precisely at Liane's house in Roscoff, an acquaintance who the princess had just introduced her to made the spontaneous gesture of treating her with warm feminine complicity. "My husband, when he was young, was madly in love with you…," she commented jovially. "And not only him: he says that all his brothers' classmates at Stanislas quarrelled over who would get to see you when you went to visit them!" It didn't often happen on first meeting that anyone would allow themselves not to be intimidated or disconcerted by her appearance, by now almost naturally virile; and she felt immediate gratification, obviously not at all related to the evocation of her charms from before the Flood or their supposed effect upon love-struck adolescents.

Perhaps this is where femininity resided, in that immediate recognition characteristic of a secret society or sister-hood that, more than on distinctive emblems, is based on details imperceptible to outsiders and often indescribable to members themselves, but of proven efficacy. For men, the opposing brother-hood, the situation was quite different, and defined itself in essentially negative terms. Either they excluded her directly, or on those occasions where she achieved acceptance, something unspecific told her insidiously that she was not a man.

She never felt like a woman amongst men. Even less on the very few occasions that she had had direct, corporeal relations. Everyone in Paris knew every detail of the episode of her unconsummated matrimony. But very few knew of the two real episodes that had situated her body to body in the same bed with vigorous representatives of the other official sex. The first had been orchestrated by a cousin of hers, madly in love, he said, who pursued her relentlessly, calling on every possible feeling, past and future. His objective appeared to be: "At least once!", as if that concession were the equivalent, on the part of someone as inaccessible as Missy, of a declaration of eternal love. Since his demand was not fulfilled, he resorted to expeditious methods, wielding the threat of suicide. Missy was impressionable and she gave in. It was all brief and harmless like a revolver shot that misses its target of flesh and embeds itself in a bit of bare wall, forgotten and without context. The presumed suicide arm, though, was strangely lightened with its chamber emptied as if the essence of that love were concentrated in a single bullet that could have been shot off in one direction or the other, without distinction.

The second case, at a stage when Missy sported all the attractions habitually attributed to mature men, was that of a charming young man of noble family, who called her "father!" whenever he got excited and formally proposed matrimony. Distrustful and cautious as a scalded cat after her first marriage, she decided to test it out. The experience lasted a little longer this time, as Missy condescended to lengthen the term to a week. What defined the two experiences for Missy was the feeling of her whole self being turned into a void for an instant, as if the space of mystery illuminated by even the most fleeting love or complicity of a woman, were emptied out at once, with the precision of a lighted cigarette meticulously destroying each embroidered flower on a valuable invisible tapestry, leaving nothing in its place.

When Colette left her, those flowers that occasionally came into her perception, tinted with thick fog, took on the scandalous colour of live blood. Then femininity became identified with a wound. More than that: with mutilation. But not with the sensation of privation or absence that the term usually evokes; rather with an excess of suffering concentrated in the very place that had earlier been occupied by the harvested part. And so the night was illuminated suddenly with a full moon of sorrow.

Renée had died a few months previously. And for the first time Missy deeply understood her sadness and her poetry, which was a sadness with the flesh, blood and skin of words. As if she had drawn to herself all the pain in the world and it had become her most essential identity, which she could not abandon without betraying either herself or a kind of unwritten pact, beyond memory. As if that which for Missy was a concrete, finite moment, unrepeatable in its intensity, was for Renée daily living, permanent and without truce.

It was also the first time that Missy understood the hidden sense of an episode that had left a touch of terror in her memory, but at the time had remained opaque.

It must have been in the autumn of 1907 or 1908. Not long after the scandal of the Moulin Rouge. Colette was radiant to let her know that Robert H., a neighbour of hers and Renée's, had decided to organize a costume party at the Théâtre des Arts, with the possibility of representing paintings and pantomimes.

Colette knew how crazy Missy was for everything to do with the theatre and performance. Not in vain had she acted with her as the masculine partenaire in private clubs and, from time to time, staged little mute works by the marquise herself. The death-defying triple jump that had catapulted them so unfortunately on to the stage of the Moulin Rouge – and that unleashed the noisiest ire of Tout-Paris at the sight of the first passionate kiss between the actress and supposed actor – had killed all possibility of repeating that singular pleasure. From then on, Missy had to resign herself to the annual Carnival in Nice, along with carnivalesque soirées and various masquerades, which were fortunately frequent in Paris during the entire season when it was populated by people of note. She had also accompanied Colette on music-hall tournées, but limiting herself to the role of obliging offstage escort. It was precisely on one of those tours, in the Riviera, that they had learned of Pauline's death.

But that was a few years later, whilst during that autumn of 1907 – or was it 1908? – Renée, with a vitality beyond reserve, enthused and tried to recruit the two of them into an exceptional performance. She had recently seen the painting by Delaroche that had caused such furore in the autumn show of 1847 at the Louvre, depicting the execution of Jane Grey. That adolescent queen – almost a child – who paid with her life for an involuntary reign of just ten days, victim of the most diverse intrigues and the masculine ambitions of a convulsed sixteenth-century England, represented for Renée the paradigm of hunted and immolated femininity: moral superiority, beauty, intelligence and subtlety, demolished by the victorious blows of mediocrity and stupidity. "The victors of history have always been the mediocre ones, the cheats, the unscrupulous... the barbarians," she would often avow. Therefore, women, the vanquished by antonomasia, must be linked to exactly the opposite virtues, which unfailingly attracted defeat.

Confronted with the objections one might make, beginning with the fact that it was a woman who ordered Lady Jane's execution, Renée would hardly have batted an eyelid: "There are women who do not deserve that name...," she would have replied without hesitation. For her, femininity seemed to be that which made women objects of punishment without blame, under an essentially culpable law. Any women who were counted among the ranks of the victors necessarily had to have abdicated from their most genuine selves; they had to have lost their essential innocence.

Obviously, Renée wanted to play the role of Jane. The project of that strange pantomime prospered, perhaps because it knew how to sink its roots, unexpectedly, into that secret space that even the most harmonious of beings reserve for their most sinister fantasies. Exultant, Renée prepared herself with an extreme unction. When the hour came, she advanced majestically toward martyrdom, her eyes transfixed in a glorious trance. And it was Lady Jane herself who came forth, charged by a luminous and tragic destiny, the supreme, synthetically intense accusation of all secular injustices perpetrated against the female sex, symbolically embodied in that gesture of heroic assumption.

Missy recalled a long, misty-eyed look of gratitude. Before placing her head proudly on the block, she dedicated to the world an indefinable expression of extreme vulnerability and lucid scorn. Then she rolled to the floor, extenuated, and with bated breath, at the very moment when Missy let the axe fall.

THE NOTEBOOKS OF SALOMON THE WISE – III

July 1926

Liane, my incomparable Eva, has consulted me about some lines of the *Inferno*, which, in the lamentable distress she's been brought to by the peccadilloes of her prince – that dear spoiled brat – she herself relates to jealousy. A jealousy that, in her case – I dare to suppose – wounds with a double-edged sword: it was not difficult to guess, through the translucent veil of an exquisite discretion, her tender solicitude toward little Manon, who has striven to repay the favour, in spades, as they say. The "Blue Notebooks" can only be fortified by an episode that will enhance them in variety and documentary value regarding the daily existence of too-idle beings. I have tried my best to subtly suggest to Liane this possible point of view on such a spiny question. She must be distracted as much as possible from the temptation to represent herself in the role of an Ariadne abandoned by Theseus at Naxos.

To get back to the reason for her consultation: Dante apart, it is true that the sentiment of jealousy is the worst punishment with which love can torment lovers, and passion can seldom escape it; Pauline is a paradigmatic example. But Liane's interpretation of the famous line is completely inadmissible, if you consider the context. The currently most accepted translation is: "Love, which absolves no lover from loving". And it goes on: "seized me for the pleasing of him so strongly that, as thou seest, it does not even now abandon me. Love brought us to one death".

However, I also find the ordinary interpretations of the first line absurd, which, if translated with good faith, should

278

read: "Love that does not pardon anyone who is loved". Most Italian commentators understand this ingenuity, defying the most elementary proof, as being that love must always be returned! Impossible to be more naive! I must say, at the risk of scandalizing the ears of devotees of the great Florentine, that Dante, tyrannized by the demands of rhyme and in possession of a yet imperfect language, often writes things that are imprecise and vague. I follow Voltaire's opinion on this point. We must add to that the fact that we do not have the manuscript, only copies of copies, so there must be endless errors of transcription.

What does the verse mean for me, ultimately? The general idea is quite monastic: the power of love and its ravages swoop down not only on the lover – that is, the seducer, the active element and therefore the "guilty" one – but also on the "innocent" one, seduced and passive. And in the case of Francesca de Rímini, both of them – she, who believes she is the instigator, and he, the beloved – go to the same death. The distinction is not one of gender, but of activity versus passivity. It is precisely in this way that the traditional roles are inverted: he even weeps as she speaks.

I am surprised that there is no reflection of this canto in Pauline's work, where Dante's footstep is explicitly present, and where love and death come together in inimitable verses. She herself is an example of a seduced being against whom love appears to exercise its wrath. Exclusively so: I see Flossie still very far away from even the most modest *Inferno*.

21 July 1926

Yesterday I returned to Paris after a week of work and excursions in Nîmes and its environs. I had the honour of initiating into Pauline's cult the current queen of the Félibrige in Avignon, who had no previous knowledge of her. She is a lovely, charming native and former friend of Mistral, called Jeanne de Flandrésy. I very much enjoyed seeing her admiration grow as I recited "Vanquished" down to the final lines:

Isis, let me find in the depths, the bare plains
where obscure poets who know of their affront
pass by singing their unknown rhymes
in the eternal darkness that weighs on their brow.

In return, Miss Flandrésy kindly offered me her hand and arm to steady the vacillating steps of an old man along the hillsides and when the grass was slippery. In some places one feels remote from all civilization, but the echoes of Frederic Mistral's *Mirèio* can be heard everywhere. The picturesque, the archaeological and – of course – poetry all combine there in harmony.

September 1926

The first Friday of the season at the salon on Rue Jacob: the hostess has returned! I remember that some time ago I reproached Flossie for the carmine on her lips, appealing to the unfading vivacity of her natural colouring. With an elfin expression she insinuated that the carmine had not in fact come from a lipstick tube... and that there had been some effusive displays of tenderness between her and Liane. Yesterday, the artificial red raddled her mouth again... yet it was obvious Liane had nothing to do with it: my Eva languishes, at times getting irritated at the poisoned echoes her divorce proceedings arouse in the press. She does not seem at all predisposed toward consoling effusions... Romaine B., on the other hand, the notable American painter who has been the habitual companion of Natalie these last few years, has the good sense to save all experiments having to do with brushes and pigmentation for her paintings...!

By the way, the honour is mine of having introduced those two ladies destined to please each other. Romaine had known Pauline only very slightly, in passing, during the last years of her life. Even so she seems better prepared to endure the versatile and curious humour – labile, I would even venture, borrowing a more picturesque but accurate word – of the Amazon.

5 December 1926

No matter how hard I try, I have not been able to discover who is hidden beneath the character of San Giovanni in *A Woman Appeared to Me*. This roman-à-clef – as all novels are at heart, no matter how difficult the code might be to decipher – does not strike me as a good story, although it is a supreme source for Pauline's biography. It is a pity that the divine being, motivated no doubt by a false sense of modesty, refused to write memoirs, a genre which is, to me, much more interesting. All the same, I cannot deny the pleasure I have derived in unveiling – the veils ceding painfully slowly, one by one – part of the mystery. As far as the above-mentioned character is concerned, the one that so stubbornly resists my interpretation, Charles B. insists that it is imaginary – a sort of alter ego of Pauline herself, with the name obviously taken from the work of Leonardo which appears on the frontispiece. Yet, in spite of that, I know he has the letters.

Fragments, and in some cases entire letters, that were simply transcribed into the novel. Charles B. told me all this when, at Natalie's suggestion, I asked him directly, but he refused to tell me where they came from, let alone the identity of the woman to whom they are addressed: a mysterious Suzanne. I hinted at buying them, but he would not hear of it. He would not even consent to allowing me to copy them, as the incomparable Flossie did. Instead, he refers me back to the novel. I have not even been able to take a peek at a heading or date to testify to their authenticity. I consider Charles B. absolutely incapable of any sort of hoax, but there is a strange reserve in his attitude, if we take into account how helpful he has been on other occasions.

I can understand that he does not want to write a biography of Pauline, as he has been asked to do repeatedly: our times are completely unworthy of it. Furthermore, he remains quite sceptical about the next century having anything better to offer us mortals. I can even understand that he does not wish to facilitate the work of future scholars on the marvellous poetess. But that he should stubbornly obstruct it by withholding valuable information he has in his hands is absolutely inconceivable to me.

Even if the letters did not exist, I cannot bring myself to believe that San Giovanni is an invented character. It would be the only case in the novel. In the 1905 edition, it is true that the personage is a little vague and immaterial, but in the 1904 one, it is very clear that it is not just a symbol: there is a concrete, even physical, presence. In spite of the name, it is a feminine character, but with the *hands of an androgyne*. Does that expression refer simply to large hands, or to some other, more imprecise peculiarity? Besides that, San Giovanni is a poet. If not, one's imagination might drift toward a person like Missy, even though s/he has something more than the hands of an androgyne. A few months ago I actually ran into that unique aristocrat as I was leaving the Opera. I was not sure, at that moment, whether it was him/her, so I made no greeting. To address a fine, well-dressed fellow with the phrase "Good evening, marquise", is simply too risky if there is the least shadow of doubt. Liane has offered to act as a bridge for us. Those two ladies had distanced themselves just after the marriage of my Eva, but it must be about two years since Liane rekindled the relation, at Natalie's request: it seems that Romaine was interested in meeting the famous transvestite. In the event, Romaine left before acquaintances could be made and Flossie back-tracked, making a great fuss over the defects "of a woman who dresses like a man and has no talent or spirit". I will draw a veil over the indignation Liane suffered at this volubility; however, she was happy to reencounter the one she oddly calls "my father-in-law". Paris society is hardly forgetful by nature, and there are few real aristocrats who rival each other to present their respects to the former "ivory princess".

Further peculiarities reported to me by Liane about this eccentric *grande dame*, which add to her picturesqueness, if that is possible, include the fact that she is such an extremely finicky eater that it is difficult to invite her anywhere. A long list of foods she never touches is lengthened by whims such as: of lettuce, only the stems; of leeks, only the stalks; of rabbits, just the feet, etc. On the other hand, she is the inventor of a liniment for gout – my Eva proclaims its efficacy from personal experience –, an ointment to make fingernails shine, a cream for cleaning copper, a folding stair, etc. She even claims she invented tanks! If the reconciliation did not serve Natalie's purposes, at least it was to the greater honour and glory of Pauline. Through Liane the memories kept by the marquise will enrich my legacy for the coming century.

In the meantime, I still cling to words my Eva said about her: "If, as I defend, dear Nathanaël, man comes from the Monkey and woman from the Angel, mustn't uncle Max be the only being who is simply human?" I could not fail to tell her that her joke connected marvellously with some rabbinic commentaries on Genesis, from the Book of Splendour (*Zohar* in Hebrew). According to this vision, the first man, Adam Cadmon, would have been created male and female at once, in the image and semblance of an androgynous God. Furthermore, in his *Dialoghi d'Amore*, Judas Abravanel – popularly known by the heteronomous name Leo the Hebrew – attempts to find an esoteric meaning in the notorious contradiction that opposes the two passages of the first book of the Pentateuch narrating the process of creation. In his reading, it was original sin that introduced the division of the sexes to the world. By all evidence, this author tried to reconcile biblical tradition with the famous story his admired Plato put in the mouth of Aristophanes in the Banquet.

To these two sources – the Greek and the Hebrew – both surely indebted to a common orphic-babylonian influence, one must add Ovid's *Metamorphoses*, where the Latin author presents the same process but inverted twice, in the figure of Hermaphrodite: the Double Being – to use Pauline's terminology – does not exist in the beginning but as a result of the transformation, nor does it typify at that stage the original state of perfection, but rather the fall into monstrosity. Leaving aside the juicy lucubrations of the alchemists on that theme, I will limit myself to providing the three major founts that have given course to the waters that feed both the ludic transvestism of Shakespeare's *As You Like It* and Balzac's *Seraphitus-Saraphita*, to name only two of the greatest authors.

But let us return, after this digression that Pauline would have liked, to our mysterious San Giovanni – Suzanne, it seems, in reality. The relationship between her and the narrator protagonist in *A Woman Appeared to Me* contrasts with that she has with all the other characters, in being completely spiritual and platonic, as if she were honouring the proverbial chastity of the biblical personage of the same name. Or might Suzanne also be a pseudonym? Without the unpayable – in the strict sense of the word – help of Charles B., the mystery remains inscrutable.

WHERE, BY THE GOOD WORK AND GRACE OF THE NARRATOR, HIDDEN FROM THE JEALOUS SALOMONIC GAZE, THE VEIL IS RAISED AND THE MYSTERY OF "SUZANNE" VANISHES, IN SO FAR AS IS POSSIBLE.

Paris, 1927

"SUZANNE, ANCIENT SHE-GOAT WITH THREE HORNS, ANIMAL FAVOURED BY BEELZEBUB; WHY, FOR CHRIST'S SAKE, DON'T YOU SEND ME MY LETTERS...? I NEED THEM FOR MY NOVEL!"

The letters, three centimetres tall, still dance before the eyes of Charles B. It was in the April 1903 letter, half-joking, half-conjuring in tone, like one of those ceremonial spells of initiation or buffoon baptism, that the transformation had occurred. After that, nothing was the same. A year and a half later, a grave illness which took him to death's door was to complete and redefine, cathartically, the meaning of things. But in the beginning, he floundered in the darkness and felt that the mask she imposed on him was no more than an ambiguous indication of their reciprocal double nudity.

Just before this, she had said to him in another letter: "Man's love is always the supreme affront." And suddenly, from then on, she had always called him by a woman's name...

Lines that capture in words a concrete, lived experience are, after a time, a second memory that can prop up recollection, like a crutch, or even substitute it, like a usurper that easily expels an evanescent rival. The images that Charles had secured with words both affirmed and defined, against vague reminiscences, a trail of unformed, burning sensations: here, those of London, in August of that same year. The lawn which seemed alive with incandescent fireflies. And they, Pauline and he, closing Dante without reading another word:

And that day we read no further.

That was the last verse they read. But in their case, there were no touching lips. In a measureless perturbation, an invisible kiss emerged, like the soul of a stillborn that abandons the body before living. A vibratory breath ran through the marrow of their bones, moistening their skin. What fountain rose up like a miracle, bespangling all the air? From the contained fire and storm came the rain that calms. The water splashed down, bringing fulfillment. But suddenly the sunset lit the hills in the distance, creating a halo around her forehead, a girl's forehead, as if a child now carried the weight of Charles's entire destiny. The display of menacing light announced the wild wind of tomorrow. But "put my head on your knees, Lady, sister, my soul, the instant that tightens and sweetens the silence. Let us close, close the *Inferno*. Let us reap this hour, so brief, like the sweetest fruit of a paradise without blame."

Eugénie was at the home of friends in Montpellier. As usual when he was leaving, she had cried a little. "You work too hard", "take care of yourself", and the clear gaze of someone who had just energetically washed away all suspicion. Only the blue of her eyes had faded a bit. Pauline was calling for him: "Suzanne, you have to come to London with me. You must correct piles of my verses." She needed him: "My donkey-brain can't do without your wise council." She teased him, as she often did, about more and more intimate themes: "Don't tell me that you still haven't sampled a youngster... Alas, that way you'll never please a turn-of-the-century virgin...!" That was when she gave him the golden tie pin with the pearl, that "trifle" as she called it, that had made Eugénie's hands tremble for a moment and that was a symbol of "a not-at-all-banal sentiment".

In the letter that accompanied the jewel, she tried to define the sentiment, as one who tries to determine the configuration of an energy that escapes one's control... To discern the ambivalent components and sum it all up in the expression "fraternity without phrases", wasn't that to put order into incipient chaos? Perhaps it was to tell herself: it is not love. But that is only said as a negation of the suspicion that has cropped up in a secret part of oneself. It is not love, it is not literary inspiration. It is not love because it is not literary inspiration. "It is an involuntary camaraderie, a nuanced intellectual admiration, that is perhaps impregnated with equally involuntary scorn, of unconscious friendship and conscious hostility." To which she added immediately: "You, too, have scorn for me (so what I just said won't shock you at all), friendship, hostility, unconscious camaraderie, and fraternity without phrases." Absolute reciprocity, in Pauline's mind. A reciprocal disquiet that both of them, at that moment, ventured to deny. It was not love, they told each other without saying it, without even thinking it. Pauline loved women. She rejected "masculine ugliness". Why, then, had she baptized him with a woman's name?

Charles had just finished reading the *Lettres intimes à l'amazone* which the *Mercure de France* brought to light, twelve years after the death of Gourmont. They are like the other side of the coin of the public letters: behind the brilliance of the discourse, the naked wound. The painful void on the other side of creation and of the full, unlimited adoration that Pygmalion experienced toward the sculpture he himself had created: that was the Amazon. But Natalie, the model, seemed to be taking her revenge for that presumption, affirming her independence. In the end, Gourmont's eyes had also created her independent. Just as Renée Vivien's – Pauline's – words and gaze had made her a siren.

Many years earlier, Charles had found in the relation that united Natalie with the recluse of Rue Saints-Pères a certain parallel with his own bond with Pauline. Now, the similarities were emphasized in some ways and substantially diminished in others. Gourmont had rebaptized Natalie with a masculine name and in private he called her nothing but Natalis...

Even though at first glance this could accentuate the similarity, there was no doubt it had a different sense in the two cases. Leaving aside the significant fact of who rebaptized the other – man and woman respectively – the name Natalis was a sort of spell, the expression of a taboo that the heterosexual man raised between himself and his desire for an inaccessible woman. To think of her as masculine was an antidote – not a very effective one, though, by all appearances – against the emotion that invaded him. In Renée's case, the name change seemed to open doors, not to close them. It took down a wall rather than raising one. What coincided was that both cases implied a negation of difference and converted the other into sameness. After all, as the ancient heretics of Albi knew so well, souls have no gender. Or else they have all genders, it's all the same. For this reason, at the moment of extreme consolation, the dying were greeted twice, once as a man and once as a woman. This was a lesson the world had not yet learned. The old civilization had died, like Renée, a fragile marvel crushed by a brutally inferior milieu. In both cases, there remained a most beautiful moment of human poetry.

"This is what the serpents taught me with regard to passion: Avoid the act of initiation, low as thievery, brutal as rape, bloody as massacre, and worthy only of a drunken and barbaric soldiery. If the woman you love is a virgin, leave to a stranger the first violation of her modesty. Love should be pure of everything that is not wholly passion."

That paradoxical advice to the "ephebe" included in *A Woman Appeared To Me*, was directed to him – who else? – he, who at twenty had published his own *Chants d'éfèbe*? And what other virgin could it be if not herself? Again, a proscription, a negation, placed the fundamental ambivalence in relief. But wasn't such apprehension logical in a girl who has not known the dissimilar embrace, feared, yet perhaps – he wanted to think – unconsciously desired?

The sense of coherence in all the preceding facts, which together seemed to point in only one possible direction, assaulted him for the first time in London. It was thus that a possibility which until then he had not dared imagine, radiated from alien eyes and reverberated in the mistiness of his own conscience. His presence, a masculine presence, next to Pauline had been received in the family atmosphere like an alleviating, tranquilizing surprise. In spite of the social differences between them and his accredited role as a salaried professor, the sentiment that united them shone before the others like a pale, rare pearl. And the others, like mirrors in which the convexity or concavity was carefully positioned to modify that which they reflected according to traditional moulds, returned the image of a concrete link, the only one allowed by convention between a man and a woman of different families. The very same simplification worked for a short lapse of time in Charles's thoughts, and after initial instinctive rejection, became stronger with an ardour he now considered bold and unworthy. To enter the trodden path, to leave behind the unbounded territory of naked feeling, was both feasible and easy. He was blinded by the impression of having at hand, without ever having desired it beforehand, that which suddenly seemed his most genuine desire. At that point, a radiant Pauline appeared with an old copy of the *Commedia*. "When I was young" – she said it like that, at barely twenty-six years – "Dante was my best companion: I learned Italian by reading him. I translated him into French, thus forgetting my exile… He, too, was an exile!" And later: "I must read my favourite passages to you." She began her reading, in Italian, with the passage of Beatrice's apparition which had given title to her novel:

Donna m'apparve sotto verde manto
vestita di color de fiamma viva

And she continued with the verses of the *Inferno* dedicated to the love of Paolo and Francesca.

Now Charles was convinced of having misinterpreted a series of signs, burdening them with a wish for excessive precision, that were essentially ambiguous, equivocal, and destined to take on a vague significance like dreams or poetry. To reduce it all, as he had done, to the concrete limits of a conventional relationship was to trivialise the mystery and trample on sacred territory without removing one's shoes. In the end, excessive physical proximity, like that which his masculine desire had dared to dream of, would have destroyed Pauline's dream, so clearly expressed in the name SUZANNE. The distance that she suddenly, conclusively placed between them, as a result of his confession – materially present in the six-month break in their ten-year uninterrupted correspondence – was indelible proof.

At times the idea crossed his mind that perhaps Eugénie's existence – unknown to Pauline until then – had been the obstacle, and in those moments he cursed the sincerity that led him to speak of his semi-matrimonial situation. As Pauline herself had said many times, love's principal enemy was sincerity. Like art, love proposes to create beauty, an illusion of absolute beauty, for the eyes of the beloved. Like Beatrice for Dante. Sincerity introduces the ugliness and banality of the real into the wondrous space of irreality. Had this been his sin? Charles abandoned the idea. Because, in fact, reality had always been present in their relationship, even though up to then it had only been expressed by Pauline.

Sometimes it appeared she wanted him alone to be the depositary of her experience of reality, while making every effort to mask and embellish it in the eyes of others. Charles had been able to read, exclusively, her disillusion at how touristy and banal Jerusalem was; her limitless disappointment when she received the photograph of Kerimée in western dress. He knew all the details of her tricks, subterfuges, and guile in treading the tightrope between Natalie, Eva, and Kerimée, while invoking Love with a capital letter. He had even intervened in very delicate, bothersome affairs like the time, at Pauline's request, he had to ask Miss Natalie B. to cede her share of the villa at Mytilene to the Baroness.

But all those things came much later. Was he to attribute them to an intensification of confidence, or rather a redefinition of the relationship? Hard to know. He had always instinctively known that Pauline was more sincere with him than with anyone else, but during the time preceding his stay in London, she seemed to mix sincerity with a sort of instinctive and wise art, as if she were playing an unconscious game of seduction. As if with the authentic fibres of her spirit and experience, she were weaving the mask she wore before him, the mask that both freed her and kept her inaccessible at the same time.

Perhaps it had always been so, after all. When Charles thought all this, he couldn't help but evoke the photograph Pauline had offered him in her last years, in which she appeared dressed *à la Turque*, with her face half-covered, mysteriously beautiful. He couldn't quite tell whether that increased beauty came from her eyes, emphasized gracefully by the sinuosity of the muslin, or from the defiant gesture with which she seemed to offer herself and to herself alone all the secrets so suggestively hidden, or owed to the fact that he knew by heart each one of the traits the veil sought to maintain in mystery. Perhaps it was all three, superimposed, but above all the last one. More or less the same was true when it came to her soul. To the degree of creating something of a paradox: he, the one who knew her best in all her imperfections and defeats, was also the one who had been able to see her best in all her perfection through the living tale of herself that were her letters and her confidences.

Vestita di color de fiamma viva.

293

The distance that resulted from his confession was a tremendous blow. Suddenly, nothing made sense to Charles outside of the strange, outrageous passion that threw him into delirium and fever. When the illness subsided, Charles had seen the face of death. He came out purified.

While still convalescing, he received a message from Pauline, in which she delicately and very solicitously offered her villa in Nice for him to go to rest and recover. And significantly, she clarified: with Madame Suzanne. For Charles, the invitation had the force of law, and he did indeed spend a few days there with Eugénie. At that point, the broken thread of their correspondence was mended once more.

Salomon R. had been pressuring him for days. He wanted him without fail to write Renée Vivien's biography. For the year two thousand, of course. The illustrious archaeologist considered it counterproductive to divulge in the present all the details of Pauline's life, especially her feminine loves. "It would be best to simply produce an abstraction of her thesis and speak only of her powerful, harmonious genius," he had written. Charles saw great difficulties in making an abstraction of a thesis that impregnated every line of Renée's writing, every verse of her poems. It was in literary form that Pauline's loves made full sense and where they ought to be situated, with no shame and from the very beginning. Her literary genius required the inspiration of beauty. It wasn't enough to be Beatrice, she had to be the singer of Beatrice as well. Nor did Charles see any need to muddy that ideal love, purified by poetry, with prosaic indiscretions, even after seventy years. Finally, he agreed to write a sort of memorandum.

As a matter of fact, his collaboration with the erudite

Israelite already dated from some years back. In the period just after the war, in order to spread Pauline's name and fame, Salomon R. bombarded the press with questions about Renée Vivien, answering them himself under the name of Charles B. – with his permission, of course. Charles had often given in to his insistence and told him many things, but he withheld, within a jealous, closed shadow, Suzanne and the secret of San Giovanni – that character in *A Woman Appeared To Me* in which he recognized some of his own traits and which was also a sort of *alter ego* for Renée. Just as Renée was for Pauline to some extent. A fictional personage in which the two of them were inextricably blended and which his past blindness had led him to think was a precursor of another kind of union. That being with androgynous hands – Charles had fine, svelte hands, no bigger than Pauline's long ones... – was a product of a kind of game of mirrors. Mirrors that are so very important to us given the impossibility of knowing ourselves directly; mirrors that appear when we search for our existence, our image, in the eyes of those closest to us. The figure of San Giovanni was the superposition of two crossed images: his in her and hers in him. Charles was horrified to have jeopardized, in a moment of weakness, the strange perfection of such an indestructible bond.

December 1927

Aside from the murky point about San Giovanni, which I have yet to resolve, *A Woman Appeared To Me* is now completely transparent for me. I finally have all the keys. It took me a long time to realize that the "Beatrice" of the work, called Eva, was the Baroness van Z. de N. At first the name took me down far-off paths. Along with the red hair, imbued with all the attributes of autumn. It all seemed to point unfailingly to Flossie's childhood friend Eva P., to whom Pauline had dedicated the poem "*To the Sunset Goddess*". I have met this charming creature who now dedicates herself to suppressing her American origin in order to bring Delphic ceremonies back to life. She is the one who introduced Pauline to Sappho, and as I have reported elsewhere, on at least one occasion she acted as mediator between her and Flossie. Her very long red hair, encircling her head like a crown of fire, left very little room for doubt: Beatrice reborn by the work and grace of the brush of a Rossetti or a Burne-Jones… But in this case, Charles B. set aside his usual discretion and assured me categorically that Eva is the Baroness: Pauline often called her that.

It takes a lot of imagination to see "the red of martyrdom" in chestnut hair that barely veers toward mahogany. Let alone the graceful and almost immaterial profile of the character in the solid, massive corpulence of Hélène van Z. No matter. All this goes to show the distillation literature exerts over life. Because I cannot doubt what Charles B. assures me without hesitation. He has even provided me with some possible explanations of that name, taken from scattered comments by Pauline herself. Once, for example, she told him that the Baroness was like the biblical Eve, who abandoned Adam at night to seek the angel, the androgyne – that is, herself – at the gates of paradise: "The bible doesn't tell that part," she would add, laughing.

Another pseudo-biblical interpretation went in another direction and led her to identify herself with Adam (Did she know the Zohar version, which also considers him an androgyne? – I cannot help but wonder). Like Adam, she had the love of Lilith in the beginning, but the enchanting creature had found her equally unworthy and had abandoned her. She was referring to Flossie, of course. Eva was the consolation, the "final piety of destiny", a woman of "sweetness", not of "desire", if we go back to Pauline's own nomenclature in some poems. What about the fall, and sin? Charles B. had asked her: "Oh, in order to gain happiness on earth, which is Eve, you have to renounce paradise."

There are other interpretations, for Pauline kept turning and returning to themes, just as she baptized and rebaptized characters and rewrote her works without respite. In the last version reported by Charles B., she, Pauline, was Lilith, Eve's real temptress, thus making her adulteress of Adam again. However it goes, it is now at least diaphanous: Eva is the Baroness, no matter how much imagination it takes to superimpose the two images. One must agree that the charming Eva P. offered a better vision, and in the end I cannot absolutely deny her role as inspiration. Perhaps the key lies in an ideal fusion, by which Pauline has attributed the beauty and image of an admired rival to a character who the faithful reproduction of the flesh and blood being represented would have deprived of all physical attraction. That is simple enough. More complex explanations would require of us an excessive dose of malice and would attribute to Pauline's acts – in this case a simple literary transposition, no doubt innocent – the same taste for perversion to which a vulgarised and therefore degraded Freudianism has now accustomed us.

2 February 1928

By a very odd chance, through an illustrious colleague of my wife, Doctor Jacobson, who has her as a patient, I came into contact with Miss Marie G. Friend and occasional travelling companion of Pauline's last years – a still undetermined period for me – this peculiar lady had been her piano teacher many years ago. Their sharing, more than once, of habitual Wagnerian pilgrimages to Bayreuth no doubt stem from this. Concretely, I know from Flossie that they were there in 1905, the year of their re-encounter preceding the mythical sojourn in Mytilene. "Melodious island, that inflames caresses…" Pauline would write on that occasion. Once again, one of her lines comes to my mouth, like versicles from the scriptures on the lips of preachers.

I just wrote "I came into contact with Miss Marie G." improperly, since the initiative was hers, quite incomprehensibly for me. According to reliable sources, she was the principal instigator of Pauline's *in extremis* conversion, which I have no qualms about calling – in private – the lamentable final masquerade. I say in private because in public I take advantage of this circumstance to heighten the glory of the divine creature, since I know the influence such conventionally edifying conversions have on the masses.

298

It is difficult to penetrate what could have induced a woman affected by such staunch apostolic zeal to seek the attention of the author of a book like *Orpheus*, which, leaving aside all false modesty, has had the merit of infuriating the entire hierarchy of the Roman Catholic Church, and of irritating even the least irritable members of its docile flock.

29 March 1928

I went to visit Liane. I found her most distressed because Mimy F., the young Venetian related to the Rothschilds who consoled her with such effective tenderness during the famous escapade of the prince, has consoled herself, in turn, for her abandonment – brought about by the return to the flock of the wayward sheep… – with Émilienne d'A., no less. I recall that I questioned Émilienne around 1920, and afterward, curiosity led me to re-read the verses Pauline had inspired in her: pure ignominy, so bad they were. Still, I could not help but feel a certain admiration – perhaps transmitted by Liane – for her intrepidness. It comes to mind that shortly after our interview, at the festival of Caen, she dared to get onto a plane; upon landing, the pilot could not avoid an inopportune tree. Result: the pilot died in the act, and Émilienne, alive by a thread, but alive!

7 July 1928

The first interview with Marie G., Pauline's old piano teacher, has finally taken place. I was surprised to find someone who renders a pious posthumous cult to Pauline, which I have to sympathize with. Even now, sixteen years later, she dresses in mourning out of respect for her memory – something she points out with open pride. The motive that has enabled her to overcome her expected mistrust for me – surely existent not just for motives of religious fanaticism, but also due to a latent racial prejudice of which she is perhaps not even aware – seems attributable to her apprehension, not at all off the mark – about her state of health. I know it because of information from my wife. To prefer that her relics, some of which have inestimable value, and her memories be saved by an infidel (however proven my good faith when it comes to that which brought us together) before they succumb to death or chance, does not fail to honour her greatly. I sent her a questionnaire, which she promised to answer shortly and place in my hands together with a diary Pauline wrote from time to time during her adolescence, Miss G's own diary, corresponding to the last months of 1909, and finally some manuscripts of the few religious poems Pauline managed to write – she specifically mentioned the mediocre "Mary's seven lilies" and some with musical themes, like "The sin of music…"

While waiting for her replies, I will record some points which will not be reflected in the questionnaire, largely because it was formulated before I encountered the unexpected information that our conversation brought to me.

In the first place, Miss G. takes credit for a fundamental role in Pauline's known French patriotism: it seems that she was buried with a ring Miss G. herself had given her many years ago, which bore a sapphire, a ruby and an aquamarine, in tribute to the colours of the *Tricoleur*. According to her, the gift dated from a trip the two had taken together to Koblenz in 1893, through occupied Alsace and Lorraine, in order to visit the tomb of Miss G.'s brother who died in the war. In fact, there was no such tomb, just an old battlefield under which they piled up the young French cadavers. This lamentable fact inspired an early poem of Pauline's, is conserved in manuscript form, which will also enrich my legacy for the next century, or so Miss G. promises.

During a journey along the banks of the Rhine, Pauline expressed a great interest in seeing the rocky spot of Lorelei. It is a landscape that lies between Sankt Goar and Obermesel, along a stretch of the river particularly dangerous for navigation, something that no doubt inspired Brentano's well-known ballad. Pauline confessed to Marie G. that when she was small, a German servant had told her several times about the legend of the seductive mermaid of the Rhine to scare her before going to sleep, but according to her own words, what had kept her awake was the tragic beauty of the character. Miss G. is unaware how she came to know Silcher's *lied*, with words by Heine, but that for her part, she had spoken of the opera of the same name by Alfredo Catalani, premiered at Turin around that time. That operatic detail intrigues me because the most famous opera by that vaguely Wagnerian composer is *La Wally* – a story, like *Loreley*, of love and death – which seems to have unexpectedly suggested the name for Flossie in the first version of *A Woman Appeared To Me*. The change from W to V can be explained since the name came to Pauline not in writing, but out loud, pronounced the German way. In the second version of the novel, the name is changed to Lorély, which Flossie had been called from very early on, according to precious information from the interested party. Interrogated by me about this detail Miss G. does not feel capable of affirming or denying anything specific.

As far as the thornier question is concerned, and contrary

to what I initially expected, Marie G. claims no fundamental role in Pauline's final-hour Catholicism. She says she only gave water to the thirsty. According to her, seeing *Parsifal*, her stay in Jerusalem, and especially the figure of Joan of Arc, whom Pauline had revered since childhood, were much more decisive than her own persevering assiduity. Even the fact that Rome had made a significant step toward the beatification of the Maid of Orléans that same year could have played a crucial role. Still, the basic, contributing element – according to her special interpretation – was Pauline's innate religious sentiment, which, after wayward and inadequate paths, had finally led her to the right destination. And paraphrasing Barrès without realizing it, she exclaimed: "After all, Pauline lost her virtue but not her innocence…" So, if Flossie proclaimed one day that voluptuousness, wanting a religion, invented love, Miss G. on the other hand, believes that the much-disputed invention should be attributed to a religious spirit, led astray or imprisoned by voluptuousness…!

I am afraid that at this point I have to agree with the lucid Gourmont in his sixth letter to the Amazon – in which he had the deference to associate my name, if only to disagree with my point of view, to Flossie's glory – when he writes: "Religion is the hospital of love: only Pauline's extreme weakness, in illness and desperation, could explain the liturgical attribution of the lily to the incomparable Flossie being deflected to some sad, ordinary Madonna. A similar process must be blamed for the fact that Jesus usurped in her mind the distinguished place of Sappho, with manifest abjuration of one of the highest moments of her poetic genius: "If Jesus watched me at the hour of passing / I would tell him serenely: lord, I know you not / Your strict, sovereign law / was never mine and I've been a simple pagan..." culminating in the wonderfully labial verse, half challenge, half apology: "The kiss was the only blasphemy on my lips."

Nevertheless, the presence of ravens around remains is well known and notoriously effective.

24 August 1928

A postcard sent by Flossie from Honfleur. Just the following words, like a seductive threat: "I'm getting closer!" During her stay in Capri with Romaine she gave no sign of life. Unsurprisingly, since no one is more enemy than she of wasted efforts. Even so...! I remember the last Friday at Rue Jacob, before she left... During one of the few moments that I had a chance to have a word with her, I commented on her fingernails, which she must never cut. I had just re-read one of Pauline's poems where "the long and cruel nail" appeared, and I had the nerve to allude to it. "One must be able to defend oneself!" she replied.

6 October 1928

I got back a few hours ago from my archaeological and museum-bound tour of the North. Trains are now functioning once more with some regularity.

Taking advantage of my visit to Boulogne, I went to question Marie F., who was Pauline's chambermaid during the last six years of her life. She was suspicious and defensive at first, but later she became more trusting. No need for me to divulge the details of the transaction.

Boulogne-sur-Mer, autumn of 1927

At herring time, everyone knows: six days of downpours and the seventh, floods. Today, though, the men have gone out to sea: just a drizzle, like a fine shepherd's rain. By noon it has dispersed altogether. While I was mending nets, they came to get me from my parents' house: a gentleman from Paris who arrived on the twelve-o'clock train was asking for me… I have to confess that at the beginning, I had no idea who it could be or what he wanted of me, but after a moment I got all dizzy, because they told me he was one of those fine folks, like a professional, and then I thought: a lawyer, or a notary, or someone who deals with law stuff. When I arrived and he said right away that he wanted to talk about Miss Pauline, may heaven keep her, my legs started to tremble like two new birch leaves. Later I calmed down, when I saw that the will and the pension weren't being discussed, and besides, this gentleman – who doesn't half have a Jewish name… Salomon something-or-other… he told me his name was! – has no dealings with the English or with the Baroness, which would be the same: because for the last months of the Miss's life, her sister and the Baroness were hand in glove. I think the Miss's illness brought them together, for both of them loved her very much, that can't be denied at all. Holy mother of God, how much time has passed since then. And with the war in the middle, it seems even more. It's all so far away, as if I were another person. Before the war, things were very different, and I was so young! Sometimes I cross myself and say: Marie, you've been halfway around the world, China, Japan, Constantinople... I don't even know, to so many places I can't remember the names. And now, here mending nets, it all seems like a dream. Not that I'm complaining, not at all, things have gone so well for me, they couldn't have gone better, and in the end there's nothing like being mistress of one's own house... but sometimes it seems strange and my head fills up with a thick fog. Like I say, as if I were someone else and had never left Boulogne, as if I were still that girl who went to watch the boats coming in, looking for the head of the Virgin in the spines of a hake. I remember that to do anything I had to stuff my braids into my apron pockets, so long they came down to my ankles. I've always loved the sea, and when I went to work in Paris, I swore to myself that when I'd saved up, I'd return. It was a mania, one of those that gets inside you and is always there, even if it's not making much noise, and I was convinced that it would take lots of years to make it go away. But since the Miss died so young and she left me what she left me... like I always say, she was an angel. As for the rest of it... after all in this life whoever isn't hump-backed has a limp, and you're either carrying it or dragging it along behind you. Sometimes it seems the world is like a big rag: full of holes and tears. Of course, dirty linen is usually well hidden. And often the ones who have the most to hide are the ones who sniff around other people's laundry... I know a lot about that sort of thing, because when you're in service, you put things together in a hurry. The cook on the first floor says things, the chambermaid on the second yacks, the one on the third swears she's seen it all with her own eyes...! So it goes. I've never liked to poke around in people's garbage. Lots of times I've had to keep my mouth shut, because the Miss's lifestyle was a magnet for all manner of gossip. I heard all sorts of things as soon as I arrived… So much that I was ready to leave the house after three days. But then I thought about it and decided to stay strong. The salary was very good, and I thought that with just one person, I wouldn't have much work. I was completely wrong about that; the Miss gave me more work than a regiment. Always here and there, although I liked travelling, especially by ship… By train, not so much, since I'm from the sea and must have salt water in my blood. Anyway, after I thought it over carefully, I could see that the job had advantages… And even though there are things that I can't condone at all, not then and not now, sometimes you have to stick your head in the sand. Live and let live, that's what I say. Too much fussing doesn't lead anywhere. And sometimes… I've seen many who thought they could touch the sky with a finger. Up, up and away, and then splat, back on the ground! With rich people you never know which way the wind's going to blow, it's always like you're out in a bamboo boat. At least at her house, there was no danger of the kind that leave trails behind… one sees so many maids get fired without a thought when they can't tighten their girdles any more and the mistress sees what's going on… And the husband or son, rascals that they are, with their tails between their legs. For me, the truth is that, aside from all kinds of foolishness she did, may God forgive her, and the fact that sometimes you had to take care of her like a kid in nappies, and sometimes she took my breath away, I still only have good things to say about her… An angel, yes sir!, and that's what I told the man from Paris. Thanks to her, I am where I am, with the boat and the house… And the kids, well fed and fattened up. With the times we've been through!

Perhaps some will think that I didn't do right, not telling the family, the English, that I'd got married. But you can't take chances with things like that. It's very clear to me that I deserve what I have, that I earned it with my own hands. Because the four years I spent with the Miss were something else. Especially the last two. It nearly left my brain in shreds. And my heart. The truth is she left me with a terribly sad pain, very deep, of the kind that gnaws you up on the inside without you realizing it, until the day comes when you've lost your compass and you don't know where you are… Because she'd lost hers for sure. As you see, I take things seriously, and become fond of people right away! I had to muster strength out of weakness just to keep going. Yes, I deserve what I have, and then some. I'm sure that the Miss would agree, if she were alive. It's true she always said: "Marie, never get married!" And she'd add that she would leave me a lifetime pension in her will so I wouldn't have to. "For life as long as she has no other means of support…" is exactly what the notary read. I've got that engraved in my head. In any case, who knows what notaries might understand by other means of support. I don't want to find out. On the other hand, the Miss wasn't so clear on how she felt about matrimony. On one hand, lots of "Marie, don't get married, Marie, don't get married." But I never saw her as happy as when her sister got married and she was the maid of honor. She dressed all in white. And she'd been wearing dark clothes for a long time, as if she were in mourning. Black, grey, or violet, and that was it. And then in London, it was as if she were the bride… And when the baby was born and they named him Paul after her, but the masculine form, she went crazy with joy.

Oh, Miss Toinette was a bit old when she married, more than twenty-five. One day, I heard Miss Pauline say that her bad reputation scared off her sister's suitors... I don't really believe that, because there's a lot of sea between Paris and London. It's true that on clear days you can see England from Boulogne. But things don't get found out so easily, and besides, she had published her books under another name. And it was the books, after all, that caused her bad reputation. Because the rest of it... Whatever happens indoors and does-n't leave a trail..., I've always heard it said: a sin when hidden is half forgiven. Although, hidden, really hidden... Well, it doesn't matter. When I arrived at that house, Miss Emmanuelle was still there, like a confidante, the head housekeeper or something... She was a discreet person, just the opposite of the cook, who talked out of turn and had a mean tongue: I remember that just a few days after I got there, she came to me with gossip... she had a great time say-ing that the Miss's favourite dish was lamb's testicles with mayonnaise, and that maybe it all came from there, that she'd always heard that what you eat is what you grow... I cut her right off. At the time, I didn't know Miss Pauline, but I could see she was a woman from head to foot, delicate and femi-nine. Then I found out that what she really liked was sweet-breads, which is entirely different, but one day, I don't know why, they gave her one thing for another and she didn't even realize it. That doesn't surprise me, because sometimes she really had her head in the clouds. After that, she didn't eat many sweetbreads, because the price wasn't the same either... that evil cook deceived her... On the other hand Miss Emmanuelle was another type of person. Pretty soon, when she saw that I knew how to hold my tongue and could be trusted, she told me lots of things I've never said to anyone, until today when that Mr Salomon asked one question after the other. It seems that in the beginning, when the Miss's first book came out, she and Miss Natalie had an idea that tickled them both, and it was for Miss Emmanuelle to present herself as the writer whenever someone wanted to meet her. I can imagine people's faces! What an uproar there must have been. Because Miss Emmanuelle was ugly as sin and she had an enormous mole on the tip of her nose with a wart on it, like a witch... Miss Emmanuelle told me right away to call her Emma, but I bring myself to do so, it was too hard, and it was because of that, she inspired, let's say, respect in me. She herself was quite proud of that fact. And she claimed that, thanks to her skill the Miss could live in peace, for she had shooed off all the ne'er-do-wells buzzing around. In those days, she says they lived together, Miss Pauline and Miss Natalie, over on Boulevard Pereire. Miss Natalie had caused quite a stir a few years earlier, because she made the girls they called of "easy morals" fall for her. But not just any girls, no. Sweeties of kings and foreign princes, rajahs and first-class bankers... And all of them, I don't know what they saw in her, but they fell madly in love to the point of leaving it all behind to follow her. They've even assured me there was one who stabbed herself out of jealousy during a Carnival party... and she almost died. No, sometimes things start out in fun, and later the tears come streaming down. I barely knew Miss Natalie, because during the time I was serving there, she didn't come much at all to the house on Bois Avenue. But I know that Miss Pauline was crazy about her – really nuts! Miss Emmanuelle... okay, Emma thought that's where all the trouble came from… She lived through some of those things from up so close that even now, when she told me about them, her eyes swelled up as if she could cry, but from rage, because tears didn't come easily to her. Me, on the other hand, sometimes it seems like I have a sponge on my neck. But in that house I couldn't let myself go at all, because the torrent would have drowned us. So, Emma told me that Miss Pauline had a very good friend from when they were little, whose name was Violette, and she died of typhus. That's where the Miss's mania for violets came from. And it was a real mania, too: at Nice, in the Clos-Fleuri garden, she had them planted everywhere: white ones and violet ones. She always wore a bouquet in her sash or at her neckline. She had them engraved on stationery and all. And the colour… for ink, clothes, bound notebooks, all violet. And of course, she had tons of books. She always said I could read them, all I wanted-ed. That wasn't half unusual, and the truth is, I never did, because even though I knew how to read, they weren't the kind of books I liked, and besides, it felt a little weird… but I was always grateful to her for offering. Speaking of reading, at the beginning something happened that still makes me laugh. The first time I saw the Miss, she asked me right away if I could read and I didn't know what to answer because I couldn't tell if she wanted a yes or a no and I didn't want her to catch me off balance right at the start. She thought I was silent because I didn't know and was ashamed of being igno-rant. Then she said that it couldn't be, that the great misfor-tune of women was ignorance, and that she would remedy it. She blathered on along lines I don't remember too well about how being knowledgeable opened lots of doors and if you didn't know anything, you might as well forget it. Then she showed me all those books with violet covers, which were all that colour because of her dead friend whose name was Violette. Okay, I'll get back to the subject… so this friend of hers was in Cannes when she took sick and the Miss rushed off as soon as they told her how serious it was. In the meantime, in Paris, Miss Natalie wasn't missing a beat, and she even invited a young Englishwoman to the house they shared, a conquest of hers, to be sure. They even went so far as to take a little honeymoon, shall we say, to Venice. Miss Emmanuelle had to go with them, and when she told me about it, her eyes sparkled from wanting to laugh but trying not to, so considerate she was. Because when they got to Venice, they paid for their sins; Miss Natalie and her English sweetie caught some terrible fever, called malaria or something like that. They couldn't get out of bed… even if they'd wanted to. "In the end – Emma told me – it wasn't so terrible, but it spoiled their fiesta. And then when Miss Pauline got back after the death of her friend, it broke your heart to look at her. She was undone." Besides that, I don't know how, but she found out about the shenanigans they pulled off while she was away. That part isn't strange at all, because Miss Natalie wasn't one to hide behind the sails, nor was she one bit ashamed of her seamanship. Maybe she was even the one who told her all about it. And then she didn't know why my Miss was crying. That's all she did: cry and cry some more. Shortly afterward, Miss Natalie went to America, because she was American, from North America, from a part of the country where there were even Indians. I think she was very American! Miss Pauline didn't want to go with her, no way. Absolutely not, she said. And that was it. That's how they separated, in the end. Because Miss Natalie stayed away for a whole year, and when she returned, the Baroness was there and Miss Pauline didn't want to see her at all. That's when Miss Natalie really turned on fire, by all accounts! She wouldn't leave the Miss alone…! One time, they came to serenade her under the window! All the neighbours came out and there was all kinds of hubbub because the singer was a super-famous opera diva, whose name was also Emma, like Miss Emmanuelle: Emma Calvé. I don't know anything about opera, but everyone had heard talk of "Carmen." Well, she was the one, in person. Oh yes! She was a smoothie, that Miss Natalie, for leading people down the garden path! But Miss Pauline, was having none of it, firmer than a mast. She had suffered enough. And she didn't even want Emma to read Miss Natalie's letters. She had them thrown out as soon as they arrived. And it was Emma who answered, making things very clear: the Miss had found peace and she wasn't about to lose it for anything in the world. Not to write to her anymore. Leave her alone, for once and for all. What she really wanted was to work. But the other one nagged and wheedled until she got her way… Now, as far as work goes, Miss Pauline really worked hard. One book after another. Sometimes alone and sometimes with the Baroness. She corrected stuff over and over again: there were days when Mr Charles B. came over three or four times. She sent him a message and the coach with the chauffeur. He came so much I think he and Emma were kind of courting. That's what the cook said, anyway. But no, she was just guessing. Because later we found out that the good man had a wife, not married legally because she was divorced. They did get married as soon as they could. I was at the house by then, and the first years both of them were invited over often. I think after that they went to live outside Paris. And today I remembered something strange. It's like she had two names. Her husband called her something like Eulalie or maybe Eugénie. Others called her Mrs B. of course. But Miss Pauline used another name and always called her Mrs Suzanne. I hadn't thought any more about it until a while back, when that Mr Salomon asked me if I'd met a friend of the Miss called Suzanne. I didn't think of it at first, but before I had a chance to say no, that I didn't know anyone like that, it came to me in a flash. When I told him who Mrs Suzanne was, his eyes got as big as plates. He said it couldn't be, no way. I said yes, he said no. He tried everything to convince me that he knew for sure that Charles B's wife had another name. As if I didn't know that... That's no reason, I told him. I insisted, but I don't think he could bring himself to believe me. And it's odd. In the end, if it's true that he found out as much about Miss Pauline as he says, he must have known that she enjoyed changing people's names. I don't know, it must have been some kind of a game. Funny thing is, she never changed mine. And that was normal for maids, that they would go changing your name wherever you worked. "What's your name? Célestine? Well from now on you're Françoise!" But she liked my name from the beginning. She said there was no name like mine, that the Maries in her life had always done right by her. That my name was a good omen. I know that when she was small she had a friend with that name. And then there was Miss G., her old piano teacher, who wouldn't leave her alone those last years. She was a dried-up old prune, flat as an ironing board... the kind that sweat holy water... I'm not crazy about the excessively devout types, but I must say that thanks to her the Miss had a good death. The Miss called her Auntie Marie, but she wasn't related, as far as I know. I said to her one day that her mother had the same name too. She protested: "No, Marie, her name is Mary, it's altogether different... Marie has that i that raises up in song... it's feminine, sweet and sharp at the same time. Like Natalie, but without the harsh t that nails the two a's to the ground. No, Mary is something else completely." I remember as if I were hearing it now, because no one had ever said anything so pretty about my name. And because it was the first time that I heard her say the name of Miss Natalie. Later on, not long before she died, she started to write a book about a queen of England called Anna something-or-other whose husband had her head cut off, and she was telling me that queen also had a chambermaid called Marie who was always consoling her, just as I was doing with the Miss... the truth is that she spoke of that Anna as if it were her own self in the flesh. I don't know what got into her all of a sudden: that last year in London, just before she pulled that stunt that nearly cost her life, she wanted to dress up like the queen and she had three or four photos taken... She took the pose and the dress from a museum painting... She was accompanied by Mr Willy, at a good salary, too. Mr Willy had been the husband of a neighbour of the Miss who worked in music-halls and was also a writer... What was her name? I can't think of it. I went to London too, of course, because the Miss was so weak you couldn't leave her alone. Since she wouldn't eat! We'd have had to stuff it down her... Skinnier than a spindle! What a difference from the Baroness. Stately as a tower... and sparkling! It was great to see her eat! And she wasn't fat from nibbling crumb around the trough, no... on the other hand, not the Miss. And she would suddenly get the obsession that she was gaining weight... and then there'd be fasting and abstinence. And as if that weren't enough, she'd wear herself out with so much walking... Once, when she was supposed to do some kind of performance with friends of hers, another one of those stories of queens on the run, she had me going up and down the forest of Saint Germain-en-Laye for four days because she said she'd gained a couple of pounds! I was panting... and not for missing a meal. For her, tea, a spoonful of rice... and liquor, for sure. Better not to get into that. So the day of the fiesta, she had managed to lose the two pounds, but she fainted in the middle of the play. The Baroness was very worried and wanted a doctor to see her, for sure. But there was no way. She had one come two or three times and he couldn't get past the door. Finally the Baroness said to me: Marie, if you really do love the Miss, you must help me. I said yes, of course, and she told me to watch every single thing that happened to the Miss and to tell it all in detail to the doctor that she would send me. And maybe that way we could do something even without saying anything to the Miss. "You know how much she trusts you – she said – she won't suspect anything, and it's for her own good. I don't need to tell you how much all this depends on you." The truth is that she treated me with more consideration ever since I saved the Miss when she tried to commit suicide in London... Before, she was a little smug with me... I'm not saying she treated me badly, not at all: she was very generous, I mean she knew how to grease a palm, but sometimes you felt like you were nobody, she'd look past you and keep going, as if her gaze were going through glass. Not that that was strange, it was more or less normal, but I wasn't used to it. Then, other times, she would start speaking English so I wouldn't understand her. Especially when Miss Toinette was there, because Miss Pauline never did that. As if there could be secrets from me, in that house! In the end, though, the Baroness realized that and saw that she needed me. In any case, it didn't help because no matter how hard I tried to explain everything to the doctor, he must not have understood me, or maybe there wasn't any remedy for the illness. The medicine he gave me didn't hurt, but it didn't help either. And the poor thing never even knew she had taken it. That day I understood that maybe in life, things can happen just like in novels and people can die of poisoning without even knowing it. I felt terrible for deceiving her like that. And all for nothing. Besides, she drank like a fish. Not that she got really legless; I mean, a few times she fell right down and I had to help her get in bed and tuck her in like a babe in arms, but I can count the times that happened on the fingers of one hand. She usually kept herself straight and didn't lose her way. But she soaked it up like a sponge. And that couldn't have been good for her at all. Besides, when she drank alone she got so terribly sad. I remember one day when she came back from Longchamp. The Baroness was crazy about horses, and I think Pauline went with her just to make her happy. When the Baroness went away – because the truth is that the Miss behaved better when the Baroness was around – she started to drink without stopping. She said over and over again that at the races everyone stared at her and said bad things about her, and that from then on she would never go out again, she would shut herself up in the house... I tried to console her, telling her she had to shake off what people said about her, like water off a duck's back, and besides it was all in their imaginations... I told her that to try to calm her down, because the truth is there must have been something in what

316

they were saying. Since she had such thin skin, everything hurt her down to the bone. Completely different from the Baroness in that way. And from Miss Natalie, too. That one really trod heavily. But she wasn't around during that time. By pure coincidence, the day she showed up was the day the Miss died. Someone must have told her that things were very serious... but she didn't get beyond the door. The Baroness made sure she was kept out. All told, there was never a more beautiful dead woman than the Miss. She looked like an angel. All white, with her hair spread out, and those long, thick eyelashes of hers... As if they'd switched her around. Because when she was alive those last years, she looked pitiful. Worse than an old hag... Dark rings under her eyes and her face all yellowed... and those legs that couldn't even hold her up...

I don't know. Mr Salomon asked me a lot of questions about the Miss's death, and I didn't know how to answer most of them. It was all one big to-do. The truth is that during her last moments, I was so exhausted, with my brain and heart in pieces, that I took the advice of the Miss's friend, the one who was also named Marie and who was her piano teacher, and I went to rest for a few hours. They didn't even tell me to come and dress her, and that really hurt a lot. Because at the moment of my Miss's death, her friend had also gone home to rest, and the only ones left at her bedside were the friar who was attending her and a new maid, too young for such headaches. The poor girl even fainted and everything, maybe from the strong smell of the candles... But she started to spread it around that the Miss had died cursing her mother, and that frightened her, and that's why she got dizzy. Lucky that Miss Marie returned and put a stop to it. As for me, I never believed that story. I'm the first to know that the Miss and her mother weren't exactly bosom buddies. More than that, during that last year, Miss Pauline only spoke badly of her. But she would say one thing and then another: she would complain that when she was little, her mother didn't give her enough to eat, or she made her wear tattered old shoes, and the next minute she was criticizing her for only paying attention to her bodily needs. Once I even heard her say that if she was wretched, it was because her mother hadn't made her learn Greek! What I sometimes think is that mothers are always the scapegoats..., I mean, since they're the ones who brought us into the world, when things don't go well and you don't know who to blame, they're the first to get it... Whatever the case, that year Miss Pauline didn't want to see her own mother, not even once. Even though her sister kept insisting on it. And the Miss was incapable of denying anything at all to her sister. But where it came to her mother, she was as firm as a mast. I don't know what must have happened, because a couple of years earlier it seemed they were on better terms, and shortly after Miss Toinette's wedding, in the summertime, she said to pack our suitcases, that Mrs T. wanted to take a trip to Honolulu and Miss Pauline had decided to go with her. And that's what we did. On the way, we went through Japan. I think that was the Miss's idea, because she'd been crazy about all things Japanese for some time. The very bed she died in was Japanese and it was really a knockout: all lacquered in black and gold, shaped like a boat, like a great big crib. One day the Miss told me it was the appropriate bed for a traveller like her, that she would like to make her last voyage in it... That was very painful for me, because I could see she was thinking too much about death again, and after the calamity in London, I was always very wary. She also had a couple of breath-taking silk kimonos. One was red, a bright cherry colour, with a dragon embroidered on it, that she never wore, and she said she'd give it to me. After she died, I looked all over for it, because I thought she would want me to have it. I couldn't find it anywhere. Someone else must have beat me to it. Miss Pauline said it was very old and worth a lot. She bought it when we were in Nagasaki, and I think she intended to give it to her mother, but she changed her mind. Nagasaki was so lovely! I remember it as if it were now, with the little woods of lemon trees and the hilly little streets, and so many yellow-faced people hopping around on wooden stilts… And the port, all lined with strange-shaped boats like I'd never seen before… That's where I found out that Japanese eat raw fish… each to their own, I suppose… From some city, I don't remember now, we got on a steamship called *Siberia* for Honolulu. I had never crossed the Pacific. It was a long trip, but for me it could have lasted another week. If I'd been born a boy, I'd have been a sailor. And a great sailor, too! But Miss Pauline suffered, and she arrived weak and tired. In Honolulu, her mother wouldn't let her rest for a single second. Mrs T. had friends and acquaintances there by the boatload, and I think even some distant relatives. Visits and receptions, dinners, parties and gatherings… And it's true that the Miss never liked that sort of thing… But she put on a brave face for her mother… She went everywhere with her. I know for sure she even paid for most of the expenses. At least the great dinner they had at the hotel was on her, where they invited all of Mrs T's friends. And what a spread, sweet Jesus! All kinds of dishes and drinks kept coming, enough to bring back the dead. And Miss Pauline, pale and thin, putting up with the onslaught. I never saw her make such an effort for anyone. She was eating a bit more... She even got the urge to get dressed up and put make-up on, something I hadn't seen before. One day, when I was helping her with her hairdo, she told me that when she was young she had even been presented to Queen Victoria! Her eyes shone, and suddenly she looked like a little kid that wants to impress you... And it seems all that was for her mother, because Mrs T. was an exquisite lady, always dressed to kill, one of those ladies who seem born to please and be in the limelight. And that's a gift you can't buy with money. Her daughter was very different. But during that time, she was most anxious to please her mother. Lots of hustle and bustle, and money-spending, I could see that well enough. Poor Miss! She was always too generous, never had anything she kept for herself... I must say that if I'd been another sort of person, I could have feathered my nest in that house... The Miss had a great collection of keys. There were all kinds – gold, silver, iron, big, medium and small, but no one knew which lock they opened or closed... One day I asked her about it and she said she just liked keys, not that she used them for anything. So, all kinds of armoires and consoles and drawers were always unlocked. And all stuffed with beautiful, expensive things... With just what she brought back from that trip! Especially a bunch of little Japanese statues, small enough to hold in your hand, in the form of animals or odd-looking people. And of course, who knows how many buddhas. Because she got carried away with buddhas. At first, they made me nervous with those bellies and fat-folds and breasts like a plump lady. But you get used to everything, and from putting apples and rice in front of them every single day, I began to like them and in the end, I thought they were even quite nice. That had already happened to me with turtles, and with frogs, and with serpents. And they'd scared me so much at first! Luckily, she didn't have cats any more when I came. Because there's nothing I can do about cats: as soon as they get near me my eyes swell up and inflate so it makes people suffer, the way I look! Anyway, I was talking about the buddhas: she had a real mania, for sure. I even think she quarrelled with her mother again because Mrs T. made some comment about them that must have stung… Good thing that the friar who helped her die well let her keep them, otherwise I don't think she would have converted. Because she was one to stick to her guns. Miss Marie had been all mulish about it for years, and little by little she made inroads… I don't know, but I think what counts in the end is to not hurt anybody and to help whoever you can. Anything else is leaves blowing in the wind. Like I said before: if I'm glad about the way everything went, it's because I know the Miss had a good death. And I know it because a few days earlier, before anything had happened, I heard her tell an acquaint-ance of hers she would have liked to die Catholic. And in the evening when I helped her get undressed and prepared the bath for her, nice and hot like she liked it, she whispered to me, real quiet like she was in confession, that Queen Anna whatshername, the one whose maid was named Marie, like me, was lucky to be Catholic because that way she could face death without fear. I told her what I thought of that, and then she started talking about her friend Violette who had died of typhus… It seems she had been dreaming about that for days. And she said Miss Violette had also converted.

Mr Salomon thingummybob – I'm no good with names, I say them and then forget them! – asked me some very delicate questions. For one thing, he wanted to know how my

Miss and the Baroness had got along in the last years. It seemed to me he knew more about some things than he let on, but with others, he pretended to know more than he did, trying to see if he could coax a truth out of me by using half-lies. It was a real tug-of-war.

I made the Baroness look good. She had her faults, like everybody, but she really did love the Miss, no denying that. She watched over her vigilantly, trying to get her to eat, to take care of herself... as I've said before. And when she didn't know what to do, she consulted with me. It's true that there were tricks. And that I hadn't known what to think for the last few years. The cook, who never stopped gossiping – the tongue is better off kept in the mouth! – , well, the cook told me that she knew from a good source that the Baroness had another sweetheart, and that she was Russian. That made sense to me, because there was a time when she wouldn't have left the house, she wouldn't even let the Miss take a breath without her, and suddenly she started coming over less. But it's strange, Miss Pauline said it was the other way around, that the Baroness was very jealous, that she watched her like a hawk. She said she had told the Miss that if the Miss deceived her she would kill her, and crazy stuff like that. I'm sure the crazy stuff was just manias and I don't know how they got into her head. Maybe because she wasn't what she used to be, and her nerves were all in a jumble... One day she even had me pack suitcases, in a big hurry – but not without a couple of her favourite buddhas, of course! – and we grabbed the train to Marseille. She told me we would get on a ship and head for Mytilene, because she was in danger and she wouldn't be safe anywhere else. Mytilene, Mytilene, always Mytilene. What madness, my god! I don't know what she found so wonderful on that miserable island. With that sun that left you fried. But whenever she could, it was like they need people there! It's true that her mansion there was lovely. She'd had it all fixed up, she put in a perfect bath, with a water-heater and everything. And the garden was splendid, I couldn't even describe it, full of golden birds in golden cages hanging from the trees. But people talked and whispered… because of course in that corner of the world, nothing like that had ever been seen. They even went so far as to gossip that the Miss was the daughter of the Prince of Wales. Since they realized she was English… You never know your luck? Yes, I've seen it all, so I have. Anyway, it didn't surprise me that we were going to Mytilene, just the way we went about it. Like she was hiding from everything and everybody. I'm not saying the Baroness was a saint or an angel, but to think that she would do harm to the Miss…! But it all went so badly. Halfway there, the Miss opened her purse and all her money fell out. She was like that, sometimes she seemed like a numbskull… Then she started to worry that they were going to rob her, because, of course, what can you expect if you show what you've got?… all that cash, just like that. Anyway, in Marseille we ran into a sort of secretary of the Baroness who was waiting for us to make us go back! I don't know how she knew so much, but she was on top of everything. She must have been having her followed, otherwise I can't explain it. And the Miss was as docile as a sheep, back home we go. I preferred it that way, because the last time we were in Mytilene, I had a fright it took me days to get over. The Miss disappeared. She went for a walk on the seaside, as she always did, but she didn't come back. And what a terrible storm there was! It was raining cats and dogs. When evening

323

came, I got scared and decided to call the gardener, to get him to round up some people. I was nervous, even though the London trouble hadn't happened yet. We found her all right, drenched, soaked, on a rock with a big crack in it, there she was, battered by the rain and the waves. Sometimes when I think of Miss Pauline, I remember her as I saw her that day. Because her face and her eyes, I don't know if I dare say it... were not of this world, a little like I imagined the women of the sea when I was small, those water sprites who had a terrible sorrow and the sea called and called. In the legends, they always ended badly, and I felt so sorry. It wouldn't have surprised me at all if that day the Miss had thought of taking the wrong turn, and who knows how it would have ended up if we hadn't arrived when we did. But what was I to think at that moment, she had such a happy face she seemed blessed... We had to bring her around, and it wasn't easy, she almost caught one of those colds it's hard to get over. The poor Miss, she really did put me through the mill sometimes. And that Mr Salomon from Paris wanted me to explain it all, every single detail... He got me to talk a lot, some people know how to hook you in and which bait to use in every case, but about some things, not a word. If I told him why the Miss died, it would have opened the floodgates. I've taken a lot of criticism for being too docile. But she would say, "Marie, do this." I couldn't do otherwise. "Marie, prepare me a nice hot bath," and I prepared it with water that would almost scald you... "Marie, fix my hair," and I fixed it. "Marie, have a cocktail ready," and there it was. Even more. She'd say "Marie, sit right here and don't move, and when I give you a signal, hand me my glass." That was when there was company. She would come to where I was with whatever excuse and she'd toss down the liquor in a gulp, as if she were throwing it down a well. Then, so her breath wouldn't give her away and no one would know, she'd rinse her mouth with rose water. I didn't like that at all, but all I did was say "Miss, you'll ruin your health." That's how it went. The kind of cramps that she got so she could hardly walk, it all came from the same thing. She would get all choked up and then of course her food would go down the wrong pipe. That can be very bad: in no time at all the lungs get blocked and you're in a hole. That happened to Miss Pauline, even though she ate like a sparrow. At least that's what I understood, because I don't know my way around all that stuff with doctors and diseases.

Mr Salomon told me that the Miss is very important, and that in years to come she'll be renowned and famous. Yes, that's it, I thought, canonise her now that she's dead… I guess he didn't even meet her, but when he read her poetry, he was good and hooked… and it seems reading her isn't enough. What I never tire of saying and repeating is that Miss Pauline was an angel… and the rest is nobody's business.

19 March 1929

While rereading *À l'heure des mains jointes* I came across a note I had written in pencil dated 1917: "The Countess of Noailles bragged to Romaine Brooks that she had left unanswered some flowers and a letter from Pauline, qualifying her as an unworthy woman. Romaine told me that." A strange caprice of memory has radically erased from my mind the circumstances under which this confidence was made to me. Since Romaine is far away and inaccessible at the moment, I interrogated Natalie about the matter to no avail: she says she knows nothing of it.

Still and all, the episode seems more than probable. An offended Pauline could only say this about a poetess: "You will not gather Sappho's roses". This could not possibly mean: "You will not know my love", for that would be of a presumption quite unlike her, and in bad taste. Nor could it be addressed to a man of letters. On the other hand, Romaine is incapable of inventing such a story, and in view of my unpardonable lapse of memory, I must depend on my testimony written at the time. So, an addressee has been identified, with all the appropriate reservations, for the poem "Without flowers on your forehead".

9 September 1929

I was in London for a week at a conference, accompanied by two nieces. I cannot help but note down how lovely the weather was for that trip, with a velvety sea, almost meridional in aspect. Even the Thames seemed transparent, at least between Hampton Court and Westminster Bridge. Every time I've set foot in this city in the last few years, I think: Pauline lived here. But I have failed to detect the slightest resonance of London in her work. Aside from the island of Mytilene, though, is there any scenery that has a real referent? As Charles B. said, it is the changing scenery of her soul that she evokes in her poems. Even so, sometimes there is an extraordinary exactness of detail. Last Friday, just before I left Paris, I saw Flossie for a moment, bronzed by the sun and blonder than ever. That wondrous verse of Pauline's came to my mind instantly:

The sky mixed gold with bronze and crystal.

Bronze was the darkened skin; gold was the hair; crystal was her clear gaze. Surely the prophesy of the withered lily is still very far from coming true!

During my sojourn on the other side of the Channel, I did not forget Pauline's glory, and as usual I advertised and celebrated her whenever I had the chance. Three ladies at my table were speaking to me of Verlaine, and I revealed the name of Renée Vivien to them, reciting in a low voice some of her most beautiful lines. The effect is always immediate, breathtaking in impact: where can we find these masterpieces? One girl especially, whose name I did not even know, caused me great pleasure. I was reciting the second of two sonnets Pauline addressed to the girls of the future, the first of which opens with hopeful, vital movement, later buried under the sad conviction of being drowned in oblivion. When I finished reciting the last lines:

None of you will remember me
I who would have loved you so gravely.

The girl exclaimed in her native English: "Oh! gravely, how lovely that is." That gravely really is a touchstone: those who enthusiastically admire that adverb, without having been advised of its beauty by the reciter, are truly worthy of admiring the rest. So here you have it that an archaeologist and specialist in painting in the eyes of the world shows himself to be privately more interested in other things. But I never recite Pauline's verse to any man. To them, I speak only of archaeology and politics. I have never forgotten what Liane, my incomparable Eva, told me one day – unjustly as far as my own person is concerned, but true in general: and she should know. What kind of interest could this passionate literature inspire in those who bear the heavy animal skin with which the Eternal dressed Adam after the fall?

6 October 1929

I gave Liane several works of Chateaubriand, among them the novel *René*, which led her to ask me if that work was related in some way to Pauline's pseudonym. Up to now, oddly enough, I have not mentioned this theme in my notebooks, so now I will describe the state of my information and conjectures.

Charles B. is the one who helped her to come up with it; he confirmed this himself. Still, I am not satisfied with the explanation he offered about its origin and underlying meaning: simply an ambiguous first name and a last name from medieval epic. For the first name, apart from its obvious symbolism, I think Liane's intuition is on the mark: exile, forbidden loves, uprootedness, the *mal du siècle*, all present in special form in this novel, are all part of Pauline's vital and literary vision, and also her greatness of soul, befitting a great sorrow. Furthermore, Chateaubriand's mark is no more imperceptible in Pauline's work than that of Baudelaire... And while her first book was mysteriously signed R. Vivien, on the cards she had printed to accompany it, René in the masculine form is clear, that is, the exact name of the protagonist who gives title to the short novella by the gentleman of Combourg. Only later would she give it the definitive feminine form.

As far as the surname is concerned, without refuting completely Charles B's thesis, I am inclined to complement it significantly. Even though it is futile to seek out traces of epic Vivienesque cavalcades in the more than eight thousand of Pauline's verses, in contrast the magical forest of Bronceliande, Celtic folklore, Merlin, and above all Viviane, do find a presence. At least three poems are explicitly dedicated to this last character, which, let us remember, in its English form is Vivien (that is how it appears in Tennyson's *The Idylls of the King*, which is surely the source of inspiration for the famous painting by Burne-Jones, today in the Birmingham museum, which Pauline no doubt knew, given her interest in the Pre-Raphaelites). Are we confronted, then, with a hybridity of gender doubled by a hybridity of language?

At the same time, if it is true that at first glance the Viviane of the poems seems to be simply another of the numerous advocations of a unique but multiform Flossie, we must not forget that according to the most extensive version of the legend, the fairy bewitches Merlin on the basis of a spell he himself taught her: might this not be Pauline's secret dream with respect to the one who initiated her into the mysteries of the Island…? The spell also has the virtue of sealing them both up together in a glass sarcophagus: a destiny that Natalie would have fled in horror, and which in contrast would have pleased Pauline as a tomb for her imperfectly corresponded love. In any case, it is a marvellous metaphor for poetry. I do not offer this hypothesis without a last scruple about the identification of Merlin with the Amazon, closer to the cruel and light arts of Epona, the Gallo-Roman virgin warrior, than to any weighty wisdom, whether magical or prophetic. Furthermore, I cannot help but tremble when I read the verses Pauline places in the mouth of the enchantress, as if they were addressed to me personally:

"I'm sorry for you, thinker, whose gaze avoids me, / for you haven't known, you who know so many things / the pallor of poppies and the laughter of roses / the ardour and languor of lips towards nightfall…".

21 November 1929

The lecture about Pauline is over. The day and the hour kept me from attending that "Friday" on Rue Jacob, thus depriving me from catching the odd smile or some distracted – priceless – word from the hostess… From this point of view, then, I feel completely inadequate: never until yesterday had circumstances imposed on me such an impossible choice between Pauline and her Lorély. But that schedule also assured me that Natalie would not be in the audience, thus sparing me from being submerged in a confusing and lamentable state: how could one speak of Pauline in her presence!

I do know, however, that she censures the central thesis of

these arguments. And I understand this: It is her pride as a goddess that cannot abide me placing at the centre of Pauline's work the axis of glory rather than that of love. Furthermore, she's too much her own person to understand the need for such diplomatic sinuosities: most people need to be offered the pot by its coolest handle. After all, perhaps glory is just a posthumous form of love: the only form with the capacity to raise the dead.

Private Papers of Sara T. (10)

Where the narrator rediscovers Sara T. a year or so after having left her in Mytilene in intimate colloquy with the ghost of Renée Vivien

Barcelona, 21 November 1985

Dearest Chantal,

Finally I can send you a copy of the screenplay... You could say that I have just written the final full-stop. I bet you thought the time would never come. Suddenly, I have the impression that from one moment to another I could begin to fly. I feel like one of those balloons from the era of Renée and Co the very moment after dropping the ballast over the side.

Even so, I can't quite shake off a certain sense of regret. It is as if the screenplay I have ended up writing was nothing more than a terrible copy, a distant replica, of that which I had intended. A sketch, perhaps: it contains broad brush-strokes of what I wanted to say, but is essentially incomplete. This, which is perhaps in itself a statement of the inevitable, is somewhat graver in my case. Because a screenplay is always little more than a sketch. So, then, my text is nothing more than a sketch of a sketch. And if the sensation of incompleteness has grown with each attempt to put things down on paper concretely, it terrifies me to think what will happen when we pass to the level of the image. Or maybe not: because if at one level the image is more concrete, it also permits, in its own way, to play with suggestion and to multiply ambiguity. Whatever the case, just thinking about this, some lines by Renée have come into my head.

Le charme douloureux des ébauches m'attire.
The painful charm of sketches attracts me.

And then it has seemed to me as if the idea of the sketch, accepted consciously, is precisely what is needed to evoke her life synthetically. Not just because she was cut down in the "flower of her life", as people here say. Every life is always radically incomplete, in one way or another. Or, indeed, complete: to the extent that death unfailingly writes the final full-stop. And it is, after all, from this ending that the narrative takes its definitive meaning. Someone who dies at 32 will as a result be from the day of their birth someone who has to die at 32. What is more, in the case of Renée, the intensity and vertiginous rhythm with which she exhausted her existence seem to defy the very limitation of such a brief time. What seems crucial to me is her lucid yet unsubmissive consciousness of being a sketch, that is, of incompletion, and, at the same time, her intuitive certainty that any attempt at real plenitude would be fallacious. Only dreams – desire? – can fill this void, this immoderate and overpowering yearning, always frustrated, for totality, for the absolute. And intimately linked to these dreams and this desire, we find literature.

Through Renée I believe I have come to understand what it means to intermingle literature and life inextricably, to live each day "literarily", or rather, "poetically": every gesture, every moment is a rhetorical figure, and systematically the humble, limited, poor signifier knows that it is not up to the requirements of the slippery Signified: the part that stretches and is broken in its efforts to represent the Whole; the totality that realises, with sadness, that it is in the end nothing but an infinitesimal part. The lack of today, which is only the symbol of another darker and more mysterious Original Lack. The minor mutilations, which both stand for and are the effect of the great causal Mutilation. Each concrete woman returns us to the abstract Feminine. And the Feminine can be embodied in Sappho and her mythical island. The Inaccessible, the Abyss, is crystallised concretely in the one that escapes and at the same time attracts without remedy: Natalie-Lorély. Each love longs to and yet cannot become Love – this is why "with each love" one is "further removed from Love". This is why hers is a "one-eyed love" and her Venus a "Venus of the blind". It is in this permanent fissure that Renée feels herself to be alive. The words that attempt to close the breach do nothing more than represent it, recreate it and reconstruct it time and again. This is her great break with the order of the world, mirrored in another that also represents her metaphorically and thus reinforces her: her revolt as a woman and her clear defence of sapphic love.

On finishing this long paragraph, I cannot help feeling again the sensation that I am trying to encircle, delimit and define something that is complexity and movement and that you constantly have the sense is escaping from your hands. Perhaps Renée Vivien too has become for me a metaphor of the inaccessible, one of those impossible, unsatisfactory (?) loves for which I seem to have such a penchant. I don't think I have ever spoken to you of the process by which I was seduced by her. Perhaps I can do so now that I have reached the end, and from here, looking back, I can see a more or less precise track... If I try to remember I know that at first she captured me by identification. The other day I spoke of it in a lecture, during the symposium: and the truth is that that poem which had moved me so, was met with the most absolute indifference. Those lines which had for me been like a mirror, turned out to be opaque for everyone else. Or maybe not, who knows. Not long ago I read somewhere that if you wanted to be sure of your success with women you had to talk of feminine ecstasy and pleasure... and it makes sense. After all, where does poking in the wound actually take us? It must be unhealthy. In anticipation of the objections of the supremely healthy and conscious collective unconscious, I read a few other fragments. Not from "Vanquished" nor from "The Pillory" nor from "The Moat". Univocal, linear, affirmative ones.

The image, sweetened by this angle of the mirror, could be recognised. In vain, I tried to continue to bet on the other side, the darker side:

The dawn has the furtive step of a she-wolf
and the eyes of a jackal.
With my hands I dug out the moat,
I built without vassal
the tower of black walls that encloses you,
Your terror watching grow
with the blind swelling of a goitre
my feudal love.

Further on in the same poem, there is that really peculiar verse that gives evidence of the contradiction in her between "ideology" and "passion":

I am as cowardly as a man,
And I order you and summon you

To languish in my kisses as
In a narrow prison.

"As cowardly as a man": how many times have I myself reflected that with my excessively possessive way of living love, I was simply copying, grotesquely, the feudal masculine. And I wavered, as Renée did, between this pole and that of believing myself the greatest lover in the world, with the same amorous megalomania that is at base – and with deference to Ausiàs March – so very feminine. The seduction had begun with that kind of miracle-mirage of the mirror. And I was taken in by it: I had all of her poetic oeuvre copied to me by international interlibrary loan. Then something strange happened, which, I don't know why, I haven't told anyone before: I experienced a momentary movement of revulsion. All at once, all of it seemed to me like a great funeral monument that had been built for herself by someone who did not believe she had the right to live.

Amidst the ashes of Gomorrah, for a moment all I could smell was the stench of death and open wound, deliberately buried under mountains of lilies, violets, arums, rushes, spikenard, roses, as well a whole shower of other flowers, candles, torches, sandalwood, belladona, datura, aconite... I am not her, I thought to myself. And it was the truth, but this did not become evident to me until the very end. Then, disconcerted, without knowing why, I persisted in delving further into that particular kind of disorienting wood. The essential likeness that I had known instinctively, could not just be forsworn as easily as that... The Renée I had forged in my image and likeness could not just disappear without leaving a trace... And I began to pursue her, like a true lover. (Between brackets I will confess that this love for a dead woman has served as a counterweight for another love; one more dangerous for me, potentially more obsessive). I had the absolute certainty, in advance, of my love being requited. Through that strange privilege that poets appear to have, Renée could speak to me from the almost immaterial world of texts:

> *Vous pour qui j'écrivis, ô belles jeunes femmes!*
> *Vous que, seules, j'aimais, relirez-vous mes vers*
> *Par les futurs matins neigeant sur l'univers,*
> *Et par les soirs futurs de roses et de flammes*

> *You for whom I wrote, oh lovely young women,*
> *You whom, alone, I loved, will you reread my verse*
> *On future mornings snowing on the universe,*
> *During future evenings of roses and flames?*

In the original she addressed me in the plural, it is true – don't go thinking I'm brushing over that fact –, but in this case I could permit myself – miraculously – the luxury of not being exclusive. And I felt the rare emotion of having already satisfied the implicit desire she herself believed to be impossible in the second part of the poem. Queer power this: to elect to give or not give meaning to figures from the past; to allow oneself either to become or not become blood for the nourishment of these strange vampires that are the texts which depend on us for survival. But Renée's poem did not just offer – or demand of me? – literature:

> *You will think for a moment, amidst your charming disarray*
> *Of dishevelled hair and robes undone:*

337

"This lady, in her sorrow and in her joy,
carried everywhere her looks and lips of a lover".

Pallid and breathing your perfumed flesh,
in the magical evocation of the night
you will say: "This lady has the ardour that flees from me...
If she was alive! She would truly have loved me!"

It is curious: at first I had made this last line my own. I had thought this very thing of Renée Vivien: that she would have loved me. Afterwards, after going into her story, I have seen that this feeling, like so many other things, was based on a fallacy. A fallacy of the type that when seen in the light of day does not offer the slightest simulacrum of truth. In the real world it is possible that Renée would have loved me – in the strong sense that she gave to the word love – if I had managed to embody before her eyes the image of an unachievable dream, of Desire always renewed. Something like what she used to say Natalie meant to her: "you are my self glorified, transfigured, almost inaccessible and ungraspable except in certain rare moments of joy or pain" – the Amazon must have understood perfectly what Renée meant, when in a message designed to reconquer her she offered, explicitly and with all the words, only that: desire, regret, sorrow. And me? I ask myself from time to time, how would I have responded before a Renée – a Pauline, rather – of flesh and bone? Perhaps something similar would have happened in my case to what I have said of her, but in attenuated form, at least. Even though I have a certain penchant for exaggeration, for radicalism, there is no real comparison! Apart from anything else, I am still alive and, by my age, Renée was already dead three years.

Right now, I know that Renée and I could only have met in the way in which we have: above and beyond this abyss that time and oblivion have tried to establish between us. Equilibrium is only possible through this kind of – momentary – overcoming of death that is a poem, a book, a film... and which each of us has attempted on our own terms. Perhaps, in the end, only a slightly more convincing simulacrum.

The narrator, who up until now has played the role of a strange coryphaeus, officiating amidst a heterogeneous and often rebellious chorus, now decides to take on the role of death and, making show of her proverbial arbitrariness, break the course of the narration at this point.

Final Monody

London, 11 June 1877-
Paris, 18 November 1909

In the future as grey as an uncertain dawn, someone, I know very well, will remember us, when they see burning over the amber plain the red eyes of autumn. A being amid the beings of the earth, O my Voluptuousness, will remember us. A woman who will bear the sweet and violent mystery on her brow. She will love the light mist fuming daintily and the olive trees beautiful as the sea, the flower of snow and the flower of foam, night and winter. Saddening the coasts and shores with her farewells, she will know the sacred love of virgins… For nothing is sweeter than love… I scorn wine, I despise honey, I want only the taste of kisses. Neither the trembling of water nor the swirls of the sky equal the rippling of your body in my bed. Ah, the perfume, ah, the poison of your lips, venomous flowers. Your eyes reflect the sky of Mytilene.

A woman, I know very well, will remember us.

Oh the trembling of the nape where my breath burned, oh the shadow of the fuzz reflected on your lips, oh the beauty of lips alike in a kiss of love. Our heart is the same in our woman's bosom, my beloved, our body is made identical. The same heavy destiny has weighed upon our soul. I am more than yours: I am your self. I translate the smile and the shadow of your face. My sweetness equals your great sweetness. In spite of the aggressive, savage vehemence of all desire and its latent cruelty, my mouth would not ever be able to harshly bite your mouth. Listen to the soft murmur of this hour I love, that passes and flees and dies in a poem... I think my pain is someone else's... Miraculously I see life's laughter, the brightness of stars spreads through the marrow of my bones... Vertiginously I attain the stars... I return to the love that transfigures all around it into gold, to the charm of the poem, to the laughter of love...

Often, I fear nothing but oblivion.

For today I rejoice to be a woman: praised be fate in its most obscure designs: my body is the mirror where you will see your breasts and your deep haunches. I am no more than your faithful mirror. I plunge into you to love you better. I dream of your beauty and it confounds me. What could you love that I do not love...? What can you think that I do not think as well? Every one of your torments is my trouble too. O sadness, O rancour of dreams soon snatched away. O tedium of aconite and belladonna... Grapes of bitter juice of a disenchanted night... Our pain equals a burst of joy. Our mad-eyed joy equals pain.

Here is the palace of pain.

I am tired of the days, the voices, and the faces, of stifled tears and mute sobbing... I have lived within a troubled dream, searching for eternity in the briefest minute. The day slips by through the stained glass like a wild one, hunting me down in my sorrow. She has entered and glares at my naked soul. Curse you, O day, unto the far off limits of time, you, who caught my anger and my hate. Curse you, day, you who with your clear eyes have been able to see the hideous immensity of my terrible love. I am of those laid low by light. Under the implacable face of day, memories devour me like abject vermin. And at dusk when I hear the groaning of the unfortunate land, I have felt in excess the horror of having been born. Who, then, will bring me the hemlock in their hands? Night slithers, slowly and subtly, toward the opal of the hill. The soul resuscitates in the tenebrous shadows.

Like a serpent in hiding, my pain begins to sleep.

O Wind, my old friend, come into my house and unite your voice to mine, weep! Let us weep for the day, for the evening, the night with the voice of women mourning over lost youth or love in flight: we are friends for we weep together. O wind, you raise in me the widest wings, carry me off, oh you who master the immense sea… the slow heavy sail lingers in the port, she who once was capable of defying the strongest storms: for her, the rest is the same as death. Oh the bewitching danger of the magnificent storm, thunder that clashes like a cymbal, lightning that slashes the night with a radiance too bright. Let us go to the high seas without clinging to the shore, without fearing the terror of bitter spaces. I know not where I will go, nor what gust carries me. But I will not return unless dead or triumphant… The masts are raised… but the sail is rotting in the urn of the port.

Yesterday I was the solitary traveller…

I have seen too many oceans, too many countries, the gaze fades from my dazzled eyes. My look was fresher than the moon of the north, green and shrouded like English seas. I learned of the taste, the odour, the desire of death, the flight, the grey exile on grey cliffs. I have seen too many landscapes, too many oceans... I return, my friend, and humbly, tenderly, joyfully I give you all that I have seen: here is the offering of my eyes. Contemplate the colours of shadows. Like a pink flower, I have seen the moon blossom, smiling on dreams without pain, the hypnotic, subtle meditation of blue nights, and while listening to the crying of owls of mysterious flight, I have seen sparkling nights of gold. I have seen, next to the silent waves calmed by night, those lush gardens, the pride of Mytilene...

I will hurl myself into your eyes where sadness rhapsodizes.

Like those who return from their travels, my fingers have traversed infinite horizons. Slowly, now they tremulously follow the line of your hips, the curve of your flank, shoulders, neck, and your breasts of poppy and magnolia. Clairvoyant, my fingers linger over the trembling of your flesh under robes of the sweetness of petals. I raise an altar of gold to good Lentitude, which teaches the forgetfulness of hours and days, friend and protector of poets... Oh you, who make a beautiful song softer, who know how to retain more time and make a soft kiss even softer. Today, though, my delicate desire refuses the kisses. It passes nearby and languishes in white voluptuousness.

O form that hands cannot retain...

The white flame of your body burns into the depth of my solitude. For you alone have I dressed and adorned myself. I have brought jewels. Will they be lucky enough to please you? The ebb tides of the sea shimmer on your dress. Here against my flesh, I have your flesh, glowing naked. The evening is replete with sandalwood and spikenard. My soul is all perfumed with the white roses of your flesh. Our caresses are a melodious poem. Your hair is a golden, aromatic rain in my hands. Fluid and insinuating like sea algae.

I will make a shroud of your hair in which to bury my dreams.

My heart is heavy and the veil light. I have not been able to triumph over my heart.

The shadow follows my steps, recriminated by the dawn. Like a reproach my shadow follows me. Straight and long like a cypress, with steps of a she-wolf, my shadow pursues me like a regret. Here you have me: the great source of culpability. I had the inexcusable audacity to want the sisterly love made of light whiteness, the furtive step that does not wound the grass, and the sweet voice that allies itself with the night... I am not one to be celebrated by the crowd, I am one the crowd hates, for I have dared to imagine that a virgin in love is lovelier than a man...

Hate has united us, much stronger than love.

Our heart has inherited the grief, the gasp, the agony of the women of sullen and pale brow. Just like the voice of a

344

beast, deep and rumbling, our revolt becomes resonance and roar at once. Let us hate the aggressive face of all males. Let us hate the zeal that soils desire. Let us hate the masses and the Laws of the World. They had forbidden me your hair, your pupils, for your hair is long and full of fragrance, and your eyes have a strange ardency with which they cloud over in rebellious waves. They have pointed at me angrily because my gaze sought out your tender gaze. I am a woman: I had no right to beauty, they had condemned me to the ugliness of men. And your eyes sang for me the sirens' song.

You, who judge me, you are nothing to me.

I do not feel pride from your praise, nor do I feel fear of your calumnies. The law I transgress is vile and abject. Like a statue among passersby, my soul is serene. You will not blanch the piety of my passion for the beauty of women… No one has seen that my gaze was clear. No one has seen that I chose you with simplicity… And they have said, who is this cursed woman silently gnawing at the flames of hell? On my lips the only blasphemy was the kiss… What does the judgment of men matter to us? What do we have to fear if we are pure before life? Let them defend their impure morality. Oh songs of mine, we will not feel shame or sadness at the scorn of those we scorn. The fire dances, the stars watch over fading books, the furniture is our friend. I no longer know the glacial look of the street where everyone passes by with growing haste… I do not know whether they speak badly of us, nor whether they still speak at all… Here, words do not hurt. Let us keep the doors closed. Souls without hope have the solitary pride of islands.

O sweetness of my songs, let us go to Mytilene!

Here, beneath the violets of the sunset, is Lesbos, regret and nostalgia of the gods, sacred exile of song. Across the unequal centuries, I again find your waves, your olive trees, your vineyards. Be the altar of yesterday's drunkenness, welcome us with goodness, receive a feminine couple in your gardens, O melodious island that inflames caresses... The vine that reddens under the sun pours into my goblet with the waves, at the laughter of the Bacchantes... We will perfume our bodies with roses and myrrh, where the fury of wine will burn like a sacred ferment. Your charm fascinates me, sinuous like a serpent. I feel the emotions of the thief before rare booty. Love, O eternal thief, who steals the heavy treasures of the heart and the secrets of dresses...

My feudal love grows like a goitre.

I am as cowardly as a man. I love you with my one-eyed love. I watch you with my only eye, my sinister eye where the rage of rum shines. I follow you with my look, lustful as an ape, drunk like a balloon without ballast. I pant toward the lure of vibrant breasts, of the subtle torso where grace joins strength... Give me kisses bitter like tears... Open your lips to me with rage and I will slowly drink in bile and poison. Like a male in heat, roaring and howling, I will make your bones crunch under my weight. Oh the voluptuousness of feeling the pearls of your blood adorn the flowers! The soul of conquerors, barbaric and violent, sings in my triumph as I leave your bed.

The evening has reddened the violet trees.

Flee from this satyress of haughty eyes, with a gaze bleached by the glare of the sun: her long savage hair is like a mane and her step is the nocturnal pace of lions. She seeks the intense hour when brightness fails. It is the hour she awaits to carry off her prey of inviolate breasts, of purest eyes and forehead, that she impregnates forever with her dark desires. Her step sullies the freshness of fountains, her breath corrupts dreams of the infinite... Oh nights devastated by the horror of voluptuousness. I will go to savage depths, pale from solitude, drunk from chasteness!

Today I am chaste like the moon.

O moon, huntress, with light arrows, come to destroy my lying loves, false kisses, false hopes... You who know how to disperse lies, dispel the huddled flock of nightmares. Sharpen the bow of blue silver that shines, and grant me the hope of a ray of light in the night! Calm the devil that feeds off me, and cross my forehead with the gesture of peace.

The moon consoles from all arduous pain, from all resentment, with the sweetness of a woman, hinting like an obscure good deed... The sweet hands of women have the gestures of a priest... Oh, the soft blessing of your hands!

Beyond death, Desire persists.

Those to be born after us, in this world where songs are hoarse, will cast a sigh toward me, who loved with profound anguish, toward you, oh my Desire. On the morrow, when fate spins and weaves, future beings will not forget us. Undulating days, nuanced by light, nights of perfume will eternalize our tremblings, our ardent suffering, and our kiss.

Well do I know that a woman will not forget us…

May my greeting follow you beyond the sea and the purple sunsets, O woman who sails towards Mytilene, with its living walls like flesh… Go, foreigner, announce to the ardent Sappho who emerged from Times blue, only flower of the Graces, that I too have woven slow verses without flaw. Bitterly jealous, despotic and cruel, song has come to reign over my soul. Slavishly, on my knees, I serve the imperious poem, adored beyond the beloved woman. What do I care that the wind disperses my verses to the darkest folds of the dark universe, since I have sung for my joy alone. Forget me, for I am a passing soul…

Whoever speaks of me, will be lying without doubt.

I am tired, I wish for nothing but oblivion. I leave without rancour, without hate, like those who have neither relatives nor friends. I leave as one who returns, lightened, enraptured, to finally forgive love and life. Without haste or fear, I enter the night once more, alongside all that slithers, all that flees. My paradise is a sweet prairie of violets where song will rule over silent souls… a music eternal. Nothing will survive here but love and song… Mytilene, jewel and splendour of the sea, like her, versatile and eternal… death cannot obliterate these gardens… do you remember, O Sappho, the perfumed island, the garden where the breath of lyres triumphed, and the flowering apple trees where the breeze halts... Return to us... Since the dark laurel will not adorn my forehead, fill once again the goblet of gold; fill it with joy for me... Pour into it wine from Cyprus and Lesbos... And you will see me walk toward the azure, sit among the gods, before the banquet of stars... I think I have been speaking up to now in complete delirium...

Let us forget, then, what I have just said.

The Passion According to Renée Vivien is a novel inspired by the life of the poet of English origin and French expression, whose real name was Pauline Mary Tarn (London 1877–Paris 1909). Surely we find ourselves before the first poet since Sappho to sing of her open love for other women in a clear, unequivocal way. Her name shines, then, with its own light amid a tradition that certainly existed, but only underground, the victim of invisibility and silence.

Renée Vivien revealed herself to me through her verses. The intense and complex singularity of her voice attracted me to her personality, to her biography. Thus, the novel you hold is the result of that fascination and of the process of research which it inspired. I began to write it in 1984, and with an intermittent rhythm, continued until this year.

Following in Renée Vivien's footsteps for the next ten years, I travelled, read manuscripts and culled bibliography of the most diverse sort and I even, like some of the characters in the work, copied many letters and unpublished poems by hand. I could have continued indefinitely, for Pauline Mary Tarn's correspondence is most extensive and moving; it should one day be edited. [N.T.: Some has been published; see that of Amédée Moullé].

The novel, structured on the basis of sketches of real, documented events, is nevertheless a work of fiction. Even though I have not invented any of the people surrounding Pauline/Renée, nor have I made up any of the episodes of her life, all those people and episodes constitute only a starting point, a mere initial bare outline. For that reason, the characters generally do not appear with their complete names in the text unless they are mentioned as historical entities, without literary elaboration. For my sources of information, I must first express my debt to the excellent biography by Jean Paul Goujon, published by Régine Desforges: she is an author and editor who has republished several works of Renée Vivien since 1977, including all of her poetry.

In my story I have tried to present the protagonist in an indirect way, through other characters who remember or take a special interest in her, in order to present a multiple, complex, at times even contradictory perspective on her and her environment. There could be many other points of view, obviously, for the possibilities are endless: for that reason the text leaves an open space, and its structure represents an outline, a sketch, to be filled out. I have also intended that readers enter inside the story without a chronological line; rather that they reconstruct it in their minds on the basis of fragmentary bits of information that they accumulate, affirm, or question as they read on, in apparent chaos, in the same manner that information about events or people, whether past or present, usually comes to us. The novel, then, deliberately represents a sort of half-done puzzle. The voice of Renée Vivien is often heard directly and explicitly through her texts; especially in the "Final Monody", which forms a collage in the strict sense, for it is composed wholly from sparse verses of the protagonist. The words of other characters appear more sporadically and sometimes without referencing throughout the text.

For the fragments from Sappho and Dante, I have relied on the Catalan versions of M. Balasch and of J. M. de Sagarra respectively. [N.T. Here we have drawn both on the Charles Norton version and on a miscellany of other translators voices].

In closing, I would like to express my gratitude to all those who helped and encouraged me with this project – friends and family who have offered their contributions, great and small, to the work. In particular, Felícia Fuster, whose generosity and hospitality made possible my many long stays in Paris; my mother, Maria Serra, for her irreplaceable collaboration during the summers, along with everything else; my daughter Heura, for her understanding during my absences and her constant support; and Fina Birulés – who followed *The Passion of Renée Vivien* step by step from the beginning – for having read version after version untiringly, and for her steady and unconditional involvement.

Barcelona, 26 October 1994

TRANSLATORS' NOTE

Our heartfelt thanks goes to Sílvia Aymerich Lemos, poet,
translator and founder of Multipleversions, for suggestions
on the translation, especially poetic ones; to Anna Wilson,
Natasha Tanna, Alice Hagopian and Vicky Buffery for being
such careful readers; and to the Faber Residencies, in Olot
and Andorra, for lovely places to work.